DICTIONARY OF AMERICAN FOLKLORE

DICTIONARY
OF
AMERICAN
FOLKLORE

Marjorie Tallman

PHILOSOPHICAL LIBRARY

New York

A

absentmindedness

Subject of many of the folk tales popular in New England. Man whittled off his finger by mistake. Another man gouges out his eyes in mistake for oysters.

Horace Greeley was well known for his absentmindedness. A hostess passed him some doughnuts. Continuing to talk he ate them all up. He next consumed the entire plate full of cheese cubes. When ultimately questioned about the situation he commented, "No disaster."

absquatulate

An artificially created term common to the West, meaning to leave or depart, usually hurriedly.

Acadian customs

In that portion of Nova Scotia that continued to observe some of the feudal customs transferred to New France it was the practice of the farmers to give every twenty-sixth bushel of wheat to the Church. The story is told of this same region that one farmer with a large family announced his desire to dedicate his twenty-sixth child to the Church also.

When the residents of Nova Scotia were removed by the British in 1755 some of the inhabitants joined their former countrymen in New Orleans where they introduced the activities associated with the Mardi Gras which they had originally brought from France. Since some of the Acadians only moved over into the St. John's Valley of Maine there too they introduced some of the practices similar to the Louisianan Mardi Gras celebrations though of a more modest character. These carriers of the French traditions to Maine would put on

1

costumes and visit from house to house for dancing, home-made wine and much laughter and merriment.

Adam's Tavern (later known as Wadsworth's)

This tavern is claimed as the oldest in Connecticut having remained in use for over two hundred years. Tradition asserts that the General Court, the colonial legislature, met there in 1687 with Andros, the King's representative, who was threatening to take the colony's charter away. While the precious document lay on the table it is claimed the candles were suddenly blown out. The charter disappeared, not to reappear again until James II was exiled and Andros was recalled.

Adirondack customs

See: SPRUCE BEER, BLUE LINE ACTIVITIES, THEODORE ROOSEVELT GUIDE, HONESTY IN ADIRONDACKS, LEON LAKE HOUSE, MAPLE SUGAR, MURRAY'S FOOLS.

Adirondack guides

When the Adirondack country became a popular resort area the services of guides became an essential service to the thousands of summer visitors who have poured into the region for the past seventy years. These native residents were divided into significant grades of whom the "hotel guide" was the lowest category. He was paid by the hour by those who sought out his services. He might row the ladies as desired or lead a group on a hunting trip. "House Guides" were attached to a private estate and were paid by the month to help where needed. The aristocrats of the guides were those selected by a special clientele and known as "private guides." They were reserved far in advance for week or month and paid very well. A certain village is still called "Easy Street" for this is where many of the guides spent the winter waiting for the next season of work. However in those early days their work would not be considered easy. A good guide would have to provide the boat and sometimes row twenty to thirty miles a day. Hauling over portages was also a very arduous task, so much so in fact that a special type boat was devel-

2

oped for that purpose, a canoe built like a row boat. The builders took off extra weight until they had one not much over sixteen feet in length weighing by itself only seventy-five pounds. Guides had to be expert also in finding the best camping spots, establishing effective smudge fires, cooking good meals. Guides were usually specialists being known for a particular region and never working outside of that district.

"Old Mountain Phelps" was a colorful guide during much of the nineteenth century. He was called "a primitive man." He hated soap and could do amazing things to the English language. He lived to be eighty-eight telling stories of his early exploits and selling guide books and pictures of himself.

Ah Quong's Inn

In the mining area about Bridgeport, California there is a legend about a fantan game run by a Chinese owner of a kind of inn where liquor and supplies were bought in the gold mining days. An Indian, Poker Tom, was known to have won one night over $300, and then never to have been seen again. However about a month later his head was found out in the woods by a squaw gathering pine nuts.

A search for the rest of his body was instituted at once in the hope that the cause of his death might be discovered but without success. Finally one of the Indian's white friends decided to stay at the place under suspicion, Ah Quong's Inn, and see what he could discover. Perhaps foreseeing the ultimate solution he was careful, so the story goes, to eat only rice and fish while he stayed there doing his best to inspect all the premises. Eventually he lifted out of the pickel barrel what was enough to assure him that his search was over!

There was indignation among the boarders of course, but the court found the evidence "of too fragmentary a nature" to be acceptable. However, before Ah Quong could leave the court four stalwart Indians entered and carried him off. Two hundred others were in the street. The telegraph wires were cut. The sheriff was out of town. The neighbors decided that the Indians had more imagination than they had given them credit for.

3

albino animals

American Indians paid marked respect toward white animals. White dogs or buffalo calves were chosen as especially effective instruments of sacrifice. A White Coyote was thought by a California tribe to be the father of all other coyotes on earth. White deerskin was also particularly favored and used for ceremonial dances. White animals were also thought to have supernatural powers and therefore were often feared as well as desired. To see a white animal according to an Algonquin Indian belief would mean bad luck.

algerines

This was a term created in Pennsylvania for log-pirates. These were men who stole logs floating down the Susquehanna. They sawed off the brand which had been placed on the end of a log during logging operations for identification purpose after all the logs had been collected at their destination. The Barbary pirates of Algiers led to the application of the name.

All quiet on the Potomac

This expression was said to have originated with General George McClellan during the Civil War while he was waiting to make his much delayed attack. The term has been carried over to apply to any circumstance where a person is waiting in peaceful circumstances for something to break forth. A recent usage has developed in reference to the "lady-in-waiting" whose pregnancy is advancing according to schedule.

"All the Law West of the Pecos"

This was the position taken by Roy Bean a Kentucky-born Texas judge in the 1880's who according to frontier legends, and the sign in his saloon was the center of law and order for many years. He held court in a town he managed to have named "Langtry" because he had fallen in love with the picture of the famous Lily. All his trials began with the request to "step up to the bar and have a snort of poison." The actual performances were unique enough in themselves but

4

the retelling for generations has embellished the material to a high polish. His trained bear drank beer at the bar and often helped in sobering drunks. As coroner he fined all dead men all the money on their person. Perhaps the most repeated tale concerns the problem of the killing of a Chinese laborer. He released the defendant because he could find nothing in the Texas lawbooks that condemned murdering a Chinese.

alphabet recitation

There is an old theatrical saying, that words and meanings of lines are not as important as the ability of the actor. Any actor worthy of the name could earn applause by reciting the alphabet with varied intonation.

Al Smith

Many of the stories told about Al Smith have already become part of the body of folklore. His brown derby and many of his pithy sayings illustrate the point. "Let's look at the record," "I think I'll take a walk" have pungent meaning for politicians.

alum

Southern Negroes claim that it is valuable to stop bleeding, cure blindness and prevent conjure spells.

ambulance chaser

An expression created for a lawyer who is especially alert to obtain a case to defend a person who has had an accident and may want to bring suit as soon as possible, that is, he is so alert that he may arrive following the person who has been brought to the hospital in an ambulance.

Amish customs

See: AVOIDING, ASCENSION DAY, THROW OVER THE FENCE.

animals in folklore

Animal anecdotes, cures, nurses and tales all have a part in Indian folklore and also in the various aspects of American folklore of the various localities of the United States. From Babe, Paul Bunyan's ox, through all the mythological

5

creatures popular in the tall tales of Arkansas, the Ozarks and the Northwest to the wily Brer Rabbit of the Uncle Remus Tales, animals form part of the pattern of American folk stories.

See: BEAVER, BIG OWN, BRER RABBIT, CAT, CHAMELEON, COW, CRICKETS, FROG, GOAT, LOBO, MOLE, MUSKRAT, PORCUPINE, SHEEP, SNAKE, TOAD.

anti-macassar

This was a little doily of lace or linen placed on the back of upholstered chairs or lounges to prevent soiling. The term originated because of the prevalent fashion for the gentlemen to dress their hair with an oil that was called macassar, so since these materials were against the oil, thus anti-macassar.

Arkansas Traveler

A well-known piece of American humor symbolizing the mythical state of "Arkansaw." There are many versions of its origins but general acceptance centers on its being a medley of tales accumulating during the 1860's and typifying the frontier distrust of strangers. A lost and tired Traveler seeking shelter for the night comes upon the Squatter. A lengthy dialogue ensues based on a number of deliberate misunderstandings. At last the Traveler wins acceptance by being able to play the balance of the tune the Squatter has been sawing at during most of the talk. Many of the jests had been popular long before they were incorporated in the dialogue and were retained over wide areas for popular entertainment purposes. A well-known one has to do with an account of a fair and square tapping of a barrel of whisky with a spigot at each end by a husband and wife who keep the drinking equal by each paying the other for the drinks taken. The Currier and Ives engraving of the incident was very popular.

Army folklore terms

See: Fat boy, guardhouse lawyer, gremlins, pentagon lore, hash marks, shave-tail, sick book rider, snow birds.

asafetida

This was an ill-smelling gum that was worn in a bag around the neck. The people in the Ozarks claim it prevents any digestive ills.

Ascension Day

Among the Amish of the Pennsylvania Dutch this is a day observed by a religious festival. Throughout this region there was a belief that no work should be done on this day, especially no sewing or bad luck would follow as a form of vengeance by the Lord.

aspen leaf

The leaves of the aspen are said to tremble because the Lord's cross was made of this wood, ignoring the fact that the long flexible leaf would be likely to be acted upon by any breath of air anyway.

as straight as Pearl Street

This comparison was a common expression in New Amsterdam with a distinctly satirical implication for this was one of the main streets of the town and swung around meanderingly on its way up town.

Astor of Waldorf

John Jacob Astor came from the town of Waldorf in Germany to New York City where he began in a very modest way his fabulous business career. He was a peddler, first of cakes and later of fur skins and of cheap jewelry. Other accounts of the man to be the richest in America tell of his working for two dollars beating furs in a step in their preparation for sale. During this occupation he quizzed all the trappers with whom he came in contact so thoroughly and seemed to have acquired such a grasp of their work that the owner of the shop in which he was working sent him up to the Indian tribes in the Adirondacks and Canada to seek out skins for him. Astor learned to bargain most expertly and was always remarkably close-fisted, weighing every penny he dispersed. Starting to trade for himself his profits rose to

7

unbelievable heights particularly because of monopolies he obtained.

Later another fortune was accumulated by him by his shrewdness in recognizing real estate values. A story that has gained popular acceptance illustrates this point. He offered to sell a piece of property near Wall Street at what was for the time a rather low price of eight thousand dollars. He was told he was foolish to do that because within a few years that property would be worth twelve thousand dollars. However he explained his action by showing that with the money from his down town property he would buy eighty lots above Canal Street and by the time his Wall Street property was worth the twelve thousand his uptown property would have advanced to eighty thousand. Such farsightedness did soon bring him remarkable profits, but it is doubtful whether he ever explained his position in such a fashion for he was far from loquacious. Of his old age another story is told. He had learned from his business agent that a poor woman was unable to pay her rent for reasons so pitiful that the agent had not the heart to press her. However Astor insisted and soon the agent reported he had the money. Astor praised him for it, but actually his son had put up the money secretly.

"avoiding"

This curious custom was developed by the Amish, a religious sect among the Pennsylvania Dutch. The Amish refused all participation in election activities as a mark of unworldliness and they also avoided the use of buttons on coats and vests, still employing hooks and eyes in their place. If a member is censured by his church he is "avoided" also and must be ignored by all other Amish, his family included.

B

Babbitt

The main character in Sinclair Lewis's novel of the same name. He is shown as a simple likeable fellow with faint aspirations to culture that are smothered in the crude all enveloping activities of earning a living and "keeping up" with the Joneses. In this sense the term Babbitt has become synonymous with the typical American business man engrossed only with money-making schemes, unconcerned with any of the artistic or cultural activities of his community unless they in some way lead to financial contacts.

Babe, the Blue Ox

The legends about Paul Bunyan contain a great deal about his companion and chief assistant in his logging operations, Babe, who was of enormous size and had a tremendous appetite. In fact, he met his death by eating a great quantity of hot cakes, stove and all. Babe was so heavy that his footsteps formed the lakes of Michigan and of Oregon.

Baby's first lock of hair

It was not sentiment alone that started the practice of preserving the first lock of hair cut from the new baby's head but an old superstition that if this hair were preserved in a safe place the child would live to a ripe old age. There was an idea also that if the child's hair were cut as he grew up it would adversely affect his eyesight; therefore both boys and girls were decorated with long curls.

baby removed from dead mother

This theme is common among many of the Indian tales from the Atlantic to the Pacific, though the Plains area is especially associated with them. In a Shoshone story, "The Wolf and the Geese," two such women are involved and a baby girl is taken from one and a boy from the other. The girl can immediately walk and travels about with the Wolf.

bachelor buttons

This term might be used for any type of flower with button-shaped head like a corn flower. A lovelorn young man would carry one in his pocket to discover his future state; if it lived he would marry his sweetheart, but if it died he would have to find another.

backstone (actually back hearthstone)

A raised section of the hearth formed a sort of partial ledge that was built across the back of the hearth in the colonial period. The two sides of the fireplace acted as natural reflectors of heat to this spot and here pies, bread and tarts were put to bake. Later the backstone was a large iron disk ever so slightly dished out, either suspended from the crane or supported on a spider.

backward action

Performing a normal action backward may cause a person to acquire magic power. On the other hand to change some article of clothing put on backwards may bring bad luck. Flying a flag upside down is an accepted symbol of distress.

bacon and.greens

In parts of Virginia they claim that the eating of bacon and greens is required for the making of a Virginian.

bad dress rehearsal—good opening

A Broadway proverb that is part of the body of stage folklore.

badger

The Hopi and other Pueblo Indians look upon the badger as having special curative power since he is associated with the digging up of roots and plants. His paw is kept near a woman in childbirth in an attempt to encourage a speedy

10

delivery since a badger can dig himself out quickly. His tooth is held to be a good cure for toothache.

badgers

This was a name for the miners who stayed all season in Wisconsin in the lead mines around Hardscrabble and New Diggings. The badgers with their stamina to stay all the year around were more admired than the miners who went south in the fall and this was part of the reason for naming Wisconsin the Badger State.

bad man

The "Bad Man" in American folklore may be traced to the wave of banditry following the Mexican War and to the continuation of some of the guerilla activities of some of the units that were active during the Civil War. The wars between the cattlemen and the sheepmen also encouraged the rise of such lawless individuals who took action into their own hands. With many colorful figures involved the average man tended to look upon the "good" bad man with considerable respect. In this category would be classed Jesse James, Sam Bass, and Pretty Boy Floyd, especially since each was killed finally largely through treachery. Others of the killer class would have no less popular appeal with the accounts of their viciousness growing with the telling. Billy the Kid claimed he killed twenty-one and ten of them single handed.

Balaam's basket

A term used by printers to refer to a receptacle containing stereotyped bits of information used by them to fill up small spaces left vacant on the page being set up in a newspaper.

balance and swing

An American square dance term which calls for the gentleman to swing the lady completely around him once or twice.

ballast for fish

White Pine Tom told great tales in the Michigan lumber camps. One winter he was selling fish to such a camp. He had

11

loaded them with sand to make them weigh more. Finally this trick was discovered and the cook challenged him to explain his seeming cheating. Tom was not stumped at all. He explained that Lake Michigan was so deep that the fish ate sand in order to take on ballast and get to the bottom of the lake where the feeding was good.

Ball the Jack

A dance originated by American Negroes which is accompanied by handclapping and chanting. A "highball" in railroad slang meant to go ahead fast and the jack was the locomotive. The refrain would be, "And I ball the jack on the railroad track" while there would also be a rolling movement of the hips of the singer.

"balloon lines"

Rudolph Dirks, one of the earliest creators of comics had originated the "Katzenjammer Kids." After his first few experiments he introduced speeches for his characters which he wrote above or near the speaker and encircled with a line drawing forever afterwards known as a balloon.

Bals du Roi (Kings' Balls)

Kings' Balls were held in New Orleans on Twelfth Night, January Sixth. An elaborate cake was always served as a crowning part of the festivities. The finder of the bean in the cake was designated host or hostess at the next celebration. This custom begun long ago still continues. After this opening celebration there are a whole series of balls until the culminating activities of the Mardi Gras on Shrove Tuesday the day before Lent begins. There is one other great ball in the midst of Lent the mi-careme, or St. Joseph's night on March 19th.

Baltimore, gastronomic center of the world

Oliver Wendell Holmes is supposed to have coined this phrase after having dined at the home of Mrs. Du Bois Egerton on Madison Street where all the delicacies for which

Baltimore was justly famous were served, such as, canvas-back duck, terrapin, an oyster roast or chicken à la Maryland.

bandanna

The cowboy would indeed have been lost without his essential bandanna. He used it at the water hole for a towel. He tied it around his neck to make a neat appearance at breakfast. Later he might use it to blindfold his horse while he mounted. Perhaps he wanted to put a calf to one side for branding, he would use his bandanna for a "pigging string" to hold its feet. He had protection from the sun for the back of his neck, or for his face as need arose, or he could use it as a mask if the day was dusty, or as a shield if in a blizzard. It mopped the sweat away, or saved his hand from hot handles. He could drink from it in necessity or make a sling of it, or finally be buried in it.

band wagon, to get on

It was the custom in early election days to carry the band along on a wagon during the pre-election campaigning. Local political leaders desirous of showing their support of the candidate for whom the parade was being staged might jump up on the wagon to make a few remarks in his favor between selections or while passing from one town to another, thus the expression came to be applied to any action where the public went along with a popular program or to designate approval.

Bang-All

The famous gun of the redoubtable Mike Fink. So skillful was he in the use of it that he was eventually excluded from all contests.

banjo

A musical instrument resembling a guitar; it was brought to the United States by the Negro slaves from West Africa and became popular as an accompaniment for singing and dancing. It was held to be an instrument of the devil by pious people who thought its use kept the frivolous ones out of the churches and led them to evil ways. When minstrel shows became widespread a five-string banjo was used for the rippling, strongly rhythmic music, soon known and loved all over the United States. "Old Dan Tucker" was a favorite piece for the banjo picker. Some of the tunes were carried over for square dancing and the words often combined ballad-type material covering any subject from wooden legs to mine disasters.

bank barns

The tremendous barns built by the Pennsylvania Dutch became a standard for such buildings in America. They were often sixty feet long by forty feet wide and sometimes as long as one hundred feet made with an inclined approach or ramp that made it possible for wagons to drive into the upper level. Here were the great threshing floors with lofty mows rising on both sides. The basement was used as a stable for horses and cattle with further passages closed by divided or "Dutch" doors.

barber's cat

Sea slang for a talkative messmate.

barber shop mugs

These china and clay mugs had a tremendous vogue from the 1880's on and could be ordered from large catalogues in an enormous quantity of styles or materials. They were often decorated to indicate the occupation of the individual for whom they were kept on the shelf in the barber shop. Sometimes a chaste and simple design was employed but often gold lettering and elaborate coloring were used. Hundreds of emblems were available as choices to fit the individual desire.

barnstormer

A ham (amateur) actor on tour. Also used for the early airmen putting on flying demonstrations after World War I.

barrel house

A term used for a cheap saloon about 1900 where the barrel of liquor was freely accessible to the drinkers and where an early type of jazz developed.

barrel treatment for drunkenness

At Fort Snelling the commandant tried to keep his troops from drinking or selling liquor to the Indians as steam boats began to ply the Mississippi about the 1830's. As punishment he walked the guilty ones up and down under guard bearing the statement, "I was drunk last night." In this small post he once had forty-seven of the garrison in the guard house for this offense.

barrenness

This was a condition for which American folklore offered many charms or treatments for its correction.

Barricke Mariche

A legend in Berks County recalls that a German family of four women found life uncomfortable in Germantown during the Revolutionary War and so left for the Oley Hills of Pennsylvania where they were forced to endure a hard life farming. At last Mary alone was left alive, but continued to do the difficult job of making a living for herself by working the farm alone for thirty years until she was seventy-five. She was tender-hearted and did much good in the neighborhood despite her inaccessible position. A marker on her mountain road states:

"A pioneer nurse, comforter of body and soul,
   benevolent, pious, brave and charitable
She hath done what she could"
                    died 1819.

Bartholomew baby

The term doll did not come into use until the Eighteenth Century but a child's plaything that was an elaborate forerunner of dolls was known as a Bartholomew baby. Images

15

made in the shape of human beings were sold in great quantities at the Saint Bartholomew Fairs held in London. Some of the figures were elaborately dressed and were used to convey fashion news as illustrations are used today. The Puritans tried to stop the Fairs while they were in power and to discourage the "babies" from being popular but they were quite unsuccessful. Later the term Bartholomew doll did come into usage, but it was used to refer to a tawdry, over-dressed woman who might resemble those who attended the fair rather than the figures that were sold there.

basers

A certain style of singing American Negro spirituals developed in which these "basers" rendered the response following a narrative line sung by the leader. They were usually so quick to respond that an impression of continual singing was given.

Basin Street

This was a street in the French Quarter of New Orleans in a notorious Red light district where a special type of musical composition was first experimented with and now is looked upon with nostalgia by some as the birth place of jazz.

bathing beauties

A man had built some gorgeous Roman Baths at Miami Beach in the 1920's. His wife while taking swimming lessons wore a one piece bathing suit which caused a minister to condemn her action. The resultant publicity was claimed as sufficient to develop the idea of "bathing beauties" to advertise such beauty spots.

Battalion Day

Among the Pennsylvania Dutch this was a day celebrated upon Whitsunday until nearly 1900. The local volunteer militia was mustered out after having held a review and parade. When the men could afford gay uniforms it was a colorful and largely-attended program.

16

Battle-ax beliefs (Pennsylvania)

A group led by Theophilis Gates introduced a novel and amazingly modern set of beliefs, but astonishing to the straight and narrow Philadelphians who first heard of them. He argued for a religion which would not bind him forever to his wife, but neither did he want one which would tolerate free love or promiscuity. He developed, therefore, the creed of the Battle Ax. Marriage was not intended to be permanent. Men and women should change their partners if they could not live in peace and harmony. Other converts joined their faith, which gradually began to assume other curious customs. Opposition developed of course, but the Battle Ax followers had an infallible method of silencing most pastoral criticism. After just having participated in one of their own services a Battle Ax member marched naked up the aisle of the church of a speechless clergyman who silently departed from his church.

bayberry candles

Burn one on Christmas Day. If the flame burns bright and the light shines clear, then heaven will bless you all the year. To prepare the candles the directions were to boil great quantities of the berries in water. Upon cooling the wax coating of the berries which had been melted off would have formed a crustlike gray-green ice upon the surface of the water. This crust was removed and remelted in deep pans. A candle wick was dipped into the melted wax and then redipped each time as a layer hardened and the process was continued until the desired size was attained. Material for wicks was in short supply during the colonial period. Molds were later used made of a great variety of substances such as glass, pottery, china, stone wear, tin, pewter, iron and wood. Candle sticks were made of any of these materials and anything else the individual might think of such as whale bone or cattle horn, too.

Bayou State

The state of Mississippi has won this designation be-

17

cause of its many creeks, or marshy overflows of rivers and lakes.

bear-hunting, Ozark style

When you fire at the bear, injure him but do not cripple him, he will then be so angry that he will chase you all the way home and save you the trouble of packing the meat home yourself.

"bear traps"

The river near Mauch Chunk, Pennsylvania in the early mining days sometimes ran very low. After a severe drought in 1818 artificial means of making the stream navigable had to be developed. A sluice gate provided artificial freshets. These arrangements are very curious looking and when questions were asked as to the purpose intended for them the first responses were that they were intended to catch bears. The term "bear trap" stuck for a long time afterwards. There is a street in Mauch Chunk still called Trap Alley after these units.

bearwalkers

The Indians in the Michigan peninsula believe that there is a force or power for evil that may haunt the neighborhood. They call this strange force a bearwalk and they try to kill it before it can kill them. It has no power over a white person. It may try to put a person to sleep or take the shape of any animal in order to attack an enemy.

A person can catch a bearwalk with the right medicine and have its power transferred to him. Shooting will do no good for then he will go off and the person after the bearwalk will get no benefit. Most people fall over in a faint when they see a bearwalk but those who are able to withstand it will live much longer than those who faint.

beats my time

A western expression meaning to do better than some one, or more especially to win the right to call upon a young lady.

beaver

Beavers have musk-producing glands which secrete a substance almost as valuable as their skins themselves and which the superstitious claim are valuable for the curing of toothache and a number of other ailments. The common belief in the great activity of the beaver as shown in the popular expression, "as busy as a beaver" is more folklore than scientific fact.

The interpretations of the beaver's activities for weather prediction is not any more dependable though there are those who maintain if he stores up a large supply of food that means a long, hard winter, and that if his coat is heavy that indicates the same possibility.

bed-rock, to be down to

Slang for being down to one's last dollar. Also used by miners to indicate that they have reached the bottom of the vein that will produce any more "pay dirt" or ore of any real value.

bed superstitions

So widespread has been the belief in the bad luck resulting from getting out-of-bed on the left side that it is common to refer to a person who is cross as having gotten out of bed on the wrong side. To the ancients the left or sinister side was likely to bring danger under any circumstances. In this case his remedy was to go back to bed, backwards to reverse the effect of the action and then get up again the right way, that is on the right side.

bee

Mississippi Negroes believed that to have a swarm of bees come to you of their own accord was sure to bring bad luck. Even to dream of a swarm alighting on a building portends misfortune. There is also a superstition that dead bees burned to ashes and sprinkled in the shoes will cure flat feet.

It is probably unwise to count on one other belief about bees that they will not sting a person if he holds his breath, clenches his fist or otherwise produces a tension.

19

Beecher's Bibles

This term was used for the "aid" sent by the abolitionists to help those trying to keep slavery out of Kansas in the bitter period when the Kansas-Nebraska Act had opened the territory to the principle of popular sovereignty or the vote of the people. The Reverend Henry Ward Beecher was an ardent Abolitionist, pastor of the Plymouth Church in Brooklyn. He heard of the assistance various groups in Connecticut were trying to render to those opposed to slavery in Kansas and he helped to raise funds for this purpose. Two articles it was felt were particularly needed—rifles and Bibles, so both were shipped in together in boxes labeled "Bibles." The Sharp's rifles or carbines were the "Beecher Bibles."

beeswax candles

A children's service on Christmas Eve in the Moravian churches is usually concluded by a candle light service. In Bethlehem, Pennsylvania, everyone carefully preserves the remainder of the candle used at this time for it was especially prepared as a symbol of the Christmas season.

belaying-pin soup

The rough treatment, or threat of such extended to merchant seamen by bullying mates in a sailing vessel. The belaying-pin could make a formidable weapon if it reached its goal.

"Bell don't make bump"

Because many of the Pennsylvania Dutch had led a somewhat isolated existence the older folk did not often speak English. However when they did learn they developed some amusing corruptions as in the case here where the intention is to say that the bell does not ring.

bells of Conestoga wagons

Five of the six horses that pulled a huge Conestoga wagon had a bow of four bells across their backs. These were worn for more than their attractive chimes since it was very useful to have it known far in advance that this heavy and lumbering vehicle was on its way. Each driver took great pride in his bells the possession of which indicated his ability to take care of himself successfully. If stuck in a mud hole or some such difficulty and forced to appeal for help his bells were the price he had to pay for any help, for it was understood that to the rescuer went the bells of the rescued wagon. This was a severe humiliation for a tough driver to accept. From this wearing of the bells arose the expression "to be there with bells on," that is to be on the Lancaster Pike, where the Conestogas ran, ready to advance.

Belsnickel

The Pennsylvania Dutch borrowed a custom from Holland and the Rhineland where there was a figure the opposite of Saint Nicholas. He was a Nicholas in fur. A neighborhood boy might dress in a shaggy bearskin coat and cap and visit the children who lived in the vicinity. Over his shoulder he would carry a bag with switches sticking out. When admitted to the kitchen he might tap the window with a switch to let the naughty children know what they might have in store for them, but if the children were found to have been good the floor was strewn with candies and nuts from his bag. The Belsnickel no longer makes these visits for he frightened the children so he was not felt to be in keeping with the Christmas spirit.

Ben Delimus

Ben became an almost legendary figure in Alabama after the Civil War. Upon his discharge from the Northern army he went back to Alabama whose fertile soil he had particularly taken note of during his campaigning. There he played upon the gullibility of the new freemen. He appealed to them as a close friend of Lincoln and Grant and warned them that the baptisms made while they were slaves would not be adequate. For a dollar he rebaptized all those who came to him. When he had exhausted the possibilities of this "racket" he claimed that they had to be remarried also. When he had milked this situation dry too, he began to market a liquid

21

to take the curl out of Negroes' hair for which he charged a dollar a bottle and prospered greatly.

Seeking new fields to conquer he decided to run for political office. At the nominating convention he contrived to put the other candidates at a disadvantage by opening the convention with a prayer that was really a political harangue. Supposedly his opponents could stand it no longer and one interrupted crying, "Who is this who dares to condemn us? He is the one who crucified the Lord." The Negro audience was aghast and Ben could feel them turning against him. He then cried "I could not have done that. It happened over two thousand years ago and I am not that old; and in addition I would have stopped it if I had been there." He won the election and remained a strong influence in the community for many years afterwards.

"best wore out"

A French Canadian expression meaning that something has been well broken in as shoes or harness or something of that type.

Bet-A-Million Gates

John W. Gates was a well-known betting man at the turn of the century and the situation involving the famous Coal Strike of 1902 looked like a sure thing to him. He said he would pay odds of 1000 to one that the miners would give in. However as cold weather approached pressure became so great on the operators and Mitchell the organizer of the strike was so firm in his demands Gates lost out on his great gamble.

betsy lamp

One of the earliest and crudest means of illuminating the colonial homes was this type of lamp which was really only a saucer or shallow vessel with a spout which burned grease.

bezoars

Stones found in the stomach, liver or intestines of some animals, but particularly the deer, possess magical properties

22

in the eyes of their Indian finders. The stones often attained large monetary exchange value because of the intense interest with which they were sought by many.

bibliomancy

Divination by means of books, but more particularly by means of the Bible. Where the Bible in pioneer households was often the only book besides an Almanac in the house considerable store was set by the practice of opening the Bible at any random spot in order to obtain an answer to some question being asked at that time. A somewhat oracular quality was given to the practice by the means employed to interpret the appropriate verse to meet the situation involved. Cliodomancy was a somewhat related practice in which a hanging key was used, the swinging movements of the latter requiring interpretation.

Big Owl

The Apache Indians believed in an evil creature who would come to eat them up but from whom they would be rescued when one of their heroes would kill him before he could place them in his basket to be carried home and eaten.

"Big Runaway"

The flight from the Tories in 1778 down the North Branch of the Susquehanna from the Wyoming Valley near present day Wilkes-Barre was such a wild rush it has been given this colorful title. Hundreds fled on boats, canoes, rafts, on anything that would float, in wild distress fearing the ruthless attack of the Indian allies of the British. The men marched single file on each side of the river to try to guard the women and children on the water. Often the women had to leap out of their boats to push them past some obstruction. The hastily loaded boats carried tables, spinning wheels, bedsteads, kettles and cows. Their occupants in some cases just barely made their escape. One woman who actually lost her scalp lived seventy years thereafter.

Big Sea Day

A colorful outing celebrated on the Jersey coast on the

23

second Saturday in August for many years until the shore was preempted for more distant vacationists. Whole families were loaded on the wagons and drove out to the sea from the pine woods area of southern Jersey. Everyone went bathing in whatever clothes they had on that day and stood around and dried off in the sun. There were some who tended to call this day, "Farmer's Wash Day" because of this aspect of the celebration. For those who for various reasons were unable to attend on the second Saturday, at Sea Girt, there was a Little Sea Day celebration, on the third Saturday in August.

Billy the Kid

From the brief outline of the facts of the life of William Bonney, Billy the Kid born 1859 a strange collection of stories has developed. In the eyes of many the legend about him has grown to heroic size and does not seem likely to diminish with the cult of the bad man still going strong. Strangely two almost exactly opposed views of him can be easily put together. To the Mexicans he seemed friendly and helpful. They found him so brave and handsome and generous. Even after he had begun his killings nothing seemed to weigh on his cheerful nature, said some reports. On the other hand his one authentic picture shows a "nondescript, adenoidal, weasel-eyed, narrow-chested, stoop-shouldered, repulsive-looking creature." Just the same stories of his activities grew through the years though the accounts of his twenty-one killings in his twenty-one years seem highly exaggerated. Though supposedly shot in the dark by Sheriff Pat Garrett there were even in 1929 still rumors that he was hiding out in Texas.

Binghamton's Origin

In 1785 the Indians gave up their claim to Ochenana, a place of seven hills where the little Chenango river joins the wide Susquehanna. The next year a Philadelphia merchant William Binghamton bought this area and with his friend Joshua Whitney organized a chopping bee to clear his Chenango Point land. He planned to give this land to form a community for "a quiet and industrious people who may give a good reputation to the neighborhood as well from their skills as from their orderly moral conduct." These new citizens were so appreciative they named the town in his honor.

bird in the house

In Alabama for a bird to fly into the house was considered a sign of good luck. Other areas look upon it with favor if a bird builds its nest in the house. Yet it is claimed that wall paper does not have bird designs because some people think it will cause luck to fly out the window. A bird tapping on the window of the house was believed to be a bad omen on the assumption that the bird's soul was inviting another soul to join him meaning that there was going to be a death in the household.

bird lore

See: BUZZARD, BLUEJAY, CANARY, OWL, PEACOCK, PIGEON, ROBIN, WHIPPOORWILL, SEA GULL.

Birthday folklore

A popular rhyme about this subject states:

Monday's child is fair of face
Tuesday's child is full of grace
Wednesday's child is sour and sad
Thursday's child is merry and glad
Friday's child is loving and giving
Saturday's child must work for a living
While the child that is born on the Sabbath Day
Is blithe and bonny and good and gay.

Another popular belief associated with birthdays has to do with the spanking usually administered at that time.

One to grow on
One to live on
One to eat on
One to get married on.

These are usually considered extras in addition to the one for each year of the person's age. Blowing out the candles on one's birthday cake has a number of interpretations. One version claims you get your wish if you blow them all out.

birthday superstitions

Old wives' tales have provided a large quantity of beliefs surprisingly many of which are still in current acceptance. It was said that a woman lost a tooth for every child she bore. It was falsely claimed that she could not conceive while she continued to nurse the new baby. Notions that prenatal influences may have a bearing so as to leave a mark upon the child are of very old duration. To be born with a caul has had many superstitions associated with it. They say if the caul is red the child will have prophetic insight, if blackish, misfortune will follow. The possession of a caul was very valuable to a sailor who then could expect a safe voyage, so that the midwives did quite a business in surreptitiously putting them aside for future business.

Biscaino, Don Pedro

A Basque adventurer who settled on the Florida keys near Miami-to-be from whom was derived the name Biscayne Bay.

black birding

An expression used to describe the practice of secretly picking up African tribesmen and bringing them to the South as slaves.

"black cat"

A term used by the fishermen and sailors on Lake Superior for a boat that has had a spell cast on it and which can never get a full crew to come aboard.

"black grains"

When Philadelphia was about to be attacked in 1745 even the Quaker pacifists could not completely overlook the danger to the colony of the possible attacks by French or Spanish privateers. They therefore voted an appropriation of four thousand pounds to be expended in the purchase of bread, meat and grain for the city. It was then liberally, and deliberately, interpreted that "black grains" (gunpowder) were to be included.

Black Hawk

This chieftain was hated and reviled by the people of the Upper Mississippi while the Black Hawk War was raging. Young Abraham Lincoln led a force against him. This much-surprised chieftain found himself well treated after his capture. He was taken to Washington with much honor. "Black Hawk could not understand the ways of American generals who were sent against him." Havinghurst.

"Black legs"

A term used for fastidious gentlemen dwelling in Mississippi and Louisiana in the 1880's. Well groomed and elegant, though quietly dressed, they abhorred temperance, favored racing and cock-fighting. On occasions they acted as "chaperons" for wealthy young men whom they would take on trips on the Mississippi steamboats, at which time they might quite legitimately relieve them of their surplus cash in little gambling matches.

"Black Robes"

In 1831 a delegation of four Indians, probably Nez Percés or Flat heads, reached St. Louis seeking a Black Robe, a Roman Catholic priest, whom they had heard about from some Canadians in the upper Missouri area where they lived. Protestant missionaries heard of the "call" and went out to satisfy the request. But the story goes that the Indians would have none of them since the Protestants had wives and did not wear crosses or offer the "Big Prayer" in which they were interested. A Jesuit father, Pierre de Smet, eventually reached the area and became well-beloved in his ministration to the Indians from 1837 to 1867. He was later instrumental in arranging a peace treaty with them, the "Treaty of Laramie."

blood beliefs

Blood was held to be in every sense a life-giving substance so that if you wanted to dispose of evil creatures you tried to get a drop of the blood to work with. In reverse some of the Indians drained all the blood out of the animals they were going to eat so that none of the animal spirits would enter into them. The drinking of blood was looked upon as being equal to a transfusion. The superstition that a dead body bleeds in the presence of his murderer has long been held. The covenant of blood brothership in which the participants exchange a drop of blood in various ceremonial rituals indicated the high regard in which blood was held and also a feeling for its magical properties. That "Negro" blood was different from that of a white person has been one of the most deeply ingrained of the racial prejudices. Allied to this were the beliefs that considered the possibility of "bad" blood transmitting criminal or physical characteristics.

bloviating

President Harding recognized that he belonged to the old school of political haranguers and used this term to describe his rather bombastic kind of speech-making. Others were less kind and called him sententious and meaningless.

"Blow Gabriel Blow"

In a small town on the Eastern shore of the Chesapeake Bay a famous Methodist preacher was supposed to have produced considerable consternation among a large number of his followers who were listening to him in an overflow meeting in the church yard. After much exhortation he started describing the angel Gabriel with a silver trumpet in his hand, and then by prearrangement, (he had met a small colored boy on his way to the meeting trudging along with a horn in his hand,) the lad had blown his horn when the preacher had cried "Blow Gabriel Blow." The congregation fell to the ground crying for mercy at this too literal answering of a prayer. When the trick was discovered the people were annoyed but the preacher warned them if a

28

small boy could scare them that much what terror would there be in their hearts when Judgment Day really came! The tale lost nothing in the numerous retellings to which it was subjected.

blow the grampus

An old Merchant Navy term for pouring water over a sleeping sailor to bring him to in a hurry.

blue-eyed boy

One who enjoys special favors in the business world or the armed forces. "Fair-haired boy" is an equivalent expression.

Blue Hen's Chickens

Raising a regiment in the early days of the Revolution Captain Jonathan Caldwell's Delawareans brought with them two game cocks hatched from the eggs of a small steel blue hen. In honor of the two birds who could outfight any others with which they were matched, the men from Delaware when they marched off to battle called themselves the sons of the Blue Hen, game to the last. In time they changed it to the Blue Hen's chickens which title the troops from Delaware have proudly borne ever since.

Blue Hill Hermit

John Mason desired to flee from all contact with women so he built a strange octagonal tower near Sunbury, Pennsylvania which according to some leaned as much as thirty-five degrees. Here he lived alone for many years known as the Blue Hill hermit. When the Susquehanna froze over he would skate to Harrisburg always carrying an umbrella. He was ultimately buried by a deep precipice near his tower.

bluejay

The bluejay is personified in the trickster category by the Indians. The Apache particularly tell a long cycle of tales showing him as a hero anxious to outdo his rivals. The blue-

29

jay also has the power to direct the activities of all the birds and animals.

"Blue line" activities

The Adirondack State Park's final boundaries were drawn in 1922 and on the official maps these areas were enclosed in blue lines. It became common practice when referring to some special regulation to say that these applied because they were "inside the blue line." On the other hand if the rules did not apply because the area was in some of the privately owned regions intermingled within some of the Park Reservations they were called "outside the Blue."

Blue-noses

A New England term for the inhabitants of Nova Scotia. It is the name of a potato which the Nova Scotians claim they produce to the greatest perfection and boast is the best in the world. The Americans have therefore countered by calling the producers of this popular item blue-noses.

blues

Shortly after the Civil War a special type of song developed out of the Negro work songs, the hollers and spirituals which became popularized under W. C. Handy about 1912 and have continued to have a great appeal. At first just concerned with vocal effects the blues have spread to instrumental types and been "modified" to such an extent as to include "boogie-woogie" and other jazz forms that seem far removed from the original folk forms but may really represent a growing body of "modern" folk manners. Musically they represent a very special form of syncopation with a slight flatting of the third and seventh intervals of the scale producing the characteristic "blues" notes.

In the early usage singing the "blues" was a way of indicating one's despair over one's lot in life in a way not possible in ordinary speech. This "sorrow" aspect resulted in the reference to the songs as "the po' man's heart disease". Even when the songs became more sophisticated and the center

30

moved north to Chicago it was that same "sorrowful" quality that continued to have appeal.

Blue-Tail Fly

An American Negro minstrel song dating from the 1840's contains some portions of authentic Negro folksong, especially in the refrain, "Jimmy crack corn and I don't care".

blutz-wagon

A farm wagon without any springs. An expression used by the Pennsylvania Dutch and copied by their neighbors.

Bodie, California

This rough gold mining town had a reputation for being a very unsavory place and much in need of spiritual uplift therefore a minister was assigned the task. Out of this situation came a well-known tale. The minister's little girl is supposed to have said piteously when she learned of their proposed trip, "Goodbye, God we're going to Bodie". Another version has it on the word of the editor of a local paper eager to defend his town's fair name that what she actually said was, "Good, by God! We're going to Bodie."

"body masters"

These were the chapter heads of the widely organized Molly Maguires who planned the executions that the organization felt were necessary, or carried out the destruction of bridges and similar sabotage. They were skillful enough to perform a "clean job", an undetected one in most cases. However a "Pinkerton man", an employee of the famed investigation company actually managed to become a trusted member of the body masters and ultimately testified in court about all the actions of this group leading to the final dispersal of the organization.

This Jim McKenna had been a member of the Mollies for two years when he finally accumulated all his information. He had been accepted as "the best Molly of them all".

bonanza

This expression originally meant fair weather at sea.

31

In America it came into common usage in application to the great ore discoveries in the Far West where many a big strike was called a bonanza.

boneshaker

A term used for an early type of bicycle made of wood and very heavy with iron tires and built quite high. The diameter of the front wheel was sometimes three and even four times that of the rear wheel.

bonnyclabber

A term for sour milk prevalent in New England but borrowed from the Irish.

boogie-woogie

A style of piano playing. The left hand maintains a heavy repetitive pattern over which the right hand improvises at will. The various patterns are sometimes described as "traveling", "climbing" or "walking". Its origin is placed in Chicago where parties were held to help the tenants collect enough contributions to make up the back rent they owed. This type of blues playing reached nationwide popularity about 1936. They say Cou-Cou Davenport gave it its name from "Boogie" the devil, or all the troubles in life.

bookmaking customs

Among the bettors on horse races it was customary to refer to a "Dutch book". That was one in which the bookmaker so arranged the odds on the horses running in a particular race that he lost money. For example he would be paying out $100 to the winners but would have received only $90 in bets placed. A "Round book" was one where the bookmaker just broke even.

boomers

Workers on the Railroad who wandered from job to job either because of incompetency, drunkenness or seasonal rushes. They usually were an independent group, insolent, humorous, worldwise, and given to bragging.

boom rats

A term used for the men who worked on the booms, the accumulated mass of logs, in the early logging days. These very skilled workers either pushed together the felled trees so that they were formed into the booms which made the mass of lumber more manageable, or after their destination had been reached pushed aside the logs marked as belonging to their employers by the brands or stamps they bore. Williamsport on the Susquehanna reached its golden age in those logging days when the boomers fed into the saw mills over three hundred and eighteen million board feet of lumber in one year.

The folk tales of this period claim as evidence of wealth the fact that the ladies of this community had a higher ratio of Paisley shawls than any other community in the nation.

"boom town" game

Children in parts of Los Angeles heard so much about the succession of booms in real estate starting with that of 1887 that they played a game patterned after the bogus schemes of the big promoters who laid out a paper town, took in enough money to buy options of a neighboring area and started the cycle all over again—until a bust came along. Then a succession of new arrivals started all over again and the children would rearrange their sandlot plans incorporating into them the many wild plans for dams, highways, race tracks until the whole area should be destroyed as actually happened to many of the grandiose schemes of their elders, leaving mute evidence of these inflated plans in boom hotels in deserted areas, trolley lines running to empty lots and other "debris of a weird civilization left as land marks"—and ready to spring to life when more desire for getting rich quick springs up. In 1889 assessed valuation in the booming AZUSA dropped from that of the year before fourteen million dollars. In an encircling area sixty towns were projected, 77,000 lots sold but only two thousand or so inhabitants attracted.

33

boot, boot camp

A boot was a new camp especially set up for that purpose in either the Navy, Marine Corps or the Coast Guard.

Boot Hill

Name given to a cemetery in Dodge City which set pattern for such names in many Western towns where the unfortunate victims of town violence by the cowboys were buried by the community.

The name comes from the fact that the deceased probably having met an abrupt and turbulent end was speedily buried with his boots on.

borderer

This term is equivalent to the expression "backwoodsman" today. They were the people living on the edge of the frontier, on the border of civilization. All their supplies were carried on their own back. As the fur trade increased, the pack horse was introduced and permanent roads began to be used. This encouraged the arrival of more settlers who began to bring in their families and soon the "borderers" were moving on further West.

Boston titles

In Puritan Boston you might be called MISTER if you had the franchise, that is, owned property which had a value of forty pounds sterling. A common person without the right to vote was called GOODMAN and his wife GOODWIFE or in common speech "Goody". By the revisions in the Charter of 1691 which brought down the qualifications for property ownership in order to vote, the adult male title of MISTER was extended to about one-fifth of the population.

"boughten bread"

This term was used for baker's bread in distinction to homemade bread. It implied a definite feeling of disapproval for any poor unfortunate who was forced to eat bread not of the superior quality made at home. In the country districts this attitude lingered long after the city folk bought "Baker's" bread as a matter of course.

bowling at pins

Fact and fancy get easily confused in this field. The Dutch brought it to America as lawn bowling to which Bowling Green in lower Manhattan is a continuing reference. Washington Irving also immortalized reference to the sport by calling attention to the thunder in the Catskills being really the clash of bowling ball on pins.

The popularity of bowling with pins increased greatly after 1835 but soon gamblers became interested so that the game was banned in Connecticut. However as the wording of the measure specifically outlawed bowling at nine pins a new game developed, bowling with ten pins. Out of the need to organize this game the American Bowling Congress arose.

box-cars

In throwing dice in betting sessions a double six is called a box-car probably because it seems as heavily laden as a freight car.

Boxer Day

A day observed in England on December twenty-sixth was observed in and about the state of Michigan by some of the immigrants of English origin. Collection boxes in the churches were opened on that day and sometimes the apprentices went around to their master's customers for small tips.

brakeman on the railroads

The new brakeman on a train provides the subject for many tales in railroad folklore. The new recruit once called a boll weevil could pull many a boner as was shown in the case where a freight train made a painful trip and finally attained the top of the hill. The engineer heaved a sigh of relief and stated his fear to the brakeman that they might have stalled and rolled down the hill backward out of control. "Nothing to worry about," the new man told him, "I went back and set all the brakes." Another subject for tale telling arose in regard to a conductor who was asking a brakeman how it was that he had not seen any fuses burning after they had a slight delay.The brakeman looked surprised and explained he had thrown out several fuses but had not known they were to be lighted.

"brave man"

By constant usage there had developed in Northern Pennsylvania an accepted folk definition. "He was not afraid of bears, he had heard Ethan Allen swear." This referred to the time Allen had attempted to organize some settlers into an independent state and had shouted defiance against the opposition so mightily that the country side claimed they would never hear its equal.

bread dance

Many Indian tribes such as the Iroquois and the Shawnee have spring and fall dances that represent a plea for plentiful crops and for good hunting. These were usually participated in by women since the growing and preparation of crops was assumed to be woman's work.

bread superstitions

It is held by some to bring bad luck if the loaf of bread is cut at both ends; if a piece of bread and butter is dropped on the floor it is considered bad luck in every sense if the buttered side falls to the floor. There are those who are convinced that if a loaf of bread is weighted down with quicksilver it will float along in the water until it stops over the dead body being sought.

break a mirror

Although many believe in the superstition that such an action may bring bad luck, there are others who claim that if one pounds the broken pieces to small bits one may overcome the handicap.

break broth

A savory broth served only at breakfast in colonial days on Cape Cod. All usually ate out of the same bowl.

36

"breast stones"

This is a term used for the gravestones of the Moravians in their burial places around Bethlehem, Pennsylvania. Placed presumably upon the chest of the one buried they attempted to show the equality of all in the eyes of the Lord. The dead were buried, not by family, but in most cases by the order in which they died. Little boys were placed in one section, little girls in another. Single men were buried apart from the married men and other related categories were grouped accordingly.

Brer Rabbit

Rabbit was the center of the trickster tales common particularly among the Gullah tribes in African folktales and it was not surprising that the transfer was easily made when later, as slaves, they made rabbit stories a large part of their story-telling repertoire. Negro fondness for these tales was probably due to an identification of themselves with the meek and timorous rabbit who yet is able to hold his own against far more powerful animals. Joel Chandler Harris' versions of the tales of Brer Rabbit are held to be closer to literature than folklore, though his folk art has been so good in many respects that they have retained their original attractiveness in a new setting. On the other hand with the popular development of "Peter Rabbit" of the modern bedtime stories the rabbit has become purely comic and whimsical rather than retaining its original trickster traits.

brick making, colonial style

Bricks were very scarce in America before 1800, most of those used before that time had been brought from England but about that time Philadelphia began to be a leader in the production of bricks and New Jersey a close competitor. Timothy Pickering made recommendations that a single brick at a time be prepared in a mold "shod" with iron. He also suggested that after molding they be thrown into a tub of fine-sifted dust and not into water to prevent their sticking. He thought a proper brick making crew should consist of a

37

man to mold the bricks, another to work the clay, and one to wheel it to the tables, and a boy to bear off one brick at a time. This group he thought could make two thousand bricks a day.

bridal knots

This attractive custom was developed in connection with the wedding bouquet in order to hold the good wishes for future happiness.

Bridal Veil Falls

A popular custom of honeymooning couples visiting Niagara Falls is to throw pennies into the Bridal Veil Falls so as to ensure them good luck during their married life. This idea may have had its origin from the custom of paying "tribute" to the gods of the seas in ancient times.

"broad horn" boat

When a flat boat was propelled by two great oars on either side it was thought to resemble the long-horn cattle of the early West and was given this designation. With a steering oar in the rear to lend resemblance to a tail the appropriateness of the title was felt to be very great.

broken striper

A popular expression used in the Navy to indicate a warrant officer because of the type of stripe worn upon his sleeve.

Bronx cheer

A custom supposedly originating in that Northern part of New York City were people made a crude and rude noise with their lips to indicate a large degree of disfavor. Also known as giving some one the "raspberry."

Brother Jonathan

This designation has come to be almost the equivalent of Yankee but there are some who consider it equally applicable to the whole nation as "John Bull" for the British. However there actually was a Brother Jonathan who was the governor of the State of Connecticut at the time of the Revolutionary War. So frequently did General Washington say that certain situations had to be referred to "Brother Jonathan" that the refrain was picked up by others and became associated with the whole section.

bruder pleger (caretaker)

Young people of the Moravian sect were very well supervised in all their activities. In Nazareth and the nearby communities of the Pennsylvania Dutch the chaperon of the young men was the bruder pleger and the counterpart for the girls was the Schwester Pleger or matron in charge of single women. They assisted in the arrangements for marriage for these young people who had no opportunity to meet those of the opposite sex. The final choice of a wife was made by lot on the assumption that God would direct the choice. The girl could refuse but so much faith was placed on the divine aspect of the choice that a girl seldom refused the man thus determined for her.

Bruneau John of Idaho

John was a member of a local Indian tribe in Idaho though friendly to his white neighbors. He reported to them that his fellow tribesmen were about to attack. However the warning was ignored and the attack was made upon a large freighting outfit on its way to Bruneau. The men were all killed and horribly mutilated. The loyal John was wounded and was thus not forced to take part in the excesses. While destroying all the supplies the Indians came upon a supply of alcohol and all became speedily drunk. John then slipped out of camp and in a wild ride much enlarged upon in the retelling warned all the white people in the Bruneau Valley of the danger in which they were. They safely fled to a neighboring valley. The Indians finally awakened and discovering their prey gone destroyed all the homes instead and then returned to their camp. John was made a scout and won a silver medal for his exploit.

brunswick stew

As made in North Carolina this popular dish may include practically everything produced on the farm including chick-

39

en, beef, veal, squirrels, beans, corn, potatoes, tomatoes, butter beans, vinegar, celery, mustard and plenty of red pepper. Bread should be available for dunking. Such a repast used to be served out-of-doors from a large iron pot by means of a long-handled ladle and placed in a boat-shaped receptacle made of thin wood. An appetizer of bourbon and branch water was popular and a barbecue of roast pig often followed. The Kentuckians call a similar dish burgo (q.v.).

brush fires

The inhabitants of the Ozark Mountains have developed a wonderful body of folklore. One of the stories they find to their liking has to do with the frequency of brush fires in that neighborhood from September to December. When they finally butcher a hog in the spring they discover he is already smoked.

buckaroo

A term for a cowpuncher West of the Rockies. It was a a corruption of vaquero, a word derived from the Spanish (vaca means cow) which at first was limited in its application to Mexican cowboys.

bucking board

In the early lumber camps of Michigan this term was used to refer to the bulletin board on which would be posted a list of the teamsters working at that time and giving the number of board feet of logs that each had hauled. A reward went to the man with the greatest amount to his credit, usually a fine mackinaw. An illiterate French Canadian was observed studying the list bearing the designated winner. He was peering very closely and seemed very annoyed that he had not won. "Best show me," he muttered, "that goddam Monsieur Total."

"Buck Private"

A popular expression used in the Air Force as a name for their light, two hundred pound helicopter.

buckwheat cakes

In colonial New York State buckwheat cakes were already popular and this housewife's recipe was copied by those who went West also. Stir into your buckwheat flour sour milk or buttermilk and add some yeast left over from the morning's baking. Put in a big pitcher which is then placed in a pan for after standing in the warm room for several hours the liquid will rise and begin to overflow. It must be "stirred down" frequently to make the best cakes.

bull

This popular name for the many portions of rough water found on the Wisconsin River was taken over from the French voyageurs, in whose Canuck style of reference a "bulles" was a rapid. The names they gave are retained in many areas, for example, Grandfather Rapid was "Grandpère bulles."

bulls and bears

Horace Greeley it is claimed while touring in California near the mother lode of the Sierras witnessed a fierce battle between a bear and a black Mexican bull. He sent a graphic description of this to his New York paper, the Tribune. The account is supposed to have given the Wall Street operators reason for calling the activities of financial rivals by the same terms.

bull boat (Missouri style)

This boat borrowed from the Indians was very commonly used on the upper reaches of the Missouri River. A hull resembling an oversize open-work basket was prepared of willow sticks lashed together with strips of green rawhide. As the last step the entire boat was covered with a single buffalo hide of the freshly killed animal. The skin dried taut on the frame some of whose willow shoots were ten feet long and as thick as a wrist, and about eight to ten inches apart, some woven at right angles to one another. The usual weight, about thirty pounds made it possible for the boat to be carried on a squaw's back; yet it would take

41

a load of over two hundred pounds and several people safely across the river, providing a very essential means of communication.

Buller legends of Lake Superior

A Cornishman, Dick Buller was gifted with a fine basso voice by means of which he won all the singing contests of the vocally musical Cornishmen of the Central Mine of the Copper Country. His voice they claimed could penetrate ten levels underground and could be heard ten to fifteen miles away on the surface. Accounts abound of his extraordinary feats.

"Bullet Barons"

Thus the gangsters of Chicago came to be called in the gang wars of the Prohibition era. Hired assassins were not a new idea for Chicago but these men did things on such an ornate style as to form a colorful part of folklore. Rival gangs were held to be responsible for twenty-five murders a year. A big shot's funeral was attended by hundreds, many representatives of the city administration attending. One was famous or infamous for his $10,000 silver-trimmed coffin brought from New York in a special baggage car. Truckloads of flowers accompanied the funerals.

"bull jine"

From 1731 to the Civil War fire fighting in New York City was done by volunteer companies who took great pride in their work and in their machines. When the apparatus was especially heavy and powerful, it was lovingly designated as a bull engine which became corrupted into the popular term "bull-jine."

bull whacker

The man needed to whip the mules on the treks to the West was held by those who had an opportunity to listen to him as the most profane of all the Westerners. He would keep the mules going with a great whip twenty feet long

42

and ten inches in circumference at the "belly." The men became very accurate in the use of the whip. Many bets were made on the ability to cut a coin from the top of a stick.

bunk fatigue

An enlisted man's expression for those in the Army who are resting or loafing.

bunny meat (rabbit food)

A common expression for referring to food or a meal made up of green vegetables, or salads without any real meat.

Bunyan's animals

Everything that was associated with Paul Bunyan was gigantic and wonderful; not the least so was a herd of cows which he maintained in his so-called home camp. To the milk which "Boss" gave you only had to add salt and you already had fine butter. That of "Suke" made very wonderful hot cakes. "Baldy's" never soured and made the finest cream gravy. S'manthy's milk was pretty poor stuff because she ate so many balsam boughs, but in the winter time it was in great demand as a potent cough medicine.

In the Bunyan tales they also refer to the gilly grouse which nested near Big Onion River and laid square eggs which Bunyan's men used for dice. There was an ax handle hound that ate all the ax handles and peavy handles that were left around. Finally there was a shagamaw, a timid creature who wandered the tote roads. He had the claws of a bear on his forefeet and the hoofs of a moose behind. He prowled around devouring coats and mittens which he found on stumps and made a great nuisance of himself.

burgo

A dish particularly associated with Kentucky was made in a variety of ways but there was pretty general agreement that almost anything around the house could be used in this vast stew-meat, corn, celery, turnips and potatoes were basic. Usually just three meats were included, beef, chicken

and any animal in season, all cooked down for hours to complete disintegration forming a paste that all Kentucky believes to be the finest possible persuader for political rallies and conventions, and a vitalizer for court days.
See: BRUNSWICK STEW.

bursting horns

In the winter of 1886 it was so cold on the plains of the Far West that the horns of the cattle actually burst in some areas. Other conditions were equally bad. An owner of a ranch there asked a cowboy to report on conditions, but the young man found them almost indescribable. Instead he painted a picture for his boss that showed the state of affairs so well that his career as a cow hand was ended, that of Charlie Russell, artist began. His rise to fame started with the poignant scene "Waiting for a Chinook" and grew steadily thereafter.

bury the hatchet

An expression used in the Northwest and Southwest, borrowed from the Indians, which means the maintenance of friendship because a dangerous weapon has been disposed of.

Buster Brown

Having originated what was probably the first comic strip character in the "Yellow Kid" in 1896, Richard Outcault by 1902 had started another famous character whose influence has survived to some extent to the present day. Buster with his dog, Tige, who made penetrating comments on human frailty followed a fairly set pattern in most of his series; the prank for the day, the resolutions, and the comment from Tige. The spread of his fame was so great that practically every other kid was called Buster and he in turn has retained an ageless quality of appeal because of the very universality of childhood that he illustrated.

butter-and-egg man

The title of a play by George S. Kaufman was applied to a group of newly rich men who did not conform to the

44

ordinary designation of "Big Business." They were making their money by playing the stock market in the period just before the Depression of 1929 and though temporary millionaires were called "big butter-and-egg men" in sarcasm for their rather ostentatious living and lack of refinement by the New York columnists.

butter-making

Many supernatural tales about difficulties with the making of butter center about New England dealing especially with the bewitching of the cream so that the butter will not come. A heated horseshoe dropped into the cream burned out the witch according to one example.

butterfly beliefs among the Indians

The Blackfoot Indians believe that dreams are brought to us in our sleep by butterflies therefore the mother embroiders the sign of the butterfly on a piece of buckskin which she ties on her baby's head when she wants him to go to sleep.

The Zuni believes when white butterflies are seen warm weather may be expected, but if they fly from the southwest rain should be expected.

butterfly beliefs in other parts of the United States

A butterfly in the house is a wedding sign.

In Maryland they say if a white butterfly comes into the house and flies around you, you will die, however in Louisiana, they believe it means good luck.

Some believe if a butterfly flies in one's face it is a sign of cold weather coming; while others specify it must be a yellow butterfly which strikes your face to bring the kind of weather which will turn the leaves yellow in a week.

buzzard

Buzzards because they eat carrion are associated with death and therefore have come to be regarded with awe by the Negroes of the South who believed that if a buzzard's shadow touched you, death, illness or some ill fortune would

45

touch you. The Pueblo Indians, on the other hand because he is a scavenger regard him as a purifying and cleansing power. Buzzard feathers are used in all cures. The Shaman brushes away evil with a buzzard feather. The Hopi say he is bald because he pushed the sun away when it got too near the earth.

In slavery days the Negroes thought the buzzard was a thief-finder and there was something more to this than legend for if one of them had stolen some pork and hidden it away on the roof the resulting decay was speedily revealed by the buzzard when the sun had been at work on it. In several parts of the country they believed that if a buzzard caught a child he would pick its eyes out.

C

cabin fever

This was a generally acknowledged condition among prospectors and others who were likely to "hole up" for the winter where they would be isolated with just one another for a long period of time. No matter how much the regard each had had for the other or how close the relationship before very long they were getting on one another's nerves to a great degree and often ended by not speaking to one another at all.

caboodle

In the Southwest where the term was widely popular it meant the whole lot or accumulation. It was often combined with the expression—"Take the whole kit and caboodle." In this sense it has also been a common term among New England long-shoremen.

caboteurs

Traders in the Southwest who carried on a profitable business along the rivers and bayous. They were later supplemented by the colporteurs, especially the sellers of Bibles for which the South was an especially good market. Also doing a similar job were the "marchand paquet," salesmen who peddled their wares on foot.

cactus

The cactus was of special religious significance to many of the American Indians. Those participating in the Zuñi ceremonials are whipped by cacti to give them strength and luck in hunting. Pieces of cacti are put in the corner of each Hopi house to give the house roots.

Café Society

A fabulous figure of the World War I period was Maury Paul better known as Cholly Knickerbocker who wrote of high society. About 1919 he made note of the fact that he saw four members of the most aristocratic families all eating out at the same time in the swank Ritz-Carlton Hotel. This was a situation that had not been noticeable previously and Mr. Paul gave this new order of things a name. He called the group Café Society, a name which became more and more popular. It was copied as the title for a movie and by night clubs. It became the accepted designation for anyone who wore a white collar. A law suit was even instituted to discover the bonafide originator of the term. In 1939 Cholly Knickerbocker was finally awarded the honor of having first coined the phrase.

See HIGH SOCIETY, FOUR HUNDRED.

cahoots, to be in

To be in a partnership with or to enter into some plans with, according to the cowboys of the Southwest.

cakewalk

At dances originating among Negroes in the South, a cake was awarded to the person who walked most stiffly erect; but gradually the "walk" developed into a high prance entailing a high degree of exhibitionism and ultimately attaining considerable vogue in public entertainment in the 1910's.

calash

This was a special kind of hat that resembled the calash or carriage top of the period. The wearer could pull the hat forward when out doors and push it back when she came in.

calico queen

A frontier term for a woman of the "honky tonks" or a prostitute.

California melon picking

Foremen in the Imperial Valley claim that only a Mexican

48

can tell the exact day when a cantaloupe should be picked—just twenty-four hours before the melon is ripe. No one they say but a Mexican knows and he does not know why he knows—he just knows.

California sock

A cowboy unable to procure any other covering for his feet might create a substitute out of a neckerchief. He would fold the corners and the front end over the top of his foot, then bring the other end up in back over the heel and wrap it around the ankle. The term "California collar" was often a cowboy's calling for a hangman's noose. When he talked about "California pants" he meant those made of especially heavy material.

calling the wind

The Negroes of slave times had a custom of "calling the wind" when a breeze was needed to carry on some task. They would say "Co' wind" three times followed by a long whistle. This was done when rice was to be fanned, when a sail hung idle or when a field was to be burned.

callout dances

A practice established at the great balls held in New Orleans in the period from January sixth to Shrove Tuesday, just before the beginning of Lent. Call-out cards are issued to the young ladies who are to attend with their original invitations. The girls are seated in special call-out seats when they arrive at the ball. There is much anxious seeking after such honors. The carnival organizations (Krewes, q.v.) issue the call-out cards to their membership who then fill in the names of those they desire to dance with. Choice by leading officers constitutes an important recognition of social standing in a very exclusive society. Membership and high position in these organizations represents an almost unattainable goal to an ordinary outsider. Business or professional position may be of no significance but poverty and blood may have far more important standing. Even Hollywood has not been able to force these doors open.

49

calumet

This is the peace pipe of the North American Indians the smoking of which indicates an acceptance of peace if all the correct ceremonials are observed. To invite a stranger to smoke the pipe is a mark of friendship, to refuse to offer the pipe meant that open hostility was intended. The pipe was usually about two and a half feet in length, the bowl of which was made of polished red marble with the stem made of a reed usually highly decorated.

The Indians looked upon the smoke-offering as being particularly sacred. Fire, ashes and smoke are endowed with purifying and life-giving properties. There was a form of native symbolism in the inhaling and then exhaling of the smoke in that it represented the breath of life itself. As the smoke rose thus also did the soul of the smoker arise with it. There was a parallel with the Oriental custom of using incense.

Cambridge Common Exhibition

At a grand review held by George Washington during the Revolutionary War British spies had trickled in to report on the results of frontier recruiting. They saw 1400 riflemen rough and crude in their clothes but leaning on the longest barrelled guns ever noted in that part of the country. Poles were set up for targets at what was held to be an unbelievable distance—250 yards. The riflemen fired nonchalantly and in a few minutes a whole fusillade of bullets had knocked down all the targets set up.

camel express

An enterprising man thought to use camels on the Great American Desert but the project failed about 1857. There are those however, who claim to have been startled by a camel appearing there as late as the nineteen twenties.

camphor superstitions

For years there was and, perhaps still is, the practice of wearing a block of camphor on a string around one's neck to ward off any infectious diseases. In rural areas they believe

50

that a piece of camphor placed near the bed of a sick person will prevent a fever from developing. Such mothers think that rubbing the breast with camphor just before a baby is born will cause the milk to dry up and the baby need not be nursed.

can

A Navy expression for a depth charge.

can openers

Western slang for spurs.

canary superstitions

The popularity of the canary has created a number of beliefs about it that are not always consistent. When the bird is silent for a long time it is assumed that evil is in the air. This sensitivity to odors is also interpreted as indicating the likelihood of a catastrophe coming. If a cat kills your canary you will not have good luck for two years. On the other hand there is a general belief because of the conjugal faithfulness of these birds that their presence in a home brings joy and harmony to the home.

Canal Street (Buffalo)

A district symbolizing a small and sinful neighborhood in Buffalo in the middle of the nineteenth century. Here a sucker could be speedily separated from his money and many other shady performances originated. A Mother Carey was supposed to have provided "cooks" as feminine companions for the lonesome captains of the canal barges. Even Sheriff Grover Cleveland is supposed to have failed in his efforts to clean up the area. Tales abound of the murders occurring there averaging some claim one a day. The Canal there has now been filled in and the stories of the region constitute a gruesome portion of folklore.

cancellation of letters

A device used by young people as a means of foretelling if affection is returned. The boy crosses out the letters in a girl's

51

name that are found in his and then repeats the refrain, "She loves me, she loves me not."

"Candle-maker"

In rural Vermont there was a woman in many communities who was the official candle maker. She would visit various homes to help in the tricky task of shipping hand made candles to market, an occupation that continued up to 1880.

candlewood

This material was sometimes confused with pine knots but though they came from the same tree candlewood was cut from the heart of the tree, the "fat" wood. It was cut in thin strips about eight inches in length and tied into small easily handled bundles. After being allowed to season well with their rich tarry content they provided winter lighting for many families in our early history. The idea was supposed to have come from the Indians as early as 1633 who had "split pine into shivers."

Cape Cod houses

The early Cape Cod houses were not built for display but for use. They often had five rooms on the ground floor and two in the attic. The parlor was usually to the right of the entrance and had a separate door, commonly called the "funeral door," for that was the purpose it usually served. The mother's and father's room was on the left. In the back was a big kitchen and a dining and living room. An ell might be added to the back making space for a few small bedrooms. One of these was kept cozy and warm and was called the "borning" room, another might provide needed isolation and was called the "measles room."

Cape Cod lore

See break broth, cup plate, Goodie Hallet, Joseph's boats, long-tail sugar, Mashpee Kingdom, moon-cussing, Nauset, Praying Braves, remembering acres, Sargo Lake, tarpaulin tarradiddles, time-telling, Timothy Dexter.

Cap Cod named

It is claimed that Bartholomew Gosnold, an English captain was sailing off the shore near where the Pilgrims had landed when he came upon a school of cod and saw the Cape at the same time. He therefore gave it what he considered an appropriate title. The King is supposed to have tried to change it to Cape James but popular usage made Cape Cod more acceptable. This was especially true after Cotton Mather had stated that it was a name which would last as long as shoals of cod fish could be seen from the hills.

capping a tale

This was a device used by many a teller of tall tales in the West. The principle was to finish off the story with a still bigger exaggeration after having already built up to a wopper. For example, a story was being told based on the need to construct an enormous kettle. Hundreds of tons of metal were to be needed—But what was the kettle to be used for? Why, of course it was to be used to cook the tremendous turnip that the previous speaker had indicated was growing on the fourteen acre patch he had been describing.

card playing superstitions

There are those who believe that one can change one's bad luck at cards by turning one's chair so that it stands with its back to the table. In bridge, there are those who having cut the high card for the deal, want to use that pack for good luck.

Carnegie Legends

Though Andrew Carnegie was somewhat of a tyrant in his beautiful Fifth Avenue home requiring his guests to be down to breakfast at eight o'clock in the morning and forbidding smoking in the house, he had a genuine affinity for the common man. When he discovered that the lawns and gardens about his Ninety-first Street mansion were enjoyed by his very humble neighbors on the back streets near him he ordered his gardener "to keep the flowers pretty so those outsiders could enjoy them." Even his widow remembered

53

his desires and would tell the gardener before each annual pilgrimage to Scotland to be sure to plant her husband's favorite bloom, red geraniums in the flower beds. She said he would want something bright in the yards for the people who rode the Fifth Avenue busses past his home to see. Despite other aspects of his austerity Carnegie had a fine appreciation of good liquor which was not dimmed by his moderate habits. He arranged for a regular shipment from Scotland of a very special brew the Queen's Vat whiskey which was the choice also of the venerable Queen Victoria of England.

Enjoying the praise he received for this fine product he began to provide a few carefully chosen friends with a supply. Benjamin Harrison while President accepted with pleasure his gift though facetiously wondering whether it might be looked upon as a political bribe. Many other persons of eminence thanked him for his "golden liquid fire." However there was one occasion when his offer was made under unusual circumstances and became a well repeated tale. On a certain Sunday noticing Mr. Rockefeller leaving church surrounded by his usual admirers, Mr. Carnegie called over to him in front of this crowd, "Oh, I've just received a new consignment of whiskey from Scotland. I'm going to send you some."

Though renowned for his large scale contributions for charitable purposes and he gave away over $350 million in his retirement, he was usually impatient with modest support of scattered worthy enterprises. When approached for five dollars for such a purpose he is said to have snapped back, "I'm not interested in retail philanthropy."

Carver's Cave

Carver's scrip. About 1777 a New England shoemaker was commissioned by Major Robert Rogers, founder of the famous Rangers to survey the area of the Upper Mississippi and to prepare a map of the region. His activities were later not recognized nor paid for. To seek some redress he went to England where he died. In that same year a volume was pub-

54

lished supposedly by him describing his early "Travels." Later criticism repudiated much that he was supposed to have written and served to put in doubt claims made in his name for certain territory along the Mississippi. However on the basis of this early account a cave is still pointed out on the Mississippi near St. Paul, under Dayton's Bluff where at a solemn ceremony two Sioux chiefs supposedly granted to Carver and his heirs a large track of land. Scrip based on this transaction remained in circulation for a long time for there were many claimants to the land and many gullible enough to buy the unsubstantiated claims. A controversy still exists as to whether Carver actually wrote the account published. Congress ultimately repudiated the alleged treaty between Carver and the Indians.

casket girls (filles a la casette)

At one time in the early history of New Orleans orphans were sent out from France to provide proper brides for the over abundant male population. The authorities had provided each girl with a chest containing some clothing and personal effects. Occasional reference may be found to the role played by these girls in the writings of the nineteenth century.

casket shortage

The tale is told very seriously about Denver a century ago when a pneumonia epidemic struck the city and the number of deaths outstripped the limited supply of caskets. An enterprising undertaker was caught building up his reserve in an unusual fashion. He was digging up at night the caskets more recently used and still in good condition.

cast down and cast off

Terms used for country dances. In the first the dancers turn outward and move backward along the set, in the second they turn outward and dance outside the set.

Castella Legend

In California, near the Upper Sacramento supposedly a

United States pay train was ambushed by Indians while picking its difficult way across the newly acquired territory, and all connected with it were killed. However, there are those who claim that hidden somewhere in the region is the supply of gold the train carried. There remains the suspicion that the tale was started out of whole cloth by an old timer oversupplied with leisure.

caterpillars

There was a belief that these wormlike creatures were made by witches with the devil's help, those of German descent held they were "teufelskatze," the devil's cats. For their use in weather prediction see "WOOLLY BEARS."

cat superstitions

The suspicion that a cat really has nine lives is so widely accepted that it hardly seems a superstition to some. Considering a black cat's crossing your path as bad luck is in the like category. Southern Negroes warn against kicking a cat lest you suffer from rheumatism or drowning a cat lest the Devil will get you. In Maine they find a cat looking out of the window a sign that it will rain. That a cat should never be left alone in the house with a baby is a precaution exercised by those who think cats jump up on the weak and delicate and suck their breath thus suffocating them. Many believe that cats are able to see in the dark.

catfish troubles

A tall tale of the rainy delta region in Louisiana lists the many sufferings a man in that area must endure. His hide sprouts water cress; and his dog has crabs instead of fleas, but the payoff comes when he starts catching catfish in the sitting room mouse trap.

Cattle Kate

Ella Watson was hanged for cattle rustling (see NECKTIE JUSTICE) though not proved a thief. Many tales about Cattle Kate grew up out of this incident vigorously retelling her widespread activities.

cat with wooden leg

A popular tall tale of the Vermont area tells of this unfortunate cat who hit his prey with his conveniently acquired permanent club. He could only eat things which he had caught himself.

"caulk off"

A Navy expression meaning to sleep from the reference to the caulking mats upon which seamen had formerly slept on deck.

Cave-In-the-Rock, Kentucky

This cave near Louisville, Kentucky was a rendez-vous of thieves and murderers about 1795. It was ideally suited for its nefarious purpose. Many stories are told of how kind-hearted strangers were tricked by means of pitiful tales to enter this impregnable hiding place and who were never seen again, nor whose goods and "possibles" were ever found. Held by some to be Kentucky's bloodiest bandits these men had a host of tricks for obtaining hostages. They might secretly bore a hole or holes in a vessel about to sail down the Ohio near their cave. They would then "rescue" the travellers and steal their supplies.

cayuse

A Western term for an undersized horse. The term was originally applied to the wild horses of Oregon taking their names from the Cayuse Indians.

chair rail

This was a special piece of wood installed along the wall of the colonial homes as a protection from the universal habit of tipping back the chairs in those days. This rail was particularly needed in the light of the fact that all the chairs then in use were remarkably hard straight-backed types, which probably accounts for the fact that they were so generally tipped back in the first place.

chameleon

Common belief accepts the unproved assumption that this

57

little reptile can change color on purpose as a means of defense despite evidence that he is actually responding to emotional changes due to fear, anger or other excitement. A popular superstition states that to wear or own one of these little animals will ward off evil influences. Others claim that worn as a charm he will protect the wearer from disease.

chanson des voyageurs (chants of the woodsmen)

In Northern New York where many French Canadians were employed, they claim if one hears one of these plaintive songs high in the air one will know that another French inhabitant has become so homesick that he has sold his soul to the devil in order to return immediately to his home and his loved ones.

chaparejos (chaparereras)

These are leather breeches or strong overalls worn by the Western cowboy when he needs protection as he rides through brush, cactus or rough chaparral. He calls them "chaps." They may protect him if he is thrown off a horse or against cold or rain. They are usually promptly removed when not immediately needed since they are hot and bulky made possibly of fur, hair, angora, bear skin. They are sometimes called bull hides, grizzles, hair pants, riding aprons, chivarros, chinkaderos and many related terms.

chaparral fox

A Western term for a sly tricky person, a sneak.

charivari

The original French form for the boisterous custom of serenading a newly married couple. The idea was that such a noisy demonstration would frighten any evil spirits away. The custom was carried North and the term was modified to Shivaree. In Creole Louisiana it was a noisy display continued until refreshments or other distractions were offered. If an old man had married a young girl there might be the likelihood of some rude observations.

Charlestown (South Carolina)

An old saw with some implication of correctness was popular among the Carolinians to the effect that near Charleston the Asley and Cooper rivers join to form the Atlantic Ocean.

cherry-tree deer

Hunter's tales may all incline to be a little tall and this one too which has its counterpart in many sections of the country. A deer hunter was finishing up his lunch and had thrown the pits from his cherry pie down beside him. Glancing up unexpectedly he noticed a deer approaching and discovered at the same moment that he was out of ammunition. However he quickly grabbed the cherry pits and fired. Unfortunately the animal was only stunned, picked himself up and ran away. But, amazingly, the following year at the same spot the hunter was astonished to see in the distance a deer with a number of trees growing among his antlers.

chew the fat

To become unnecessarily involved in an argument or discussion often when other duties should be carried out.

Chinese funeral customs in Idaho

In the mining days of the Old West Chinese laborers were much in demand so that there was a rather large Chinese population in the mine fields of Idaho. When one of their members died the tong, a Chinese secret society followed a careful ritual in the burial procedure. The deceased was followed to his grave by an orchestra consisting of a gong, a reed instrument, and another instrument resembling a banjo. Twice a year the Chinese officials went out to "feed" their dead. Bowls of rice, pork and whiskey were set out by the graves. These were inspected in the morning to see if they were empty which they usually were due to the coyotes and watchful white men. After two years the bodies were exhumed. The bones were then sealed in metal containers and shipped back to China for burial, a requirement that the Chinese were very insistent upon.

59

Chinese in the early mining days

Throughout Idaho there were many tales told about the superstitions observed by the many Chinese in this region in the early days. One has to do with the death of a Chinese in a distant place. Because the Chinese were particularly concerned with the return of the bodies of their dead to their native land a quick-tempered Swede was commissioned to go to the place where the Chinaman had died and bring back the body to them in Silver City. Having recovered the body the Swede was puzzled how he was going to get it over the mountain passes and around other difficulties. At last he worked out a solution. He attached skis to the Chinese and coasted his way home. He had many mishaps along the way and was especially eager to turn over his burden to those who had hired him. However, he became resentful when each Chinese he approached passed him on to another for payment. At last in desperation he announced that he guessed he would take the body home and feed it to his pet fox. Funds were immediately forthcoming.

On another occasion in order to have a fine funeral a group of Chinese hired the local band to perform. However, the band did not have its music with them so they had a very limited choice as to what they could render. On the way to the burial they played over and over, "There'll Be a Hot Time In the Old Town Tonight." At the grave they broke into "Down Went McGinty." The Chinese were particularly pleased with the performance and profusely thanked them paying them one hundred dollars for the fine "funeral march and requiem."

Chinese were scrupulously attentive to correct care of the dead because they did not want any spirits coming back to reproach or haunt them.

Another Idaho tale tells of a man having run over a sleek fat dog. He thought he would make some profit out of the situation, so he sold it to a Chinese restaurant claiming it was mutton. A few days later having had dinner there he was told he had just eaten the "mutton" he had sold them before.

chin music

A common Western term for long-winded talk of a gossipy nature.

chin superstitions

It is a very common belief that people with receding chins are weaklings and that those with strong protruding chins are pugnacious.

Chippewa's gain fire

In the Lake Superior region Nanabazhoo (q.v.) was a famous demi-god and one of the legends about him explains how he was able to bring the use of fire to the Chippewa. The tale states that shortly after he was born he decided he would have to obtain the benefits of fire for his people. Changing himself into a hare he let himself be captured by the daughter of the owner of fire who saw with sympathy the poor little bunny wet from the lake. Nanabazhoo is allowed to dry himself out before the fire and when the sparks start burning on his skin he rushes for his own tribesmen and thus fire has been won. As a reminder of this action the hare continues to turn brown in summer (burn his coat) and becomes white again in the winter.

Chitlins or chitterlings

At the fall hog-killing the frill-like small intestines of the hogs become available in large quantities in many Southern communities. After these had been soaked, cleaned and parboiled, they were fried like an oyster and represent the most delectable ambrosia to many.

cigar store Indians

A wooden Indian had indicated the location of a cigar store as early as 1700 in Boston. The fashion then spread all over the country and even to the present there are devoted collectors of this type of Americana.

These practical statues were required to be made in full detail with all the feathers of a war chief's bonnet made to show up clearly. One well-known carver claimed there were

61

more "Indians" of the wooden variety within a mile of Old Fort Dearborn than there had been alive at Potawatomie at the time of the massacre.

City ordinances requiring that the sidewalks be kept clear finally drove the "Indians" and their closest competitor, the stuffed bear, off the streets.

Old Walter Campbell long the carver of fine statues got even with the changing time in his last models for he included a handcarved watch and chain with a carved Masonic chain, a pistol in place of a tomahawk and corn cob pipe.

"Cindy"

A popular banjo or fiddle tune for square dances. The first verse gives an idea of the charms and complexities of a somewhat bewildered backwoods girl:

"I wish a' I was an apple,
Ahangin' in the tree
And ev'ry time my sweetheart passed,
She'd take a bite of me.
She told me that she loved me,
She called me sugar plum,
She throwed her arms around me—
I thought my time had come."
Chorus:
"Git along home, Cindy, Cindy, (repeat three times)
I'll marry you some time."

circular story

A rambling tale told by a cowboy concealing a "sell" for the benefit of a greenhorn. The sucker may not fall for the trick quickly and the story may get back where it started with the teller starting off again. Ultimately the inexperienced listener will fall for something and produce the laughter sought originally.

cisterns

Early colonial homes in Boston used these articles resembling a water cooler as a means of serving beer or cider. The people of that time distrusted water greatly and for a

62

long time so that these means of providing a substitute beverage were very popular. Some were quite expensive because of the elaborate carving made upon them or because of the silver hoops with which they were adorned.

Civil War greetings

A classic exchange of words is credited with occurring frequently throughout the South during the period of the slow advance of the Northern armies especially in the Shenandoah Valley, called the valley of humiliation by the inhabitants. Rebel meets Yank. "Where are you going Yank?"

"Going to Richmond."

"You'll never get there."

"Oh, yes, we will, swap generals with us and we will be there in three weeks."

clean shirts for sea captains

The sea captains of Cape Cod were understood to be very fastidious gentlemen. Stories about a few of them seem to prove that very thoroughly. One captain came home with three hundred soiled shirts each hand-made by his wife. He had worn a fresh one every day of the voyage. It is claimed that Sumner Pierce of Barnstable came home with seven hundred to be laundered and that it took Mrs. Pierce all summer to get caught up.

cloak and dagger merchant

The security officer who is on his own "secret mission," or one responsible for the maintenance of full security regulations.

coal as fuel

Though some Indians were aware of the fact that what they called "stonecoal" would burn, it was not used in the colonies as fuel until the 1770's when a Connecticut blacksmith living in Wyoming Valley of the Susquehanna which is now part of Pennsylvania, began to use it in his forge. In 1808 a poorly paid judge used his home as a tavern. To increase its warmth and thus attract more customers he developed a grate made of iron in which at first he burned hickory withes but soon he learned of the coal that the blacksmith had been burning and began to use it also. By practical demonstration he began to show the advantages of this type of fuel. Pretty soon the cumbersome barges which had been navigating the Susquehanna began to carry supplies to enterprising blacksmiths who early saw the advantage of this fuel. Gradually fascinated citizens began to purchase coal and a vast new enterprise was started.

coarse materials known to the colonial South

Crocus was the term used for such a kind of wool. Druggets were made of looser woven wool. Printed calico came into use by 1758.

cob iron

An andiron for the support of logs. Made by a blacksmith of wrought iron. The irons were placed in the fireplace lengthwise from front end to back in pairs so that logs could be piled on them from both sides. Popular in Revolutionary times.

cockroach bosses

This uncomplimentary title was given to the men who gave out work to the sweat shops around Paterson, New Jersey, where at one time two-thirds of the silk goods being produced in America was manufactured amid tremendous rivalry and cutthroat competition between the employers.

codfish superstitions

Off the Jersey coast if they see the codfish running in October rather than as usual in December they will announce a hard winter to come. The earstones or otoliths of a codfish are regarded by superstitious sailors as especially lucky. Possession of a pair of them will protect the holder at sea.

coffee pot sailor

A term used at the beginning of the twentieth century to indicate a sailor who had transferred from a sailing vessel to steam. The early steamships were called "kettle-bottomed coffee pots" by the sailing fraternity.

"coffin-notices"

These were messages sent out by the Molly Maguires (q.v.), to those whose actions they objected to. These threats of death were illustrated by crude drawings of the persons to whom they were addressed appearing as a corpse in a pine box surrounded by grisly skulls and crossbones.

coin flipping

To flip a coin to make a decision is still a widespread practice of those who would probably not admit to being observers of folk customs. "Heads you win, tails you lose" settles many a dispute without any resulting hard feelings since it is regarded as an entirely impartial performance. Some carry a "lucky" coin especially for this purpose. The large old-fashioned copper penny has been often carried for this reason.

cold brand or hair brand

A rustler may brand a young calf with the correct brand to pass inspection, but do it through a blanket so that just the hair of the animal is singed and the hide not seared. The following year the hair will have grown out over where the brand was supposed to be and the man with dishonest purposes in view may then pick out such a cow and put his own brand on it.

cold sores

Sores on the lips, or chapped lips had many superstitions connected with them, some of them quite contradictory; one of which was that the person had had too many kisses. Another version states that cold sores mean that one has told a lie.

cold thunder

When it gets cold in the Ozarks it does so in a very superior fashion as is guaranteed by the teller of tall tales. It is explained that in a cold spell the water in the rivers freezes,

65

and expands so much that the banks have to be pushed back. This performance resembles an earthquake and is known as cold thunder.

"Colonel Colt's equalizer"

When Colt had his gun in widespread distribution it was agreed that its possession made any slight weak man strong. It was in use in the Mexican War and had already been popular on the range.

colonial drinks

The most popular drink of the colonial period was flip (q.v.) made of beer and rum. Apple jack was common also and when particularly potent was called Jersey lightning. Gin was especially cheap and was called commonly "Strip and Go Naked." A rum fustian was a more elaborate drink to prepare. It consisted of beer, sherry, gin, yolks of eggs, sugar, nutmeg all fused together when a red-hot poker (*see* LOGGERHEAD) was thrust into the mixture. Rum was the one ingredient that was not included accounting for the use of the word fustian meaning a coarse, cotton twill, an imitation or substitute for velvet.

"coloring in early America"

The housewife who performed every step in the process of dressing her family from caring for the sheep through the spinning and weaving had also to produce the necessary coloring matter and appeared to be quite successful in this undertaking though it required ingenious planning and plenty of time. Peddlers brought the indigo to the more distant communities in the form of lumps of material which after having been softened and mashed in little bags were placed in a lye solution in earthenware or wooden dye pots. Blue wool "frocks" resembling our artists' smocks were worn for work by many farmers. Part of the hand-carded wool would be left white and the remainder dyed blue. When woven a pretty check was attained by using the white yarn in one direction and the blue in the other. Blue and white wool scarves and socks were produced by tying strings tightly

66

around the skeins of yarn, then they were left in the dye pots for several weeks. When they were removed they were an interesting variegated pattern of blue and white.

Most of the coloring in this early period was done in the yarn stage. Butternuts were used for brown, the bark or the shucks producing different shades. Among other materials used were walnuts, saffron, petals of St. John's Wort, sassafras and onion skin which was the cheapest. Cochineal provided the red dye. Elderberries and sumach gave a purple shade while the purple flag colored white wool a soft violet. All these vegetable dyes seemed to improve the lasting quality of the wool. To set or make the colors last copperas was used. The green crystals were applied to the dye water.

color symbolism

The Pueblo Indians used colors for directions. White denotes the East, Yellow or Blue the North, Blue (more frequently) the West, Red or Buff the South. Cherokees have a color symbolism also where Red indicates success, Blue trouble, Black death, White happiness.

"Colt on Revolvers"

This was a popular expression in the early West to indicate that justice was dependent on who was better armed or who was quickest on the draw. In one court case the defending lawyer laid a pistol on the table in an attempt to intimidate the judge. However the judge drew out a Colt six-shooter and announced that his authority, "Colt on Revolvers" outweighed the other man's authority.

Columbia, Pennsylvania

This town was known as Wright's ferry in its early history. It was located at a likely spot for crossing the Susquehanna when leaving Philadelphia. Sam Wright thought the Federal government would select this place for its permanent capital and changed the name to Columbia in expectation. He had the whole area laid out in lots. He then went ahead to sell chances on this one hundred and sixty lots at the rate of fifteen shillings a ticket. For a while he profited greatly for the rumor persisted that this town would make the best choice for a capital as it was accessible from the East but represented also the interest of the early West. However the scheme fell through though the town retained some importance as a link in the network of waterways that formed the Pennsylvania Canal in 1830.

Columbus circle or balloon tire

A colloquial term on the stage for a circle or sag under an actor's eye.

comancheros

A term applied to the Mexican traders of the Spanish settlements who hunted on the Staked Plains and did business with the Comanche Indians. These Mexicans furnished a good market for stolen cattle, horses and other plunder taken in raids on the Americans and thus were an encouragement to the Indians raiding the Texas frontier. Though thus sure of a market the Indians were always very much cheated in the transactions; for example they might receive a keg of whiskey for a mule or ten pounds of coffee for a pack horse.

comb superstitions

Since it was widely believed that the hair was a place where evil spirits might easily lurk—witness all the superstitions about having the head properly covered—it is not surprising that there are also many superstitious customs developed about the use of combs. Actors and singers are known to be quite concerned about dropping a comb before a performance since it may bring hard luck. As a countercharm they step on it with the right foot when picking it up. Other such beliefs include the following; to use the comb of a dead man means one will become bald, never let a man carry your comb if you want him to continue to be interested in you.

come-all-ye

A type of ballad singing which was popular with the

68

shanty boys, the railroaders, the miners and the cowboys. It takes its name from the opening lines, "Come all ye jolly sailors," or "all ye sons of liberty" or some similar expression.

A variation of one of these may be seen in the song of the "Buffalo Skinners."

"Come all you jolly cowboys, and listen to my song
There are not many verses, it won't detain you long.
It's concerning some young fellows who did agree to go
And spend one summer pleasantly on the range of the
buffalo."

The following seven stanzas tell of their hunting skill.

"Come up and see me some time"

This quip of the fabulous Mae West has reached practically legendary proportions as an expression implying a visit to a lady from a gentleman for purposes that might not be highly approved by Society. "Come up and see my etchings" has come to have similar connotations.

compressed hay

In areas of the Southwest where wood for fuel was not easily accessible this was a term used for dried cow chips—end result of much eating of hay.

conches

These were the early settlers in Florida and were mainly of British descent, having come over on the boats trading from the Bahamas. They earned their living from the sea thus accounting for their name. As original characters they were a close second to Georgia Crackers (q.v.) who came south by land. Conches lived on sea food and pigeon peas, limes, and saodillas, commonly called "sours and dillies." Another unique characteristic was their habit of putting a "squizzle," a squeeze of lime in their morning coffee.

conestogas—"stogies"

A special type of cigar was produced by the Marsh factory in Wheeling, West Virginia. It was particularly pop-

69

ular with the teamsters who drove the great lumbering wagons, the Conestogas, along the National Road and it was a corruption of this word that led to the creation of the term "stogie" for any cigar.

See BELL OF CONESTOGA WAGONS.

conjuring lodge

Tent or hut of North American Indian tribes in which mediumistic practices were held. The Negroes of the United States also pay regard to the conjurer. Their belief in his ability to practice magic was one of the most sharply retained of their African customs.

conner

A variation of the word canoe. The term is still used in tidal Virginia and along the Eastern Shore of Maryland. It closely resembled the early canoes being handcarved from a single log hollowed out for this purpose.

contagious magic

Belief that harm may be rendered to a person through rites observed over objects which once had contact with that person such as hair, nail parings and similar objects.

"cookem fry"

This odd expression is a survival of those lawless days when sailors had reputations so bad that they never expected to be candidates for heaven and were, therefore, reconciled to "cook and fry" in Hell.

cookie-pusher

A young, junior diplomatic official whose time was thought by some taxpayers to be too much occupied with unimportant details, such as passing the plate at official receptions.

Coolidge humor as Vice-President

"Silent" Cal has probably had more legends associated with his name over what he did not say than otherwise though there are a few apt phrases that he coined. To illustrate his taciturnity, upon his first arrival in Washington, the following tales are still repeated. A young woman sitting next to him at dinner announced brightly that she had bet her friend that she could get him to say three words. He glanced at her rather disdainfully and stated, "You lose."

On another occasion in much the same vein a young man again beside him at dinner noticed his visible suffering at that particular dinner and asked him why he continued to go out when he obviously did not enjoy it. His reply was, "Got to eat somewhere."

coon skin of Davy Crockett

A very much repeated tale involving Davy Crockett, tells of his use of a coon skin to obtain some liquor at a bar. The story is elaborated to show how necessary it was for him to have the rum since he must satisfy his constituents' thirst while he makes speeches to them. Upon returning after the first time he offered the coon skin, he is out of cash and wonders how he can promote a deal to get some more liquor. He sees his coon skin lying beside the bar where it had been tossed when he paid it over the first time. He sees an opportunity and grabs it back buying another jug of liquor. All this goes over so smoothly he actually is supposed to be able to put through the deal ten times with the same coon skin and to boast of what he had done later.

coon, to go the whole coon

A popular Southern expression equivalent to —to go the whole hog—to see the thing to the bitter end and never mind the consequences.

Cooney-caboose

In some parts of the West the cook kept a bag or sack under the chuck wagon for carrying fuel for the cooking; perhaps the scarce wood but more likely cow chips picked up when available.

coontie

A food favored by the Indians of the Everglades made from the foot-tall, ferny green cycad, whose great thick roots

71

were grated and squeezed and sifted to make flour. One of their legends tells of a time when there was a great famine and the Indians prayed to the Master of Breath, who sent his Son, God's Little Boy, to walk about at the edge of the pineland and the 'Glades. Wherever he walked, there in his heel marks grew the coontie, which the Indians immediately began to prepare as food. In the early days the white man sometimes called it compte, which they grated into a starch, known today as arrowroot.

cooper

A Negro roustabout who handled the great hogsheads of tobacco that were auctioned off at Louisville at the turn of the century. Some casks might weigh as much as two thousand pounds. The men would roll them to the auction and stand them up to have samples taken from them. These samples were called "breaks" and weighed about ten pounds. If that load were not sold promptly, then the next day another "break" would be made. There were those who claimed that a whole hogshead might finally disappear in this fashion.

coopers

In New York State the coopers made two types of barrels. One was called "slack," was made by less expert individuals and was used to load flour, salt and fruit. The other was called "tight" and required that the wood be dressed and shaped more carefully, and that the staves be beveled for accurate fit. This was used for cider, whiskey and meat.

Cooperstown, New York

William Cooper had first considered the area at the southern tip of Otsego Lake in 1785, and was inspired to start a town there when he took over and offered for sale forty thousand acres of land he had picked up at a sheriff's sale. He adopted a wise policy of land sale, giving the buyers adequate time to pay off. He was a Federalist, with considerable resources available, and he helped his purchasers to found a successful settlement.

Cooperstown became a county seat and Cooper was the

first judge of the County Court. His son, James Fenimore, did not have his father's successful ways with his countrymen, though he won nation-wide acclaim for his Leatherstocking tales garnered from his home-town locale. The crotchety son of William Cooper would not even allow picnickers on his property and was involved in many lawsuits over this issue, which immediately established the legal point that one may not attack the character of another without producing evidence.

Cooperstown acquired many legendary characters, such as the amazing publisher, Phinney, who predicted in his popular Almanac that it would snow on the Fourth of July and was astonished to discover that a few flakes actually did fall that morning. But real popularity for Cooperstown was derived not from its early history but from the fact that in 1939 the Baseball Hall of Fame was established there, a museum and exhibit that thousands visit annually.

Coos Bay

According to the tales about Paul Bunyan, his enormous blue ox, "Babe" (q.v.), once became sick. Without the help of his powerful ox in bringing the logs out of the forests Bunyan's whole logging enterprise would fail, so he was vitally concerned. But nothing seemed to help the ailing animal. At last Bunyan learned that whale's milk would save Babe. In order to obtain a supply of this valuable commodity, Bunyan scooped out a big piece of the Pacific Coast near Seattle and lured a herd of whales into it. Unfortunately, the treatment did not help Babe, but after the whales were released the great hollow remained and was known as Coos Bay. The great mound of earth thrown up for its construction became known as the Cascade Mountains, the highest peak of which the people in Seattle called Mt. Bunyan, the people of Tacoma called Mt. Tacoma and tourists know as Mt. Rainier.

copper captain

A sham captain, a man who struts about with the title he

73

has no right to. Washington Irving noted its use in his *Knickerbocker History.*

corduroy roads

On the frontier of the South and the West the use of these primitive roads represented at least to some degree, the approach to civilization. In the very earliest stage of our road-making, simple packed-down earth was sufficient, but over swampy areas the first corduroy roads were laid. They consisted of logs six to eight inches in diameter, sawn in two longitudinally and laid transversely. They thus presented a ribbed appearance similar to the cotton and linen cloth of that day and so were called "corduroy." Soil was piled over the logs to even up the road but this slight improvement only lasted until the next rain. The traveler over such roads might find the experience a devastating one. He could expect to be thrown in a heap in his carriage one minute and suffer contusions from contact with the roof the next. For the next stage in improvements, *see* PLANK ROAD.

corn

Maize was a native American product which the Indians introduced to the European explorers and immigrants, who mistakenly applied to it their general term for cereal grains —"corn." Corn enters widely into the mythology and religious practices of most of the Indians. The plant is referred to as Corn Maiden or Corn Mother. Various parts of the plant are used ritualistically. Major ceremonies occur before the corn planting and after the harvest. The famous Green Corn Dances of the Pueblo Indians are fragments of ceremonies now enacted secretly in the kivas. It embodies for other tribes the idea of thanksgiving for bountiful crops and a form of worship of "Our Grandmother." The Iroquois Festival lasted for four days in early September. Not only is the spirit of Corn addressed but the two additional life-giving sisters, beans and squash, come in for recognition.

Longfellow incorporated in *Hiawatha* an account of the origin of corn as being a gift from a goddess.

corn freight

A term used to describe wagonloads of goods sent out West pulled by mules. Because of the nature of the country, feed in the form of corn had to be carried for the animals, which took up some of the valuable space of the wagons and raised the freight rates. However, even at this high cost "corn freight" was more efficient than transportation by other methods in the early development of the West.

Cornish customs

See COUSIN JACK, PLOD-JESTS, "PASTY."

"cotton boxes"

A special type of flatboat, used on some of the Georgia rivers. These light-draught boats by having high sides could carry large cargoes and keep the cotton perfectly dry without capsizing. The "boxes" themselves were broken up and sold for lumber when the boats arrived at their destination on the coast.

The up-river freight went on pole-boats. These had keels to keep them straight in the current and their bows and sterns were pointed to reduce resistance to the water.

counting-out games

Games to determine who is to be "It" have an infinite variety, but by far the most popular in the past has been:

"Eeny, meeny, miney, mo,
Catch a nigger by the toe;
If he hollers let him go,
Eeny, meeny, miney, mo."

Various attempts have been made to substitute "feller" or some other term for "nigger." A host of local alternatives have developed but it is an interesting comment on human nature how resentful a person may become when, having learned one system or rimble, the "correct" or familiar version is not used.

courtship limited in New England

The thoughtful father of about 1700 prevented the suitor

75

for his daughter's hand from staying too late by reducing the oil in the kerosene lamp to an amount he estimated would last an hour or so.

Cousin Jack, Cousin Jenny

A popular term for Cornishmen in the Michigan peninsula, probably derived from "cussing" Jack. The men from Cornwall, England, were attracted to the mines in Michigan because of the skills they already had and in the expectation of better working conditions. They were thought to be very droll characters. They were famous for their singing and for the "pasty" (q.v.) which their wives made, a delicious meat and vegetable pie. Another dish for which they were especially famous was made of scalded rich cream which was heated until it would hold up a weight. It was served on treacle and bread and butter and called thunder and lightning.

cowboy modern style

The entertainment world has developed a number of outstanding "cowboys," of whom each has a devoted number of followers. Among these would be included Roy Rogers, Gene Autrey, Hopalong Cassidy, and the Lone Ranger. These "cowboys" are in marked contrast to the old cowpunchers in many respects, the most conspicuous of which are the requirements that they may not cuss, spit, gamble, shoot pool, or step into a saloon. They are restricted in another way also: romance is frowned upon. All affection is to be expended upon a suitable object, the horse.

Their wardrobe attempts to follow the "typical" style of the traditional cowpuncher: chaps, broad brimmed hat, high-heeled boots, elaborate spurs decorated in a Spanish pattern, Colt .45 six-gun, a Winchester in a scabbard, stock forward, rope at saddle fork on the right, and flamboyant scarf.

cowboy of the Pecos

Everything that one usually thinks of in regard to a man who works at punching cows, herding horses, only more so! The Pecos represented a very wild region; therefore, it was especially necessary to be rugged in order to survive in its wildness. The land was hot, infested by snakes and avoided by all who could do so, except those who felt it advisable to hide out there.

cowboy terms applied to Indians

"Beef issue" referred to the food distributed by the government agencies on the reservations. "Cuitan" was used for an Indian pony of the coastal tribes, while "yakima" was used for other types of Indian ponies. "Fire-water" was used to refer to whiskey and supposedly came into usage because it was customary to demonstrate the strength of the drink by throwing some on the fire to let it burn. "Grass money" was used to indicate the rent paid for using Indian lands for grazing. "Hair lifter" might mean an Indian intent on scalping his enemy, or be used for a situation that was extremely precarious. "Siwash" would be used to refer to anything of Indian origin not considered up to the standards of white civilization. "Wickiup" was a primitive type of Indian hut and by transfer might mean anyone's home.

cowboy terms borrowed from the Spanish

The cowboys of the Southwest were quick to create terms where they were needed so that it was especially appropriate that they should borrow many expressions already in use by the Spanish-speaking cowhands doing the same type of work. "Hoosegow" was the cowboy's attempt to pronounce the Spanish "*juzgado*" a court of justice. By easy transfer "hoosegow" became the universally accepted term for jail. In the same fashion he altered "*jaquima*," meaning a halter, to the commonly used "hackamore." "Chaps" became his term for the "*chaparejos*" (q.v.). To "dally welter" was to take a half-hitch around the saddle horn after a horse had been caught, that is, "*dar la vuelta*," Spanish for the same thing. His word "lariat" was from the Spanish, "*la reata*," meaning a rope with which to tie up animals. The term "reata" alone might be used as much as "lariat" in the Southwest with "palin rope" serving toward the North.

77

Cowboy's Lament

A ballad of the West about a young man who gives details for his funeral for "I am a young cowboy and I know I've done wrong." It is borrowed from an Irish song, "The Unfortunate Rake," which was the lament of a dissolute soldier who wanted a military funeral. The drums and the fifes were preserved in the cowboy version:

"We beat the drum slowly and played the fife lowly,
And bitterly wept as we bore him along;
For we all loved our comrade, so brave, young and handsome,
We all loved our comrade although he'd done wrong."

cowboy usages

See DEATH TERMS, GIRTH, GRAB THE SADDLE HORN, "HEAD FOR THE SETTING SUN," "QUIEN SABE," DEADMAN'S HAND.

cow casualty

In one of the minor wars of the nineteenth century, the Aroostook War over the Maine-New Brunswick boundary, a strange casualty was frequently referred to—an unfortunate cow shot by a guard near the St. John's River boundary.

cow chips

A cheap fuel easily obtainable from the droppings of cattle in the early days of the West and badly needed since wood was very scarce. This "prairie coal" made a hot fire but burned out quickly and was hard to get started.

cowpuncher

There are those who claim that this term is not equivalent to "cowboy." It is of more recent usage, having been applied first to the cowhand who had to prod the cattle placed on trains so as to keep them from lying down on the floor of the overcrowded freight cars. Probably, too, the cowpuncher was not so reckless or wild an individual.

cow superstitions

If a cow lies down immediately after going out into the

78

field, it will storm before evening. If you cut off a piece of her tail, she will make no effort to run away. If she does not bawl when her calf is sold, there will soon be a death in the family. Cows born when the moon was waning will not be good breeders.

Coyote

Most of the Indians of the Plains and the Southwest have stories concerning the trickster activities of Coyote, who appears to have a dual character, at one time performing acts that have a nuisance value as a bullying, greedy dupe, but at other times serving as a hero who imparts knowledge of the arts and sciences, provides game or brings fire.

cracker

A term used for poor white folk in the Southern United States, especially Georgia, who have developed a distinct back-country flavor akin to the hillbilly. The expression is of nineteenth-century vintage and is supposedly derived from their common practice of cracking their long whips very noisily. In Florida they settled around Miami with a favorite diet of cowpeas and collards, mustard greens or white bacon, though in Georgia style. For contrast *see* CONCHES, their close neighbors. "Rednecks" is a synonym for crackers.

cranberries

One version of the origin of this Cape Cod specialty states that they were known to the earliest settlers as "craneberries" because the cranes were seen eating them. Since the inhabitants remained primarily concerned with whaling it was almost two centuries before notice was again taken of the common berries. A family experimented by boiling them and adding sugar. This relish became so popular that before long Cape Codders were raising millions of bushels.

At first all the neighbors participated in the harvesting. The girls wore sunbonnets and sewed oilcloth across the front of their dresses for they had to kneel in the damp bogs to pick the berries. They were paid after the harvest was completed, probably using some of their earnings to buy new

79

dresses for the Cranberry Dance which was a high point of the social season.

Now the picking is done by the Portuguese who have moved into the Cape in large numbers, and bringing with them their own colorful customs.

crazy as a sheepherder

The isolated and lonely life of the sheepmen of the West was supposed to have a depressing effect upon these recluses and to render them at least a little "queer."

crazy quilts

In parts of New Hampshire the bride had lovely quilts or samplers made for her by her mother's friends. The quilts would be stitched with scraps of silk and velvet in designs of birds or flowers. The samplers might try to show designs of well-remembered little cabins or of favorite hills.

Creole funeral customs-coffin material

Along the Louisiana bayous or inlets it was an accepted custom that loose boards washed up on the shore could be used by those in poor circumstances to make a coffin upon the death of someone in their family. It was the unwritten law that such lumber could not be refused by the one on whose property it rested if it were not nailed down. Some shrewd individuals speedily nailed such pieces of wood into any sort of impromptu structure so that they were not committed to "giving" them for some unfortunate purpose.

crickets

Because crickets like warmth it is not surprising that a quantity of folklore has grown up centered about hearth and home. A chirping cricket in the house is quite generally looked upon as bringing good luck. However, it must never be killed lest a member of the family meet the same end shortly thereafter. To hear one chirp on Christmas Eve is the best of all good luck. If the crickets sing louder than usual, expect rain. The Cherokee Indians believed that a tea made of dried crickets would make them good singers like the crickets themselves. In the South there is a popular custom of calling the crickets "Old Folks," in deference to their fireside-sitting propensities.

crookneck squash

The residents of the Ozark Mountains, profoundly conscious of their steep, hilly farmland, explain with succinct detail why they plant squash instead of pumpkins in their cornfields. The crook on the squash hooks onto the corn stalks when they ripen but the pumpkins might just roll down the hills!

Cross my heart

The expression, "Cross my heart, and hope to die," used after a statement has long been considered an effective means of guaranteeing the truth of the assertion just made. Though popular with children, there probably remains within the adult using it a slight feeling of superstitious awe as to the consequences should the oath be falsely made.

crosshaul

When the old logging days were at their height, the only leisure of the loggers fell on Sunday, when they were sometimes hard put to it to find amusement. One of their favorite means of relieving the tedium was to haze the greenhorns. A popular routine would be to send one of them to the cook to ask for a crosshaul. After the irate cook had thrown out the intruder the men would then explain that a crosshaul was a track in the woods at right angles to a logging road.

crossing

A crossing in Missouri steamboating days meant a place where the current crosses the bed of the river from one side to the other. This condition created great difficulties for navigation and was very dangerous because of the uncertainties of depth and the possibility of being swept down stream.

crossing little fingers

If two persons chance to say the same thing at the same time a special formula has been developed which should be followed if one wants a wish to come true. One of the persons says a word. The other responds immediately with an associated word. Then the little fingers of each hand are linked together and snapped after each has made his wish.

> "I say chimney, you say smoke
> Then our wish will never be broke."

One explanation claims that the crossing of the fingers was a symbol of the three stages—the speaking, the crossing, and the response—involving the Trinity symbol.

croup

Chicagoans had a curious treatment for this disorder in the city's early days. They sent the afflicted child down to the gashouse to sit and breathe for an hour.

crow

The crow has earned an evil reputation both for the things it actually does which have a nuisance value—such as its thievery and its raucous cawing—and for what has grown into a collection of beliefs as to its appearance or flying bringing bad luck. "Crow on the fence, rain will go hence. Crow on the ground, rain will come down," shows the popular view of the crow as a weather prophet.

The Navajos of the Southwest used the word "crow" to refer to the missionaries because of their black robes.

crow-bar hole

In the Ozarks you may be regaled with an account of the terrible winds that sometimes blow in that vicinity. One of the tests of the velocity of the wind was to have a hole in the cabin wall through which an object could be projected and the wind speed could thus be safely gauged. Usually one stuck a crowbar through the opening—if it merely bent in the wind then it was safe to emerge.

culture hero

A character in mythology, folklore or legend or even of historical origin who has come to be regarded as contributing

82

some form of idealized teachings to his people. All good or useful things have been introduced or improved by him. He may have brought fire or originated corn or invented alphabets or developed medicines or perhaps have been just strong and powerful. The tales of his prowess always grow with the telling and there is often some expectation of his future return.

cup plates

This combination of a saucer and a plate had a practical value for the early dwellers on Cape Cod and now has even more value for the seeker after antiques for its use was eventually discontinued. The Cape Codder wanted to enjoy his tea in comfort, so he poured it into the saucer to cool while he placed the cup back on the "cup plate." These dainty china plates were made in lovely shades of lavender, pale green and raspberry and were sometimes called "sentiment plates." Those with hearts on the rim were often used as Valentine gifts, but they were all finally retired when drinking from a saucer came to be frowned upon.

cures

For a burn one should recite the following:
"As far as the East is from the West
Come out fire and go in frost."

For freckles one should wash in the first snow and then step over a stone, three times backward and three times forward.

See TUBERCULOSIS.

curfew

In Charleston, South Carolina, there was an hour after which Negroes were not to be out of doors. This was announced by drum beat through the town. Horseback riding after this drumming was also forbidden.

In New England, through French Canadian influence, the original literal meaning of covering the fire for the night was carried out by using the term for a flat pan with a cone

83

over it which was put over the fire to diminish it but still have it available in the morning.

cuspidor

A cuspidor, also known as a spittoon, was a refinement that came rather late to some sections of the West. There is a tale of an old-timer visiting a well-appointed home in New York whose hostess was apparently striving to preserve her floors, for she elicited this comment after having moved a cuspidor into a number of strategic locations. "Pardon me, ma'am, but if you keep moving that darn thing around I'm liable to spit in it."

customer's yachts

Billy Travers was reputed to be a great wit in both the resorts he frequented, Saratoga and Newport. A popular story about him tells of his looking out to sea at a beautiful collection of yachts he was told belonged to a number of Wall Street brokers. "But where," he inquired, "are the customer's yachts?"

He topped this once when he went to Bermuda for a rest and change by stating, "Yes that was what I went for, but the waiters got the change and the hotel got the rest."

cut a swath

To make an impression. An expression arising in early agricultural sections, referring to the amount of grass a man could cut with one sweep of his scythe and thus show how important he was.

cutting out

One of the most important jobs of the cowboy is to cut out, that is, remove a group of cows from the main herd for some definite purpose. Of great assistance in this work is a good cutting horse. So highly esteemed is a well-trained horse of this type that the highest compliment one can pay a person is to say he is "as smart as a cutting horse." Many folk tales have arisen through the telling of the brilliant performances of some of these horses. If one particular cow out of the whole herd was wanted, a cowboy might take his bridle off his cutting horse and let him do the work himself. When a larger group was to be cut out, a fine degree of co-operation could be worked out, each anticipating the other's move.

D

daddy-long-legs or straddle bug

The belief is common that the daddy-long-legs will help find strayed cows. One says, "Grandaddy, Grandaddy, where did my old cows go?" The bug will then point a leg in the direction in which the cows may be found.

daisy folklore

The daisy was considered a symbol of fidelity and was thus of value in the divination of one's love affairs. Pluck the petals and figure out whether he loves you or loves you not. One may also take the center yellow disc, and break it up by rolling between the fingers. The pieces are then tossed on the hand from the back to the front; those remaining determine how many offspring the participant will have.

Daisy folklore also involved babies and children. It was lucky to step on the first daisy seen in the spring, but if one uprooted a daisy plant then one's children would not thrive. A somewhat related belief stated that if one forgot to place one's foot on the first daisy, daisies would grow over one or someone dear to the person would die.

A curious belief insisted that daisies fed to a puppy would keep him small, perhaps originating in the low-growing habit of the daisy.

Dalton Gang

The five Dalton boys were the sons of a Kansas farming preacher, whose strict methods of rearing his children seemed to have had a contrary effect upon them. The Daltons met with almost uninterrupted success during a long career as bank robbers. Their finish came in a battle royal on the morning of October 5, 1892, when they rode in on the Whiskey Trail toward Coffeyville, Kansas. This engagement, certainly the most famous street fight in the history of the old West, resulted in the killing of four Coffeyville citizens and four of the Daltons. The fifth Dalton was captured in the fracas and served fourteen years in prison. Emerging reformed, he became a lecturer on the folly of a life of crime and wrote pamphlets on the subject.

damnyankee

In the degrees of strained relations between Southerner and Northerner it was understood that the distinction between a "damnyankee" and an ordinary one was that at least a Yankee had enough sense to stay where he belonged whereas the damnyankee might actually inflict his presence upon the South.

dandelion divination

When the dandelion has gone to seed (often called a "blowball"), a girl holds the head by its stem and blows on it to learn whether her lover thinks about her. If one seed remains after three blows she knows for sure that he does. In some districts the same device may be used to discover how many children the blower may expect to have. The method may also be used to determine whether a wish will come true. If after three blows a seed still remains on the head, the answer is positive.

dander

"To get your dander up" means to get angry. It was used along the Atlantic coast but was probably originally introduced by the Dutch.

dangers on the Missouri River

There is a popular tale told on the Missouri about a timid old lady asking the captain of a steamboat about the dangers of drowning while on board. The pompous reply was as follows: "My dear madame, you must not believe everything you hear. I have never met a man who was drowned upon the Missouri."

87

Daniel McGirth

Florida is rife with tales associated with the name of this stanch American patriot in the early years of the Revolution. However, when it became a question of giving up his magnificent horse, Gray Goose, Daniel McGirth, the rugged individualist, transferred his allegiance to the British. On the other hand, he did not remain true to them very long and was soon participating in border raids, at first against the Spanish only, but soon against the Americans also. His colorful maraudings came to an end with his final capture by the Spanish authorities, who were extremely indignant at his having allied himself with the Indians with whom he had hidden away in the deep forests between the St. Johns and St. Marys rivers. Feeling that simple execution was too good for him, they had him walled up in one of the unlighted cells of a Spanish castle, in which he was kept alive for five years and is said to have gone mad.

dark and bloody land

A term applied to Kentucky by the Indians before Daniel Boone's time, when it became even more appropriate.

deaconed off

In early colonial days Congregational churches in Boston conducted their hymn-singing by having the deacon give the line and then having the congregation repeat it in unison. Since no musical instruments were tolerated in these early churches the process of "deaconing off," or giving the line to the members, sometimes produced a degree of disharmony. Eventually a pitchpipe was surreptitiously used.

In more distant areas where deaconing was beginning to lapse, they called singing in harmony "tuning the psalm."

deacon's seat

In the Maine logging camps, conditions were very primitive a century ago. Almost the only furnishing was a long bunk or ledge upon which the men slept. In front of this, across the bunk, was a long bench which, from its resemblance to the seat reserved for the deacons in the front of New England churches, was given the same name. It served as a table or bench as needed, and suggests the limited conveniences available to the loggers in those early days.

dead beat

In original English usage this meant to be exhausted, but Americans have used it as a noun meaning a worthless person or one who does someone out of payment due him.

deadheads

Those who have been admitted without having to pay, such as in a theater or on a train. They are "dead" in the sense that they represent no possibility of profit.

Dead Horse Chantey

This was a chantey common on American and British ships. The crew had to work, as they considered, for nothing for the first month on board ship because their wages had been advanced to them while they were ashore and already been spent. When the debt had been worked out, a dummy horse of rags and straw was dragged around the deck and then thrown overboard to the tune of the chantey.

Deadman's Hand

Since the time of Wild Bill Hickok it has been the practice to refer to a poker hand containing two black aces and two black eights as a "dead man's hand." This was because Wild Bill was killed in a saloon in 1876 while playing poker. As he was being removed there dropped from his hand this combination of cards, which ever since has caused superstitious gamblers to beware if they draw such a hand.

deadwood, to get the deadwood on you

This old Ozark expression, meaning to have someone over the barrel or to have them fixed so that they cannot do any harm, has its origin in a popular folktale about a heron. It seems there was an old heron who found upon swallowing a particularly lively eel that he could not digest it. According to the Ozark tellers, he had only one gut and the eel kept going right through. After this had happened several times the old

89

heron thought up a remedy. He backed up against a dead sycamore tree, swallowed the eel again, and stayed jammed against the wood until the eel was digested. Thus the Ozark folk saying, "I've got the deadwood on you."

death terms of cowboys

Cashed in his chips. Hung up his saddle forever. Last roundup. Sawdust in his beard (if shot down in a saloon). Fried gent (if burned to death in a prairie fire). Put to bed with a pick and shovel.

death warnings

Many New Englanders in the past had a firm belief that no death occurs without a warning. They believed also that certain individuals had a gift of second sight to forewarn of such tragedies. Among seafaring folk it was believed that a sick person on board a ship would not die until the tide ebbed.

déchargé

In the region around Lake Superior it was frequently necessary to transfer from one body of water to another. On some occasions it was necessary to remove only the human cargo to lighten the canoe, leaving in the rest of the freight. This partial removal was called "déchargé."

deer meat swamp style

The dwellers in Okefenokee Swamp, when they had deer meat to prepare, first skinned and quartered the carcass. They cubed, seasoned, and pressed it into tins, then steamed it until it was a tender mass in a thick jelly of its own juice. If a little melted tallow was run over the top of the tin to seal it, the meat would keep all winter.

Deer Woman

In the tales of the Western North American Indians there are widespread accounts of a human being marrying a deer wife. In the legends the wife is frequently offended by references to her eating habits. She then often leaves her husband after bearing him a son. Another variation tells of an abandoned child raised by a deer woman, who finally recognizes

90

that the fleet and sturdy young boy must be returned to his people. Arrangements for this are made but his human mother is made to promise that he will be first kept in a darkened room for four days. But during this time the mother cannot resist the temptation to look at him. The child then takes the form of a deer and gallops north to find his adopted mother.

demon dancers

Many Indian tribes had dances which ventured to imitate supernatural powers. The Iroquois and the Apache used them to bring about a cure of some kind, while the Californian rites of the Kuksu were to bring prosperity, especially of the crops. Among these tribes a feeling of danger was attached to the impersonation since madness or illness might result from a misstep in the dance.

Derby Hat (American style)

The people of Norwalk, Connecticut claim that one of their early citizens invented the derby hat when the economical colonists complained that the costly beaver hats (price, seven dollars) were not lasting the full life expected of them. To meet this situation, the long-enduring bean-pot derby was developed, made on a rounded block, to bring a new and prosperous industry to the town.

devil in New England

Supernatural tales of this region are filled with "evidence" of the visitations of the devil. Gargantuan outlines of a cloven hoof are seared into rocks all over New England and "testify" to his frequent appearance in that part of the world.

Devil's Island influence

A poor boy on the Eastern Shore of the Chesapeake, Joshua Thomas, has been credited with bringing about the conversion of thousands of sinners in the vicinity of Tangier Island. Though it all happened a long time ago, tales of it are still fresh in the people's minds. One incident has to do with the occasion when Thomas addressed 12,000 British troops on the eve of their intended attack on Baltimore

91

during the War of 1812. He told them the Almighty had revealed to him they would fail and suffer much. Their morale was very low and it was afterward reported that his warnings had so haunted them that they may have contributed to their defeat. In time Devil's Island became Deals Island and a section on it called Damned Quarter became Dames Quarter.

Diamond Horseshoe

Before 1883 the Academy of Music on East Fourteenth Street had been the great musical center in New York City. But the house had so few boxes available that many of the rich devotees of music were forced to sit in the lowly orchestra stalls, where they felt they were looked down upon by the haughty occupants of the boxes. This condition they could not endure, so they arranged to finance the construction of a much more magnificent building at Thirty-ninth Street and Broadway. Thus the Metropolitan Opera House came into being and soon drove its competitor out of business. After a serious fire in 1892 the management, noting how successful had been its policy of catering to those who desired boxes, outdid itself in the restoration by producing a tier of boxes that sparkled in matchless glory. This, plus the wealthy and fashionable appearance of the boxes' occupants, led to the coining of the term "Diamond Horseshoe." The second tier, occupied by a slightly less glamorous assemblage, was known as the "Golden Horseshoe."

"Dick Smith"

A term the lumberjacks of the Michigan peninsula used for a man who bought himself a drink alone, a rare situation. When such an occasion arose, six "honest" jacks would toss him over the bar and he would be forced to stand treat. It was, of course, more common practice for a man to stand treat as long as he had any funds. A particularly generous character at this activity was one Barney Wates, whose invitation, "to snow the road," was well known in the area and meant to come and enjoy the treats.

92

"dig for wood and climb for water"

This strange contradiction may be observed in Texas, where mesquite roots, dug up and dried, provide a fuel, and the necessity of climbing gravelly canyons is a preliminary to finding water in some regions.

diggings

Lodging places. Use of this term may have originated from the practices of the Galena lead miners of Wisconsin, who lived in the parts of the mine they had already dug out. The name was then carried over to any type of dwelling.

dimples

There are many who believe the pleasant myth that a dimple is a mark left by an angel's finger.

"A dimple in your cheek,
You are gentle and meek.
A dimple in your chin,
You have a devil within."

Still others think that the possession of a dimple brings you good luck.

dingle

A term used in the Maine logging camps to describe an open shed where the fresh meat brought in by the hunters would be stored. A man was usually hired by the owners of the logging camp just to maintain this supply of meat.

dipping

In the big cities "dipping" was the term used for picking pockets. It was better to work with a group, to distribute the responsibilities and to give added protection. To "fan" was to jostle the victim lightly to discover where the man kept his wallet. The "stall" was the member of the gang who distracted the attention of the subject, perhaps by rattling a newspaper in front of him or by other such devices. The "Hook" was the most skillful of the organization, who used his "duke" (hand) to extract the "poke," after which he

93

would speedily pass the wallet along to one of his assistants on the outer circle, so that if anything went wrong he would be in the clear. If the victim discovered his loss the pickpocket "blew," while one of the gang began to make loud complaints over the accusation to cover up the retreat of his confederates. The member holding the wallet might temporarily "ditch it" on an unsuspecting bystander, to be picked up later when the "heat" was off.

dirty boy or despised boy

This is a popular subject of many Apache tales, in which a boy lies around dirty, unkempt and lazy, but eventually proves his great running ability and courage. The tales are often drawn out into a long series of adventures.

"dish turner"

In the early colonial period many of the family dishes were made of wood. This task was usually undertaken in the wintertime when other jobs were not piling up and the men of the family had time to spare. However, one man of the community often made a business of making the dishes for all. Since he used a lathe to "turn" the wood, he thus earned the title of "dish turner."

dive for the oyster

An American square dance figure. The first couple dip under the upraised arms of the second couple, who come back in the same fashion.

divination practices

See BIBLIOMANCY, DANDELION DIVINATION, DEATH WARNINGS, DOG'S HOWL, PEEL OF APPLE.

"Divine Right Baer"

A tale retold often enough to have assumed the dimensions of folklore has to do with George Baer, president of the Philadelphia and Reading Railroad at the time of the great railroad strike of 1902. Baer had won a nation-wide reputation for his action in continuing to decline outside

94

mediation. He said, "Rights of workingmen will be cared for by Christian men to whom God in his wisdom has given the control of the property rights of the country."

Dixieland

There are several versions of the origin of this term but a well-substantiated one traces it to the activities of a New Orleans banker. In a period when there was a great deal of inflated and insecure paper money in circulation, his bank issued a series of sound and dependable ten-dollar bills. This money, printed in French, had the amount indicated as "dix" (ten). Gradually up and down the Mississippi and in neighboring areas, people began to refer to the land from which the "dixies" came, and then finally called the whole south by that expression. Another version claims that a Mr. Dixie, a Southern landowner, treated his slaves so well that the news got around and all the slaves dreamed of reaching that heavenly place, Dixie's land.

Dizzy Dean's English

Already a large body of folklore has developed about the weird language used by the former baseball star in his activities as a broadcaster. He would say that So-and-So *slud* to second. Another would be *throwed* out. Or he might declare that someone had *swang* and missed. Hesitating to predict that a certain play might be disastrous, he stated that it could be *goodastrous*. The phrases are still being assembled from this rich source.

dobe walled

A cowboy's way of saying that a person had been shot standing in front of an adobe wall.

do brown

In Yankee terminology, if you were able to take advantage of someone you had done them brown. A "sell" is the term used in another section to give the same idea.

docey-do

The Western square dance form of the dos-a-dos position,

where the dancers pass about one another keeping back to back.

dock weed

A plant used by the Indians in Aroostook County to cause an infected scratch to heal.

dogie

An undersize calf in Western talk. One version of the origin claims that they were young lean animals that were first taken on the long trail to northern regions for fattening, whereas the other cows would already be fat enough to market. Others say they were the forlorn orphans left after a very severe winter and that in their underfed state they looked like "sourdough," then called "dough-guts," and finally named "dogies," to be claimed by who ever spotted them first.

dog's howls

It is a country-wide superstition that the howling of a dog at night is the forerunner of disaster. Even today many think that the dog sees an apparition of death invisible to human eyes.

dogwood

The flowering dogwood of the common American variety was used as a medicine by the Indian tribes of the Eastern United States. They made a decoction of the bark which they gave to warriors fevered with battle wounds. The colonists used this remedy for malaria with good results, understandable since we have identified the active principle of quinine in it. It served the same purpose for the doctors of the Confederacy during the Civil War when the blockade cut off outside resources. The Catawbas say the raw berries are good for chills. In Tennessee it is thought that if you chew dogwood you will lose your sweetheart. Many of the Indian tribes would pass their children through the branches of the trees to make them immune to childhood diseases and as a cure for rupture. However, those who went through this

96

process were supposed to subject themselves to pain when dogwood sticks were burned in the fire.

doo hicky

A mechanical device whose name one has forgotten. A modern version of "thingumajig" or "thingumabob."

door signs

Objects may be placed over or above a door according to the community's lore. The horseshoe appears in various parts of America and tramps have been suspected of leaving signs that indicate to their fellows where to expect good meals or where to avoid harm from dog or man.

dory

From "*duri,*" an Indian word meaning "dugout." This type of boat was the oldest in America and was literally "dug out" of a tree trunk in the earliest period of its manufacture. It had flaring sides but was tapered at the stern. The people of Maine claim it was double-ended like a pea pod. Flat on the bottom, it can carry as much sail as can be put on it. It is very steady and can be rowed standing up, going backward or forward.

dowser

One who is thought to be able to locate springs or other objects below the earth's surface. There are many even today who claim that there really are persons with an uncanny knack for indicating the spot where water can be found.

"drive the river"

An informal day of celebration was enjoyed by the residents living on the Susquehanna where it dips down into Pennsylvania, at the end of the spring planting. The settlers would build a willow-woven barrier across the river, where it ran in two channels. The children were assigned the task of creating a disturbance in one channel so that the fish would be driven into the other. On the morning selected for the activities there were usually thousands of shad coming up the river to spawn. The adults would push the barrier down

97

toward the fish, rounding up great quantities. These would then be thrown out on the shore. Each person would take home his allotment to be salted down for the winter.

droop-eyed calves

When rustlers stole young calves, they did not want them to give the show away by going back to their mothers; therefore, they would cut the muscles which supported the eyelids of the calves so that vision would be interfered with. This gave the calves a droop-eyed appearance.

drowning superstitions

There are those so convinced that a body will rise to the surface three times after drowning that they probably could not be convinced that it is only a legend.

drums for church service

Boston Congregationalists looked upon any instrumental music as sinful. In the early colonial period they even frowned upon tower bells and so summoned churchgoers by means of drums.

dry gulch, to

To throw into a ravine. In the bitter feuds between sheepmen and cattlemen in the West many murders occurred. A simple and speedy means of disposing of the bodies was to roll them to oblivion in some inaccessible deep hollow.

duck

A customary expression for designating an amphibious truck, which can operate as a power boat on water and as a vehicle on land, to transport men and materials in combined land and sea operations. The official term was "DUKW."

duck dance

Many North American Indian tribes perform imitative dances. The Kutchin wave their arms realistically, while the Iroquois merely cry "quack, quack," as a means of increasing the accessibility or the numbers of the birds. Some have dances, which include a duck walk, suggesting a waddling gait in a curious hip-displacement manner.

98

Dunker love feast observance

Among the Pennsylvania Dutch there is a religious group called Dunkers, somewhat related to the Amish, and belonging to the Plain People who observe an impressive ceremony in their celebration of the Last Supper. The women wear a variety of sheer white caps, the older sisters dressing in simple garb with no ornamentation, subdued and drab in tone.

After a scriptural reading describing the Last Supper, the congregation puts on white aprons. The women are seated on one side and the men on the other. They then wash the feet of the neighbor nearest them, using foot tubs provided for that purpose. As they finish with one they exchange a kiss and a handshake and repeat the ritual down the line. After a lengthy period they all rise and pray, then eat a meal that usually consists of meat, bread and a thick rice and beef soup. Each spoonful is carefully protected on the journey to the mouth by a piece of bread to catch any possible dripping. When the eaters have consumed their fill, they stand and offer thanks again, and the hand of friendship and the kiss of love is once more given. Communion concludes the observation. The bread is unleavened but very rich with butter and eggs. Each square is clearly marked with five sharp nail prints as symbols of the wounds of the Saviour as He hung upon the Cross.

Dutch courage

For no outstanding reason the person who has become brave by the addition of a quantity of alcoholic liquor is said to have acquired "Dutch courage."

Dutchman's breeches

Patches of blue in a stormy sky. If one can see enough of these patches to make a pair of breeches one may presume the weather will clear.

Dutch Tea Parties

In New Amsterdam tea parties were popular and were usually held from three to six in the afternoon. Olykoeks (doughnuts) were served. Washington Irving in *A History of*

99

New York describes an economical old lady who, when holding her parties, instead of putting a lump of sugar at each place, suspended a large lump on a string from the ceiling so that it could swing from mouth to mouth. "An ingenious expedient," he states, "which is still kept up by some families in Albany, but which without exception is followed in Communipaw, Bergen, Flatbush and all our other uncontaminated Dutch villages."

E

"eager beaver"

Originally the expression meant one who was very busy, and then gradually it assumed the implication of being a busybody. It became the nickname for a six-wheeled 2½ ton truck which can be operated both on land and sea.

eagle

The eagle has a varied role in Indian folklore, being one of the major animal characters, the symbol for the eagle dances where its actions are imitated. Eagle feathers were used for ceremonial costumes, headdresses and other ceremonial objects by nearly all American tribes, who looked upon the wearing of eagle feathers as a privilege extended only to the brave and the most worthy of this honorable mark of distinction. The eagle also stood as a warning bird and as a symbol of swiftness, keenness of vision, and longevity.

The eagle is also identified with the thunderbird. Because of its power to make long, sustained flights that carry it beyond the clouds it became associated with rain, thunder and storms.

eagle myths of the Cherokee

Since the eagle was a sacred bird to these Indians it was a matter of great difficulty to obtain the feathers of the bird needed in their Eagle Dance. The eagle-killer had to go alone into the mountains to fast and pray for four days. By using a deer's carcass as a decoy and uttering the proper magical songs he would manage to kill the bird, which he would leave lying at the place where it died until certain rites

101

had been performed. The Indian would proclaim that a Spaniard had done the deed so as to spare the tribe retribution. He would return to his people and announce that a "snowbird" had died to further protect them. Finally they would go to collect the feathers they desired and then hold their Eagle Dance.

"early candle light"

This was a way of designating the time for holding meetings when watches were not generally owned. It was used for the time of the weekly prayer meeting and for the singing, particularly in North Carolina. Though there might be some lateness due to varying interpretations of the hour, it seemed to get the people there about as fast as the specific statement of an hour would have, and the expression continued to be used almost up until the 1900's.

ear-puller or ear-swinger

An idle seaman who loafs at the dockside borrowing money from former shipmates.

ears burn

It is a very common superstition that someone is talking about you when your ears seem to tingle. If the person then repeats the names of his acquaintances the name at which the tingling stops is the one who was talking about him. To stop the gossip, make a cross with saliva and then touch the ear.

earthquakes

Earthquakes are often accounted for by supernatural means and thus become the subject matter of folklore. The Indians imagined that when the god or hero who supports the earth moves, he produces a quake.

Easter before Lent (Paques avant Careme)

This was an expression used by the Creole folk of Louisiana to indicate that a baby had been born too soon after the wedding.

102

"easy boss"

Thomas C. Platt was the political boss of New York State and made his home town of Oswego a second capital. His invitations to "Buckwheat breakfasts" in the town's outstanding hotel, the Ah-wah-ga, were commands not lightly ignored. One of the most lavish was given in honor of the election of Theodore Roosevelt in 1904. The dining room was decorated with prize pumpkins and tall cornstalks and there were prodigious mounds of crisp buckwheat cakes and quarts of maple syrup that quickly disappeared.

eat crow

Be compelled to do something very objectionable. An American hunting between the British and American lines during the War of 1812 was encountered by a British officer who by a ruse obtained his gun and then forced him to eat the only item which he had managed to kill, a crow. The American, recovering his gun, forced his former captor to eat the remainder of the crow, thus doubling the disagreeableness of the situation.

eat dog

The eating of dogs was a custom at councils held by various Indian tribes. Later when an occasion arose for white men to meet with them, a problem arose, for the white man did not want, knowingly, to eat dog, but neither did he want to give offense if a treaty or concessions were to be won. Therefore an arrangement was reached whereby a silver dollar could be placed in the serving dish and the next guest would eat the other's portion of dog.

ecclesiastical bricks

Also called hand bibles; they refer to the holystones which seamen had to use for scrubbing the decks.

eclipse

The eclipse of moon or sun was a matter of grave importance to a primitive people, so various propitiatory rites had to be indulged in to make certain that light returned. There

103

was also a popular belief among some Indians that an animal, bird, dog or snake was eating the moon or sun. In many tribes noises were made to frighten the attacker and bring back the light. Others made their dogs squeal by twisting their tails, shot arrows into the air, turned over vessels, thumped on canoes, or concocted special medicines.

"economic royalists"

This was a term created in 1936 by Franklin D. Roosevelt, intended as an insult to his well-to-do Republican opponents. It has become practically a legend in political discussion in reference to the opposition to both the New Deal and the Fair Deal.

egg superstitions

It is good luck to open an egg that has two yokes and you will get your wish if you make it while you are eating such an egg. It is a Southern Negro belief that if you take an egg out of a guinea hen nest you must do so with a spoon for the hen will never return to a nest which a human has touched. Eggs have been held as having a value in the reduction of fever. After the egg has touched the sufferer it is buried to transfer the heat to the earth.

The giving of Easter eggs or their hiding away for children to find as a gift from the Easter bunny is an extremely common practice, as is the coloring of eggs at Easter.

Eileschpijjel tales or Eulenspiegel tales

This immigrant from the Rhineland is the subject of many stories among the Pennsylvania Dutch. One tells of his making a bet with the devil over how much heat each could stand. They agreed to settle the argument by getting in a large oven under which they had built a large fire. After a minute or two Eileschpijjel could not take it and was headed toward the door. The devil inquired where was he going. His reply—"Oh, I think it is getting a little chilly in here. I'll go put some more wood on the fire"—so astonished the devil that he ran away, swearing the whole time.

elbedritsche

A mythical animal that young men of the Pennsylvania Dutch use as a device for fooling naive or guileless visitors. The victim is taken to catch the animal in some out-of-the-way place and left literally holding the bag, while those fooling him slip away making guesses as to how long he will continue his useless vigil.

electric "fluid"

When the first crude attempts at marketing electricity were undertaken in the early 1880's there was much confusion and misunderstanding as to its use. A barman complained to the electric company about the rates rising, from June to November, from twenty to forty dollars a month. He stated that if the cost reached sixty dollars he was through with buying the fluid.

Even J. P. Morgan was annoyed at what he considered extravagance or overcharge for the service. He ordered that everyone in his employ record when the current was turned on and when it was turned off. With this information Morgan lodged his complaints with the company about the excessive amounts for which he was being charged. At last Edison himself was called in to investigate. He discovered that no one had thought to warn the janitor, who was using all the light he wanted without making any record.

elephant as a symbol

Because of admiration for his size and shrewdness it is not surprising that the elephant has been widely used as a good luck charm. Just how he came to be the symbol of the Republican party is not quite so obvious. However, it is supposed to be connected with a cartoon published by Thomas Nast in 1874. In this cartoon appeared an elephant labeled "Republican Votes." Several years later he repeated a like device until the association became widely accepted.

Emancipation Proclamation Day, August 4

In the spring of 1880 a group of Negroes from the South

who sometimes called themselves the Exodusers founded a settlement in Kansas which they named Nicodemus, after a famous ex-slave whose heroism they much admired. They built the typical sod houses of the area, established a Methodist church, and then determined upon a top holiday—August 4, when the whole community would celebrate the Emancipation Proclamation with a gala all-day picnic. The annual event still attracts the curious, and visitors have come from as far as Chicago to participate. The town itself declined considerably, its annual celebration remaining the only indication of the brighter days of the past.

epilepsy

Since there is much social ignorance connected with this disease, there are still those who look upon the sufferer of such seizures or "fits" as under the control of an evil spirit. There are many folk cures suggested, such as to wear a necklace of nine pieces cut from an elder twig, or to heat a church key red-hot and lay it on the patient's head. Others say one must cross running water before sunrise and then swim in it.

escape tales

A basic pattern used for folktales all over the country may build up to an elaborate or simple account of escape, leading to the question in the listener's mind, "How did you do it?" Of course the climax is reached by the unexpected response: "I didn't."

Ethan Allen

At the time of the Revolution Allen was organizing his Green Mountain Boys despite the price placed upon his head by the British, who were more than eager for his arrest. On one occasion he is supposed to have entered a popular tavern in Albany where a number of politicians were assembled and after ordering a bowl of punch dared anyone to try to take him for the reward.

ethnocentric viewpoint

Many Indian tribes of the Eastern woodlands claim to have

been created on this basis,—that is, their tribe was created first "at the heart" of the world. Ethnocentrism may be expressed when the narrator of a myth assumes that the language of his tribe was the language spoken universally.

eucalyptus trees of San Francisco

A missionary, Father Taylor, while on a brief visit to Australia, is said to have sent back to his wife in California, a few seeds of the eucalyptus tree, which she planted on the dunes of the bay. These soon spread to the ranches roundabout, providing what is now one of the most characteristic aspects of the landscape of the bay region.

evil eye

Superstitious belief as to the influence the evil eye may have upon one has been incorporated into our language in a number of expressions, such as "if looks could kill," "withering glance," "to jinx," "to put the Indian sign on."

eyebrow superstitions

Beliefs about the fate of a person whose eyebrows meet are very contradictory. In some regions this means a happy marriage, but in others it means no marriage at all. For some communities it is a sign of beauty, while in others it is the sign of the werewolf or witch. Some women make a special effort to have them plucked, for they have heard it said that such a sign makes a poor wife.

eyelash as means of predicting the future

If the eyelash is laid on the back of the hand and a blow of the right palm dislodges it, one of two solutions may result: if it is not moved, the wish made is lost; if it disappears, it is assumed to have gone to bring the wish. This belief has very widespread acceptance.

107

F

Fair Play Boys

A group that banded together on the Fourth of July in 1776 to protect their rights to the lands they had staked out along the Susquehanna. They jumped the gun on the Revolution by their activities.

falling stars

According to a belief once popular in New York State, the star falling represents a soul selling itself to the devil. If one makes a sign of the cross, one may save the falling soul from damnation.

false faces

This term refers both to the masks worn in the Indian ceremony involved and to the people who took part. The False Face performers were men who dressed in a bearskin suit, wore carved wooden masks, used a cane and carried tortoise-shell rattles. They did not speak and were accompanied on their rounds of the village by other masked figures whose masks were made of braided corn husks. The Iroquois carved their masks out of a block of wood that they chopped from the living tree. They expected their performers to be ritually clean and held the curious belief that if he were not he would be seen not as the fully clothed person that he was, but naked.

"false front" architecture

In the quickly established Western cowtowns, particularly in Kansas, a high broad façade was often built onto a store or house front to give the illusion that the building was two stories high, though it was perfectly obvious that it was not. This was such a common form of architecture usage that many remnants still remain in parts of the West.

family record

A folio found in most New England households with birth, baptism and marriage certificates done with careful penwork, and often embellished with little water color pictures and a border of leaves and flowers.

Fasnacht or Shrove Tuesday

This religious holiday is celebrated by many of the inhabitants of the Pennsylvania Dutch areas by gorging themselves on the delicious doughnuts dedicated to this day. The last one in the household to get up is "*die alt Fasnacht*" and must not only do a number of extra chores but also may be looked down upon for the day as a slow poke. Festivals and dances were also held on this day, in many instances as a continuation of the customs started in the Rhineland before the German-Dutch ancestors migrated.

"Fat boy"

An army slang expression for the atomic bomb dropped at Nagasaki.

feather merchant

Army slang for a loafer or shirker.

Febold Feboldson

One of the great company of Paul Bunyan, he is credited with a number of minor miracles such as cutting the Great Fog into long strips and burying it along the roads so the farmers could go on with their work. He also is supposed to have invented popcorn balls. About 1928 a newspaperman writing as Watt Tell created the character in the Gothenburg (Nebraska) *Times*. Another resident of the town, Paul Beath, is responsible for giving Febold wider circulation. The anecdotes and yarns about him may have had some historical basis in the life of a Swedish pioneer who settled in that part of the country and was the hero of many a local story. Adding

109

this tradition to the already popular Bunyan tales is a familiar instance of the mingling of tall tales with regional conditions.

fees for preachers

New England preachers often received their fees in kind at the whim of the committee in charge. By subtle hints in their sermons they might complain of the shortages they were suffering under. For example, this was the subject of one preacher's sermon: "Where no wood is, there the fire goeth out" (Proverbs 26:20).

fence cutter's wars

When the little cattle rancher was striving to survive against the competition of the big cattle "corporations," he might find himself completely encircled by the richer companies who could afford to protect their herds by fencing in their holdings. The little man would discover that he had no way to get out to market or to water holes and would be forced to sell out cheap. However, masked raiders formed secret organizations and tried to cut their way out. Cattlemen retaliated by burning houses and crops until finally population increases brought law and compromise.

feu follet (will of the wisps)

In the Delta country about Louisiana they fear these "things" may come after you but no one has ever discovered for sure what really happens to you if the feu follet actually catches up with you—though some are daring enough to say they are nothing but marsh gas.

field day

Navy slang for general cleaning day aboard a ship.

fillee

A ration of whiskey given to the boatmen on the Mississippi River in Mike Fink's day.

"finding the bean"

At the masquerade balls which took place in New Orleans on January 6 or Twelfth Night, called King's Balls, a king

110

cake or Twelfth cake was cut. The one finding the bean in his portion was declared to be the host or hostess of the next great celebration.

fingernails

A quite general folk belief states that a child will become a thief if his nails are cut before he is a year old. Mothers therefore bite them off, for a while at least. Another belief declares that cutting the nails strengthens the eyesight. If you cut them during a waning moon they will not come back too fast. To cut them on Mondays will bring news, on Tuesday new shoes, on Wednesday cause you to travel, on Thursday may bring you an illness, while on Friday you will either gain money or a toothache. By cutting them on Saturday you will make sure of seeing your lover on Sunday, but if you cut them on that day you will have bad luck, get into a fight or see blood before morning.

Nail parings also serve many valuable purposes. Your own soaked in wine served to the one you love will restore affection. Those of a dead man buried under your enemy's doorstep will give him an ague until you remove them. The parings of a person buried in a walk where he will walk over them will put that person in your power.

fingers crossed

Common belief in the United States that such action may protect one from danger or bring one good luck; especially useful when passing by a cemetery. One "crosses out" the wickedness if the fingers are crossed while telling a white lie and thus protects one's soul.

Finglish

A dialect developed around Lake Superior where a large number of Finns have gathered and maintained much of their Old World folklore and sing many of their old songs.

"fining judges"

In the early West, an alert judge would make it his business to be wherever some "crime" was likely to be com-

111

mitted, drunken cowboys shooting their guns in town, and like situations, so as to be able to levy a fine immediately.

Finnigan to Flanagan

In 1897 a reporter for the Richmond *Palladium* wrote a poem about some railroad men which attained immediate success and nation-wide acceptance and is still remembered by many. The poem was about a quarrel over the long-winded reports of accidents that the superintendent claimed his trainman made. After he has received several more reprimands for not condensing his remarks, the concluding lines of the poem indicate this report on the derailment of the train concerned:

> "Bilin down's report was Finnigan
> And he write this here: 'Mister Flanagan
> Off ag'in, on ag'in,
> Gone ag'in, Finnigan'."

Finnish custom

See SAUNA.

"fire-eater"

An expression usually applied to a politician who, either sincerely or for dramatic effect, appears to be impetuous and fierce on certain subjects. The practice has been so widespread and so characteristic of many Southern leaders as to form practically a body of folklore in itself.

fire engine panels

The volunteer fire companies before the 1870's were extremely proud of their equipment. On the side of their engines they often had elaborate paintings. These contained many examples of genre painting and pioneer art, of which fortunately a number of examples have been preserved in art museums.

fire-fighting companies' rivalries

Fire-fighting in the cities before 1870 was handled by volunteer companies which had important social standing in the

112

community, so there was a great deal of honor connected with being the first company on the spot to start operations. To attain this supremacy the rival companies often resorted to many tricks. The minute the location was given by the alarm a few especially designated members of the nearest companies would be ready to dash off immediately to take over control of a hydrant for their special "masheen." These men sometimes carried a barrel which they would place over the source of the water supply to hide it from a rival scout. Some fierce fighting for possession of the hydrant often delayed attention from the fire. On a few occasions in the dimly lighted streets of those days the group might discover they were fighting over something which was not a hydrant at all.

fireflies

The presence in the house of these little beetles produces various kinds of good luck according to many superstitious persons, and the more there are, the better luck to be expected. Just one firefly or lightning bug indicates a visitor, while two means a marriage if the occupants are unmarried.

firemark

A cast-iron plaque called a firemark was issued in Philadelphia by the fire insurance companies for the homes they had insured. All the volunteer fire companies would answer the alarm but the one who found his company's plaque displayed would continue to fight the fire. These cast-iron markers are still to be found in some old homes and others have been collected by antique dealers and hobbyists.

fires in rooms

Comparatively few rooms had fireplaces in them up to 1850. They burned only wood at first, but when coal became available grates were introduced into the fireplaces. Later wood stoves were introduced, forcing a change in the chimney, for a hole was provided in the back of the chimney going to the cellar below through which the surplus ashes were pushed. In the early period these wood ashes had been precious for they were saved for soapmaking.

113

"fire sticks"

These were devices used in early colonial history for providing light. Very crude means were employed, such as birds or fish suspended on poles and set aflame for temporary lighting. Resin wrapped in leaves and fastened to a stick was a more common torch, though plain pine knots were used by the Pilgrims. A knot of the pine tree cut off just below the joint was used, the slender part supplying the handle and the knot the lighting fluid of pitch. This made a light which could be carried about easily in the home or on the farm, and could also be fastened on an iron spike for stationary use. Simple and helpful as this arrangement was, it had one drawback—the possibility of the pitchy drippings doing some damage—though this was somewhat obviated by fastening the stick over a stone in the chimney corner where possible.

fire trumpets

These were instruments like megaphones used by the volunteer firemen to shout directions over the noise and confusion that accompanied early efforts at fire-fighting. They are very scarce items in the Americana of today.

firing of three shots

Throughout the Creole region of Louisiana it was the custom to fire three shots if any critical circumstances arose, in order to attract the attention of the otherwise inaccessible neighbors. The same action was performed to announce the death of a member of the family so as to bring together those who would start preparations for the funeral.

First Families of Virginia

This distinguished group, often called simply the FFV's, constitutes the basis for many legends and stories of the South even before the War Between the States (as Southerners prefer to call the Civil War).

"First Gringo"

The first non-Spanish settler in Los Angeles was a Boston

114

Yankee called "El Ingles" who had been shanghaied on board a boat that had sailed for the California coast and, acting as a pirate, made attacks near Los Angeles about the year 1818. After a succession of these pillaging attacks upon the missions along the coast, a boatload of the pirates was captured. Included among them was the legendary figure who was to be called the first white man—John Chapman. Though held in prison by the outraged Spanish grandees, the wounded Chapman was ordered released by an imperious young lady whom he was later to marry. Held in a form of parole he was "loaned" out to the various missions, where he performed astonishing services of a practical nature and gradually became indispensable to the whole community. He won a pardon, became a citizen, and married Guadeloupe Ortega, who had originally saved his life.

first star seen

A superstition still very widely practiced, although perhaps a bit cynically, involves the recitation of the following lines when one notices the first star in the evening:

> "Star light, star bright,
> First star I have seen tonight,
> I wish I may, I wish I might
> Have the wish I wish tonight."

First Ward Parties (Chicago)

In the 1890's shortly before Christmas a party was regularly held for Lame Jimmy, a crippled piano player at one of the neighborhood parlor houses. In 1895 a drunken detective shot and critically wounded a fellow officer. A great outcry of public indignation followed and the order throughout the First Ward was no more such affairs. However, as regrets were widely expressed, a politician active in the First Ward Democratic organization had an inspiration. A ball should be given in the Seventh Regiment Armory for persons unknown. Word got around and tickets were sold by the hundreds. Waiters paid five dollars apiece to serve in the expectation of fabulous tips. No occupation was too low to

115

fail to have representation. Bathhouse John, a colorful local character, let his love of garish pomp have ample expression. Another bathhouse owner led the grand march. Resplendent as his outfit was, many surpassed him. "His tail coat was a crisp billiard-green, his vest a delicate mauve. His trousers were lavender, as was his glowing cravat and his kid gloves a pale pink. His pumps shone a gleaming yellow and perched on his glistening pompadour was a silken top hat sparkling like glass."

The newspapers were filled with glowing accounts of all the wonders. Churchmen raised their voices in horror over the tribute to organized vice. It was called a Saturnalian orgy, a black stain on the name of Chicago and worse. But $2,500 in profits for the "cause" was raised, and a legend was to grow in the telling.

Fish House Punch

This was a special drink popular with Philadelphians, most insidious and authoritative, with a brandy base and a grand blending of a quantity of other items.

five beans in the wheel

A western expression referring to the fact that most cowboys, having a cautious regard for firearms, did not fully load their six-shooters, but because of the hair-trigger arrangement on the guns would keep the hammer down on an empty chamber. Most cowboys figured realistically that if they could not do the job in five shots they had just as well get away in a hurry.

flint and tinder box

These means of obtaining a flame were in use for more than two centuries in America. The ordinary box was round in shape and held the piece of iron mixed with carbon (the so-called "steel") and the piece of hard quartz with a sharp edge which was to make the spark, as well as a "damper," which was an inner cover of tin with a flat handle fitting just below the cover of the box and used for smothering the tinder (any easily inflammable material) once the flame had

116

been obtained. A "spunk" transferred the fire from the tinder to the place where it was needed. These spunks were slender strips of wood dipped in sulphur. Later improvements provided a trough-like box with a steel wheel at one end which could be spun with a thong drawn tightly and hitting against the flint with the box. Since the early process might take as long as a half-hour, this later development was much appreciated because of the shorter time involved. Coals borrowed from a neighbor were often a quicker way of getting a light in that early period.

flint rocks dispose of a bear

In the Ozarks they swear this is a true tale of how a bear was disposed of when a man without a weapon met one unexpectedly. He picked up a flinty stone and threw it at the bear. It knocked out her teeth and went down her gullet. As she turned around with pain he threw another flint rock. This landed under her tail and "tore out her innards." When the two flints met inside the bear she caught fire like "a barrel of axle grease" and burned up completely.

flip

This was a drink made of a mixture of rum and beer seemingly as popular in the 1700's as soda water today. The directions for making it stated that to a quart pitcher two-thirds full of strong beer there should be added enough sugar to give the beer a sweet taste. To this mixture should then be added about half a pint of rum. Heat the contents of the pitcher by thrusting into it a red-hot poker called a loggerhead to give it a burnt, bitter taste. If a fresh egg was beaten into the mixture, the froth poured over the top of the mug and the drink was called a "bellows top."

The glasses used for this popular drink are now eagerly sought museum pieces, and are also accurate gauges of the wonderful capacities of some of our New England ancestors. Some of these glass tumblers held three or four cups apiece.

floating gin palace

An expression used by ordinary seamen to designate a

117

passenger liner with its elaborate bar and pleasure-seeking passengers.

flock paper

An early wallpaper used in seventeenth-century homes was made by printing the figures with boiled linseed oil. While the oil was still sticky the "flock," a powdery substance made of fine flecks of wool sheared from wool cloth and dyed, was blown across the paper. When the excess was shaken off the figures looked like appliqué. Feathers, silk and fur might be used in a similar way.

Florida lore

See CONCHES, CRACKER, SAND IN YOUR SHOES.

Florida sunshine

The modest claims of the residents of that state have long been that their wonderful sunshine will cure anything. The only difficulty is that California is running them a close second in making the same claims.

flower lore

See BACHELOR BUTTON, DAISY, DANDELION, DOGWOOD.

flying box car

Air Force slang for a bomber plane.

fofurraw

A term, probably a corruption of "fanfaron," used for everything showy, effeminate and unessential by the trappers who kept away from civilization. Applied especially about Texas, "faradiddle" and "fumadiddle" were probably further corruptions, meaning fancy dress.

footprints

Some Southern Negroes believed that if you picked up the earth or sand that held the impress of a footprint and put it in a bag and carried the bag with you, you could make that person follow you around.

footstoves

The unheated churches of New England were made a

118

little more cheerful by the use of individual footstoves which the church members brought with them each Sunday.

forgetfulness

There are those who say that if you have forgotten something and go back for it you must sit down and count ten in order to avoid difficulties.

forty-miler

A term used by carnival folk of an enterprise that does not get more than forty miles from its home town. For bigger outfits on the move a "small jump" was a trip up to a hundred miles, while a "big jump" was one of two to four hundred miles.

forty-niner miner's laundry troubles

Labor shortages were so great during the Gold Rush that many services were all but unobtainable. Men threw their soiled shirts away as cheaper than trying to have them washed. One tale has it that outside one hotel they piled up to the second-story windows.

Four hundred

The Four Hundred as an expression referring to the elite of society was apparently originated by Ward McAllister, the great fashion arbiter of New York City in the 1880's and '90's. The figure was not reached by a deliberate count of the number of eligible society folk who merited invitation to the balls for which he was often asked to prepare the invitation lists, but by the process of elimination. He had declared that if one began with a certain number one could then recognize that half of that number were outsiders who would not be at ease and would keep the others from being at ease, and were better not included. Cynics, however, stated that the number four hundred was agreed upon because that was the capacity of Mrs. Vanderbilt's ballroom. McAllister's fame was due not only to the popularizing of this expression but to his many clever, but often biting witticisms, which were

119

eagerly awaited by those whom they amused and direly dreaded by those eager to stay in his good graces.

"Foxy-grandpop"

This early subject of the comics, about 1900, was a prankster who surprisingly turned the table upon the youngsters who were the more familiar subjects of the first comic strips. Oldsters are still referred to as "foxy grandpops" when they are the authors of some shrewd move.

"Freedom Road"

An area in New York State formerly called "Nigger Hollow," a woodland trail along which slaves were led secretly as part of the Underground Railroad arrangements by which slaves were helped to reach Canada and the life of free men. This portion of the route was near Columbia and the west branch of the Susquehanna.

"French Creeks"

This term was used for the coal flatboats operating on the Monongehela, especially the smaller-sized barges (160' x 24' x 6'). This usage developed because one of the first such towboats had been built up the Allegheny River, one of the tributaries of which was called French Creek.

Frick Legends

The stories have it that there was considerable social rivalry between the former steel partners, so that when Henry Clay Frick was told that Andrew Carnegie's beautiful mansion on Fifth Avenue, which he called a cottage, had cost over a million dollars, Frick at first growled and then said, "I'll make that place look like a miner's shack compared with mine." He then went to work and ordered constructed what became the great Frick Museum for an original outlay of $75 million and eventually at a far greater cost for the magnificent paintings he installed and for the needed upkeep. Though Carnegie mellowed with age, Frick was not ready to end

120

their estrangement. When a mutual friend suggested that Carnegie wanted to shake his former friend's hand before he died Frick replied, "Tell your friend that I will see him in hell where we both are going."

Friday superstitions

So unpopular is Friday among superstitious people that on that day they will refrain from taking a trip or starting a new enterprise or signing a contract. Needless to say, Friday the thirteenth is the day when most care must be exercised by the superstitious. Witches were declared to hold their meetings then.

frog superstitions

Country folk had many variations on the way to prepare a soup of frogs but all agreed that it was a sure cure for whooping cough. A wish made upon seeing the first frog in the spring if kept secret will come true. If you find a frog when neither the sun nor the moon is shining and cut off one of his hind legs it will cure gout, cancer and tuberculosis. Because of the tremendous number of eggs that a frog lays, it has become a symbol of fertility also.

The belief that the croaking of frogs indicates that there will be rain has had very wide acceptance and may have some accuracy because of their susceptibility to atmospheric changes. The Indian belief goes further for they have on occasion enclosed the frogs and then tapped them regularly to get them to produce rain during a drought.

frontier appetites

The men of the West had very healthy appetites and fortunately a very bountiful supply, for it was a common expression that one turkey was too much for one but not enough for two.

full dress

In the colonial period full dress at first meant that the material out of which the clothes had been made had gone

121

through the long and complicated process applied by the fuller in the fulling mills.

See FULLER.

fuller

As early as 1650 there were persons involved in fulling cloth after it had been woven and before it could be made up into clothes. Knots and fuzziness had to be picked out with tweezers. The material had then to be pounded in the great troughs of the fuller with heavy oaken hammers, well soaked with hot water and prepared with fuller's earth so that all grease and stains could be removed. This also shrank the woven threads together for greater strength and warmth. Then the goods had to be dressed. This was done with the head of the teasel plant, which was grown for this express purpose in the fields about the fulling mills. These prickly plants raised the nap of the goods without injuring it. The wool cards used at the beginning of the process for preparing the wool for the spinners were used again in the final preparation of the wool for the tailors and dressmakers. For the very last stage the material was stretched on tenterhooks (q.v.). In the older meaning of the word "full dress" meant material given the full process. During the Revolutionary period patriots would not wear goods thus processed by equipment brought from Britain but indulged in homespun instead.

funeral customs

Among the Sac and Fox Indians every relative of the person to be buried was careful to put something into the grave, whether it had value or not, for fear that the ghost of the deceased might come back and claim the forgotten gift. Among the Southern Negroes the body might be placed on a cooling board below which a plateful of ashes would be placed which were expected to absorb the diseases in the body and which were later thrown into the grave for final disposal. The wearing of black is not just out of respect for

122

the dead but definitely reflects an Old World custom of trying to avoid the possible return of the ghost. In parts of Georgia even the domestic animals are decorated with a bit of black during the funeral period as a means of avoiding the contamination of the ghost. There are still many persons throughout the country who consider it bad luck to meet or cross the street in front of a funeral cortege, probably a hold over of the earlier idea that the ghost may be a source of "contamination." The eulogy is also a part of this group of customs, for speaking well of the dead placates the ghost. Though the wearing of mourning is important for the first year the superstitious think it unwise to wear it for the second, lest a second tragedy be invited. A similar belief applies to the keeping of black-bordered paper in the house after the mourning period.

funeral procession

This ritual brings forth many superstitious acts associated with the fear of death, among which the following are typical. Never allow a child under a year old to attend a funeral or his life may be forfeited. Likewise a pregnant woman should not attend a funeral. A bridal couple will have bad luck if they encounter anything suggestive of death on their way to their wedding. The dead man's horse is led in some processions in the belief that he will need it in the other world.

furrow, the longest in the world

This claim was made on the basis of the work of Lyman Dillon, who started west from Dubuque to Iowa City with a large breaking plow hitched to five yoke of oxen and covering an area of over one hundred miles. It went up hill and down, over virgin prairie that had never known the mark of a plow. Dillon intended his furrow to serve as a guide to future road builders and as a trail for new settlers to follow before a road was made.

fustian

A kind of cloth known as early as the period of the Pilgrims. It was made of two materials, with a warp of flax or cotton. The word also had the meaning of bombast or boastfulness, a suggestion of which was conveyed by the material itself, for this rough stuff had somewhat the appearance of corduroy, a finer material resembling velvet.

G

garlic as a cure-all

Garlic is universally respected, largely because of its pungent odor, as having antiseptic powers which are the basis for many superstitions. It was worn as an amulet to ward off all kinds of diseases. Where it grew plentifully it was often woven into a wreath and placed over the doorway to ward off evil influences. It was also worn around the neck to prevent the action of demons or witches that one might encounter. Onions were held to serve much the same purposes.

genius

With a few spectacular cases to provide a basis for the superstition, there has been a very common belief that a person who possesses genius is unbalanced and is likely to die insane.

George

This name seems to have been universally applied to Negro conductors and Pullman porters.

ginger

A wild or Indian ginger was used by the Indians to boil with meat that was spoiled to prevent food poisoning.

ginseng

This herb was also used by the Indians for curing purposes, particularly for ailments of the stomach and for sore gums. They grated it in hot water for a stomach ache caused by gas. Sometimes the leaves are smoked as a treatment for asthma.

girth

This is the cinch or broad band of woven horsehair that is used in saddling the cowboy's horse. Among Texans it was an established custom to pronounce the word "girt."

give a lick and a promise

An expression originating in the West but fairly common all over the country, now meaning a job has been done in a very sketchy fashion, much as a cat might do if she were cleaning herself in a hurry.

"Give them Watts"

During a Revolutionary War battle in northern New Jersey, the Americans were well supplied with powder but lacked paper wads with which the guns had to be packed to make them shoot true. The minister whose church at that moment happened to be in the midst of the battlefield brought out some copies of Watts' hymnal and distributed them among the soldiers to make up for the shortage of wads. "Give them Watts" became a rallying cry that helped bring victory. As the agency that should have provided the material was known as DQMG, the soldiers altered this to read, "Damned Queer Minister of the Gospel."

"glazier and goddard"

These names were given by the Aroostook pine loggers of early days to a jumper or "go-devil," a device used to get out their heavy timbers. A "glazier" was a kind of roller that went in front to hold a squared tree, which might weigh up to forty tons, and the "goddard" was placed in back to make the tree level so that it could be rolled out for loading. By painful manipulation an obstruction in the hauling roads might thus be overcome. Glazier was the inventor of the "contraption" and a prominent lumber baron of the time.

goat gland rejuvenation

A Kansas doctor, wanting to take advantage of the growing importance of radio in the 1920's, started advertising his process for restoring youth to old men. At $750 an operation

126

he was soon making half million a year and getting 50,000 letters a day in request for information about his treatments. The red-goateed and aggressive young doctor, John R. Brinkley, found himself attacked by the press and brought to trial by the Medical Society. Satisfied customers jumped to his defense. Wives avidly related the differences in their husbands. His license revoked, he facetiously declared he would go back to Kansas and get himself elected governor. In an unbelievable six-weeks campaign he came very close to winning. The regular Democrat had a lead of only 251 over the regular Republican but neither group of party regulars dared challenge the returns because they had thrown out so many of the Brinkley write-in votes that an investigation might have ended in his winning on a tide of personal popularity. In final analysis of the unusual circumstances it was said, "Across a wide belt in central Kansas this radio play upon the mass emotions was a potent vote-getter." It embodied aspects of a Ku-Klux Klan revival, mixed with religious views of many descriptions, sympathy for his exposure as a quack, a protest against hard times, and disgust with the feeble efforts of the regular parties. Brinkley moved to Texas and was elected head of the local Rotary Club. Legends that circulated about his amazing experiences hardly matched the truth.

goat superstitions

There is a very widespread belief that goats will eat anything, relishing especially tin cans. The probable foundation for this belief is the ability of some goats to eat brushwood and weeds, for which purpose many farmers kept them. It is an old tradition that goats kept in a stable will protect the horses from harm. There are those who say a goat's horn under a pillow is a cure for insomnia, and that if you meet a goat when embarking on a business venture you will surely have success.

The phrase "to get someone's goat," meaning to annoy or frustrate someone, goes back to an ancient belief that

127

goats tended to destroy the vineyards,—they were "cutting capers" ("caper" was the Latin word for goat). To be capricious is to be goatlike.

goat that flagged the train

A song once popular with the barbershop quartets had to do with a goat that had eaten three red shirts off the clothesline. As punishment the goat was tied to the railroad tracks but just as the train drew near he coughed up the shirts and thus stopped the train.

goats used in coal mines

Many strange tales are told of the sturdy little goats who did much of the hauling in the early days of mining. They would not under any circumstances pull a third car loaded with coal. They seemed to know exactly to the minute when it was closing time, despite the fact that there were no whistles or similar warnings in the mines. It was claimed that it would take dynamite to make a goat work once the time was up.

go back and cross the t's

Ironical advice given to one steering a vessel who has followed a very erratic course.

gobble weed

The practical mountaineers of the Ozarks have a custom, they claim, of making gobble weed available to the wild turkeys. This causes the turkeys to close their eyes and permits hunters to walk right up and wring their necks. They say the Cherokees sell them the weed.

Goelet legends

The Goelets' name was not so well known to the public as the Astors' and the Vanderbilts' but stories of their wealth were followed with as much avidity by their contemporaries at the turn of the century. Goelet was the master of a magnificent estate at Glenmere near Goshen, New York, whose description ran to legendary dimensions. According to accounts, the estate was approached by two miles of winding

128

road that cost $50,000 to build. Bathrooms were as large as bedrooms and were fitted with gilt fixtures in the form of porpoises. The patio had a marble fountain containing fifteen tons of Italian marble. When the house was sold it was planned to move the fountain at the cost of $700. It was dismantled and then when Goelet changed his mind it cost $750 to put it back again. He did move his mahogany library to his Fifth Avenue home for a supposed $14,000. Society gasped when he said he had offered the estate to Father Divine.

The Goelets' relations with their neighbors were none too cordial, especially over Goelet's refusal to permit the villagers to skate on his frozen lakes. The original owner, they recalled, had granted to the Florida Water Company the use in perpetuity of the upper eighteen inches of the water in the lake over its entire surface. Robert Goelet is presumed to have stated, "Let those people use the surface of the lake, but I still control the air around it and I do not want it disturbed by their skating through it."

golden rod

This herb was used at times as a substitute for tea while the flowers were steeped to make a lotion to soothe a bee sting or for treatment of wounds and bruises. The Chippewa Indians used it as a cure for pains in the chest, to treat boils and ulcers, and to curb convulsions.

gold in their gizzards

In the area around the Sacramento River during the early period of the Gold Rush, cooks were very careful to salvage chicken gizzards because the birds in foraging among the small stones in the chicken runs were supposed to pick up an occasional nugget of gold.

gold rush supplement

Among many of the prospectors in California full beards were commonly worn. The barbers got an extra bonus when they washed or trimmed these customers for it was claimed that an appreciable quantity of gold dust was to be found in them.

129

golf stories

U. S. Grant is supposed to have been the first president "aware" of golf, but his comment was, "That looks like good exercise, but what's the little white ball for?"

gone coon

A person in extreme difficulties. Because the raccoon is hunted only for its fur, if the animal becomes treed and so cannot escape from those pursuing him he is "gone," done for. A story is told in this connection of Captain Martin Scott whom all the animals knew as such a perfect shot that when they had identified him they simply gave themselves up. They were all "gone coons."

"gone to Texas"

Newspaper accounts before 1848, when relating a story of the misappropriation of funds, frequently ended with the phrase, "gone to Texas." There, presumably, anyone fleeing the law might find sanctuary.

Goodie Hallett of Eastam

An inhabitant on Cape Cod who won a curious reputation as a witch living in the "Whistling Whale." This mythical creature was able to avoid all harpoons, upset whale boats that came after it, and make a mockery of the efforts of the good men of Eastam to catch it. Today Goodie Hallett's cabin lies in ruin, surrounded by poverty grass and sand unlike that in any other area of the Cape. It is, of course, haunted.

goose grease

The fat from the goose was looked upon with high regard in our early history and there are still a surprising number of individuals who find it useful not only for choice cookery but for various medicinal treatments. It may be blended with turpentine and rubbed on chests for coughs and colds. It helps in earaches and soothes rheumatism. Because it was very easily absorbed it was thought to get immediately at the seat of the difficulty. Weather predictions were offered by judging the heaviness of the breast bone—if thick, a cold winter is to be expected. The expression, "All is well and the goose hangs high," is taken to mean that because the goose is honking high up in the sky the weather will be good, for when he flies low the weather will be bad. American Indians held that when the wild geese went south in early August a severe winter could be expected.

goose-plucking

In colonial New England there were many ways favored for making a goose behave while it was being plucked. Some placed a heavy woolen stocking over its head. Others had especially woven baskets into which the goose's head and neck were inserted. Feathers might be plucked as often as four times a year, usually yielding three-quarters of a pound.

Gould Legends

In his day Jay Gould was so cordially hated as the result of his stock manipulations that it is hard to separate fact from fancy in the many stories told about him. Though in 1869 he ruthlessly engineered a corner on the market in gold that was almost disastrous for the country, he looked very meek and mild and was a lover of flowers, especially roses. The window boxes of his Fifth Avenue mansion bloomed with flowers regardless of whether the house was occupied. A female reporter of his day is supposed to have commented romantically, "Such a man could not be altogether bad who is such a friend of the rose."

He was taken to court many times for his financial machinations but always managed to wriggle out through some legal loophole. This so outraged those with whom he did business that they are supposed to have tried to make arrangements with a double, a man who bore considerable resemblance to the hated Gould, to play a part for $20 that would cause Gould great grief. The double was to appear near the corner of Broad Street in the financial district with his face covered with blood and to fall down on the sidewalk. Confederates nearby were to yell, "There's Jay Gould, he is

131

dying." This was to cause a great drop in the stock market and those in on the plot would sell short and reap a great profit. The scheme fell through, it is said, because the double turned the opportunity down. He was too afraid of Gould!

On another occasion when Gould attempted to bribe a Senator to vote as he wanted on a certain law, he was shown the door with scant courtesy. Telling the incident to a business associate later, Gould stated, "That man will never make an outstanding success. He is not a good businessman."

Governor John Winthrop Jr.

Winthrop was the leading figure in Connecticut affairs during his term of office 1657-1676. Legend has it that he found favor for his plea for a royal charter because upon visiting Charles II in England he offered the King a beautiful and remarkable ring which had been given to his grandfather by Charles I.

grab the saddle horn

The cowboy would call it "pulling leather" or "shaking hands with grandma."

graham bread

Sylvester Graham fell ill in 1840 from the food he ate. Because of this he began eating unbolted flour which did him so much good it set the style for the production of graham bread.

grand right and left

A term used in square dancing. Partners step in front of one another and join their extended right hands; each walks forward in the opposite direction and so comes face to face with a new partner; joining hands as before, all continue around the circle, alternating right and left hands, until they promenade back to their original places.

grapevine twist

A position in a square dance in which the leader causes the whole line of dancers to follow him in a series of loops between couples back to their original places.

132

grasshoppering

A term used to describe the way a Missouri steamboat would be lifted over a sand bar. Spars were set in the river bottom in front of the boat. As the capstan was turned, the paddlewheel revolved and the boat was lifted and pushed forward. The spars were then reset and the boat "hopped" forward again.

grease

The mountaineers of the Southern highlands were reputed to fry practically everything. Unfortunately they used a practically indigestible grease for their cooking. Their few vegetables were loaded with fat. It was pretty well understood that in neighborhoods where shootings were numerous, the irritations were directly traceable to rebellious stomachs or an overdose of greasy collard greens.

Great Barrington Legend

The vague boundaries of the early days along the Housatonic River are illustrated by an incident connected with the sale of land from the Westenhook patentees. A Dutchman had made arrangements to purchase a tract of land in this area that was to stretch from the Hudson River as far eastward as a man could run in a day. Shrewdly the purchaser employed a famous Indian runner, who between dawn and sunset covered over forty miles from the Hudson to the Housatonic, including the crossing of the Taconic Mountains.

green Christmas means a fat graveyard

A superstition popular in Idaho where the belief was that if there was a mild December the sick would die in the spring when the petals began to fall.

green'un

A Yankee term for a gullible individual, or for someone new to a situation and thus often taken advantage of. He is frequently the butt of a tall tale. For example, a townsman may collect from a green 'un a fee to enter a public park, or upon being offered a lemon the green one may eat it whole.

133

gremlins

Small creatures some airmen say existed as long ago as World War I who manage to get into machinery or motors and cause inexplicable failures. It has become common practice to blame them for mistakes that no one else will admit to.

Griffith Park, Los Angeles

Before the Gold Rush the lands later to make up the city of Los Angeles were held by the "First Families" in the form of extensive ranches. After the Civil War many of these areas were lost through speculation and bad judgment. That of the Feliz family was inherited by an American despite the claims of a niece of the family, Petronella, who was ignored in the will. Varied versions of the tale tell how she came to curse the property, which had been gained by a Welsh peasant, Felix Griffith, who had managed to marry the Spanish heiress by advertising his love for her in the newspapers. Petronella's curse foretold that though the new owner would become rich, death, bloodshed, violence, destruction and floods would be connected with the property. Griffith did become a millionaire. He shot his wife, declaring she was conspiring with the Pope to overthrow America. After a sensational trial and his later release from prison, fires destroyed the property and a cloudburst did much damage. Though the curses seemed to be coming true, the city benefited for he gave the land for a planetarium and also provided for a Greek theater. They say, however, that the ghost of old Felix still rides the hills on a white stallion on a dark night.

grind man

Term used for a ticket seller in a traveling carnival, who is continually "grinding," that is, repeating the same memorized phrases.

Grindstone Hill

Near a branch of the Penobscot a strangely shaped hill

has led to the creation of several legends to acount for its origin. One states that an Indian boy was sent for a pumpkin and detoured on the hunt. Returning home late without having carried out his errand, he noticed a little moon had been following his route. Toward this he pointed his bow and arrow and was amazed to discover that the little moon had fallen in a swamp and formed a hill which he continued to live near for the rest of his life.

Another version attributes the hill to the activities of a French Canadian officer who was leading a troupe to reinforce Montcalm's garrison in Quebec. He was so completely disgusted with the weather that he let out a tremendous oath compounded of two languages and urging that it rain grindstones. And it did. These wiped out all but one of the unfortunate party—a man who had slowed up at the sound of the terrible swearing.

Groundhog Day

Whether seriously or not, most of the adult population gives some passing attention to the superstition concerned with the activities of the groundhog on February 2 of each year. When the groundhog emerges from his burrow on this day, if he sees his shadow there will be six weeks more of winter weather and he goes back to sleep the bad interval out. On the other hand, if the day is cloudy and he does not see his shadow he is expected to stay outside for spring is on its way.

At Quarryville, in Pennsylvania, they have had a special celebration on this day for the past fifty years, and neighboring communities have been taking up the idea. They have a "Slumbering Lodge" which sends out a large delegation for investigation on February 2.

This is an American parallel to the European celebration known as Candlemas Day.

ground-lead logging

In lumbering in the Northwest it was not always necessary

to depend exclusively on traditional manpower methods. A steam donkey engine would sometimes be introduced which used a turning wheel or capstan so that logs could be yarded or led along the ground. When the same process was used to drag a tree above the trees surrounding it, it was called "high-level" logging in contrast to ground-level activities. A pulley was hung high in a tree. Through this ran the line from the donkey engine. Thus the log could be hauled in, riding free of stumps and underbrush. Eventually this led to the development of the "high rigger" a forerunner of the mechanization of the logging industry and the end of an era filled with colorful folklore.

guardhouse lawyer

Army slang for a soldier who is in the habit of twisting the regulations in his favor and of helping others do the same thing.

gundalo, also gondola and gundaloa

This boat of the Merrimac region in use off the coast of New Hampshire and Massachusetts had many spellings but was usually pronounced "gunlow." Its name was probably derived from the Italian "gondola" but not its style of construction or its usage. These boats were sailing scows; sloops rigged with a bowsprit and one or two lee boards. Some had a house forward or aft, and a mast so arranged that it could be dipped to pass under a bridge.

gunman's sidewalk

A Western expression for the middle of the street, probably the safest place for him to walk since he could thus see all around him and be less exposed to ambush.

gunman versus gunfighter

In the legends and tales of the West a distinction was made in the use of these two terms. The first was a sneaking and malicious killer who took advantage of the weak and helpless. The second was held to be a chivalrous and sportsman-like man who never shot except under conditions of fair play.

136

gunpowder for dogs

A Creole belief in Louisiana states that a dog may be rendered an excellent watchdog if it is fed gunpowder to make it ferocious.

H

Hadley's angel

During an Indian attack upon this town in Massachusetts Colony during King Philip's War an old man emerged from the woods when the colonists were hard-pressed and helped in the defense of the town until the Indians were driven off. The populace claimed an angel had been sent down to aid them. It seems more likely that the man was a William Goffe, who had come out from hiding to their rescue. He was one of the judges who had signed the death warrant of Charles I. Feeling that it was wise to leave England after the Restoration of Charles II in 1660, he had hidden away in an obscure part of the colony near Hadley, where he later died. Another judge, Whalley, was said to have hidden away in like circumstances. Over a hundred years later it was claimed that the bones of each had been found and a tablet was erected in their memory.

hair coloration as basis for superstitions

Folksay, superstition or just plain common sense, the belief that blondes can be dangerous is very widespread, as is also the notion that gentlemen prefer them. That redheads are spitfires is also a prevalent idea. Some say that thin delicate hair indicates a weak constitution. Prematurely gray hair has been held to be a sign of genius. There are many who claim that a sudden shock may turn hair white overnight, or that long hair may sap one's strength, or that cutting the hair may do the same thing. They all belong to the realm of hearsay, as does the old story that hair and beard grow in the grave.

138

Hale's Toll Bridge

This was the first bridge across the Connecticut River and it joined Walpole, New Hampshire, and Bellows Falls, Vermont. Legend has it that the builder, Colonel Enoch Hale, financed the building of the bridge by means of a mortgage arranged by a jealous rival who stipulated in the contract that if the anual payments were even one day in arrears he could foreclose. One year Hale sent his payment by means of his son who was delayed and caused the bridge to be lost. The reason for his delay, they say, was that he had encountered his estranged wife, made it up with her and forgotten his mission until too late—a costly reconciliation.

hand in one's chips

Die. Probably derived from the practice in a poker game of turning in one's counters or chips at the end of the game; therefore, by analogy, the end of the game of life.

"handkerchief heads"

A term of insult applied to what the modern Negro calls the "take it easy boys." They are the ones willing to accept compromise on segregation or who will accept white restrictions without protest. The reference is to the bandannas worn by the old mammies and thus symbolizes the Negro of slavery days.

hand of glory

This was a charm made from the dried or pickled hand of a dead man. It had much greater efficacy if it were that of a criminal, and best of all if that of a man who had been hung. Robbers were known to set fire to the fingers of such a hand before entering a home, to see if all the inmates were asleep. A finger that would not burn showed that someone was still awake in the household. In like vein was the belief that to slap the ground before the house you wish to enter with the hand of a woman who had died giving birth to her first child would render all those within unconscious.

139

hand symbols

Ways of using the hands have a place in many superstitious acts and in ritualistic ceremonials. There were gestures for warding off the "evil eye" and for indicating that a husband had a faithless wife. The shaking of hands upon the completion of a business transaction or after a wager has a superstitious implication, for the hand was once looked upon as a symbol of integrity. Asking for the lady's hand as a first step toward marriage had widespread usage. If in a confused moment of introduction two couples find themselves crossing arms there will probably be the superstition uttered that someone is to be married within the year. Churchill's famous "V for victory" has practically been adopted as a universal sign, whereas crossing the fingers as an expression of the hopeful fulfillment of some desired action is still commonplace. *See* LEFT-HANDEDNESS.

hanging

In Western style this sad fate might be expressed in many ways: wearing a hemp necktie, dying with throat trouble, guest of honor at a string party, getting the neck stretched, Texas cakewalk, used to trim a tree, rope meat.

Hanging Day

The day set for an execution in New York State was usually an occasion for celebration before 1850. Great was the discontent if at the last minute a reprieve came through to upset the spirit of holiday. A great crowd had assembled on December 28, 1827 to see a Levi Kelley hung for having killed one of his tenants in a jealous rage. An enormous scaffold had been erected from which the spectators might watch but so great were the numbers in this improvised grandstand that it collapsed. This event caused far more excitement than the quick and immediate execution of the prisoner, who seemed to be far more concerned over the harm to the crowd than over what he was about to endure. However, the event was widely acclaimed in folk tales and grew with the telling. Ballads too were written about it.

140

"Poor Kelley in this trying time
Was executed for his crime.
He hung, an awful sight to see;
May this a solemn warning be."

Most parts of the U.S. observed the practice of having hangings on Fridays.

"hanging judge"

Federal Judge Isaac Parker from 1875 to 1896 sentenced 163 men to death. His marshal, Maledon, was said to have hanged twenty-one men in one day, but this record is doubted. He did hang five men simultaneously. When asked about his possible fear of returning spirits he is credited with saying, "I did a good job and I ain't yet had a man come back and ask to have it done over."

"happles"

A popular tale in Newport, Rhode Island tells of a disdainful Britisher viewing some pumpkins an old huckster woman was offering for sale. He is supposed to have remarked, "We have bigger happles than that in Hengland." "Happles!" the indignant vendor retorted, "Them's huckleberries."

Harvey Girls

The Harvey House staffs provided the West with more than food, or even more than waitresses, for the "Harvey Girls" had to conform to high standards of appearance and decorum, so high that they were married off rapidly to many of the leading men of the various communities where they were stationed. A quantity of folklore has accumulated about their actions, sayings and "civilizing" influence. Some claim 4,000 babies were named Fred or Harvey in appreciation of the romances that budded from eating at the different Harvey houses.

hash marks

Service stripes worn on the sleeve of an enlisted man's uniform to show the number of previous enlistments.

141

hassayampers

A western expression for a liar. There was a popular
legend that anyone who drank of the Hassayampa River in
Arizona would never again tell the truth.

hasty pudding

This popular dish of the colonial period had to be made
in a very exacting fashion. The cook had to add a mixture
of rye and corn meal to boiling water grain by grain, taking
at least half an hour. She then had to continue stirring with
a paddle for an hour more. It was then turned out into a pot
and served with milk. This recipe was learned from the
Indians, who just poured in the corn and boiled it until they
were ready to eat, thus accounting for its original title. It
was not originally intended as a dessert but was served during
the meal, on some occasions the whole meal.

hatchetation

By 1890 Carrie Nation, in her horror at the evils drunkenness produced, was seeking larger pastures for her special
talents for inflicting prohibition by destruction. Upon arriving
in Wichita, then the second largest city in Kansas, she threw
rocks at a painting displayed in a bar, and then with a rod
and a cane destroyed all the bottles on the counter. To her
delight she was arrested with much ensuing publicity, which
led ladies in other cities to follow her example. She referred
to her program as "hatchetation" though no hatchet was used
in her early forays. She changed her first name from Carrie
to Carry with deliberate intent and would sign hotel registers
"Carry A. Nation, your loving home defender." She boasted
she would "carry a nation to prohibition and glory." Depending on the point of view of those who observed her work,
she was a shining evangel or she was a noisy joke and a gad-
fly. Like so many fanatical characters who come and go on
the American scene, she is now just a legend.

hat removal device

On the programs issued at matinees to ladies during the
early nineties was a shrewd statement: "The prettiest, wisest

and most charming women take their hats off during a theatrical performance."

hauling power

A farmer unable to move a heavy load on his wagon, wet the traces thoroughly and led his horse back to his house, stretching the traces. He then sat down and waited for the rawhide to dry out. As it did so the wagon was pulled without difficulty right where he wanted it—or at least so the Arkansas farmers claim.

hawks

These birds are disappearing rapidly for they have been commonly looked upon as an evil influence. If one is seen carrying off its prey, the observer will suffer a loss of money. A hawk skin is supposed to bring its possessor protection of various kinds.

hay superstitions

If you see a load of hay approaching it is considered good luck to make a wish, which will be fulfilled when the bale is broken open. If you fail to make a wish under these circumstances, you will have bad luck.

hayseed

A colonial term for a country man or rustic individual, implying that the individual has recently been in or near a hayfield.

haywire

To have something go wrong or be uncontrolled, presumably derived from the difficulty in handling the rolls of wire used to bale hay. These may very easily get out of control, with the coils springing out of the rolls and becoming very unmanageable.

"head and pluck"

This was a popular dish in colonial times. The head, heart, liver and sweetbreads of a lamb or sheep were cooked all together. They were then chopped fine and served as hash.

143

head for the setting sun

A Western expression meaning to avoid contact with law enforcement officers—which in those early days meant to go West. "Whipping a tired pony out of Texas" meant the same thing.

head right

Under Virginia law anyone who brought an indentured servant or a slave into the colony received a head right that entitled him to fifty acres of land on condition that it was occupied within two years. The title was then clear except for a quit rent of a shilling annually on each fifty acres. This was a land tax all landlords paid.

heat, to turn the heat on

Part of the colloquial usage of gangland meaning to be subjected to intense cross examination or questioning under very bright lights.

heaving

By a policeman on night duty in the old days the practice of heaving was most esteemed. The only difficulty was the need to find a place where this refreshing sleep might be safely enjoyed. Basements of furniture stores or garages were attractive spots. Once, outside a ferry slip four patrol cars were observed with seven sleeping occupants, one awake to maintain an alert eye for that great menace to heaving—the investigator or shoefly. It was a little harder for the mounted policeman to get his rest. Disposing of the horse was a little risky. However, there were some riding academies where it might be safe to take a rest. One amusing tale tells of four such sleepers caught in quiet rest by the arrival of an inspection force. Seriously worried, the four at the last minute hit upon a remedy. They wrapped their raincoats about their heads and emerged as four galloping headless horsemen.

Helena, Montana

Last Chance Gulch, now the main street of the capital city of Montana, almost gave its name to the city, but when it was considered too undignified, a miner selected the name of his own home town in Minnesota—Helena—pronouncing it to rhyme with "lena." However, the mule skinners and vigilantes would not have it that way. They claimed it was named after Helen of Troy.

"Helen-a after a darling dizzy dame
Of much beauty but spotted fame;
In pronouncing the name understand me well,
Strong emphasis should be laid on Hel."

Gossip has it they were determined to get "Hell" into the town some way or other.

Hemstitch Nettie

A term of legendary origin in San Francisco as a name for a drug addict. Its appropriateness depended on the fact that his skin would be well punctured by the use of a hypodermic needle.

hex

A wizard; or to bewitch. Some are professional men known as hex doctors and may actually do some good. They are found particularly among the Pennsylvania Dutch, where tales of animals cured by them are very frequent. Barns carry hex signs to protect animals from the evil eye.

hiccups

The number of folk cures of this disconcerting condition are myriad. Note the voluminous contributions in the press whenever a lengthy case of such suffering is brought before the public. Probably the idea of scaring the person is the first remedy that comes to mind, especially by means of a blown-up paper bag which is burst unexpectedly in the victim's face. A cold key down the back or holding the breath have been suggested often.

hickory nut milk

Due to the scarcity of cows in the early Virginia colonies children were fed hickory nuts beaten to a pulp in place of

145

milk, a trick picked up from the Indians around Roanoke Island and Jamestown.

hide and tallow factories

As cattle ranchers raised more and more cattle in the 1830's they found that the price dropped as low as $10 per animal. As they sought to find additional means of obtaining income, they recalled that tallow dips were valuable for purposes of illumination. The small packers soon found that the tallow rendered out of the carcass of the steer brought in more money than the salt-jerked meat they had formerly tried to dispose of. Until the demand for meat revived again, these small enterprises continued to operate.

high rigger

The high rigger represents the introduction of the specialist in the logging industry. He wears sharp steel spurs and a safety belt hung with an ax and a saw. He hitches himself to a tall fir 150 to 200 feet in the air and saws off the tip. He has to be very alert to the effects of the vibrations of the tree when the top branches crash to the ground. In time he may only be concerned with placing a pulley for ground-lead (q.v.) or high-lead lumbering.

hit the high lonesome

An expression popular in Idaho, meaning to depart in haste for unknown areas.

hit the silk

Army slang for making a parachute jump from a plane.

hoaxing

In practically every section of the United States the telling of tall tales is enjoyed more if the tale involves a bit of cheating. The hoax involves deceiving for the purpose of building up a good yarn—"loading the greenhorn."

hogreeves

In some New Hampshire towns it was common practice before 1900 to make the groom of every newly married

146

couple a "hogreeve," responsible for conducting trespassing pigs to the pound.

holler

A holler was a Negro improvisation of a song though it might have a close resemblance to some frequently repeated folk song.

hollering down the rain barrel

A Kansas expression used to indicate that the man's wife was pregnant.

holy clay

A community on the Santa Cruz known as Chimayo had built itself a beautiful little church and carved the image of a Christ Child. On its feet they put shoes, but each morning they found them worn out. In the meantime the whole community prospered, supposedly from the visits of the Christ Child to bless the townsfolk. Finally the people from that part of New Mexico and even as far away as Colorado and Texas came to believe the church was on holy land, and came to be cured of bodily ills and to receive a spiritual blessing. In time a large hole appeared near the church from the practice of carrying away some of the sanctified soil. A New Mexican Lourdes had arisen.

honesty in the Adirondacks

A wealthy New Yorker once left an expensive fishing pole overnight on the porch of one of Colonel Baker's hotels at Saranac Lake. Surprised the next day at finding it where he had left it, he won from the Colonel the following reply: "By Godfrey, sir, your things are as safe here as in the Bank of England. There's not a Republican within ten miles."

hooked rugs

In New Hampshire they were made primarily of scraps of wool of white, yellow, black rose, red and warm brown and gray. Peddlers sold the patterns or they were borrowed from friends. The more popular ones were Orange Peel, Double and Single Snowball, and Pine Bloom.

147

"Hook 'em, cow"

An expression of encouragement at a branding corral in the Old West and used today to show support for a performer in a rodeo. "Hooks" were slang for spurs.

hookers

These boats were a kind of barge used for lumber tows on the Great Lakes. As steam-and-propeller-driven ships took over most of the transportation of freight on Lake Superior because of their economy of operation, the older but still sound sailing craft were eliminated. However, around 1900 a boom in lumber production was under way and the increased demand for shipping space provided an incentive for a return to the old sailing vessels. They were converted into "tows," retaining one mast to add buoyancy or to carry a little sail, and were floated tandem-style behind a steam tug. These "hookers," as they were called, were the cheapest means of transportation for the numerous forest products about the Lakes until accessible supplies were practically all removed.

hoosegow

The cowboy of the early West pronounced Spanish words as they sounded to him and in many cases created new and colorful words. "*Juzgado*," Spanish for a court, was commonly circulated as "hoosegow," for the jail the cowboy unfortunately found waiting for him in some towns when he was through drinking.

hoot of the deer owl

This deep booming sound was used by the "swampers" of Okefenokee as a distress signal when anyone was lost or hurt. It would carry for miles over the swamp and effectively bring help.

hops

According to an old New York State custom, a girl kissed through the loops in the hop vine will always remain faithful.

148

horseblock class

This term was popular in western New York well over a century ago for, surprisingly, even in those days there were individuals who did not follow the accepted custom of consistent church attendance. Instead they convened outside or under the sheds for the horses in back of the church. There, it was declared, they told dubious stories or discussed horse trades until the rest of the congregation was released.

horse chestnuts or buckeyes

These used to be carried in the pocket to prevent rheumatism. There were those who thought that if fed to horses they would cure coughs and improve shortness of breath.

"horse dams"

Loggers along the Aroostook River in the great logging days of the past wanted to get their immense quantity of timber to market quickly and easily, for which they needed a good supply of water to float their hundreds of trees. After the spring freshets, on occasion, not all the wood might have been floated down. Therefore, some of the woodsmen would build flimsy dams just strong enough to hold a sufficient supply of water to finish the job after the highest levels had dropped. They often constructed their dams where the beavers had already started work. Quarrels developed when rival companies competed for facilities and the workers of one group would dynamite the dam of the other. Lawsuits would develop from the resulting damage. The whole situation lapsed when the woods were finally denuded of most of their fine timber.

horsehairs

Many children believe that a horsehair placed in water will grow into a snake or eel. There is a rather obvious explanation for this seeming phenomenon. There is a hairworm that matures in about the time it takes a horsehair to decay and these worms may give the illusion of being miniature eels.

149

horse-hunting

A standard excuse for almost any situation in the West that would cause a person's delay. Courting might even be included in this category.

horseless buggy produced strange results

A popular tale of the 1910's tells of an asylum established for motorists driven crazy over trouble with their cars. A visitor was taken into one of the wards on a tour of inspection. He could see no occupants. Then he was urged to look under the beds. The patients were all down there attempting to repair the bed slats.

"horse power toll"

One of the tall tales from Idaho tells of an event when automobiles were just beginning to be popular. An old farmer had a tollgate on a road he had constructed in northern Idaho. He charged twenty-five cents for a team to use it. He was greatly astonished when a man in a car came up to his gate and asked what he owed. The flabbergasted farmer asked the man what horsepower he had and was told that his car had about forty horsepower. The farmer replied, "Well, I guess you owe me about five dollars."

horse-shave

This was a device used in early colonial times for almost any kind of woodwork. It was kept in the kitchen where it might come in handy for furniture making or the shaping of wooden bowls then so very much in demand. It was also known as a "shingle horse" because the farmer often set himself astride the horse for convenience in the making of shingles. The amazing fact is that all this fine work was done without metal instruments. For example, the farmer working with some already prepared pieces of wood would smooth them down with long quick strokes. The horse had an attachment which held the shingles firm while they were being shaved. They might be of hemlock, cedar or spruce, and were accurately shaped by one piece of wood striking another. One side was left smooth to throw off the rain and

150

the other rough to cling to the roof better. Some of the trees used were so large that they produced shingles twenty-eight inches across, held on by wooden pegs.

horseshoe customs

There is hardly a person in the United States who does not consider a horseshoe a symbol of good luck. The magic qualities of the horseshoe involve a combination of factors. Iron is a repellent of witches. The arch is a special symbol of fertility. There are various interpretations as to which way the "horns" are supposed to be placed. As a means of protection the convex side should be placed outward, while for good luck one must make certain that the "horns" or open end are at the top so that the luck will not run out. A Pennsylvania custom places the horseshoe outside the house with the prongs pointing inside so that the good luck will surely pour into the home. Though modern times make it much more difficult to find a horseshoe on the highway and thus end all one's possible misfortunes, the great quantity of items still fashioned in the form of a horseshoe show what a strong hold this popular superstition has upon the public. Witness floral displays, stick pins, brooches, buttons and so on.

hospitality, Southern style

A new hotel was about to be constructed in a Georgia city. Its necessity was questioned when the matter of who was to be entertained arose. For if a man were a gentleman, he would be entertained by his friends in their private homes; if he weren't, he would not be wanted in the hotel!

hot foot

This was a practice used by rustlers of burning a stolen calf between the toes so that it would not go back to its mother and reveal to its former owner the false brand which the thieves had placed on it.

How!

This laconic expression has traditionally been accepted as an Indian salutation though there is reason to believe that it

151

really was "A-haw," meaning "Peace be with you" or "All is well."

hulled corn

This was a substantial dish popular in colonial times. To prepare it the housewife had to boil white ashes to get a lye solution strong enough to hold up an egg. The shelled corn was put into this liquid and boiled until the skins came off easily. Then the corn was washed well to remove all the lye. After that it was boiled again until soft. It was to be eaten warm with milk. Sometimes it was served with maple syrup for dessert. It was often fried for breakfast.

Hungry Sam Miller

Miller put on eating shows at farmer's picnics all over eastern Pennsylvania. He had started giving exhibits just after the Spanish-American War, when he found out he would not only get a free meal but get paid as well. He gave up his activities during World War I out of patriotic deference to the Wheatless and Meatless Days of that era, but he started in again on Armistice Day with two whole chickens followed by one hundred and fifty-three waffles. Practical jokers took him to the popular church socials of the day which displayed signs, "All you can eat for fifty cents." He always produced a deficit. At one picnic he ate an eighteen-pound ham. At another he ate forty-eight ten-inch pies. Once when challenged to eat a bale of hay he burned it and ate the ashes. He died at eighty having never suffered from indigestion.

hunting buffalo, Indian style

When hunting buffalo, which were for them the indispensable source of food, clothing, heat and shelter, the Indians of the northwestern plains used an ingenious device. A fleet-footed man would run ahead of the herd as a decoy. When the cows were close at his heels he would throw himself into a previously selected crevice while the fast-moving herd would see too late the gulf ahead. The following animals would push the first bunch over, all of them falling a hundred

152

or more feet to their death. Here, the Indians set to work to skin and prepare the meat for the whole tribe. Wolves ultimately gorged on the leftovers. The Lewis and Clark expedition in 1804 located such an area by the stench, and reported on the number of wolves in the neighborhood.

hunting dog's voices

The sound of a hunting dog's voice is ordinarily identified as a yelp, a whine, a bark or a howl. However, these terms are too vague for the people of the Ozarks who have such carefully differentiated subdivisions as piggle-mouth, squealing mouth, goose-mouth, and fine or chop mouth.

Hunting Shirts as Uniforms

Early in the Revolution, General Washington recognized the hysterical effect the tremendous accuracy of the frontier riflemen's fire had upon the British Army. The American recruitment service decided to play upon this panic. An order issued stated: "The General earnestly encourages the use of Hunting Shirts with long Breeches made of the same material—it is a dress justly supposed to carry no small terror to the enemy who think every such person a complete marksman."

hunyak

A term used commonly in Pennsylvania for any foreigner. It was as widely used there as "Portuguee" on Cape Cod. Its origin has been traced to the first Chinese laundryman in eastern Pennsylvania, whose name they say was Hun-Yak.

Hylan, John F.

The former mayor of New York City was looked upon as a man who had attained office only as the result of party regularity and many stories circulated to show he was not of particularly keen mental ability. In an exchange with Al Smith he was asked by the Governor, "And how do you intend to build the tunnel, by the open cut or by the bore method?" Hylan is supposed to have replied that if he used the open-cut method he would need fish to do the job.

153

I

ice house
These structures are characteristic of the period before modern refrigeration, when the winter storing of ice and its sale in the summer formed an important industry. The pieces were cut in large blocks from the neighboring lakes and then stored in barnlike structures in layers of sawdust. This harvest of ice was even shipped by sea successfully.

Idaho potatoes
Old-timers in Idaho claim that potatoes really reached some size in the past, and prove it by a yarn about a farmer who was approached by the Director of a neighboring CCC camp who wanted to buy about a hundred pounds of potatoes. The farmer told him he was sorry he could not accommodate him because "I won't cut a spud in half for no one."

"immortal poker game"
From Warrenton, North Carolina, has come a tall tale having a wide and naive following. It tells of a poker game started prior to the Civil War and still going on, in which the eldest sons take their fathers' places generation to generation. One variation adds that the game was momentarily suspended when, upon General Lee's entrance, the men all stood up to salute, but upon his joining in, the game immediately continued.

Imperial Valley of California
An amazing tale is told of the time in the 1890's when the rich Imperial Valley was almost washed away by a shift in the Colorado River. By heroic means the action was averted though the valley was for a time under the "Salten Sea."

154

Indian file

It was the custom of certain Indian tribes to march one behind the other so that each stepped in the footprints of the preceding. The last man was supposed to obliterate the tracks, thus preventing the determination of their route or numbers.

Indian-Puritan Incident

This incident, supposed to have occurred about 1700, has been claimed by several colonies but Woodbury, Connecticut, residents feel sure it happened there. After two settlers had been discussing the full implications of predestination one of them before leaving for home checked the priming on his musket, explaining he was afraid of a possible attack by an Indian. His host countered by asking what good his musket would be if it was predestined that he was to be killed by an Indian. His guest replied that if it was so predestined there was nothing he could do about it, but if on the other hand it was predestined that he kill the Indian he had better be ready for it.

Indian whiskey

This concoction, also known as "pizen" and "popskull," was sold illegally to the Indians and accounts for certain trappers getting rich. To one barrel of Missouri water were added two gallons of alcohol, two ounces of strychnine, three plugs of tobacco, three bars of soap, red pepper and sage brush, after which it was stirred well and strained.

infant population increases

There are many settings for the oft-repeated tale about the effect on sleepers of an early morning train that whistled frequently at some particular crossing, but all agree that a considerable increase in the number of babies was one of the consequences.

intermission lore

The theater critic, John Chapman, was annoyed at the practice of rather pushy individuals during intermissions in

155

the Times Square district of New York City of shaking boxes for collections under the noses of those standing and smoking and talking in the foyer. Approached by one of these collectors for help for lepers, he replied in exasperation, in a phrase thereafter much repeated, "Good. I *am* a leper."

"inveigling"

In Puritan Boston if a young man did not seek permission from a girl's parents to pay court to her, he could be brought up before a magistrate and charged with inveigling the young woman's affection—that is, trying to win her by trickery. If the young woman encouraged the man, they might both be brought up on charges of "sinful dalliance" and be fined according to the severity of the "sin."

Ipswich fright

A frequently told story relates how the community of Ipswich feared that a regiment of British regulars were about to attack them on April 21, 1775. All fled the town, fearing total extermination. Many ridiculous situations arose due to the hysteria of the people. Ultimately news of the falseness of the report was obtained and the inhabitants went sheepishly back to their homes.

Irish Indian chief

A Jesuit priest after preaching through an interpreter to a group of Indians was astonished when an Indian came up to speak to him in good English. Upon inquiry the priest discovered his "Indian" was an Irishman, who, having found he drank too much in civilization, took to Indian life like a duck to water and had been made chief of his tribe. He had an Indian wife and several children and his request was "that his Reverence baptize his five papooses and do it right this time."

ironing board story

In a certain section of the South they tell the story of a marvelous hunting dog. He always knew the kind of varmint he was to follow by the kind of board the owner put outside his cabin door for the stretching of the hide of the animal to be hunted. The dog lived up to his reputation except for one cleaning day, when consternation reigned because the hunter's wife had placed the ironing board outside!

iron plow

In 1797 Charles Newbold cast in one piece an iron plow which was a great improvement over the crude wooden plows in use previously, but it did not sell. Farmers claimed iron poisoned the soil. A wooden plow, on the other hand, they believed was a case of wood returning to its mother since wood had come from the earth. These superstitions continued for more than twenty years and then iron plows began to sell. The farmer rationalized this by stating that as iron was strong so the soil in which an iron plow was used would be strong.

iron strap for railroad ties

When the first railroads were being built in Texas, a rawhide strap was used to reduce the wear and tear on the early narrow-gauge roads. The rawhide became almost as stiff and hard as iron but did not stay in place very well. Stories are told of delays following a derailment, when it was claimed the passengers had to wait around for the conductor and the brakeman to rope a steer, kill him, skin him and replace the rawhide.

"I'se regusted"

This expression to indicate the disgust of Amos of the famous team of Amos and Andy became a household expression in most of the homes of America after 1925. Incidents in the lives of these characters, retold and followed closely year after year, assumed the proportions of folklore.

ivy

If the ivy plant grows over the house it is thought to be unlucky for the person who planted it but lucky for the one who lives there. The gift of an ivy plant is said by some to break a friendship, and is held by many to be unlucky to have around the house. Some feel that if ivy does not grow upon a grave it indicates that the soul of the person buried there is uneasy. If it grows strongly on the grave of a young woman, it shows that she died of a broken heart.

In folk medicine ivy was considered useful as an antidote for poison and as a dressing for wounds, burns and ulcers. The powdered berries were held effective against jaundice. It was also supposed to cure the itch and by some was thought effective as a depilatory and as a hair dye.

J

jack-in-the-mist
A Cape Cod term for a drowned sailor.

Jack-pine gold search
A popular whizzer, or hoax, practiced on a tenderfoot. When a new arrival was seen coming into camp, a seasoned miner would start pulling bark slabs off a jack pine. By a trick of legerdemain a nugget would suddenly appear. Of course the newcomer would want to stake out some trees immediately for his own claim and another tall tale would be started on its rounds.

Jack Rabbit
A shortened form of "jackass rabbit," a large prairie hare with long ears and legs.

Jackson's Folly
In an attempt to render the Okefenokee swamp more usable, Captain Henry J. Jackson of the Suwannee Canal Company bought a portion of the swamp from the state of Georgia and tried to drain it. However, he could not remove the waters, nor were others later able to accomplish this much referred to "folly."

Jemimakins
Followers of Jemima Wilkinson, who had given herself the title of "Universal Friend" and had started a new sect. Almost dying of a severe fever, she claimed that she really had, but that life had been restored to her body by the fact that Christ had entered it instead of her own spirit. She announced that like Christ she had the ability to walk on

water. At a demonstration she asked her followers if they believed that her body could actually perform such a miracle. They all proclaimed that they did believe it possible. Cleverly, she then announced that under the circumstances it was unnecessary to perform the action! Her followers existed near New Milford on the Housatonic around the 1780's.

jerkers or jumpers

Those associated with religious groups which encouraged the individuals to embark upon a religious ecstasy during which they often became subject to violent and involuntary twitching and shaking. In some communities the conversions amounted to psychological epidemics.

jerk water railroads

When water was needed for the locomotives on the early lines, the trainman stopped at a convenient stream and lowered buckets for water. The stops and starts involved and the pulling up of the buckets gave the name to the line and the term was later applied to any old-style railroad.

Jersey lightning

A local term for apple jack or brandy.

"Jessie Scouts"

These were Northerners dressed in Confederate uniforms who went into occupied Southern towns during the Civil War. They mingled with the people in order to trap the unwary into disastrous expressions of opinion, which resulted in retaliation against the speaker. A woman who criticized a union officer's wife found herself removed from her home and left on an inaccessible part of the highway without baggage.

jewel superstitions

Among all the jewels that come to mind, it is probably the opal that most people immediately think of as being unlucky. Women of Italian descent still believe strongly in the good effects of coral and wear it regularly or at least keep it in the house. It was said to help the baby through a dif-

160

ficult teething period. Coral was also thought to be a cure for fever in that it kept the body cool. Pearls are held to be lucky for those born in June. They are thought by some to be a protection against fire because according to ancient legend they were produced by the moon, and represent tears.

jingle-bob

To mark his cattle in a distinctive fashion without the use of a branding iron, John Chisum, a pioneer rancher in Lincoln County, New Mexico, had a deep slit made in the steer's ear which left the lower half of the ear flapping down, known as the jingle-bob. This deformity made it very easy to cut out his cows from among any others.

Johnny Mitchell Specials

A devoted organizer of what was to be the United Mine Workers, John Mitchell attained importance by winning the great coal strike of 1902. Before the strikers won, however, many of them had to leave their small Pennsylvania towns in search of some other sort of employment. They sought out the big cities and of course being without funds they "rode the rods"—sneaked rides on freight trains, which they called taking a "side-door Pullman" or riding in a "Johnny Mitchell special." Having ultimately won their strike, they established October 29 as John Mitchell Day.

John's Night

The night of Midsummer's Eve, when all the ships which have been sunk off Cape Cod or were registered there and anywhere in the world return to the home waters. The vessels form in a long procession out on the old seaway, and flash signals to one another. As dawn comes, a white horse advances before the fleet as it skirts the reefs—and then they all go back where they came from.

Johnson City

Having started as a worker in a shoe shop in Binghamton in 1881, George F. Johnson showed a shrewd appreciation of the fact that workers might want to get out of a crowded

161

city. Therefore when he started his own new factory he selected a peaceful site on the Susquehanna which became known in time as Johnson City. He provided three hospitals and built neat homes for his workers. He introduced a system of profitsharing whereby fifty per cent of the profits went to the stockholders, and fifty per cent to the workers. When Thomas Watson was thinking of enlarging his International Business Machine Company, Johnson is supposed to have warned him it was not necessary to go looking for a labor supply: "Don't move. Provide sufficient incentive for working and the skilled workers will seek you out."

George F., as he was popularly known, won the hearts of his workers in many ways. One folktale embodies this attitude well. Mr. Johnson bought a hill with a splendid view. He put up a sign reading "Round Top—Private Property— Visitors Welcome." Before long the young people discovered its advantages on moonlit nights. The police became suspicious and routed out a few couples. Someone protested to Mr. Johnson that something would have to be done to restrict entrance to the grounds. "You are right," he is supposed to have replied. "The police will have to be kept out." He won out in other ways also, for Johnson City is still known as the "Valley of Opportunity."

jook

Originally a shack somewhat off the main road where a Negro could go for a snort of moonshine or maybe a bottle of bootleg beer. After Prohibition ended many jooks were opened for white people. Some were very elaborate establishments, but others were definitely on the crude side. Entertainment was often provided by a jook organ, a piccolo or a jook band, rhythm instruments. The major role of such places was to cater to people who often could ill afford to pay an admission charge for their entertainment, let alone a cover charge or other minimum payment. In fact, some guests were just "lookers" who avidly watched all that was going on. Prices of drinks were remarkably low, whiskey fifteen cents a glass,

162

beer ten cents a bottle. Mixed drinks were considered unfit for human consumption. Occasionally additional business was sought in the renting of adjoining "cabins for tourists."

Josepha Carrillo

Tales of love and adventure abound throughout southern California. A colorful one is connected with the names of several still famous families who were pre-eminent in the period before the Gold Rush. A famous Spanish beauty of early Los Angeles was Josepha Carrillo, who was loved by the Governor and by a handsome Spanish Don, Pio Pico, of an outstanding family. However, she fell in love with a visiting Yankee mate. Despite his feelings for her, Don Pico aided in her elopement and she got safely away on her lover's boat. Upon her return two years later she and her husband were arrested and there was a long ecclesiastical trial. The final decision was that their marriage was not legitimate but neither was it null and void! They were ordered to do penance in a variety of ways, one of which was to give the little Plaza chapel of Our Lady the gift of a bell weighing at least fifty pounds. Its gentle tolling continued to sound through the California countryside for decades thereafter.

Joseph Choate

Ambassador to Britain, leader of the New York Bar and an internationally famous wit, Mr. Choate was bound to have many a popular tale associated with his name. On one occasion he was asked, "If you were not Joseph Choate, who would you wish to be?" His reply was, "Mrs. Choate's second husband." At another time he assured a resident of a certain town that he could be certain that he had become a permanent resident. He had just bought a lot in the cemetery. That was also the time he stated that it was not necessary to build a proposed fence around the cemetery, for those inside were not going to try to get out, and those outside were not going to try to get in. When someone warned against the Chesterfieldian manner of a lawyer on a case, Choate said they had more to fear from the Westchesterfieldian manner of his opponent.

Joseph's boats

An attractive folk chronicle of Cape Cod accounts for the many old dories laden with growing flowers that were once popular along the coastline of fishing towns. The story goes that the elders of a small church felt that their devoted but rather naive minister, Joseph Metcalf, needed to be reprimanded for his worldly fondness for his brightly colored garden and for his stated intention of spending a small legacy on a boat in which to take his ease. Since he had raised ten children on a trifling income and given his whole energies to the community, this seemed unnecessarily harsh criticism, but he bowed to their demands. That night, however, during a violent storm the minister died and strangely enough a dory was washed up to his door. Since his garden had also been uprooted someone chanced to put the minister's solely surviving rosebushes into the dory. Later, some of his parishioners out of a tardy feeling of appreciation for his efforts threw some soil into the boat, and still others brought varied slips to be planted. The flowers prospered and in time a pleasant custom had been established.

journey-proud

A term used among North Carolina's hill folk of a person who has been upon a trip and cannot stop talking about it, wearing every one's patience thin.

"jumping Frenchmen"

There were those who believed that French Canadians along the Maine-Canadian border were affected with a curious nervous disorder. They assumed that the hardships endured when they were driven out of Acadia by the British were so harrowing that their descendants became "jumpers," who upon being startled would react with prodigious jumps or by rushing blindly into the forests or jumping into fire or water.

jumping over the broom stick

It was the accepted practice in inaccessible portions of the

164

swamplands of Louisiana that if a couple wished to wed and the curé (priest) was not immediately available, they would "jump over the broomstick together," thus announcing their intentions and being considered temporarily bound. It was understood that when the curé did come, they must obtain a license and be joined by a real ceremony.

junkers or junkereeren

The term used for some of the holders of large estates in colonial New York, such as Frederick Phillips after whom Phillips Manor was named. Years later when vaudeville had made its appearance, the routine often included the question, "What are junkers?" By giving the word its correct German pronunciation, they made a pun on the city of Yonkers, next door to New York. Some think that is the actual derivation of the town's name.

Jupiter Pluvius

This nickname was applied to J. P. Morgan for a number of appropriate reasons, probably the chief of which was his behavior as the "Storm King" of Wall Street, where his widespread activities sometimes had the effect of a downpour.

Pierpontifex Maximus was another title conferred on him, referring to the supposedly Jovian characteristics of the senior Morgan. He was supposed to have few friends and many enemies, among whom was numbered President Theodore Roosevelt. When the latter was embarking upon his trip to hunt wild animals in Africa, Morgan is quoted as stating, "I hope the first lion he meets does his duty."

Justin's

A cowboy would use this term to refer to his fine grade of boots. These represented the most expensive item in his clothing, for he wanted them of the best-grade leather, high-heeled, thin-soled and well stitched to keep them from wrinkling. The firm of Justin's, founded in Texas in 1879, set the style for the best, as Stetson's did for hats and Levis for overalls.

165

K

Kansan Paul Bunyan

As a subject of innumerable tall tales, Lem Blanchard occupies a position in the folklore of Kansas resembling that of Paul Bunyan, though on a somewhat less ambitious scale. In order to survey his cornfield more effectively, Lem climbed upon a stalk. This was during the great July growing season and when he started to come down he discovered that the stalk was rising faster than he could descend. Various conclusions are popular: one states he was rescued by a balloonist, another that his neighbors, having at last located him on high, shot him to save him from slow death by starvation.

katydid

The sounds made by this green, long-horned insect related to the grasshopper are the subject of various interpretations. Some claim that frost will come within six weeks of the time it is first heard. In Missouri the sound indicates the time to plant corn. In New England they say the chirping of a katydid in the house foretells death.

keel boats used on the Mohawk River

The Mohawk River above Albany before it flows into the Hudson has many shallows, a circumstance which led to the development of a boat that was flat-bottomed, with a heavy timber about four inches by four inches running the whole length of the bottom. With this construction a boat could withstand the shock of running aground. Its length might be from forty to seventy-five feet and its width between seven and nine feet. It might carry a mast or depend on long oars called sweeps or upon poles. The latter would be oper-

166

ated by men who walked the length of the boats on boards laid for that purpose while they continued to push on their firmly planted poles.

The style of construction of these boats represented a basic pattern and they derived their names from the locality where they were used—Mohawk boats, Susquehanna boats and so forth.

keeping his branding iron smooth

A description applied to a rustler in the early West because he changed brands to hide his stealing. He never allowed his iron to rust or to accumulate scale because of its constant usage.

Keller's Wild Animal Circus

This was an enterprise organized by a college professor who was a resident of Bloomsburg, New York. In this unique circus all the workers were college professors who claimed that they found their summer a quiet and restful experience after what they endured during the year.

Key West

On one of the islands of which Key West is made up, there was a Cayo Huesco or Bone Island upon which a great heap of bones was discovered, causing much speculation. At first it was thought to be the site of a battle, but later the bones were presumed to be due to the death of a whole village or villages from disease.

King who became Queen

This title used by people of the Eastern Shore of the Chesapeake Bay referred to the capabilities of the daughter of one of their early respected families. Sir Robert King, one of the early settlers, had a daughter who married a Francis Jenkins, and later a minister named Henry, and still later another named Hampton. Throughout her long and distinguished career she was most imposing in her appearance and most queenly in her conduct. Her reputation for elegance and authority became famous throughout the region.

167

"kin to kaint"

This was a means of indicating the length of a day in South Carolina in the 1880's. It meant that one worked from daylight to sunset, or from "can see" (the light) until "cannot see" (the darkness).

kissing bridge

In New York in the colonial period an interesting bridge crossed an indentation of the East River at what is now Second Avenue. It was understood by the young people of that time that a kiss could be exacted from one's companion whenever the bridge was crossed.

Kitty Knight

This young woman of a prominent Kent County family on the Eastern Shore of Maryland has long been credited in legend with having prevented the British from burning her home during the American Revolution. However, her account of it in her old age was that there was a very old and delicate lady in a house that the British had already fired. Her urgings induced them to put the fire out, though they went on to set a neighboring house afire which might be equally dangerous to the old lady. Kitty was able to beat this fire out with her broom. As a last defiant gesture the British boarding party thrust a board ax through a panel of her door, a mark which it is claimed could be seen until recently.

knife superstitions

To drop a knife accidentally means that company is coming and if it falls on its point the direction in which it is leaning will indicate the way from which the visitor will come. A fork falling means a female visitor.

knife throwing of the "Roaring Fifties"

The technique, contrary to that of movie villains today, used in the wild period after the first Gold Rush of 1848 found the well-prepared fighter holding the knife like a fencing foil, with fingers extended, the forefinger along the base

168

of the blade to provide extended reach. Two well-matched opponents, serapes draped over their arms as shields, might drop from exhaustion after a match, with the blankets in shreds yet neither having a scratch. One trick that would start operations in a hurry and pay off quickly with success was for the accuser to dash a sombrero unexpectedly in his opponent's face and kill before the other could recover from his surprise.

Knights of the Golden Circle

This was a secret organization in the South which spread as far north as the Susquehanna Valley. Its purpose was to denounce the Union, the Civil War, and particularly the drafting of troops. Many of the members won the title of "Copperheads," meaning traitors to the Union. Many difficult situations arose wherever these groups appeared. An example occurred when a Union sergeant attempted to arrest a deserter attending his sister's funeral, and Northern and Southern sympathizers started shooting at one another. On another occasion an officer was killed attempting to enforce the draft. A church service was interrupted by the Knights, who questioned the minister on his "position." They said if he was a Democrat he could continue, but if he was an Abolitionist they would hang him. The preacher did not wait to reply. He left quickly, diving through the window for safety.

Knight of the Silver Spurs

Captain J. J. Dickenson was the leader of a cavalry corps that operated along the St. Johns River, assisting the blockade runners who were striving to bring much needed supplies to the Confederate forces. Dickenson's troops on several occasions fired upon Federal vessels plying the river. In one dramatic encounter the Confederates captured the Columbine, a Federal vessel, after having fired upon her with such deadly accuracy that only 66 of her 148 men were found alive. They sank the vessel and thus established a unique record in naval history, a ship taken by cavalry. So grateful

169

were the women of Orange Springs, Florida, for the defense of their homes and their chastity that they presented Captain Dickenson with a pair of spurs "made in our little village from old heirlooms and relics of silver long preserved with scrupulous care." For thirty-seven years after the presentation of this symbolic gift J. J. Dickenson was revered throughout Florida as the "Knight of the Silver Spurs."

knocking on wood

Perhaps the most universal superstition retained by the so-called sophisticated is that of touching wood to retain one's luck. It is generally in order when one has just boasted about something or is about to perform some difficult task. There are those who make some effort to find "raw" wood—not covered by paint or varnish—and there are those who think three knocks in rapid succession are a wise precaution. Even children follow this custom, often adding a playful request to strike a playmate's head, with the implied suggestion that it is made of wood. There are those who think the practice may have developed from the touching of a wooden crucifix in ancient times, though there are others who think that the important point is the making of a noise and that the practice was an ancient attempt to scare away evil forces.

Krewe of Comus

An organization of exclusive membership that leads the parade as part of the Mardi Gras celebration in New Orleans. The King of Comus was usually accompanied by a captain, a lieutenant, and elaborate floats, with all persons closely masked or bearded. It also led off one of the great balls that completed the evening's activities. These elaborate performances took place on Shrove Tuesday, the day before Lent, and have a history going back almost one hundred years, though some of the carnival balls are of more recent origin.

There may be various Krewes. All take their activities very seriously and supposedly never reveal their secrets. It is claimed that Hollywood, eager to reproduce the splendors of Comus and similar groups, has never been allowed to take a picture of them. It is known that the program consists of a tableau, a grand march, call-out dances (q.v.) and probably some general dancing. A supper at some exclusive restaurant or hotel takes place at midnight. Membership in the Krewes is male and exclusive, admission depending upon the death of a member.

L

Ladies Parlor

In the Victorian period when it was not considered seemly for a woman to travel alone, the hotels made available for their few women guests a dark and gloomy room, carefully hidden away in the back of the hotel, known as a "Ladies Parlor." Women were not even admitted after dark unless accompanied by a male relative, and even then, they had to use the Ladies Entrance at the side of the hotel.

ladybug

Practically every child in America is familiar with the refrain, "Ladybug, ladybug fly away home; your house is on fire and your children may burn," without knowing what it is all about. It is agreed, however, that the little red beetle will bring good luck. If she lights on your hand, new gloves will be forthcoming, if on your dress, a new dress, and so on. To kill one of them is to court the greatest misfortune. If you watch in which direction she flies away you will be able to tell from what direction your true lover may arrive.

Lafitte, the pirate

Lafitte exacted enormous wealth from those he attacked around the Gulf of Mexico in his lifetime, besides having rendered his country some service against the British during the War of 1812, but the tales circulated after his death stated that his ghost was still trying to find someone to use his buried treasure unselfishly. This was supposed to be the condition for his release from his lifetime guilt and make it unnecessary for him to go on haunting the land where his fortune was hidden.

172

lagniappe

A term used in the Southwestern United States to indicate a token given to a customer as a compliment or as a symbol of good measure when a purchase is made.

land-office business

When public land was offered for sale by the United States government, usually in the West, it was generally very desirable land and often at a very low rate, so that there a tremendous amount of business was done at the official land offices. Later the expression was applied to any activity where a great amount of business was being handled.

langue de femme trees

This name, meaning "tongue of a woman," is used in Louisiana for the cottonwood and sycamore trees because their leaves are never still, even when there is no breeze stirring. It is obvious that the naming must have been done by the males of the community.

lanterns for commuters

During the 1870's people taking a train before dawn carried lanterns to light their way. These were lined up on the station platforms, so the story goes, and serviced by the station master to be in readiness for the return trip in the evening.

latch string out

In the colonial period doors were made with a hole over the latch. If the occupant of the room wanted to make it easy for anyone to enter, the latch string would be left hanging outside, accessible to whoever might want it. On the other hand, if the door was to be kept barred, the latch string would be drawn inside and the door could not be opened from without. From this procedure developed the expression "to leave the latch string out," meaning to make welcome.

launching ceremonies

It has been a long-held superstition that if the bottle of champagne used to christen a vessel on its maiden voyage

173

does not break, bad luck may result. Therefore at all such ceremonies someone is on hand to see that the bottle is broken by some other means before the ship is fully launched. The taboo against women performing this service has gradually lapsed, as has that against a widow's participation. Friday launchings were supposed to be unlucky also. Silver coins were formerly inserted under masts for good luck.

law West of the Pecos

This "law," administered by the colorful Judge Roy Bean, was effective if not based strictly on statute. In 1889 Bean had become a Justice of the Peace and in his Texan bailiwick he became a frontier vigilante in an attempt to provide what justice was available. His native shrewdness and bluster inspired respect despite his sometimes weird decisions, which often grew stranger with the passage of time and retelling. One famous tale records his judgment that it was no crime to kill a Chinaman—since he was not human. He provided an effective deterrent to drunkenness by fastening a bear to a stake to which he also attached the drunk to sober him up speedily.

lazy board

On all the great Conestoga wagons there was a place on the left-hand side of the wagon for a board to be pulled out. As this was intended as a place for the driver to rest when he was not riding the left wheel horse or walking by the side of the wagon, it gained the designation of "lazy" board. It was usually of white oak and had to be strong enough to support the weight of an unusually big man. There are those who think this practice of using a lazy board and thus having to pull over to the right-hand side of the road to keep clear of passing wagons accounts for the American practice of driving on the right.

lead pencils

Up to 1750, when a crude lead pencil was introduced, all records were kept by means of a quill pen and ink. The earliest pencils were made of clay and graphite in a somewhat

174

unsatisfactory mixture, so that the pencil itself was thick and clumsy and the stroke of the "lead" was scratchy and rough, though refinements and improvements were not long in being introduced.

leanter (lean to)

This was a rear one-story addition to the Puritan saltbox house, where most of the household duties were undertaken, such as spinning, weaving, candlemaking and cheesemaking. The front of the house reached two stories and would contain the common room (living room) with an attic over it.

leather fire buckets and leather hose

In the early days of firefighting before the availability of rubber, buckets and hose were made of leather. These were used for parades and ceremonial functions. They were painted with the name and insignia of the volunteer fire company that owned them and were often very elaborate in design. For routine firefighting buckets of collapsible canvas or sailcloth were used.

Lecture Day

In Puritan Massachusetts Thursday was Lecture Day. All work except what was absolutely necessary was suspended. After listening to an edifying lecture or sermon in the morning, all turned to the enjoyment of sports, games, and gossip for the rest of the afternoon. Most of these activities took place on the village green. Here there was a view of the stocks which, if pleasure threatened to become too exuberant, quickly brought to mind the possibility of punishment.

lefthandedness

There is a common, mistaken belief that if a left-handed person is forced to use his right hand against his inclination he will become a stutterer. The idea that one who uses his left hand is clumsy is another hearsay that has no scientific backing. In nearly all languages the word for "left" indicates something "sinister" or awkward. All magical rites call for the participation of the left hand.

175

legal erudition

On the Western frontier in the early history of Pennsylvania there was a shrewd but untrained lawyer who felt he was handicapped in competing with other lawyers by their ability to quote learned Latin quotes. However, he thought he might be able to even things up a bit by an advantage he enjoyed over them. He defended his clients with impressive quotes from the Mohawk tongue.

Leon Lake House

This was a well-known inn in the Adirondacks which was managed by an outspoken woman called Mrs. Chase. A wealthy and impatient New Yorker and party arrived for a meal and made some critical remarks about the delay in service. Thereupon Mrs. Chase took over and saw to it that they were well served. The New Yorker expressed his great satisfaction with the meal and asked what he owed her, saying he wanted to come again. Her reply was that he owed her nothing. He said, "Oh, I could not possibly come here again if I did not pay you." "That's what I thought," said the indignant woman.

levis

Overalls. The name was derived from the first name of Levi Strauss of San Francisco, the pioneer overall manufacturer of the West. They are distinctly different from the bib overalls worn by farmers. They are made like an ordinary pair of pants except that they have copper rivets to reinforce the seams and pockets. They are usually worn with the cuffs well turned up and the cowboys have a fondness for wearing them as tight as it is possible to get into them.

Lewiston, Idaho

The people of Lewiston enjoy telling some rather tall tales about their summer weather. They say some summers in the past were so hot that the Snake and Clearwater rivers often boiled at the edges, though not in midstream where the current was faster. The streets were so hot barrels of water

176

were kept along the curbs in case anyone's beard should catch fire. They claim the first charitable murder occurred when a man with a bright red beard was drowned from too many people throwing water on him.

lights in trees to deceive the British

During the War of 1812 when some British ships sailed up the Miles River, an indentation of Chesapeake Bay's Eastern Shore, the legend has it that the townspeople hung lights out on the trees to make the British waste their shots on useless targets. One account claims that in an unexpectedly successful shot a cannon ball passed through the roof of a house and bounced down the stairs, passing the terrified wife of the householder on its way.

loaded for bear

This expression developed in the West where a hunter was wise if he carried an extra-heavy charge in his gun when he expected to encounter bear in the vicinity. The application has been made to modern circumstances in the sense that anyone facing exceptionally difficult tasks should be particularly well prepared.

lobo

A large fierce wolf found only in Mexico and Texas. One famous tale tells of "Big-Foot Wallace," who was able to hold off a band of twenty-five after he had climbed a neighboring oak. Widespread attacks by cattlemen so reduced the wolf packs that in many cases a single animal became a bandit or outlaw, often gaining an individual name, such as "Old Club Foot" or "Old Three Toes," and while forestalling capture give rise to many strange tales. One such old wolf was suspected of hunting just for the fun of it. He killed thirty sheep in one night's activity, taking only a bite here and there.

loco

A Spanish term used to mean a person is crazy, foolish or absurd. The application was derived from the effect eating

177

the plant had on the cattle in the Southwest. They are stimulated as by a drug and cannot stop eating until they go crazy.

locomotive bells

These bells were made of bronze and had a very clear tone. One stockholder, in appreciation for having a train named after him, is supposed to have put twenty-eight silver dollars into the molten solution out of which the bell for "his" locomotive was to be cast, and to have thus produced a tone of a quality much truer and higher than the average.

log cabin myth

A thesis of Harold Shustleff attempts to prove that few cabins were built in our early history. The cabin was a late-comer, built largely by Irish immigrants using Swedish or Alpine style of corner-cutting and notching. The nineteenth-century log cabins were made of rounded logs, sometimes peeled, chinked with stone and chips and daubed with mud to keep out drafts. The better log cabins of this period were made of squared logs dovetailed at the corners and pegged together.

loggerhead

This was a poker used to place the logs in better position in a fireplace, but used just as frequently in preparing hot drinks, such as the popular flip which had a unique flavor added to it by the thrusting of a red-hot loggerhead into the mixture of rum and beer. Because these tools were available in every home and were often handy while extended drinking bouts were going on, they were accessible when drunkenness slipped over into combativeness. When someone grabbed a poker to prove that he was right and the other fellow wrong, the expression arose that the two were "at loggerheads."

On the other hand, there are those who think the origin of the term goes back to the loggers themselves, who were often at "loggerheads" because they also were quick-tempered and had weapons readily at hand.

logrolling bee

After the early pioneers in western New York State had

cut down and burned over the area they were going to use for planting, they were frequently faced with a problem beyond their own unaided efforts. Then a "bee" was in order to remove the blackened stumps of trees. The whole community co-operated and ox teams skidded and snaked the charred logs to a convenient spot where united efforts put them in piles for burning. This once praiseworthy activity has its counterpart in concerted political effort when "raids" on the United States Treasury by interested groups are engineered under the same term, "logrolling."

logging berries

This was a term used by the early loggers for the ever-present prune.

logging "inspectors" in Lake Superior camps

There were a few men in the logging camps who might be classed as hobos because they had the same shrewd way of getting along without working. These wanderers were sarcastically called "inspectors." They would arrive at camp with their "turkeys" (luggage sacks) and apply for work. They would get a good supper and a bed. After breakfast they would start out with the crews to begin chopping, but would slip away after retrieving their turkeys and be off "to fresh woods and pastures new."

logging terms

"To Saginaw" a log meant that when the logs were being directed down the stream in the spring thaw the logger tried to retard the large end of the log. "To St. Croix a log" meant to help the small end gain. "Gumming a log" meant to fail to keep the two ends even.

Turkey: sack containing a logger's possessions. Corked boots: corruption of "calked boots," boots with spikes driven in them to keep the loggers from skidding on ice or slipping in the mud.

See BOOM RATS, CROSSHAUL.

Long Knives

This was the Indians' way of designating Virginians who

179

settled in the West, in the colonial period. The appropriateness of the term was due to the swords they carried.

long-tail sugar

This was an early Cape Cod expression for molasses used for fishing. Though the tale may seem a bit tall, the account goes that one put the molasses on the fishhook, threw it into the air and thus attracted bees, which as they hovered over the surface of the water appeared like flies to the fish. Humming with anger and indignation at their treatment, the bees then stung the fish to death, thus affording the fisherman success with his long-tail sugar.

"Long Tom"

A popular term for a large-caliber artillery piece.

look at the house

In theatrical circles it is considered unlucky to look out between the curtains at the audience.

"Lost on the Lady Elgin"

The Lady Elgin was a steam vessel, the largest in the world in 1851. Three hundred were lost on it when it was rammed by the Augusta. The engine dropped completely out of the boat. There were as many as three hundred and fifty orphans created by its sinking, in one ward in Milwaukee from which the boat had sailed. Irish-Americans in Chicago organized a campaign to raise funds for the survivors. For decades afterward music hall singers throughout the Middle West always included in their repertoire a popular piece called by this title. Prints of its chorus hung in black frames in many of the homes in the Irish colony. Brass bands played it as a dirge at the funerals of politicians and other leading citizens.

Louisiana Lottery

In the 1880's and '90's the corrupt Louisiana legislature permitted a colossal scheme for raising money at the expense of the little man who hoped to make his fortune by picking a lucky number in a great lottery, operated in Louisiana, but participated in by the whole country. It was said that their advertising campaign alone called for the placing of $50,000 of ballyhoo in one Philadelphia paper. Bank savings took a tremendous drop while the schemers were in full swing. Congress finally checked the activity somewhat by denying them the use of the mails. They resorted to the express companies, but the reform movement finally succeeded, until Huey Long started a somewhat similar performance. Superstitions naturally abounded in the choice of numbers to be played. Some of the advertisers recommended that tickets be bought at their establishments because of lucky addresses or because the seller had a "lucky hand." If the man about to buy a ticket saw a stray dog, he would play number six. If he had seen a dead woman with grey hair, he would play number thirteen. In addition to the superstitious practices, there were what amounted to ritualistic performances in connection with the drawing of the numbers in the sumptuous Lottery Building.

loup-garou

This French word for werewolf was used in parts of Maine where the French-Canadians had introduced some of their beliefs. A man becomes such a creature because of a curse or some punishment from heaven, such as for not going to Mass. Delivery from this state may be obtained through exorcism, a blow on the head, or the loss of blood while in such a condition. Though the loup-garou may eat dead bodies or other animals, his chief misconduct is merely that of frightening people.

louse removal methods of lumber jacks in Michigan

One method was tried by a young Finn who could not stand the suffering he was subjected to. He had been told to rub himself all over with the contents of a ten-pound bag of salt. The next day his partner took him down to the lakeside and told him to strip. The other lumbermen were lurking behind trees to see if the method was going to be successful. As he laid his clothes down on the ground the lice were seen

181

running down to the lake. His companion told the Finn to get dressed in a hurry and get back to camp before the lice stopped drinking. He explained, "I knowed if you fed them bugs enough salty meat they sure would get awful thirsty." Another method was used by old-timers who each had a strong suit of heavy woven underwear, all hand-made and as thick as leather. All they did was simply turn the underwear inside out every few days and thus gain some relief because it would take that long for the lice to get through the underwear to their hides again.

Loyal League

In the decade of Reconstruction, the Northern representatives of the Republican Party who were active in occupied Southern territory worked to get the newly free slaves into their organization. The Loyal League was a secret organization into which the Negro was inducted with elaborate ritual and ceremonial. There were secret passwords, special hand grips, and hard-binding oaths to be sworn to, all of which had a mighty appeal to the largely illiterate new membership.

lug pole

This was a device by which the big iron pots used for cooking in the colonial fireplaces were held over the coals. Since iron was very scarce in that time green wood was often used for the supports, but on some occasions the pole took fire and precipitated the whole dinner into the fireplace.

lumbering terms of the old days

"Crosshaul"—a track in the woods at right angles to a logging road. "Round turn"—a circular track where the teamsters could turn around for the trip back. "Deacon seat" —in front of the ledge or bunk upon which the men slept was a long bench, so called from its resemblance to a seat in the first row of the churches reserved for the deacons. This constituted the only place to sit in the loggers' crude quarters. "The Big Push"—the foreman. "Sky hooking"— stacking additional logs on top of a load. "Ground hog"—the man who pushed the logs into place with a peavey as they

182

were rolled up to be loaded. "Wannagan"—camp commissary. "Logging berries"—prunes. "Road monkey"—the workers who kept the roads in repair so that supplies could get in and the logs be shipped out. In winter they kept the roads flooded with water at night so that they would freeze smooth by morning and thus make easier pulling for the horses. On downhill routes they sprinkled hay so the load would not nip the teams; they might also cut ruts so that the huge sleds would stay in place.

lumps of glass as a means of cheating the unwary

Judge Roy Bean reportedly used this trick when mixing drinks. After some satisfactory tinkling he would find an excuse to fish it out.

"Lutheran and Democratic"

The Pennsylvania Dutch when first settling in this country were pacifist in their sympathies but before the French and Indian War they found it necessary to break with the Quakers who would not vote to buy arms to outfit the militia for defense against the Indians. With the coming of the American Revolution the more radical of these Pennsylvanians wrested control of the district from the Anglicans and the Quakers. For generations thereafter they remained radical in their political sympathies, so that even years later they would still answer when asked their politics, *"Luderisch und Demergrauchisch verdolt"*—i.e., "Lutheran and Democratic, I'll be damned."

lutins

French-Canadians of the Michigan peninsula and elsewhere believe in lutins, little men who ride the farmers' horses at night and return them with knotted mains. Sometimes the farmers place a brass ring in the main to keep it from getting tangled. On the other hand, a lutin will occasionally take a liking to a particular horse and make a favorite of it, brushing and feeding it well.

lye leach

Around 1760 farmers were using a device for improving

the soil in which an open trough was loaded with wood ashes and covered with water so that a strong alkaline fluid would seep into a funnel-like arrangement. By this means a stream of the solution was carried to sanded runnels and permitted to dry out into crystals. The best part of the powder was used for baking powder and the coarser, poor-quality stuff became lye.

Lyman Beecher anecdote

The great preacher and foe of slavery was very absent-minded, as the following incident well illustrates. He was brought back unexpectedly from a fishing trip to officiate at a service. As he stepped into the pulpit a live fish popped out of his tailcoat pocket and flopped to the floor.

M

macaronis

This expression was used in the colonial period to indicate young bloods who went to great extremes in matters of modishness, effeminacy and refinement. Presumably they ate macaroni to indicate their attainment of European sophistication and thus earned themselves the title.

McClellan's House

General McClellan's House, located on Seminary Ridge, had been fired upon during the Civil War, with the consequence that a girl who had taken refuge in it to wait for her soldier-sweetheart was killed. For years thereafter it was customary for a single woman to place her finger in the bullet hole in the hope of marrying within the year. The hole grew rapidly to the size of a cannon ball.

McDonough Day

A day celebrated in New Orleans by school children, who take flowers to a statue of John McDonough in Lafayette Square. McDonough was considered a miser in the last years of his life and held to be the meanest of men, though he had always been generous to his slaves. He was said never to have spent a cent of his fortune after he became wealthy at the age of thirty-two, and he left it all to numerous public schools in Baltimore and New Orleans.

mail clerks on railroad routes

Substitute clerks on the old mail routes were subjected to many indignities in the hazing that went on during their apprentice stage, and these form an amusing part of railroad folklore. Harassed subs would be sent hunting a "sack stretcher," a "case scraper" or some other weird, nonexistent article. A clerk might be told to even up the pouches so that all were equally filled in utter disregard of the destination of the mail. Other unfortunates, not appreciating the significance of the order in which the mail pouches were arranged to be thrown off at the passing stations, might miss one pouch and throw out the delivery of the entire run. Confusion in directions might result also as when a clerk-in-charge asked to be awakened at Dawn, Missouri and discovered he had not been called until "daylight," at the end of the trip. There was also a clerk who piled all the mail on the center table and then gathered up a supply at each stop in proportion to what he thought was the size of the population.

Main line

An expression used to indicate upper society in Philadelphia, or later its suburbs. It was derived from reference to the main or most important line of the Pennsylvania Railroad and is equivalent to the F.F.V.'s (the First Families of Virginia) or to the Back Bay of Boston.

main stem

In hobo parlance, main stem or main drag is the principal street, not for residence or business but for "stemming," panhandling.

"man bites dog"

The journalist has incorporated this expression into the body of newspaper terms, to indicate that the ordinary event, such as a dog biting a man, is never of as great significance as the phenomenal or unexpected, or as Charles Dana said, "Man bites dog is news."

Manhattan

Among antiquarians there is a tale as to the origin of the name for the universally known island of New York City. They say that "Manahatta" was so-called by the Indians because it means "the place where we all got drunk," and

186

they aver that Hudson on his first trip up the river bearing his name regaled the Indians with liquor. If the story has never been fully substantiated it is at least appropriate. It has grown as much a part of the folklore of New York as the oft-reported sale of the island by the Indians for twenty-four dollars.

"man lost"

A century ago the streets of Chicago were a morass of mud, with the result that many signs were exhibited to poke fun at the terrible conditions some of the citizens found themselves in. A hat would be placed over the oozing mud with the announcement, "Man Lost," to indicate the bottomless state of the streets. Other signs might be put out during the spring thaw stating, "No Bottom Team Underneath" or "Road to China." Another variation of the hat theme would indicate that someone should pick up the hat and acting as a good Samaritan volunteer to rescue the person found sinking underneath it. Still another variation was the reported reply of the about-to-be-rescued individual: "Never mind, friend. I have a good horse under me and I have gotten out of tighter spots than this one." Eventually Chicago undertook a tremendous task and raised the level of all its streets and the dwellers raised the buildings to match.

maple sugar gathering

In the Adirondacks there are several practices accepted as legendary: The first hole bored in the tree trunk should be breast-high on the south side of the tree. The second hole should be placed on the north side. The largest flow is obtained by tapping on the side bearing the most branches or over the largest root. The richest sap comes from the layer near the bark. Deeper holes give less syrup, of a darker color and of less value.

If the boiling down of the sugar was done in the kitchen, a lump of salt pork was sometimes hung above the kettle. If the sugar started to boil too high it would strike the pork and subside.

187

A "snow party" was a pleasant custom developing in this connection. At sugaring time you would pour maple sugar over a plateful of snow and watch it cool and turn to taffy. Two common additions to such a program in the old days were salted crackers and sour pickles. A party of twenty could eat a gallon of syrup, a gallon of pickles, and pound after pound of crackers.

marriage by lottery

The Moravian young people in Pennsylvania accepted their sect's custom of marriage by lot. A boy would make a list of the girls he was considering. When the first name was presented, two slips were offered to him, one bearing the word "yes," the other "no." He drew one and had to abide by the decision. It was not looked upon as lucky but believed that divine guidance had pointed the way to his selection of a slip. Even if the girl wanted to accept the boy and he drew a "no," she could not accept him at that time, but only hope for the possibility of another opportunity. She was privileged to refuse if another suitor happened to draw a "yes" in seeking her hand.

Mary Powell

This great steamboat over three hundred feet long was queen of the Hudson from 1860 to 1920. Her owner, Absalom Alexander, kept her lines trim for speed. Some say he had a boy just to keep flies off her rails to prevent additional weight. Others claimed he mixed whale's grease into her paint to make it easy for her to slide through the water. She was kept immaculate and respectable and worked out her days on the Dayline Run beloved by thousands.

mascot

The original idea behind a mascot was to ward off evil and then it developed as a means of bringing luck to team or club or company. The word is derived from the Provençal "masco," meaning sorceress. Not only do animals play a part as mascots, but now one can notice objects decorating auto-

188

mobiles to bring luck, such as a foxtail on the radiator cap, or baby shoes dangling from the rear-vision mirror.

Mashpee Kingdom

This was a region on Cape Cod which Richard Bourne had obtained for his Indian converts in 1665. He had been a great friend and helper to the Indians so that upon his death his influence was shown in a number of ways. The Indians claimed that they had buried him beneath the altar in the first meeting house constructed for Indian worship. (*See* PRAYING BRAVES.) The Indians continued to visit this place. They claimed that a light shone about the place where Bourne was buried and that it could cure a number of ailments.

Later the land left in trust for the Indians was taken by greedy white men, and roads and canals crossed the area.

masks

The well-to-do ladies of the Revolutionary War period wore masks, usually made of velvet, to protect their skins, which to be fashionable had to be of a delicate pink and white texture.

Massachusetts House of Representatives

In the old hall a stuffed specimen of the sacred cod has hung since earliest times to commemorate the maritime and fishing pre-eminence of the Bay State.

matches

The earliest matches were introduced into America from France about 1830. They were very scarce and clumsy at first. One of the earliest methods for making a match consisted of first dipping the strip of wood into a sulphur solution and coating this with a mixture of red lead, chlorate of potash and sugar. This finally had to be dipped into a bath of sulphuric acid. A later variation was a bead mounted on gummed paper filled with sulphuric acid, crushed with pliers to cause a burst of flame. Early and appropriate titles for these matches were "lucifers" or "brimstone matches." They

189

eventually came in sheets or rows of forty splints and could
be lighted by rubbing between sheets of sand paper. At
first they made a crackling noise but when still further improved were advertised as "noiseless lucifers." The "vesta"
was a still later development and had a slender wick of
twisted cotton covered with wax and tipped with inflammable
pastes.

maverick

A cattleman by the name of Beauregard bought up all the
cattle that a Colonel Sam Maverick had long been holding
for disposal, the increase of which had never been branded
due to the neglect of his slaves. The purchasers appropriated
all the unmarked cattle. Since 1895 an unbranded beef
animal old enough to leave its mother has been known as a
maverick. In the early days of the West it was not considered
wrong to appropriate any of the young cows you came across
that were unbranded since they were held to be anyone's
property. In fact some respectable ranchers would hire cowboys to do a "little mavericking" at so much per head.

meat biscuit

This was the description of the first canned beef, claimed
to have been invented in Galveston, Texas, by Gail Borden,
who later branched out and became a millionaire by marketing canned condensed milk, a process which he had originated.

mediatrice—The Peacemaker

A sandwich like the "Po' White Sandwich" (q.v.), made
in New Orleans of a long loaf of French bread and stuffed
with butter and fried oysters very hot. Its name derived
from the fact that it was often brought home by husbands
as a peace offering when they were outrageously late.

memory aids

There is a superstitious belief that one may aid his memory
by tying a knot in his handkerchief. Another such idea provides an aid to memory by rubbing the hand over a bald

190

man's head, the older the better, on the assumption that the older man has more knowledge. There are those also who believe that one can remember what is placed under one's pillow at night.

Mennonite wheat

Legend has it that the Mennonites who came from Russia to settle in Kansas after the Civil War brought their best seed wheat with them. So well suited was their type of wheat that they prospered where others suffered from the drought and plant diseases. When their neighbors asked the reason for their success they were told, "It is because we plow the dew under." This group firmly believed that dawntime plowing, before the dew had dried on the ground, meant the difference between success and failure. The practice plainly bespoke the frugal caution and endless diligence of the Mennonites in all aspects of their lives.

Mexican jumping bean

This curiosity contains the matured egg of the moth, which having been laid in the bean flower has been incorporated into the hardened bean itself. When the caterpillar reaches the pupa stage it feeds upon the juicy meat in the bean and frequently causes the bean to jump around.

michie

A title used by Louisiana Negroes as a contraction of "Monsieur" and popular throughout the region.

mine rats

In the early days of mining rats sometimes got into the mines with the hay that was taken in to feed the mules used for hauling. When the rats poured out of the mine, it was held to be a serious sign of danger. The rats were befriended because they actually give a warning of unexpected danger.

miner's burros

Very dependent upon his sturdy little burro, many of the early gold miners were prepared to tell fantastic tales about the cleverness of these indispensable creatures. They seemed

191

always to be smart enough to know if they were to be worked and go off and hide. One, it was said, had a toothache and wandered off. When he returned he had a gold filling in his hollow tooth. Another, they swear, kicked a hole in a water pipe to save going a long distance for water.

miner's holidays

In the Michigan mines the men will not work on Whitsunday, the seventh Sunday after Easter, or on Midsummer Day. They agreed once in 1896 to work half a day on the latter date but there was a fall of earth and a man was killed and they never did it again. They refuse to work on Boxer day, December 26. Curiously, they are willing to work January first, for they have a superstition that promises them work all year if they work the first day of the year.

See BED ROCK.

minister's pay

Eastham on Cape Cod and other New England communities voted to give the minister a part of each whale cast ashore as a portion of their annual pay. Thoreau pictures the old parsons sitting on the shore watching for whales to eke out their meager pay.

minister's tax

The minister was allowed to collect a tax for the support of the local Congregational churches in New Hampshire until 1819, when a Toleration Act was passed providing for private support of all churches.

Mississippi raft making

After loggers had sent timber down to the Mississippi, the logs were often penned up for twenty miles along the river where there were shallows—say, along the Beef Slough on the Upper Mississippi. Then enough logs were released at a time to make a raft. Three braids of logs made a unit 700 by 13 feet, which was called half a raft and was as big as was considered safe in shallow water. When the water was running full, some rafts bound together with ropes reached enormous size, as big as 1,500 by 300 feet. Sweeps were provided to move the great load, which the men operated from the rear where planks had been laid for them to walk on. The pilot had a plank walk running down the length of the raft. He had a little "cell" up in front for his quarters.

In the 1830's many of the famous steamboat pilots got their first experience on the river running these rafts laden with logs from the Black, the Chippewa and St. Croix rivers which flowed into the Mississippi. Stephen Hanks, a cousin of Abraham Lincoln, by the old accounts was the most famous. He knew every bend, sand bar, every towhead and crosscurrent from Stillwater to St. Louis.

All these early activities of the rivermen used the river's own power, but after the Civil War towboats were introduced along certain stretches of the river. They were steam-driven and were used to push the rafts because they could exert much more power. Rival rafting crews often had bitter fights, while the authorities were forced to wait until the fracas was over. Even with power, it still was a great accomplishment to get the rafts safely down. They drew eighteen inches of water and were often as much as three acres across. A skilled pilot might have to loosen the rafts into sections to get around a bend, so that the raft assumed a "C" shape or even on occasions an "S" shape. The pilots earned $500 a month for this work, big money for those days, but no one denied that they were worth every cent.

Mississippi river pilot titles

Though the pilots on this river were a well-paid and extremely skillful group as a rule, split-second decisions and unexpected circumstances could cause accidents, so the various derisive terms developed for pilots who had more than their normal quota of difficulties. "A sticker"—one who was repeatedly hung up on a sand bar. "A wood butcher"—one who struck bridge piers more than twice a season.

Missouri River tales

Shifting channels and shifting river beds have been the

193

constant condition with the "Big Muddy," the Missouri River. Many a dweller on this river when asked on which side of the river he lives will look worried and say, "on the east—when I came away." Harvesting becomes fascinating too—the crop may be corn or catfish. Sometimes the river eats away eighty acres at a mouthful and more than ten thousand in a single year—actually. Of course when the teller of tall tales gets busy he has a field day. Not only is it a real problem for an engineer to build a bridge—he then must keep the river under the bridge.

Mrs. Astor's plush horse

Mrs. William Astor, widow of the grandson of the first John Jacob Astor, was the dominant figure in New York and Newport society until her death in 1908. Her annual ball at 842 Fifth Avenue was the great affair of the season. Her gilded, overstuffed magnificence led to the expression that an ostentatiously dressed person looked "like Mrs. Astor's plush horse," or as it sometimes appeared, "Mrs. Astor's pet horse."

mister, the

The term commonly used by Pennsylvania Dutch housewives in addressing their husbands.

mistletoe

Though of ancient origin, kissing under the mistletoe is still a popular folk institution, with beliefs about it varying somewhat over the country: The unmarried girl who stands under the mistletoe and is not kissed will not be married that year. If she refuses to be kissed, she will die an old maid. Mistletoe also has a place in folk medicine. Southern Negroes claim that a preparation of it will dry up mother's milk. Elsewhere a portion of the berries is administered to produce fertility, as an antidote against poison, and to ward off epilepsy and convulsions.

mitten, to get the mitten

A Midwestern expression, mid-eighteenth century, mean-

194

ing to be refused permission to see a young lady home from some social function.

moccasin making, Maine style

For the workers in the Maine woods a soft strip of leather fourteen inches long was taken with only the front sewed up. The individual for whom it was intended was then measured and the back was sewed up appropriately.

modifications of French surnames

In Aroostook County, Maine, there were many residents who did not understand the language of either the French-Canadians or the older inhabitants, the Acadian-French, so that many of the family names were subjected to some curious modifications. For example; Anselmo Albert became "Handsome All Bear," Moreau "Morrow," Charette "Carter," Roi "King," Rossignol "Nightingale," and Levesque "Bishop." Some of those changes of course were literal translations.

mole superstitions

Many superstitions are based on the theory that like attracts like; therefore, since the mole's forepaws serve him as such excellent tools to dig the passageways to his burrow, man may gain like skills if he carries the dried paw of a mole. Teething is also made easier if such a paw is worn on a string around the baby's neck. Moles on the body are also a subject of many superstitions, particularly in regard to the place where the mole is located. For instance, it was held that a mole on the nose meant one would succeed in business, one on the shoulder meant the person enjoyed great fortitude, on the hands that one would be able to take care of oneself, on the legs that one was supposed to be self-willed, while one on the chin meant one could be sure of the loyalty of one's friends.

Mollie Maguires

This secret brotherhood represented some thousands of miners during the thirty years of its existence in the period

195

after the Civil War. Activities were particularly concentrated in Schuylkill County, Pennsylvania. On one hand, it was claimed that dictatorial leadership of the organization precipitated terroristic methods in putting over its program; on the other, it was asserted that labor spies backed by management and police caused bitter fights to arise in the attempt to weaken the control of the "Mollies." A large number of the members were arrested, with death sentences administered to eleven. Many complaints were made as to the partiality of the conduct of the trials. Out of this confused situation many strange tales emerged. The words "Mollie Maguire" were enough to strike terror in the hearts of certain groups and to arouse violent anger in others. Under the circumstances, it is not surprising that a body of stories have grown up in this connection having all the characteristics of folk tales.

Molotov cocktail

Bottled inflammable liquid mixed with sawdust, used to set tanks on fire. An incendiary grenade developed during World War II.

Monmouth Red Check

An apple raised in New Jersey, spotted, it was claimed, by the bloodshed in the Revolutionary Battle of Monmouth, though experts belittle the tale by noting that the apple was not developed until a generation later.

moon cussing

Unscrupulous individuals on Cape Cod sometimes engaged in a disastrous form of trickery when on a moonless night they walked up and down the shoreline swinging lanterns. These bobbing lights would be mistaken for lights on the mastheads of anchored vessels, and incoming ships might continue toward port and instead run aground or be wrecked, affording rich opportunities for the cheaters to benefit. Later the term was used for legitimate salvage operations, where fear of the light of the moon would not make the application of the title so appropriate. This same type of trickery was also known on the Carolina coast and by the same term.

196

Moon Mullins

A famous comic strip character created by Frank Willard in the 1920's, which remained popular until his death in 1958. He was a tough, unshaven fellow perpetually wearing a derby, who was distinctly vulgar and uncouth but who exerted a great appeal by making the reader feel a sense of superiority to the slums from which he had emerged. He virtually symbolized the folklore of tenement life.

moon superstitions

If one sees the new moon over his left shoulder, he should make a wish. The waxing of the moon is associated with the possibility of growth as of money, material possessions or of crops. If the points of the moon turn up, then one should expect rain since the "basin" of the moon will hold rain. On the other hand, if the points turn down, the weather will clear because no rain can be held in the container so formed.

mossy horns

An expression used to refer to mature cattle, usually over six years old, because the wrinkled cracked appearance of the horns resembles lichens clinging to a rock. The same term is sometimes used as a slang word for an old cowhand.

Mott Island in Lake Superior

Mott Island lies near Isle Royal and obtained its name from an incident connected with an Indian probably named La Motte, who had a Christianized Indian wife named Angélique. The two of them went to this island to maintain a mining claim for another man. Through a variety of circumstances, their supplies did not reach them. The husband died, but legends grew around the accounts of how Angélique managed to survive. She pulled out her hair to weave snares for rabbits, and caught fish with an old coffee sack. Above all, she fought the temptation to eat her husband! His frozen body was found with her. Her story became a classic tale at the campfires around the lake.

197

mouth superstitions

It is a very common belief that a large mouth denotes generosity and that a small one indicates a person with selfish traits. A protruding lower lip indicates a passionate nature, while a short upper lip shows stubbornness. There once were superstitions about lip color, but men would seem to be the only ones involved. Bloodless lips are supposed to indicate a dissolute and avaricious person, bright red lips mean you will live long, but while you do you are protected from the "evil eye," for red is a "stop" signal for bad influences.

movie folklore

Sam Goldwyn's expressions which have already been accepted in the industry as legendary. They include such gems as the following: "Include me out." "I'll give you a definite maybe." "In two words, im-possible." "Anyone who goes to a psychiatrist should have his head examined."

moving day jinxes

According to the moving companies, there are persons who object to each day of the week as unlucky. There are many taboos connected with what you should move and what you should leave behind. Salt is the subject of many of these superstitions, some saying you must take your old saltbox along to the new house, but others insisting just as strongly that salt is the one object you must not move. Others say you must never move to a lower floor or you will have bad luck, which may also happen if you move back into a house which you once moved out of.

mulligan (hobo stew)

This varying meal consisted of "hoppins"—any and all vegetables that could be begged, borrowed or stolen—and gumbo, chicken or meat acquired in the same way. Custom insisted that if one approached a hobo jungle where a mulligan was being prepared, one put something in if one took anything out. One rare tale tells of a raid on a railroad freight coach which resulted in a great haul of chickens for a glorious mulligan. It was later discovered that all the fowl had been

198

pedigreed, of rare racing stock, producing a famous "million-dollar mulligan."

murdering preacher

Cyriacus Spakenberg arrived in Pennsylvania before the Hessian troops. After his ordination he tried to marry a member of the church. He was exposed as having a wife in the German town he had left. Later he obtained another church. Upon being investigated for retention, he was sitting at the altar when he was accused by an elder who was sitting beside him. He killed the man. After his trial some members of the congregation were so impressed by his personality they wanted to have him spared.

Murray's fools

There was a tremendous influx of visitors to the Adirondacks after the publication of a book, *Adventures in the Wilderness—Camp Life in the Adirondacks,* by a minister named Murray. Since a great many of these campers had no real idea of the shortcomings attendant upon life in the mountains in those days, the local population scornfully referred to them as "Murray's Fools" for thinking that camping could be so simple. There were so many "misunderstandings" that critics called the book most unreliable. He suggested that the ladies wear a fine Swiss net material gathered into a sack by means of an elastic and worn over the head for protection from gnats and mosquitoes. He also recommended a pair of buckskin gloves with wide bands attached, buttoned nearly to the elbow. In addition she would wear a man's felt hat, broad in the brim. A short walking dress and Turkish drawers fastened tightly at the ankle completed the picture. From the protests of those following his advice one can understand why "Murray's Fools" were a constant wonder.

Murrell's gang

A group of bandits under the leadership of Murrell was active in Arkansas between 1830 and 1860. Their stealing and audacity assumed almost legendary proportions. Murrell

199

was said to have boasted that he stole and resold to their owners nearly a thousand slaves. So cowed were the people at the thought of possible reprisal that they paid the blackmailer without any attempt at curbing his rapacious demands. Murrell was supposed to have a large secret organization co-operating with him in reporting information and receiving dividends for their assistance.

muskrat superstitions

In Indian mythology the muskrat figures prominently as the animal which succeeded in bringing up earth to form the land out of the flood waters which had covered the universe. The tiny bit of mud magically expanded to the world. Weather predictions are based by the superstitious on the following points: If he builds his home higher out of the water than usual, it is a sign of a wet spring and possible floods. If he digs a shallow or flimsy burrow, there will be a mild winter. If the walls are very thick, it will be a cold winter. There is also a belief that if the furry side of the pelt is laid against the chest, it will make breathing easier for sufferers of asthmatic conditions.

mussel gathering on the Tennessee

A primitive Indian group is known to have gathered mussels from the plentiful beds that existed along the river. They tossed away the shells, collected in still preserved mounds. One called Shellmound was located west of Chattanooga. Some think that "Muscle Shoals" may be a corruption of an early designation, "mussel shoals," used by the first white prospectors who gathered shells for buttons.

N

nailing a drag
It was a practice of the railroad stiffs (hoboes) to hide by the tracks and try to catch a train, a "drag," before it got up too much steam. The risk to those who did not calculate accurately would be that of being pulled under the cars or of being smashed into the ravines along the tracks. A very speedy train, a "red ball," would only be tackled by very experienced stealers of rides.

nail makers
From colonial days on, metal was very scarce in many New Hampshire communities, so that it was the custom for itinerant workers to visit farms and melt and hammer into nails old scythe blades and other metal junk carefully saved for their coming each year.

nail puller
A device popular with young hunters in the Ozark Mountains. Since they cannot afford ammunition they shoot squirrels with nails. After they recover their game, they use a claw hammer or similar instrument to remove the nails.

nails scarce
In colonial times nails were so rare and expensive that they were sometimes willed by provident householders to their descendants. A rule was passed that the number of nails in the house had to be given the owner when he left in order to stop him from burning down the house to recover his original "investment."

naked girl tale

In the 1800's a naked girl was found bound and gagged outside the cabin of an elderly German couple who had settled in the town of Jersey Shore near the West Branch of the Susquehanna. The minister of the community took her in. Many gifts were sent to the attractive and seemingly most modest young lady. Finally the hoax was revealed. The girl had not been beaten and robbed but had figured out an easy way to gain importance and supplies. She left town accompanied by the laughter of the townspeople, who continued to tell her story for another century.

Nanabazhoo

A legendary Indian god or spirit who was supposed to inhabit a large fragment of rock bearing some resemblance to a human form and located on Lake Superior. When Longfellow wrote his famous Indian poem he used stories about Nanabazhoo but gave his main character the name of Hiawatha, a name common to the Iroquois, a different tribe from that of the god he used as his model.

Nantucket

This island, called "Far-Away Island" (Na-to-cket) by the neighboring Indians, is the subject of several legends about its origin, but Maushop, a gentle giant admired by the Indians, is connected with all of them. One version tells of an Indian warrior who could not hope to wed the princess he desired because he owned so little land. Maushop carried him to the island which he had created, Nantucket, and gave it to the warrior so that he could marry the princess, and their descendants remained very grateful to Maushop ever afterward.

Nantucket sleigh-ride

After one of the smaller boats sent out from the main ship had harpooned a whale, the whale might remain on the surface of the water and drag the boat behind him, sometimes reaching a speed of thirty miles an hour. It was hoped that the whale would soon exhaust himself and the "sleighride" come to a safe finish, but New Englanders often told tales of amazing experiences endured by the hardy whalers, sometimes ending in disaster if the whale sounded, or dove to the bottom of the sea.

Napoleonic influence in Alabama

Demapolis was a town founded in Alabama by refugees from the Napoleonic regime after 1815. The county was named Marengo, with towns called Linden, Arcola and Moscow after campaigns in which Napoleon I had been involved. Cultivations of the vine and of olive trees was undertaken. Except for a few families descended from the original three hundred or so, little remains but the place names and an original grant signed by President Monroe, though stories of the noble ladies and gentlemen who attempted to make a life in the wilderness are still told. A Colonel Cluis ran a ferry where many lingered to reminisce. This became such a practice that it was the custom in that part of the country for anyone unexpectedly delayed to be accused of "visiting Cluis."

Narragansett Road

At a certain lonely crossroads along this route suicides were buried, in accordance with eighteenth-century custom, with stakes driven into their hearts. These graves were pointed out with keen interest by the drivers of the stages as they went rattling by on their way to the lower part of the Boston Post Road.

Another display common in those days was also visible from the road. Murderers were left hanging in chains rattling in the wind until the links finally rusted through.

Natural Bridge

This curious natural wonder was called by the Monocan Indians of the Shenandoah Valley "the bridge of God," for they believed that it had been thrown across a chasm for them when they were fleeing from the Powhatans. The warriors had sent their women and children to safety over the bridge and then turned to drive back the enemy.

203

Nauset-Wampanoag Tribe

This Indian Tribe occupying Cape Cod has retained many legends of the land with which it has been so long associated. Its tales handed down by word of mouth tell of a gentle giant named Maushop. Once he killed a bird-monster who was stealing the Indian babies and brought back all those he found still alive. Another time he shook a quantity of sand out of his moccasins and caused the formation of the islands of Nantucket (q.v.) and Martha's Vineyard.

When these Indians noted the fogs rolling in along the south shore of the Cape, they would nod wisely and say that the kindly Maushop was smoking his pipe again. Maushop was also supposed to have scooped out Scargo Lake (q.v.).

Maushop had a wife who was not quite so tall, named Quant. They had five sons, all of whom were killed through trickery in an epic battle with the "Little People," pygmies who lived near the Poponesset marsh. When Maushop retaliated, he lured them all into the bay and heaped soil over the graves into huge mounds which became known later as the Elizabeth Islands, or the town of Gosnold.

necktie justice

In the folklore of the West many examples of the speedy administration of justice abound. A quick trial followed by immediate execution was not unusual in cases of cattle rustling or of the stealing of horses. This summary justice was felt to be none too severe in the latter case, for a man's very existence might depend on his well-trained horse. In some areas all the inhabitants were sworn in as deputies, therefore making arrests easier and facilitating the carrying out of punishment, though such technicalities were not always relied upon and a group of outraged ranchers might literally take justice in their own hands.

Nell Hilton, Protector

Nell Hilton was a Puritan girl who, in 1740, went to live with the Indians. On her various return trips to civilization she gained a reputation for her ability to predict the results of military encounters. Not accepting her accounts of her visits with the Indians, the British later executed her as a spy. On the gallows she promised to return if danger threatened her country. It was long believed that on March first of such years she did appear on Hilton's Neck in Jonesboro, Maine.

nester

One who squatted or settled on public land and was looked upon with disfavor by the cattlemen. The name was probably derived from the practice of the nester of making a small place for protection on the range, which seen from a distance resembled a nest. This "nest" the cattlemen were very eager to uproot since it interfered with the free running of their cattle, and would encourage additional population and additional settlements. Bitter warfare often resulted, but the settlements won out in time.

New Haven Blue Laws

The Reverend Sam A. Peters in a *History of Connecticut*, published in 1781, made a great point of the restrictions imposed by the theocratic dictators of the New Haven settlement. He claimed that a mother was forbidden to kiss her child on Sunday, along with a number of other strict regulations, but much of his account is held to be merely a collection of tales.

New York City incident

A tale that has grown somewhat in the retelling is based on an incident in 1919 when the Queen of the Belgians was officially greeted at City Hall. Politely the Queen commented to the mayor's wife, "How wonderful to be the wife of the mayor of the greatest city in the world." The lady thus addressed beamed and replied, "You said a mouthful, Queen." Grover Whalen, even then the city's official welcomer, denied the incident actually occurred, but it has been constantly repeated by those who were not present.

Niagara

This was the name of a moosehound who played a part in the legends revolving around Paul Bunyan. Niagara was so huge a creature that when he once started playfully chasing some ordinary brown bears, he not only chased them to the North Pole but caused their hair to turn white from fear, thus creating the first polar bears.

nibble and sip

The townsfolk in early Philadelphia served a lump of sugar on a saucer when they had tea. They claimed that only countryfolk put sugar into the cup.

nickel-plated

The nickel-plate line was originally to be known as the New York Central and St. Louis, but after it was completed in 1882 it was bought out by the Lake Shore and Michigan Southern, of which it would have been a competitor. According to one tale, so large an amount was paid for it, that one of its purchasers declared it must surely be nickel-plated. An astute public relations man was supposed to have heard the remark and felt it was a clever choice for a title for the road. Gradually the expression was accepted in common usage as an equivalent to high praise.

In contrast, another version states that when Jay Gould, the railroad magnate, was buying up the bankrupt line he entered a very low bid for the valuable property. When questioned about this, he is supposed to have stated he would not pay another cent, even if the line were nickel-plated.

Nieman-Marcus

There is a fabulous department store in Dallas, Texas, about which a collection of legends have accumulated in regard to the amazing assortment, price or quality of the goods some of the equally fabulous clients of the store purchase. One such item involved a customer who desired a special gift for his lion cub. An electric comforter was ultimately agreed upon. Another involved a lady who sent back her purchases when they were delivered by a truck substituting for the regular Nieman-Marcus delivery vehicle, which was under repair. Her claim was that she would buy nowhere

206

else but at this wonderful store and she wanted her neighbors to know it.

"nose test"

At one point during the raising of troops to supplement General Washington's army, the volunteers were in excess of the number needed. A recruitment officer devised this test to make his selection easier. He drew the outline of a man's nose at a distance of 150 feet. He then announced that the riflemen whose bullets came closest to the nose would be chosen. The marksmen's accuracy was due, they claimed, to their long-barreled guns, mistakenly called "Kentucky rifles." A sequel to the story tells how these riflemen made General Gage "take care of his nose."

North West Company

This was a trading company that had posts in Canada in competition with the Hudson Bay Company, which ultimately absorbed it. An early offshoot of the North West Company, called the "Little Company," was known also as "Les Petits," corrupted to "Potties," and was recognized throughout the fur-producing areas as a good market for goods.

"nothing lost save honor"

This expression was held to be used by Jim Fisk in connection with the shoddy deals by which he managed to catch the suckers on Wall Street.

"Now you've said something"

Judge Willis had two dominant obsessions. He liked a long toddy and he insisted on starting his court on time. A neighboring Texan, called as a witness, was fined fifty dollars for being late. After court the neighbor was walking beside the Judge, attempting to give cogent reasons for his lateness. Receiving little response, at last he proposed, "Judge how would you like a nice long toddy?" The reply has become a classic in the Panhandle: "Now you've said something."

Nunnehi

The Cherokee Indians had a tale about the whirlpool or "Boiling Pot" that was located on the Tennessee River near Muscle Shoals. An Indian drawn into the vortex of this turbulent whirlpool claimed he saw a race of supernatural people there beckoning him to stay with them. These Nunnehi could assume mortal form and sometimes brought visitors to their underwater home. Occasionally such people were supposed to return to normal life, but more often the tales would tell only of their ghostly return to haunt the regions where they had once been known.

O

odd year leases

Among business people there has been a superstition that even numbers are under an evil influence, therefore leases were made for ninety-nine years instead of one hundred. Since it was also considered unlucky to keep moving from year to year, leases were made for longer periods of time so that their profits would not be diminshed.

oil king

In the Navy a slang expression for the petty officer in charge of fuel oil storage.

oil wells discovered

Accounts of how famous oil wells and gushers came to be discovered fall into a pattern that is repeated in many towns of the Southwest. A heavy load of lumber intended for the newly selected site for an oil drilling gets stuck in the mud. The decision to drill there instead of at the original site usually results in the gusher coming in at the accidentally chosen place. Sometimes the theme varies slightly. The teamster gets lost and inadvertently unloads the machinery in a position that brings in a gusher.

Okefenokee Swamp

According to local folklore this region was created as a result of a war between the beavers and the Indians. The beavers destroyed the dams that they had taught the Indians to build and caused the land to be flooded.

Swampers claim that if you become lost in this vast expanse just let your boat drift and the slight but discernible flow of the water will eventually draw you toward the Suwannee River and out of the swamp.

See PINEY WOODS ROOTER.

old age

The longevity of many of the people of Vermont is a matter of pride to the natives, even in the telling of tall tales. They like to tell of two old fellows so old that they have forgotten who they are and there is no one alive who can tell them.

Old Nick

A New England term for the devil. Sometimes used in the expression, "to have the Old Nick in him," meaning to be full of the devil. "Old Harry" and "Old Scratch" are terms used in the same fashion.

Old Settler's Association

In Chicago in the 1870's the city decided to celebrate the advancement of the community by honoring the old people who had had a part in its founding. However, they made little effort to preserve the material objects which would have helped to explain the early days of the colorful city.

olykoek (doughnut)

The olykoek was introduced into New Amsterdam by the Dutch who made it as a ball of sweetened dough fried in hot hog's fat. They were usually served at the tea table between three and six in the afternoon. The teapot would be decorated delftware, with paintings of little Dutch shepherds and shepherdesses tending pigs, boats sailing in the air, and other ingenious Dutch fancies.

onion

The superstitions held in regard to the onion are very like those about garlic. However, the onion has special powers of weather prediction, as shown in the following verse: "Onion's skin very thin, mild winter coming in. Onion's skin thick and tough, coming winter cold and rough." There are those who believe that placing an onion under the bed will attract a sweetheart to the house because it keeps away those who are jealous of one's happiness by its strong odor. Before the onion will serve this purpose it must have been first "treated" by a witch.

Leave a piece of onion on the shelf and it will absorb the germs of disease in a home, so that the dwellers may remain healthy. Cut in half and left hanging on a string, it will cure a cold. Georgia Negroes say thick skins on the onions mean a severe winter, and that if you carry a red onion in your left hand or your left pocket it will ward off disease. In New England they hang a whole garland of onions for the same purpose.

onion juice

The inhabitants of Okefenokee Swamp believe that this remedy rubbed regularly on the head will make the hair grow.

Oofty-Goofty

A weird freak who appeared on the San Francisco Barbary Coast as a wild man from Borneo. He was coated with tar in which horse hair had been embedded. He ate raw meat and yelped "Oofty-Goofty" at frequent intervals. However, being unable to perspire he landed in the hospital, where the doctors had a hard time removing his tar covering and leaving his skin. He then spent many years earning tips in return for being kicked or batted on the head. He seemed to be immune to pain and could take terrible punishment in this respect. At long last, however, John L. Sullivan took a swing at him, landing such a blow that he lost his curious power. Tales of the unbelievable beating he could withstand have grown with the retelling, to produce a curious collection of legends.

Origin of the Great Philadelphia Wagon Road

This was an important link in the development of the West in early colonial times, though it was forgotten with the rise of other means of communication. Towns along the route

211

included Winchester, Staunton, Salisbury and Augusta. A common pattern would develop as the settlers began to move in. They would start at a crossroads, on the bank of a river near a ferry or a grist mill, or near a county courthouse. At these points shelter might be provided for travelers who were planning to cover the four hundred or more miles of the Wagon Road, which went through Lancaster to Harris' Ferry and then through the Shenandoah Valley. From these stopovers towns developed.

"out of the gift"

This expression is applied by the Shakers to those they look upon as backsliders. It was also considered "out of the gift" to leave anything out of order, or for any female to touch a male or even be in a room alone with one. It was held contrary to order to talk loudly, shut doors hard, rap at a door for admittance, or even make a noise when walking.

owl

When the Seminole Indian heard an owl hoot he would whistle back and if there was no further response he accepted in resignation the summons to approaching death. If the owl, on the other hand, responded with an answering "whooo" he rejoiced for this was considered a sign that good luck would follow.

Reference to the owl as a symbol of wisdom seems to be based on superstition for the bird is not at all intelligent, any more than it is "blind" in the daylight—merely farsighted and often confused by the glare of the sun. A common belief that an owl can wring its own neck has probably developed because it can twist its neck very far to the right or to the left.

oyster express

Oysters were shipped west before refrigeration had been developed by placing the live oysters in straw or in salt water containing corn meal. Oysters were kept alive for months in this fashion.

212

oysters on the Canal Street Plan

In many of the saloons on New York City's famous Canal Street they advertised: "Pay twelve and a half cents and eat all the oysters you can."

oysters on the large side

A much repeated tale in New England has to do with the reference made by Thackeray on one of his visits to this country to the large size of American oysters. He stated after having consumed some that he felt as if he had just eaten a baby.

oxcage

When the blacksmiths of a century ago had to shoe an ox they discovered that the heavy creature could not raise its hoof as a horse does, but would lose balance unless the hoof were raised in a sling or ox cage to hold the animal steady.

ox teams

In western New York State "Devons" were particularly admired. Young lads started training them when they were a year and a half old. They were liked especially for their uniform, solid light red color which made matching teams easy. Their light-footed movement was also an asset. It was the custom to refer to them as steers. The order was steer calves, yearlings, two-year-olds, three-year-olds. Only when approaching full maturity at four years of age was the term "oxen" used, and even then "cattle" was a more popular designation.

"Buck" and "Bright" were among the most common names used. As one stood behind the plow the nigh ox was Buck while his mate was Bright. Their widespread white horns were often tipped with brass nobs. Old farmhands claim that when oxen were overheated they did not need to be restrained from drinking too much, as horses did.

Ozark Mountain folk

These very individualistic mountain people provide a quantity of fascinating folklore, especially in regard to their tall tales and their unique animals. The word "Ozark" is presumed to have been derived from the words used by the French explorers claiming the region for King Louis, "aux Arkansas"—"toward the Arkansas River." The French also named the "Purgatoire River," a tributary of the Arkansas, which later became the Picketwire River.

P

pack horse bells

As the settlers began to move into the western parts of Virginia in the period after the Revolution, they imitated the first explorers who carried all their supplies on their own backs. Gradually pack horses were introduced. These animals were hobbled and turned loose at night. In order to keep track of their wanderings, the bells around their necks were "opened" at night, that is, the wadding stuffed into them while they traveled during the day was removed.

pack horse to heaven

A Connecticut tale tells of a confirmed bachelor of forty who married an elderly spinster of shrewish character of thirty-two. Questioned as to his motives when there were so many more attractive maidens available, he explained that life had been so pleasant for him that he doubted if he could get to heaven if he did not endure some suffering on earth; therefore he had chosen a shrew for a wife. When this piece of information was relayed to his new wife she proclaimed that she was no pack horse to heaven—and thereafter became the most amiable of wives.

Padilla, Juan de

Three friars accompanied Coronado into what was later to be the state of Kansas. One of these Franciscans became the first Christian martyr to die in America. Padilla was slain by unfriendly Indians on Christmas morning in 1542. Friendly Indians buried the body. According to tradition, the spirit of Father Padilla rises briefly from its resting place in a scooped-out cottonwood log every twenty years; considers the chang-

215

ing scene and pronounces a benediction upon those who witness the miracle.

"paid off with the boom"

In the old days the oyster boats on the Eastern Shore of the Chesapeake might "shanghai" unwary sailors from the Baltimore waterfront and keep the crew virtual prisoners for the entire season. They were often starved, frozen and cruelly beaten by the mates. On the way home in the spring it was often said that the men were "paid off with the boom," meaning that they were knocked on the head and thrown overboard.

Painted Rocks (near Harpers Ferry, Virginia)

The Catawba Indians who had wandered up from South Carolina into the area of the Shenandoah Valley had a story to account for the red coloring of the Painted Rocks, near Harpers Ferry, Virginia. They claimed that they had had a great victory over their enemies, whose blood had reddened the rocks permanently.

"paint her green"

All firefighting efforts before the Civil War in New York were undertaken by volunteers who were extremely proud not only of their company but of their equipment. The fire engine was decorated grandly with many bright colors and designs. At one of their regular dinners a slightly drunken member of the company was listening at intervals to the discussion as to what color scheme should be used on the new refurbishing of the machine. Waking at irregular intervals, he is supposed to have cried each time, "paint her green." His request amused the membership and became a popular refrain whenever they gathered. In time it came to be used as a symbol of the successful putting out of a fire, for they would then cry that they had painted the fire green.

palm leaf hats

In Connecticut before the Civil War a girl would have been as ashamed not to be able to make a good palm leaf

216

hat as she would if she could not bake a good loaf of bread. A bale of palm leaf might be shipped to a Connecticut village and the women and girls for miles around would take the leaf and braid it into hats; the big work hats all men wore in those days while they worked in the fields. A townsman would gather up hundreds of such hats to send them out with the peddlers who would carry them all over the country.

palouser

In Idaho a handy lantern constructed out of a lard pail with a candle stuck in it.

pastor turned General

The story is told in Virginia of the pastor of a Lutheran church in the Shenandoah Valley, the Reverend Peter Muhlenberg, who appeared in the pulpit of his church in 1775 and preached a stirring sermon on the text, "For everything there is a season, and a time for every purpose under heaven . . . and a time to keep silence, and a time to speak, and a time for war." Upon completion of the sermon he removed his somber black robe. Under it he was wearing the uniform of a Virginia colonel. He immediately began to recruit a regiment from his congregation. With this group he fought in the Revolution, ending as a brigadier general.

"pasty"

This term was used by the Cornishmen for their popular meat pie. They brought the custom with them from Wales to the mines in Michigan, where the dish is still a great favorite. The pasty originated, say the legends, because the arsenic in the air in the mines rusted the lunch pails, so that a clever Cornishman's wife coated the lunch with flour and water and then decided to make the coating good enough to eat. Tradition has it that the miner carried the hot pie on his chest to keep him warm when he went to work but as dinnertime approached he was so overheated from digging that he was keeping the pasty warm himself.

A curious reversal of the usual skill of a newly wed wife

217

came to light when a miner complained that the crusts of his wife's pasties crumbled as he took them to work but that you could throw his mother's down the shaft and nothing would happen to them.

patroon (as used in the South)

The term was originally applied to the lords of the great estates in New York but it was also widely used in the Carolinas in the eighteenth century for the Negro master of a boat. Great responsibility rested upon him of seeing to the safety of the crew and cargo, for he had to be master of the river and be aware of the changing channels, the shoals and the snags and other dangerous obstructions.

Paxtang Boys

These Pennsylvanians living near Harris' Ferry, the present Harrisburg, were organized into a strong group by John Elder, a Presbyterian dominie. This ruthless band struck such terror into the hostile Indian tribes in that vicinity that they undoubtedly protected many white settlers from massacre. However, they made no distinction as to the Indians they attacked. They took part in a cruel raid against some innocent Conestoga Indians as a reprisal against another group's attack. It was Christmastime and the doomed Indians were shot down in family groups at prayer.

This gang was also involved in the so-called Pennymite War, a quarrel as to ownership of the Wyoming Valley, a section of land near present-day Wilkes-Barre, which was claimed by Connecticut settlers as part of their province in the days before the Revolutionary War. Thirty of the Paxtang Boys led a raid and claimed the lands for Connecticut. Though powerful reinforcements were sent against them, they kept possession. As more Yankees poured in, the territory was organized as a New England township, part of Litchfield, Connecticut. Local wars continued even during the Revolution, giving a Tory force an opportunity to attack with their Iroquois allies, who did much damage. Retaliation was made later. *See* WYOMING MASSACRE.

Ultimately the efforts of the Paxtang Boys were overcome and the Wyoming Valley was recovered by the state of Pennsylvania.

Peach Bottom Furniture Boat

Once a year in the 1860's and 1870's a boat loaded with fine furniture, chests, beds and china closets of cherry, walnut and pine, was shipped from a factory at Peach Bottom near the mouth of the Susquehanna through the West Branch Canal. The articles sold from this floating furniture store were treasured highly and many are still in use, forming a body of heirlooms glorifying the production of the Peach Bottom Furniture Boat.

peacock

Superstitions about peacock feathers seem to run to contradictions, for some find them favorable and others the reverse. The Indians believed that to wear the feathers endowed one with the characteristics of the bird, making one vain, arrogant and greedy. On the other hand, to see a peacock in a park meant that a woman would marry soon. Yet peacock feathers in the house were said to drive all suitors away.

peas with honey

Though forks had been introduced into England in Elizabeth's time they were not looked upon with favor in the colonies, where their use was considered an affectation. One had to be fairly ingenious to keep all that was eaten balanced on a knife. Because of this situation a popular rhyme was often quoted in Puritan Boston:

> "I eat my peas with honey;
> I've done it all my life.
> It makes the peas taste funny,
> But it keeps them on my knife."

peckerwoods

An Ozark mountaineer term for a woodpecker, but also used to designate a "low-class backwoodsman" equivalent to "white trash." The analogy was obvious to some residents of

219

the area. A peckerwood may have the same effect upon a courthouse as a woodpecker.

peddlers of New England

The Yankee peddler, representing a footloose group of men carrying notions and tin plate about the country, seldom went over the same route in making their sales. They always made sure of a profit, and though they started with persuasiveness they often ended with various tricks so that it was not wise to return to the same neighborhood too soon after making the first "sell." So far did these tales of alleged iniquities go that there is a quantity of folklore on this subject that almost matches the tales of that equally entertaining subject of tall tales—Paul Bunyan. "Wooden nutmegs" are an example of the mildest of the forms of cheating involved. The thousand per cent profit exacted was only scaled down to reason when the peddlers discovered that they had to build up a permanent following of customers.

peel of apple as a means of telling a fortune

In the "apple" bees of the country districts, when apples were being prepared for apple butter or dried in quarters for the winter, each girl tried to keep her peel in one continuous piece. When this was accomplished she was expected to let it fall on the floor and see what initial it formed, from which she might guess the name of her future husband.

peggins

These were wooden receptacles used at milking time. They were shaped like sap buckets but had an extra-long stave at one side with which the farmer could carry the milk to the house.

pemmican (taureau or "bull")

Half-breed Indians of the Northwestern plains, descendants of French-Canadian fathers, prepared buffalo meat by making strips or chips of it. After allowing it to dry, they ground it up into a powder. Hot tallow was mixed well with it, after which it was packed in rawhide sacks which had

220

been moistened. As these sacks dried they squeezed the pemmican into a hard compact mass. This might be used upon necessity just as it was; however, when dried pounded plums or chokeberries were added, a well-balanced diet was provided known as "taureau à graines," considered to be very delicious. These Canadian breeds made great inroads on the number of buffalo in the upper Missouri Valley, one raid reporting 1,776 cows converted to pemmican at one time.

Pennsylvania Dutch Folk Art

This art represents the love of the gay and the beautiful. It was undertaken only to add color to their life and not for any practical purpose. "For fancy or for nice," said the Dutch. The tulip was represented on numerous objects, such as barns, dower chests, brides' boxes, certificates of baptism and of marriage, quilts, stove plates, and appeared so regularly on certain slipware that that kind of dish was called tulip ware. Hearts were popular too and sometimes "Distilfinks" lively bird, probably an imaginary goldfinch, and peacocks.

Fraktur (illuminated writing) was popular in the area about Ephrata. It was made up of elaborately scrolled letters encircled by stylized foliage.

Barn symbols were very diverse. Though arranged in hundreds of different patterns there were a few basic designs, such as a lily, a tulip, the sun or a sunburst, a spinning whorl or an inverted teardrop. Some were very simple, others must have been created by skilled workmen. Variety was admired and some barns might carry as many as seven signs. Occasionally an itinerant painter might have wandered through a whole community and his individual work be recognizable.

Pie plates usually received the most elaborate decorations in the pottery line. They were molded rather flat with an unbroken line so that the pie could be easily lifted out. There was no rim or base but there might be a motto around the edge.

Glassware by Stiegel forms some of the most precious antiques of the region, done in shades of blue, violet, amber,

221

rose and green that approach perfection. He is also credited with much fine work in iron, such as stove plates with Biblical scenes or primitive designs. Trivets and andirons were delicately made of iron also.

A breadbasket was made of straw and in it the dough was set to rise and then turned upside down on the bake-oven shovel. Straw hampers stored the ever-popular snitz (dried apples).

Pennsylvania Dutch Lore

See BANK BARNS, BELLS, HEX, DON'T MAKE BUMP, DUNKER LOVE FEAST, POWWOWING, PREACHER'S DINNER, SEI GEIK, ROCKAHOMINY.

Pennsylvania hitching post reserve

In line with their efforts to continue cordial relations with the Indians the Quakers of Philadelphia, represented by William Penn, negotiated an agreement with the Lenni-Lenape which was to allow them the privilege of hitching their ponies in a certain section outside the city. In theory this right continued for several centuries but the ultimate growth of the city incorporated the camp site into the heart of the city.

Penn Treaty Elm

The site of this famous tree is somewhat disputed but it is known that a pledge of everlasting faith was made between the Indians and William Penn. The wampum belt used to seal the promise of unbroken allegiance is still preserved. The chief representing the Indians was called Tammany. He later became known as Saint Tammany and was adopted as a patron figure by the Philadelphia workers, who frequently voiced their scorn for their employer-aristocrats. They sometimes dressed in Indian garb in their May Day parades, or wore bucktails in their hats. Jefferson's program for the common man was later staunchly supported by them. In time a New York organization also adopted Saint Tammany and the name began to have political implications.

Pentagon lore

Because of the great intricacy of the mammoth War Department building in Washington, D.C., it has become a custom to relay to a newcomer all the choice tales about the difficulties of getting around the vast building. A typical account tells of an obviously pregnant woman warned to take a layette and other necessary supplies with her, while a dramatic tale is made of the fate of a Western Union boy who was processed and came out a colonel.

Peoria

Much to the disgust of the citizens of the city of Peoria, Illinois, which is a pretty tough place and produces quantities of whiskey, the name of their city has become a synonym for a hick town, the home of the boob and the rube. Probably no other city except Brooklyn has been so slandered.

pepper

In Texas a piece of cotton filled with black pepper is placed in the ear to cure earache, while swallowing whole chili peppers will cure a cold, according to many accounts. Others say that pepper in any form acts as an aphrodisiac.

Peppersas

Old Peppersas, one of the famous locomotives of American railroad history, was especially built in 1869 to climb Mt. Washington, New Hampshire. Her vertically hung boiler spouted smoke from a mushroom stack, which from the resemblance to a peppersauce bottle gave her her name. Though withdrawn in 1893, a final ceremonial trip was planned in 1929 before Old Peppersas was set upon a pedestal as a permanent exhibit at Bretton Woods. The venerable, splendidly refurbished train unfortunately lost a wheel and caused the death of one of the photographers intending to take pictures of the last historic run.

perpendicular farms

Such farms have been claimed to exist in parts of Kentucky. Stories are told of a man falling out of his own cornfield and breaking his neck.

223

persimmon

If a girl were to eat nine of these unripe fruits, the folk of Alabama say, she would turn into a boy. They also say you may cure a chill if you knot a piece of string and tie it around a persimmon tree. There is also a warning not to put a piece of persimmon wood on another man's fire unless you want to drive him away.

Peruna

This was a popular patent medicine, but it was bought by a great many who professed to be temperance leaders as a partially adequate substitute for hard liquor. It was first known as Gold and Sodium tonic, but was really a cheap whiskey spiked with herbs and bitters and had a surprisingly widespread market.

pesos on the stirrup

Before the discovery of gold there were many fine Spanish families in California who produced excellent horsemen. One of the finest riders was Don Luis Lopez. The account goes that he would put a silver peso in each stirrup and another on the saddle. He would then ride a bucking horse until the latter surrendered from exhaustion. When he dismounted the pesos would still be in place.

pettiauger

A name for boats loading rice in the South Carolina region. They were used for a great variety of activities but always had in common the ability to meet any sort of freshwater emergency.

Phinney's Almanac

This was a highly popular almanac published by a Cooperstown, New York, printer in the 1840's. His weather predictions were looked upon with great respect. He once announced that it would snow on the Fourth of July and was as amazed as his readers when there actually were a few flakes in the morning of that day.

224

"picking for keeps"

The Pennsylvania Dutch brought with them from the Rhineland many ancient German customs, of which the most popular had to do with the Easter bunny laying eggs. Throughout the Dutch towns boys after Easter would test each other's eggs for hardness, and the loser would have to give the victor his gaily colored eggs which had been picked for keeping. There are those who think the egg rolling on the White House lawn on Easter Monday is derived from this old custom.

picking pockets

See DIPPING.

pie book

This was a card or booklet by which a railroad worker could obtain a certain number of meals at a given restaurant. Because the amount paid for the book could be deducted from their pay some men would arrange to have several issued to them, which they would then dispose of at a discount. They favored this arrangement because their wives would not be able to find out how much they actually earned and they could thus keep back extra spending money for themselves.

pigeon hunting

The tellers of tall tales in the Ozarks explain their difficulties about pigeon hunting as follows. They were always able to kill four or five birds at each shot but the birds were so dense that they were carried away by the momentum. Before they finally became extinct they often blew out to sea and caused wrecks.

pigeons

Because pigeons are taken to be very greedy birds folklore had made the deduction that a pigeon-toed person is sure to be greedy. If you feed strange pigeons, it will bring you new friends. If they make their home on the roof of your house, it will bring good luck, but if their home is pulled

225

down the house occupant's wife will die. Pigeons flying in a circle over a body of water indicate it will rain.

Doves are a smaller member of the pigeon family and have a great many superstitions associated with them also. Their cooing at the window is a sign of bad news coming. If turtle-doves live nearby they will banish rheumatism. The whiteness of the dove results in some contradictory practices for white may mean purity and peace but is also held to be a symbol of death.

pigs as weather prophets

Some communities believe that pigs are sensitive to dampness and that when they stack up straw to sleep on, they are trying to avoid getting wet, and therefore reveal that it is going to rain. Unfortunately there is no scientific verification of this superstition.

pig-tail coal brigade

Oriental labor was common in the West in the 1870's. Therefore the Chinese workers employed to fire the locomotives in Nevada were given this designation since they insisted on retaining their old customs.

Pike, General Albert

General Pike became a legendary figure in Arkansas history. He was supposed to have hunted geese with a cannon. On an impulse he hid the Confederate Treasury's gold far behind the battle front and thus managed to save $63,000. The tales of his eating and drinking reach prodigious dimensions. He considered himself a sage, a philosopher and a poet.

Pilgrim corn planting

Following the custom of the Indians, the Pilgrim fathers planted five kernels of corn to a hill plus a herring for fertilizer. A popular refrain explained the method: "One for the blackbird, one for the crow, one for the cutworm, and two to let grow."

226

pilot on the Mississippi

The pilots were among the most respected individuals in the Louisiana Delta region. They represented a standard so high that if food, for example, were particularly good or well prepared the marketer would proclaim that the quality was so high that it was suitable for a pilot; or, if an individual seemed to be behaving above his means, a friend would tell him, "Stop acting like you think you are a pilot."

"pinchtoe model"

When Denver was just getting started a century ago, they had their first lynching party and found no provisions had been made for the burial of the victim. A cabinetmaker was commandeered for this purpose. Since timber was very scarce in the pioneer town, the woodworker made a very tight-fitting casket, with so little extra space that it became known as the pinchtoe model.

"piney woods rooter" (wild hog)

In the Okefenokee Swamp region these large gray creatures are looked upon as dangerous animals. The natives claim they are especially vicious in hunting the diamondback rattlesnake which they tear to pieces.

pinhooking

This was a term for a little irregular trading on the part of a tobacco auctioneer which was contrary to regulations. He might buy some hogsheads of tobacco privately and try to get a good price for it at the Louisville auctions, in the mid-nineteenth century.

pinning money to the bridal skirt

A long-continued custom of the Russian-German emigrants to Kansas at their colorful wedding feasts was for the guests to pin up to the voluminous skirts of the bride money to help the young couple get started in life. The practice has continued to some extent, and amounts of from $250 to $1,000 are often collected. Another source of income came from the custom of some young buck's stealing the shoe of

227

the bride. The best man had to redeem the shoe with cash, which went into the household fund.

piñon nuts

Tales of the best way to gather the nuts of this valuable tree of the Southwest may differ, but all agree that the wood is wonderful and has heated their area for generations. The fruit (pine nuts) is high in food value, with a crop appearing pretty much any time. One approved method for harvesting advocates that the collector lie on his stomach and shake the nuts down onto a sheet. Eating them correctly is the test of a real Westerner.

pipe lighter

This was a paper spill that was employed to further the more economical use of matches, which up to the 1850's were scarce and expensive. They were often made of twisted newspapers lighted at the hot coals of a stove or in a fireplace and used to light a pipe or a kerosene lamp.

"pipes"

On canoe trips on Lake Michigan it was a common practice in the early period of travel to calculate the distance traveled by the number of pipes the guide had smoked. Three pipefuls consumed meant twelve miles completed, after which a short rest was allowed.

piquant mourette

A locust thorn tree prevalent in Louisiana. The inhabitants think that the prick of such a leaf will bring lockjaw unless a "*sorcière*" can provide a powerful remedy to counteract the "pick of death."

"pistols for two, coffee for one"

This was supposedly a popular order in the Louisville, Kentucky, coffeehouses in the 1840's when duelling was popular. It was also estimated that there were more duelists in its population of thirty thousand than in all New York City with its vastly larger numbers, and most of them sensitive as to their honor and very quick on the draw.

228

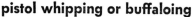
pistol whipping or buffaloing

A beating administered by a Western cowboy. The pistol would be held in the ordinary manner, with the long heavy barrel brought down with a whipping motion on the skull of the victim. It would have been unnatural for the cowboy of the early West to have shifted his gun to a position where it could be used as a club for there was too much chance that he might need to use it as a shooting iron as well as a club.

pitching horses

To the Texas cowboy a horse which pitches is a bucking horse but there is some distinction possible. There are those who claim European and Asiatic horses do not pitch. Some folk tales try to explain this by saying that the Spanish horses brought to the New World feared the panthers they sometimes encountered and thus learned to pitch, and their descendants kept it up for human annoyance.

plank roads

In contrast to the earliest roads made of trimmed trees laid parallel (*see* CORDUROY), the planks road was made of milled lumber, trees fashioned into planks, and the boards were laid in fairly well-populated areas. The first such road was built between Syracuse, New York, and Oneida Lake in 1845. Within five years there were over two thousand miles of such planking. The roads were about eight feet wide, with planks laid on one side of the road only, on the approach to a town where heavy-laden farm wagons would need firm going; but not on the other side on the route home because the wagon would be lighter and the fairly expensive planking would not be so necessary.

Joists, four by four, were laid lengthwise and beams to keep them in place, also four inches wide, were placed crosswise. No nails or spikes were used, weight alone keeping the lumber in place. A slight slope for drainage was allowed. Though comparatively inexpensive to build ($1,800 a mile), they lasted only five years. The calks on the horseshoes and

229

the decay caused by rain made dangerous holes. After the Panic of 1857 their popularity passed.

"please"

This is all the sign that the people of Boston need on the Commons to remind them to stay off the grass.

plew or plus

A prime beaver skin. Bundles of skins served as a substitute for money in the mountainous areas of the Southwest.

plod-jests

It was a custom among the Cornishmen who settled in the Michigan peninsula to save some of the Good Friday buns, which were hung on a string and left to dry until the next Good Friday, they were grated and used to cure diseases.

plogues

This was the name given to the buckwheat cakes introduced by the French-Canadians in the early Aroostook timber camps. They were eaten with salt pork and washed down by tea, sweetened with blackstrap molasses.

"plug the Dutchman"

In smaller printing plants in years past the men never had enough material with which to work, such as "leads, quads or spaces." They would sometimes keep a handful in their pockets when they went to the toilet to keep them from disappearing. When they complained about not having enough such materials, they were told to "plug the Dutchman"—that is, make out as best they could with substitutes, such as pasteboard, toothpick slivers, tin or anything they could find.

Po' Boy Sandwich

A New Orleans candidate on the list of folk cookery, made of a long crisp loaf of French bread, a "flute," hollowed out in compartments filled with various meats, such as ham, chicken salad and sausage. The name comes from the story that a generous merchant in the French Quarter used to give them to little Negro boys who called to him as he walked down the street, "Please give a po' boy a sandwich."

poke

A device like a yoke used in New England to keep animals under control. A horse poke sometimes had a long staff attached which prevented the animal from jumping over fences and getting away. Cows and sheep had especially designed pokes, often hand-carved by the farmers during the winter months.

policemen's outfits

In a style later popularized by the famous "Keystone" cops of the early movies, the Chicago police wore long blue coats, luxuriant mustaches and coal scuttle helmets. They twirled nightsticks fastened to their wrists with all the skill of drum majors.

Pontoosoc, Massachusetts, legend

Two young men, according to the still repeated tale, were wandering about Pontoosoc, the modern Pittsfield, in the 1750's when they noticed two Indian chiefs on the outskirts of the town. They killed them from ambush and thus were credited with saving the whole community from massacre.

"pooched-out tree"

This curious tree may be seen in parts of the Ozarks. A gang of possums hide themselves in a hollow tree and cause it to swell and contract with their breathing in unison.

Pool family

The Pools represent an isolated group of native-born people of mixed blood and eccentric characteristics who are looked upon with interest as representing "sociological islands." Concentrated about Sayre, Pennsylvania, the Pools were a dark-haired people, healthy and prolific, with families of twelve or more, and though often on relief they seemed better off than their more industrious neighbors. One myth as to the origin of the family has them stemming from Mary Brand, sister of the great Indian chief, Joseph Brand, and Sir William Johnson, agent of the British crown, one of

231

whose eight children, Elizabeth, married the American Revolutionary War veteran, Anthony Vanderpool, of a distinguished Kinderhook family. Further admixtures were said to have been added from the Dominican Negroes brought by the French Revolutionary refugees who settled at Azilum.

poor land

Folk tales attempting to describe the inadequacy of the soil in some parts of the Southwest say that it takes three pigs to pull up a blade of grass, each pulling the other's tail. They also declare that the dogs are so weak that they have to lean against a fence to bark.

popping corn

In the tall tales about the weather, especially in the Ozarks, it is commonplace to hear that it gets so hot the corn in the fields pops. It is perhaps a little difficult to believe that the horses sometimes mistake the corn, as it piles up on the roads, for snow and that farmers have difficulty treating their shivers and chills.

porcupine

The superstition that a porcupine can shoot its quills voluntarily as a means of offense is so well established that it would probably take a skillful naturalist to show that such is not the situation. The quills easily detach themselves, giving the impression that they have been ejected.

postillion

When the National Road first came into general use after 1800 there was a great desire to speed up the stagecoaches that traveled it. To make the expected twenty miles a day, assistance had to be rendered on the steeper hills. A postillion with a pair of horses would be ready to attach them to the coach's four and help the coach up a hill. At the top he quickly detached his pair and went back down to await the next coach. A well-known man who filled such a position was Nathan Hutton. He operated near Brownsville, Pennsylvania, and was a most thoroughly reliable man, who expected horse and man alike to "stand by his 'tarnal integrity."

postriders

The earliest American Postal route was from New York to Boston. Each post rider started out from his own city along the Boston Post Road, in use from 1673. They met at a tavern halfway, perhaps Saybrook, Connecticut, exchanged saddlebags and then returned to their home stations. The entire trip usually took three weeks. About 1763 the colonial postmaster, Benjamin Franklin, started day and night service and boasted that a letter sent from Philadelphia could get a reply from Boston in three weeks.

potato chips

In a small town in New York they tell the story of a local resident who with his mother looked in despair at an over-crop of potatoes that were already beginning to sprout. With sudden inspiration he decided to make them into potato chips and market them in transparent covers. These cellophane bags of Earl W. Wise were soon known all over the country. Some of the townsfolk have been known to say that they think a few bags were marketed to taverns with an addition of red pepper to make the customers extra thirsty.

potato coffee

In our early history when transportation costs made coffee very expensive, various substitutes were attempted. In Vermont the following method was used. Potatoes were cut in small chunks and stored away in a bag. When needed, they were roasted or burned, ground in a mill or reduced to powder in a mortar. A like method was used on parched rye, chestnuts and dandelion roots.

pottle pot

A two-quart jar made by hand of pewter in the early colonial period. It replaced horn dishes and was in turn replaced by "china" ware after the Revolution. The designation "pot" meant a quart jar. A little pot meant a pint draught.

233

Powwowing

A minor form of sorcery among the Pennsylvania Dutch that attempts to cure disease or repel evil through magic formulas or related performances. Though amulets are used, much emphasis is placed on the necessity of faith. While consulting a regular doctor for a condition for which a cure may be readily obtained, powwowing may be practiced secretly, and if an improvement is ultimately noticed more than likely the magic process will get the credit. Curiously, powwowing seems to have been effective where modern medicine has failed. The wording of the spells is based to some extent on a book by F. J. Hohmen called *Long Lost Friend,* which contains a collection of incantations for all possible occasions. For example, to stop a hemorrhage:

"This is the day the wound was made. Oh Blood! thou shalt stop and be still until the Virgin Mary bears another Son."

prairie vogages

On the great plains of the Middle West the rolling, level prairies resembled the sea, so that it is not surprising that terms used in ocean travel were introduced. The prairie schooners had "pilots" to guide them. When wagons approached one another, the questions invariably put were: "Where are you from and whither are you bound? How many days out? What kind of weather have you had?"

prayer for rain

A story that well illustrates Yankee shrewdness is one in which a Goshen minister was asked to pray for rain. He replied that he was willing to do so but did not think it would do much good as long as the wind remained in the northwest.

Praying Braves

In 1665 Richard Bourne of Cape Cod gained for his Indian converts a tract of land of 160 square miles which was entailed to the "South Sea Indians" and their children forever. The dwellers in the Mashpee kingdom (q.v.) were permitted to retain their war dances and powwows, but revealed their

234

Christian training by building the first Indian meeting house. In bad seasons Bourne fed the natives, and served as judge, teacher, doctor and minister to them.

praying mantis

In the South the mantis is said to be an agent of the devil and it may spit in your eye and blind you if you annoy it. They also call it a "mule-killer" because they think the brownish liquid it secretes from its mouth is poisonous.

preacher's dinner

A term used among the Pennsylvania Dutch to mean a sumptuous meal. Special occasions, such as a baptism or a marriage, would be accompanied by a bounteous dinner, as would any visit by the minister.

preemption tricks

In order to qualify for the purchase of land under homestead agreements various dodges were used to satisfy the letter of the law. A man might swear that he had on his property a house twelve by fourteen, though the measurement was in inches not in feet, as he allowed it to be assumed. For the same purpose some pre-emptors rented for five dollars a cabin on wheels that could be rolled on to his land long enough for him to swear that he had a house. Observers also frequently noticed one glass window, unattached, leaning or hanging upon a slab cabin to permit a witness to swear that the requirements were met. Since only widows or heads of families were supposed to pre-empt, young unmarried women might "borrow" a family for the "proving up." In many cases the officials involved connived at the situation.

pregnancy superstitions

A popular belief still held by many mothers though disproved scientifically, is that if a mother continues to nurse her child she will not become pregnant. There are those, too, who still think that a mother loses a tooth for every child she bears, though this may be true only if she has neglected the care of her teeth. The idea that a pregnant woman has abnormal dietary desires which must be satisfied is a common belief, though it has no scientific basis.

presidential comments

Some statements attributed to Presidents of the United States and aspirants to that job have become part of the body of political folklore. Henry Clay's statement in 1850 that he would rather be right than president belongs in that category. The response supposedly made by John C. Calhoun was, "I guess it's all right to be half right and vice-president." William Tecumseh Sherman produced a much repeated blast: "If nominated I will not accept. If elected I will not serve." Calvin Coolidge in 1928 contributed the famous "I do not choose to run."

A number of expressions have been associated with political figures, such as Theodore Roosevelt's, "My hat is in the ring" and "A swing around the circle," by Andrew Johnson. Another common expression politicians are supposed to stand for in general is: "If you can't lick them, join them." And appropriate in the 1890's was the sobriquet of the Senate, "the Millionaires' Club."

prize fight lore

Three-minute rounds in the manly art of self-defense were thought to be more humanitarian by those who wanted to see new regulations introduced about the 1890's, but there are others who think that some of the conditions of the "brutal" bare-knuckle era were actually less hard on the fighter. Under their rules a man who felt exhausted dropped to the floor and was able to enjoy a thirty-second respite. Back in the ring he could again fall and claim another thirty seconds without even having been struck in the interval. Some fighters used this as a means of "coasting," that is, taking it easy. In Sullivan against Kilrain in 1889, Kilrain was down almost as much as he was up. On the other hand, seventeen men in good condition were killed in 1952 as the result of fighting under the "safe" Marquis of Queensbury rules, which permit quite a beating during the three-minute interval.

236

Desiring to extend his field of followers and in need of funds, John L. Sullivan devised a new scheme for prizefight promotion in 1882 to get around restrictive laws in the various states. He joined a theatrical troupe which provided him with sparring partners who boxed with him. In this way he reached an audience which had never privately seen such performances. Twitted about paying his performers to turn in an inferior effort, Sullivan offered to pay any man no matter how big or heavy $100 if he could not knock him out in four rounds. As the story goes, so popular did this practice become that he increased the offer to the then fabulous amount of $500.

It has been customary to say that the first battle for the heavyweight championship under Marquis of Queensbury rules, with gloves and three-minute rounds, was between James J. Corbett and John L. Sullivan, September 7, 1892, and that John L. claimed to be champion on the basis of his skill in his bare-knuckle performances. This is disputed by some, who claim an earlier fight in 1885 between Sullivan and McCaffrey was the first. *See* OOFTY-GOOFTY.

prophets' chambers

In the homes about Concord and Lexington there was often a guest room maintained for visiting clergymen. This was up in the attic and was designated as the "prophets' chamber" in deference to the Biblical references usually made by the visiting pastors.

prospecting generosity

Miners were always ready to give a break to the forlorn and penniless. They would often work their "diggings" for an hour or so just to raise some gold dust to stake another miner to a start on his way to digging again.

Prosper of New Orleans

A folktale of Louisiana has it that a slave of a Creole family who was a devoted follower of opera was provided by his owner with a season's subscription. He occupied the same seat, front row center of the balcony for all performances.

237

He ceremoniously bowed to all the subscribers whom he knew. He also discussed with them afterward the fine points of the performances to such an extent that there were those who suspected him of determining the level of musical appreciation among his acquaintances.

Pullman Building

On Michigan Boulevard in Chicago stood the last great building of masonry before the advent of the steel structure. Its brick walls were several feet thick and would have been torn down sooner except for the anticipated expense of breaking the stout building apart.

Pullman porters

Many tales about the activities of the Pullman porter have contributed their quota to the mass of railroad folklore. One of the most interesting topics concerns the use of words having special meanings, such as:

"buggy"—observation car;
"tin can"—buffet car:
"battleship"—old-line sixteen-section sleeper;
"Baker Heater League"—a good gabfest.

Punch Bowl

This is a spring near Bucknell Avenue on Biscayne Bay in Miami, to which it is claimed pirates and explorers had access. It was said to be shaped like a bowl and to be reached by steps hewn out of the rocky shore by hand, probably by Spanish missionaries who came there in the 1500's.

punishment for killing an overseer

In the early 1800's cruel punishment was inflicted in Georgia upon Negroes whose crimes were held to be flagrant. Burning to death was selected as punishment not only for its immediate effects but because it deprived those so punished of even the mental consolation held by many former African tribesmen that after death they would be able to return to their own country. This bitter punishment was justified at the time as being a great deterrent to crime.

238

Puritan church practice

The lengthy and compulsory church services of the Puritans were matched by other austere practices, including the belief that heat in the building was much too soft a practice to be tolerated. There was no central heating for these buildings until after 1800. A little individual footstool for the ladies was tolerated, but even these evoked complaints because they were sometimes left in the church with a possible fire hazard involved.

Puritan restrictions on kissing

Puritan law forbade anyone to kiss his wife in public. A well-known sea captain just returned from a year-long cruise, kissed his wife when she came down to the dock to meet him. Despite the extenuating circumstances he was tried and sentenced immediately to two hours in the stocks on his first day in port.

Puritan wedding arrangements

The bride was expected to select the Bible text for the next church service after the wedding. Just before the sermon the couple would rise and turn seven times so that everyone in the church could see them. At the ceremony itself a judge or some other official would perform the rites. Though the minister might be present he could not officiate at the ceremony for Puritan law prohibited it, probably as a form of protest against the elaborate services held in the Church of England ceremonies. The usual time was late afternoon, after which prodigious meals would be served if the family could afford it. Though curfew sounded at nine o'clock, a wedding party could get permission for a torchlight parade at a late hour when the bridal couple were to be escorted to their new home. Often part of the final form consisted in "stealing the bride." In mock concern the groom would look all around the neighborhood until he found the hiding place of his bride, after which they all entered the new home.

239

push a keel

This refers to the efforts of the river boatmen going down the Mississippi to New Orleans.

Putnam Farm

This farm of Israel Putnam, Revolutionary War hero, is located on the old Boston Post Road. Once when Washington was passing over this route, he regretted he did not have time to slip over to see his former fellow officer. On this farm was the famous wolf den precariously located on a ledge, where according to tradition Putnam crawled in after a wolf he had shot and seized him by the ears, while his frightened companions dragged them both out by the rope which Putnam had tied around his waist.

putz

Christmas scenes made up of miniature wooden figures. The practice of arranging these little images of the Christ Child and the shepherds was started by the Moravian settlers, particularly around Bethlehem, Pennsylvania. In the period around 1740 it is claimed some Indians watched the scenes with great interest and many asked to be baptized when the story was explained to them. Another legend tells that when an Indian attack was being secretly arranged the Indians heard the wonderful music festival that the townspeople had prepared for the midnight service Christmas Eve and departed without making any attack.

pyrography

This was an almost universal fad overwhelmingly popular about 1900. Ornamentation was produced upon wooden objects by means of a hot poker which originally had a platinum point and resembled an electric solder iron. An atomizer filled with benzine provided the flame, and also many household hazards. Scorched lines on the wood were produced in decorative patterns which were applied to bowls, plaques, the popular "what-nots," tambours, trays and anything else the passionately addicted ladies could manage to decorate and inflict on relatives and friends.

240

Q

Quaker persecutions on Cape Cod

A cleavage existed in early colonial days between the Quakers and the regular congregations. At first the Quakers were very badly treated for their nonconformity and later were at least tolerated. However, feelings were likely to run very high at any provocation and the incident of the "pizen cow meat" showed this very clearly. On this memorable occasion the minister's daughter died after having eaten the meat of a calf which had been given to the minister by a wealthy Quaker as his church tax. Later the minister himself died after eating part of another calf coming from the same source. The people of the township (near modern Sandwich) were about to lynch the Quaker but calmer heads intervened. Finally the crisis subsided when the new minister accepted a turkey from another Quaker. However, the superstitious members of the community took it for granted that he suffered no danger because he uttered the Lord's Prayer over the bird before he ate it.

quassia cup

A drinking cup carved out of quassia wood which would impart a bitterness to water left in it overnight. This solution was a cheap way of obtaining a dose of "bitters," which some people claimed had medicinal value. Those offering the cups for sale claimed they were good for a year before the essence or virtue was used up.

"Queen of the Valley"

A train of the Philadelphia and Reading Railway established in 1846, held in great esteem by the Pennsylvania Dutch. Clocks were set by it as it went down the Great Valley every evening.

question of guilt for repeated offense

A popular folktale in Pennsylvania had to do with the defense offered by the accused on his second charge of drunkenness. He claimed he was not drunk again—he simply had not sobered up from the earlier occasion.

Quien sabe

Spanish for "Who knows?" but adopted by the cowboy of the Southwest as "kin-savvy," usually uttered with a shrug to indicate that he has no knowledge of the subject. "Savvy" used by itself as a query would mean "Do you understand?" To say that a person had plenty of savvy would mean that he knew all about the subject.

quilting bees

As a community festival there was probably no more important part of American folklore than the practices and customs that arose in connection with the making of quilts. The expert quilters were the queens of the occasion. The pattern could be drawn "by the eye" or the edge of a saucer or a pan could be used. Sometimes a string was chalked and stretched tautly across the quilt top upon which it was snapped to leave a mark. Heavy carved blocks of wood carved in various patterns would also be heavily chalked and pressed upon the quilt. Usually the small pieces of material were tacked on first by the less-experienced quilters. Then the pattern was worked out in feather stitch or other design, or the whole quilt was cross-stitched in parallel straight lines. The pieced squares might be in a geometrical design, rectangle, diamond, circle or hexagon, formed of contrasting colors of light or dark or assembled in shades of similar colors. A New Hampshire exhibit showed a quilt of 42,000 pieces. An appliqué style might also be developed consisting of cut-out motifs of flowers, leaves or wreaths in dark shades

242

against a neutral background. The crazy quilt was made up of a hit-or-miss collection of pieces. Each design had a special designation covering the fields of romance, religion, politics and history. One of the most intricate was the American eagle design. All this activity arose out of the thrifty desire to save odds and ends of material but eventually "boughten" materials were employed. The quilting queens saw to it also that business was well combined with pleasure.

R

rabbit superstitions

The carrying of a rabbit's foot to bring luck is still a much observed superstition. To be fully effective it should be taken from the left foot of an animal killed by a cross-eyed person during a full moon. Since the rabbit is one of the three animals whose rear feet hit the ground in front of its forefeet when running rapidly it is not surprising that special qualities were attributed to it. The hare and the rabbit are so thoroughly confused with one another that the folk tales about each are intermingled also. A hare passing in front of a pregnant woman was said to cause the child to be born with a harelip unless she made a tear in her petticoat. Some people used wet rabbit skins for swellings and sprains. Some talk sweetly to a rabbit if it crosses their path so that they will not have bad luck. Because of the great prolificness of rabbits, the foot has been carried by those desiring a large family. *See* BRER RABBIT.

rabbits for lambs

Newcomers to the West were always in for a great deal of hazing and the sheep-raising section of the Northwest was no exception. A popular tale tells of a greenhorn who, just before lambing time, was told to round up the sheep and bring them all in. Also, he was warned to be careful and not miss any of the lambs. The one being tricked comes back hours late with all the sheep and some rabbits. Of course there were no lambs and he had been wearing himself out hunting for the elusive rabbits he had mistaken for lambs.

race horse eggs

In Paradise Valley in northern Idaho the farmers were proud of their enormous pumpkins and were not averse to pulling the legs of their Eastern visitors. One old-timer displaying a particularly large variety explained that this huge vegetable was a "hoss egg." Carrying it along the field he pretended to stumble and drop it so that it rolled some distance down a hill. This action scared a rabbit who bounded off at terrific speed. Having noticed all this the visitor remarked regretfully, "What a race horse that egg would have produced."

"Railroad Bill"

A Negro in Escambia got into a fight with a policeman which led to a shooting. The assailant, Morris Stater, had a chance to jump a freight and get away. Thereafter he was known as "Railroad Bill" and became practically a god of Negro mythology during the 1890's. He would raid the freight trains and throw off supplies which he would then sell cheaply wherever he could. His escapes became the subject of many legends. The Negroes claimed he turned into a sheep in the field just as a posse was catching up with him. Sometimes the law got "too close" for him to exercise his conjure and he had to shoot the officers. All sheriffs in the state of Alabama were sworn to get him. The tale of one such sad encounter became a popular ballad:

> "Railroad Bill mighty bad man,
> Shot all lights out of brakeman's hand,
> Was looking for Railroad Bill.
> Railroad Bill mighty big spo't,
> Shot all buttons off sheriff's coat,
> Was looking for Railroad Bill.
> Railroad Bill was worse old coon,
> Killed McMillan by light of the moon,
> Was looking for Railroad Bill."

Other tales said that often a strange brown dog would run with the pack looking for Railroad Bill and cause the hunters

245

to lose the scent. At last he was cornered in a Negro store and his head nearly blasted off by the hidden law officers, McGowan and John, who split a $1,250 reward. The body was exhibited at Brewster, Montgomery and even in Pensacola, Florida. However, many of the people who knew of his activities would say when sitting in their shacks that he was not really dead—not *him*, they said.

raised on prunes and proverbs

A Western expression for a person who was very fastidious and inclined to be quite religious.

"Raise less corn and more hell"

Mrs. Mary Ellen Leach made this statement in Kansas when she was a colorful leader of the Populists, and it was soon being repeated throughout the country as the Populists gained strength in the 1890's. She was supposed to have berated the farmers for raising bumper crops which resulted in oats selling at ten cents a bushel, and beef at two cents a pound, with no market at all for butter and eggs. She demanded that the accursed foreclosure system be wiped out. "The bloodhounds of money who dogged the footsteps of the farmers must look out." She was a powerful speaker proud of being able to reach an audience of twenty thousand. She attacked Bryan, despite his leadership of the party, as insincere and unpatriotic. A story tells of an attempt to embarrass her in California, but the woman of iron-jawed determination donned the new-style bathing suit of that day and even a shark could not scare her. Known throughout the West as Mary Yellin', she lived up to her reputation amply.

raising the devil

A tale of varied New England locale has to do with a man frequently called Dow who was supposed to be able to raise the devil. The circumstances rested upon the fact he had learned that a woman was hiding her lover from the unexpected return of her husband by placing him in a barrel of tow. Dow being forced to show whether he could really raise

246

the devil touched a flame to the barrel and caused the devil to go flying down the street in a blaze of flame.

raisin pie as a funeral pie

In the old days of the Pennsylvania Dutch raisin pies were always included among the copious desserts served following a funeral service. This led to the saying about a person thought on the verge of death: "Yes, there will be raisin pie for him yet."

ramrod

The need for a ramrod to load the guns used in our early history provides a source for some interesting tall tales. One tells of a man who forgot to remove the ramrod from his gun when he fired. His bag included sixteen prairie chickens spitted right through the middle.

rams, ewes and moonlight

Sheepherders of the Southwest wanted a full moon when lambing began, to assist them with their chores, so they kept the rams and the ewes apart until the exact day when they calculated that the lambs would arrive with plenty of light for their often extensive task.

ramsquaddled

An early Western expression for being drunk.

rats desert a sinking ship

This belief, long accepted by all connected with the sea, is not a superstition at all, but a fact. The rats usually are the first to know that a ship is sinking; they may even have contributed to the cause, and will start leaving as if they had foreknowledge before the sailors themselves.

rattlesnake lore

According to Southwestern lore, rattlesnakes remove their fangs when they are courting so that if they quarrel they cannot hurt each other. It is also believed that when they go forth hunting food or drink they leave their poison sacs in their dens so that they will not poison their food. Mexican

247

sheepherders hoped to protect themselves by constantly shifting their feet for they believed that a snake never struck at a moving object.

People in many other areas have accepted the erroneous notion that a rattlesnake always gives warning before striking, and have tried to tell the age of a snake by the number of its rattles despite the fact that the rattles frequently wear out and break off.

rattlesnake soup

The unwary Easterner visiting the West for the first time might find the following recipe offered to him in perfect seriousness. To prepare a really good rattlesnake soup, you must not use little snakes only for then it will lack body. On the other hand, to use all big snakes will make it tough. Don't slice the snakes lengthwise or the soup will be stringy. Finally, put it all in a pail and ride off and leave the stinking mess somewhere.

rawhiders

There were men from Texas who gave their entire time to preparing rawhide, a practically indispensable product for Westerners. Cows would be killed for their hides alone. These would be carried in the wagon beds of those crossing the plains or stored as dried strips on hunting trips. When needed, they would be soaked in water and cut into long strips called "whangs." These would be wrapped around a break in the hub tongue, or wheel of a wagon and would hold it securely in place. Since nails were scarce, furniture, camp stools, wheelbarrows, and other pieces were fashioned of rawhide. Ropes, shoes, and clotheslines were made from rawhide. It patched and held together practically all the equipment the Westerner handled. The sellers of this commodity had an assured market for years until at last the nester, wire fences and automobiles put an end to its need.

razor back hogs

This very narrow, sharp-backed hog got its start on the steep Ozark hills from absolute necessity. If they got too fat

248

they just naturally stuck between the walls of the valley and starved to death.

red carpets

The use of and reference to red carpets as a symbol of the celebration of a luxurious occasion began among the socially elite in New York City in the 1890's. Carpets three inches thick were laid from curb to front door when a grand reception was planned. Mrs. Astor, Mrs. Hamilton Fish and Mrs. Vanderbilt all observed the practice, and upon the arrival of their guests usually had announcements made, that supper would be served at twelve-thirty and that the cotillion would be at three-thirty.

Red Light House

A house with a red light actually existed in Dodge City as a welcome to cowboys. In time it gave its name to the neighborhood where similar houses were established and ultimately created a term used the world over for houses of prostitution.

"Red Sea Trade"

This was a curious traffic that developed in New York City whereby respectable New York merchants loaded and sent out ships which they fully expected professional pirates to "capture." Their cargoes were then taken to Madagascar, where they were sold at a substantial profit as rich oriental wares. They eventually reappeared on the New York Market as black-market goods at a great increase in price to the mutual advantage of all involved. Many a famous New York fortune was started in this way.

refusal to wed

In New Amsterdam if the man refused to marry when a complaint was made to the authorities, he was shaved on the head, flogged, his ears bored and finally put to work for two years.

regard ring

This was a ring given by the young people on Cape Cod as a token of affection. The name was partially created because

249

of the stones used to decorate it, which consisted of an "R" for ruby, an "E" for emerald and a "G" for garnet.

Remembering Acre

A burying ground on Cape Cod where the man lost somewhere at sea has a white stone placed in remembrance of him even though no body has been recovered.

Remembrance Day

The persecuted Schwenkfelders, a Protestant sect in Europe, were given sanctuary in the New World on September 24, 1734. Thereafter they celebrated this day as "Remembrance Day." All those who have left their home communities go back for this special occasion.

Renfroe, Steve

A colorful figure in Alabama tales, he started out as a sheriff. He had many loyal friends so that though he was eventually accused of misappropriating the funds of the county, he was helped to break jail many times. Though finally convicted, he broke loose from his chain gang and outwitted even the bloodhounds. He hid out in a belt of uninhabited woods and was acknowledged by his despairing friends as an outlaw. Captured again, the tales about him say, he tried to avoid further punishment by veiled blackmail in which he threatened to reveal the names of those who in their youth were involved in Klan activities. The membership at that time had been connected with many unsavory deals which he was ready to reveal. Much as his friends had done for him in the past, this threat was too much for them. Just before his last trial twenty men visited him secretly at the jail. He was taken out and hung from a neighboring chinaberry tree. They say children still play about it and the bravest of them dare one another to cry, "Renfroe, Renfroe, what did you do?"

Stories about Renfroe were long popular, for his life was a string of exciting incidents. He was a handsome man who had a way with the ladies. No one knew anything of him when he first came into Sumpter County but he rode a milk-

250

white horse and made an imposing appearance. He promptly married into a good family and helped his neighbors put down the carpetbaggers, discourage the Republicans and organize the Ku-Klux Klan. In appreciation the town made him sheriff. Loyalty to those who had once served him was strong until self-interest finally caused his lynching.

reno-vated

A popular term created by Walter Winchell to refer to those who had been to Reno, Nevada, to obtain a divorce. Its popularity is about on a par with another expressive term created by Mr. Winchell, "blessed event," for the birth of a child.

Revere's ride

The famous ride of Paul Revere is re-enacted every April nineteenth in Boston. Usually two cavalrymen represent the leading characters one of whom, who went by the long route, few have ever heard of, though his responsibility in awakening the countryside was just as important. Helen More makes the point well in the following lines:

" 'Tis well for children to hear of the midnight ride of
   Paul Revere;
But why should my name be quite forgot Who rode as
   boldly and well, God wot?
Why should I ask? The reason is clear;
My name was Dawes and his Revere."

reversing clothes

To turn one's cap or apron backward or one's pocket inside out will prevent misfortune from striking after a bad omen has been experienced. This countermagic is best carried out if the turning is done in the direction the sun moves.

rice-spoon

This utensil was particularly popular in Charleston, South Carolina, where it was usually about fifteen inches long and always laid upon the table before a meal.

251

ridge runner

In some Western areas the term would refer to a patrol in a high point of land used by herds of wild horses to be kept alert to possible danger. In the Middle West the term refers to a man forced to live on a high point of land.

riding and tying

Travel conditions in colonial times were difficult and expensive. As a result an ingenious device to aid people of limited means developed. One couple would ride a horse a certain distance, tie it to a tree, then go on by foot. A second couple following them on foot would finally catch up with the now rested horse, and ride it on ahead of the first couple, leaving it for them in turn. Thus all four did some walking but all got a rest too.

riding the battery boxes

Tramps desirous of stealing a ride on a train would by various means get into the oblong wooden boxes which ordinarily contained storage batteries but which, when empty, would provide a good means of hiding away from the inspectors.

right foot foremost

It was an old superstition that laid the foundation for the expression "to get off on the right foot." It was considered lucky to step forward on the right foot both in starting a marriage or in starting a ship upon its maiden voyage.

right hand of executed robber provides magic charm

It was a well-founded tradition in Pennsylvania and Maryland that anyone possessing the right hand of a successful marauder, who had been punished for his crimes, would be able to put anyone he chose to sleep, rob him at his ease, and avoid any interference with his escape.

ring-boned, knock kneed and spavined

A common expression in the West indicating contempt for someone's uselessness.

252

rise and shine

The traditional cry for awakening enlisted personnel. The somewhat equivalent Navy slang would be "show a leg," that is, hurry up.

Risely Shawl

When Lafayette was visiting in the Middle West many years after the Revolution he was pleasantly entertained at a reception in a rather small town which he had imagined would have very few contacts with the fashions of the East, yet he remarked how very well dressed the ladies appeared to be. The explanation, and the start of a tale repeated on many occasions, was that there was actually one handsome shawl in the community belonging to a Mrs. Risely which was passed along and worn by most of the ladies at the party, who used great ingenuity in draping it and playing up its various possibilities.

river hog

This was a term used for the loggers about the St. John's river and in Aroostook County, Maine, in the early days of lumbering operations, when these hard workers helped to float thousands of tons of timber down to the Bay of Fundy. When they came out of the camps after the spring drive, they were something to see. Worn out from their long walk to the "outside," they sometimes covered fifty miles in a day, they were "tough" in many respects. They had long hair to their shoulders. Their woolen trousers were cut off above the ankle so that the cuffs would not catch in their logging operations. Their originally bright checkered shirts were faded beyond recognition. They celebrated their return to "civilization" with great brawls.

In the Lake Superior region they were sometimes called river pigs but they did the same hard dangerous work while there was still timber to get to market. They might spend days and nights in their wet clothes before any supplies caught up with them.

road agents

Men who held up stagecoaches in the early days of the West. An interesting tale has developed out of the discovery that one of the stagecoach drivers who most successfully withstood these would-be robbers was a widow who used her earnings to put a daughter through an Eastern college secretly. The mother's identity was not revealed until her death.

Robin Hoodlums

A happy expression for the "Beer Barons" (*See* BULLET BARONS) of Chicago of the 1920's who, while engaging in one set of unsavory practices to accumulate wealth, on the other hand ran soup kitchens for the needy in their neighborhoods and became the subjects of many weird legends.

robin superstitions

Actually it is the thrush most persons mean when they say that the first one they see in spring will bring good luck if he flies up, bad luck if he flies down. Very bad luck comes to anyone who takes a robin's egg from its nest.

rockahominy

This was ground Indian corn used as an emergency food supply supplemented by jerked venison in the days when the frontiersmen were off on Indian hunts. It was a term used by hunters among the Pennsylvania Dutch.

"Rocks and Shoals"

This is a popular expression in the Navy for the fundamental law for the regulation of the U.S. Navy. The "Articles for the Government of the Navy," the first chapter of the Navy Regulations, must be hung in some conspicuous place on the ship and be read once a month to the ship's company.

rolling roads

These roads, on which goods were literally rolled along, were in use from colonial times in the Southern coastal areas to bring the tobacco hogsheads to the wharves for shipment to England. Their meandering routes were due to the foremen's taking the easiest means of getting them to market.

254

Each "crate" weighed from eight hundred to a thousand pounds.

Rollingstone City

This was a fake city on the Mississippi, supposedly established by a group of real estate dealers who only set it up on paper and cheated land purchasers completely. Unfortunately this happened quite frequently, the only difference in this case being that it was a bigger and more complete swindle.

romal

Western cowboys preferred the use of a romal, or quirt braided to the ends of the rein. They borrowed the name from a Spanish word meaning a branch road. By having the whip thus permanently attached to the reins it could not easily be lost.

root, hog, or die

An expression arising in the West meaning that a person had to get on speedily with the hard work involved in survival or cease to exist.

ropeyarn Sunday

Navy slang for the time when clothing or some other small items of personal property are repaired.

rousters

Roustabouts, the hard-working stevedores on the Mississippi steamboats, exercised a strange kind of loyalty toward their bosses. It was common practice to boast that they had the toughest mate on the river. Many showed with pride the bumps upon their heads to indicate how much they had been beaten up. Some mates were held to be "soft" or "chain-barrel" mates if they allowed two rousters to use a device made of two poles with a connecting chain to ease the burdensomeness of the tasks they performed. The tough mate would state that a load was what two men could pick up and that one could just manage to carry. Their idolatry of old river men for their mates has a parallel in the later attitude of the admirers of such killers as Jesse James, Billy the Kid and John Dillinger.

rubbers worn indoors

Since the time rubber was first available, about the start of the 1900's, there has been a widespread belief that it is bad to wear them, or sneakers, indoors, and parents have consistently driven children to take them off. The supposition has been advanced that the sweating of the feet due to the rubbers may have created the impression that the person was beginning to suffer from a fever.

rum without cash

Many a tall tale in New England is concerned with a long-winded explanation of a Yankee appearing at a bar with a two-gallon jug already half full of water. By devious means he gets the bartender to fill up the jug with a gallon of rum. He then discovers he has no cash. The bartender removes, seemingly, his gallon of rum, and the schemer departs to work the same trick elsewhere to strengthen his weak rum.

run the gauntlet

This expression from Indian lore has become a common expression to indicate any difficult task though originally it was a ceremony imposed in some tribes upon the maturing youth and in most was a punishment forced upon captives, white or red. The type of beating or how long the prisoner had to endure the treatment differed in various tribes but it was common for the person surviving or showing great fortitude to be adopted as a member in full standing.

rush light

One of the earliest devices for lighting colonial homes was this easily prepared light. An ordinary rush was stripped bare of its outer skin and the remaining pith stuck in a quantity of grease preserved from the family cooking and allowed to harden. Sometimes these rush lights were twisted together and set in a metal holder, to give a surprisingly strong light.

256

Russell, Charles

See BURSTING HORNS.

"Russian peanuts"

The people of Ellis County, Kansas, gave this name to the dried sunflower seeds which were popular in that area. They also included dried watermelon seeds.

rustler

At first the man was just a hustler who hurried the cattle along, but in time there was the incentive to hustle some of the mavericks or unbranded cows away permanently and the term came to mean a thief. The rustler may also become expert in altering brands, which will win him the designation "brand artist" or "brand blotter." He may also be called a "waddy," a term derived from wadding or filling in temporarily.

"rye an injun"

A term for the popular "hasty pudding" (q.v.), with its mixture of grains of rye and Indian corn meal.

S

St. Elmo's fire

New England seamen accepted the belief common to the sailors of Britanny that if a strange ball of fire appeared in their rigging it meant that the patron saint of Britanny, Saint Elmo, was looking out for them and they might expect some miracle to benefit them. The New Englanders would corrupt their name for the fiery object to "corposant" from "corpo santo"—"saint's body." To spot it at the mast of their vessel they would consider a sign that all on board would get safely back to port.

St. Nicholas "on leave"

The legend states that St. Nicholas, the patron saint of New Amsterdam, left for a visit to Holland. Lacking the protection he might have provided, the city was captured by the British, though Peter Stuyvesant tried his best to defend it, practically single-handed.

St. Valentine's Day Massacre

On February 14, 1929, the Al Capone gang was active in disposing of all its opposition so as to have undisputed sway over the bootlegging of liquor in Chicago. His rivals, "Bugs" Moran's gang, had refused an offer of amalgamation. Just as Moran was arriving four of Capone's followers entered, lined seven subordinates up along the side wall of the garage and chopped them all down with machine guns. Capone was in Miami at the time and he knew enough to stay out of town for a while. Two years later he was caught for income tax evasion. His income for 1929 was estimated at approximately two hundred million. He died a natural

258

death in 1947 in Alcatraz and was buried in Chicago with practically no notice of it, though the tales of his earlier activities grew in the retelling.

Saints rewarded

Certain saints have an especial appeal for certain individuals, so the devout who pray for aid may have their favorites. In and around New Orleans the results of such intercession may be proclaimed, together with the recipient's thanks, in paid advertisements. Gratitude may be expressed by such an item as: "Thanks to the Holy Ghost for prayer answered" or "Thanks to the Infant Jesus" or "Thanks to Saint Anne for the return of my dogs" or "Thanks to St. Jude for helping my son to walk."

Sallie Ward

Miss Ward of Louisville was held to be the most beautiful of the great number of lovely women which the South had produced. An oft-told tale about her recounts that while riding one day she passed a group of Irish laborers, one of whom commented, "Painted, by God!" Unblushing, she is quoted as saying, "Painted by God," and swept imperturbably on.

Her name was used for many products but she was especially copied in the Sallie Ward walk. Her five marriages make her seem almost modern, though they evoked much gossip in her day. She also originated a fascinating custom of wearing a fresh flower in her hair to each bud of which was glued a diamond simulating a dewdrop.

Salome's Frog

A popular tale refers to the extreme dryness of a town in Arizona, Salome, pronounced to rhyme with "home," in which the authorities felt the need to provide a bathtub for a poor frog who had never had an opportunity to learn to swim during his seven years of life. He also suffered other privations; he had to water his back to keep it green and prime himself with water when he wanted to cry.

259

"salt" customs

There is hardly a person who does not feel some inclination to throw salt over his shoulder when it has been spilt. Because salt was scarce and valuable from the earliest times this superstition probably developed as a means of preserving it with care. Some people will not move salt from an old home to a new one. Others make sure that salt is the first thing that they take into the house.

"salted alderman"

A play upon the word "salt" makes an interesting tale where the necessity for real salt becomes apparent as well as the need to salt or reward some politicians. P. T. Barnum had two whales to display. They were not so big that he could not manage to contain them in a tank which the public was at first eager to inspect. However, it was discovered that the artificially salted water was not satisfactory to the whales. The problem of obtaining salt water from New York Bay was not too great as far as the laying of pipes was concerned, but a real difficulty was run into when it was discovered that the Board of Aldermen had to give permission for this and did not intend to do so. At long last, however, enough aldermen were "salted" to obtain a favorable vote for delivering the salt water to the suffering whales.

salted bullets

Among the tall tales favored by hunters there is one that explains why salted bullets were needed: the shot traveled such a distance the salt was necessary to preserve the shot animal until it could be recovered.

salter or salt cellar

In colonial times the superior cellar was made of silver, sometimes elaborately engraved, but many were just whittled out of wood or, later in the period, made of glass. Sometimes called the "standing salt," the salter was placed in the center of the table in the continuance of a custom started in England where the position of the salter indicated the relationship of the diners. The distinction was that those above the salt were of the family or its guests while those below the salt were the retainers.

Samuel Forbes Legends

In the 1770's there lived in Canaan (Connecticut) a strong-willed giant of a man who eloped with an equally tall and powerful young woman. When he brought her back home he is supposed to have thrown a rope over his barn and told his bride to pull on one end while he pulled on the other. They were so evenly matched that neither was able to pull the other. Thereupon he called her around to his side and together they easily pulled the rope to them. He then ended the incident by stating that that would be the way they would run their house in the future.

Samuel Forbes and his brother formed a combination with Ethan Allen and his brother and established the first real blast furnace in the Housatonic Valley.

"sand in your shoes"

There is a claim made with widespread support that once you visit Miami Beach and get sand in your shoes, you will never be able to stay away.

San Juan Island

Of the many tales told about Paul Bunyan one has to do with his tremendous strength in digging, which resulted in his being hired to produce Puget Sound. However, it turned out that he was dissatisfied with the arrangements in regard to his expected payment. In his annoyance he started throwing the dirt back into the sound and created San Juan Island before he was assured of full payment.

Santa Fe Trail

After a small-scale attempt or two, the first real wagon train rolled west led by Captain W. H. Becknell, who took six months for the trip and made a very large financial profit. On one of these early crossings his train, made up of twenty-one men, suffered a host of difficulties. There was an Indian

261

attack, their horses were lost, and the weather switched to scorching hot. After a dreadful struggle the men drank the last of their water, sure that the Cimarron in the next valley would provide their direly needed supply. They covered the distance they had planned, only to discover the river dried up. At this moment a mangy old buffalo wandered by. Of no value as meat, they killed him quickly and discovered his stomach filled with water sufficient to give everyone in the party a life-giving drink. Knowing that the old buffalo must have found water somewhere near, one of the stronger men continued the search, with ultimate success. The story of how the stray buffalo saved the whole Becknell party became one of the familiar legends of the Santa Fe Trail.

Santee Boats

These boats were developed especially for taking rice down the Santee River to Charleston. They had to meet the condition of shallows in the river and in Charleston harbor also. They resembled to some extent the keel boats (q.v.) to the North.

Sa Sa Na

Three young people, a brother and two sisters, members of a Mohawk tribe that had sought refuge in Canada, had become fine musicians. They came to give a concert in Oswego, New York, in 1852. While waiting at the station an engineer lost control of his freight train and the sister, Sa Sa Na Loft, was crushed to death. The family were Christians and a service was held at which long lines of mourners attended, the schools having been closed. Though the brothers planned to take their sister's body back to Canada, in the spring, the townspeople proposed a memorial. In a lovely site a marble obelisk was placed bearing these words: "By birth a daughter of the forest, by adoption child of God." There are those who claim that Mohawk tribesmen still come to visit this retreat, sometimes in the quiet of the night, despite the long journey involved.

262

saunas

The Finns have developed a large body of folklore wherever they have congregated in numbers, and this is especially so in the northern part of the Michigan peninsula. There they have followed one of their favorite activities, steam baths in their saunas or wooden bathhouses. One of the tales they like to tell on themselves has to do with a Finnish sailor captured by cannibals in the Philippines. He was placed in a pot to stew for six months. Back comes the chieftain to enjoy his meal, but the Finn says to him, "Where, please is the switcher and the towels?"

save-alls

This was a term for the little wire frames used in colonial times to hold the last bit of candle until it was gone. Since the materials for making candles were scarce in those days and candles were quite expensive, most households practiced these economies.

Sawdust War

This bitterly remembered fight was due to a strike on the part of the workers in the sawmills along the Susquehanna in 1870, when they tried to show their discontent over the twelve-hour workday. The militia broke it up.

Saybrook Plantations

Alice Fenwick and her family settled in the salt marshes of Saybrook, Connecticut, in the 1640's, part of the original group of ladies and gentlemen to arrive. The rigors of the new country were too much for the gentle lady and she died young. However, when three centuries later her bones were moved they were said to be completely enshrouded in the masses of her red-gold hair.

Scargo Lake on Cape Cod

A pretty legend has been handed down by the Indians on Cape Cod as to how this lake came into existence. The story relates that a self-willed daughter of the chieftain of that region was given a present of some fish in a hollowed-out

263

pumpkin. Scargo, the daughter, admired her fish very much but was afraid that her pet perch would not live very long under those conditions so she begged her father to do something. He called his people together and the squaws agreed to dig a lake for the fish. Filling their wicker baskets time after time, the women finally dug out a lake the required length, one arrow's flight. The rains kept it filled and there are perch swimming there to this day.

scarlet letter A

Hawthorne's novel based on an incident where a woman accused of adultery was forced to wear a scarlet letter "A" sewn on the front of her dress was taken from the real usage of the time in Puritan New England. The penalty was actually used until 1754 and remained on the records until 1785.

scenery mirrors

These mirrors were painted with landscape scenes in gay colors of blue, yellow, red and green and helped to decorate the parlor of many a New Hampshire farmhouse.

Schoolcraft, Henry Rowe

Appointed Indian agent to the Ojibwas during the 1930's, Mr. Schoolcraft made an extensive record of their life and legends, affording later researchers much valuable material.

schoolmaster barred from school at Christmas time

It was a pleasant custom in the subscription schools among the Pennsylvania Dutch to pretend to keep the schoolteacher out of his classroom on the day before Christmas until he had bribed his way in by providing a Christmas tree and cookies and making promises of lighter homework and fewer switchings.

Schwab Legends

The handsome castle that Charles Schwab, the steel magnate, had built at Seventy-second Street and Riverside Drive in New York City was as fabulous as the other great residences that were going up along Fifth Avenue around 1900, but through the influence of Mrs. Schwab some portions of it were kept as homelike and as cozy as its grandeur would permit. Many a tale was started about some of its marvels, especially the early morning organ concerts. Schwab himself was also the subject of many a legend. One account has it that he once introduced his valet to the King of Sweden. "King, this is my valet. He is a Swede too." The story went the rounds that he was an inveterate shooter of craps with the hired help in the basement of his great chateau.

scorching

This was a pastime that fascinated the Victorians, who went speeding or scorching down the highways on their bicyles. New York had a special detail of police to watch out for the sports who broke the speed laws even in those days.

scouring in colonial times

The colonial dames found a useful combination for doing their household chores in a mixture of half a cup of vinegar and a tablespoon of salt or wood ashes.

scrapple

This was a dish originally made by the Pennsylvania Dutch of all the leftover parts of the pig with spices and herbs added and the whole held together with ground meal.

scrimshaw

These were the objects the sailors carved out of whale bone and whale's teeth during the long monotonous trips on the old whaling vessels. They might make fans, yarn winders, crimpers for pie crust, combs or most elaborate and beautiful ship models.

sea clam harvesting

The diggers of sea clams on Cape Cod claim that the best time to gather them is when the tide is low and the moon full, and the best place about two miles off the shore. The beach along the Cape is extremely long to meet these conditions. These hard workers may gather thousands and pile them up on a sand bar until they sell them. Beginners are warned to

265

look out for clams that squirt, for some claim that a clam can shoot a stream ten feet into the wind.

seagulls

Sailors have been known to believe that the souls of those drowned at sea live again in the gulls. They are therefore rather careful not to shoot at them. Seagulls are also held to be weather prophets, for when they fly inland it is predicted that it will rain.

"sea lions"

A derisive term used by the early cowboys for the steers that had to do a lot of swimming on the way north.

seam squirrels

The cowboy's style of reference to fleas with which they were all supposed to be plentifully supplied—"wild, woolly and full of fleas."

Miners used the same designation for lice and had an invariable source of supply for the many races they organized —between scratches.

sei geik

This "instrument" was a part of the shivaree held by the Pennsylvania Dutch for a newly married couple on their first night home. A bull band or callithumpian band would create a special noisemaker out of the trough used for scalding hogs, across which wires would be stretched and the cumbersome device played by a "bow," a two-by-four covered with resin, and guaranteed to produce the greatest amount of discord possible.

Seminole punishment—the long scratch

Indians of the Everglades, who were sometimes called Seminoles, but were really only a subdivision of a tribe for which this was a general term, at fixed intervals held special councils at which punishment was allotted to those requiring it. Men guilty of murder or adultery were given a long deep scratch from neck to heel with a snake's fangs or with a garfish's teeth.

266

sensible coon

The sensible coon is the subject of an anecdote told about Davy Crockett that has become a permanent part of American folklore. This coon, recognizing Crockett, gave himself up for he considered himself shot. When Crockett, charmed by the compliment, patted him on the head saying, "I hope I may be shot before I hurt a hair of your head," the coon calmly walked off, saying, "Not doubting your word a bit, but lest you should kinder happen to change your mind."

"set a dumb supper"

This is a performance that some of the old Ozark folk tell about. A meal is served backward as a means of winning something you should not. It was condemned by the "good" people of the community as no better than a prayer to the devil. They claimed that anything gained by such conjuring was as likely to do harm as good.

Shake Rag Street in Mineral Point, Wisconsin

The name of this street is taken from the original name of the town settled by Cornish miners less than a century ago. When the wives wanted to call their men to their meals from the lead mines some distance away, they appeared upon the hillside waving a cloth. This old custom is still called to mind by the slightly changed title of "Shake Rag."

"shaker the plate"

This expression, meaning to eat everything upon your plate, was much used in northern New York State. It came from the practice of the religious community of Shakers of taking no more from the communal pot than could be eaten.

sharp instrument

There are those who believe that if you give a present of a knife or a pair of scissors this action will cut your friendship if you do not exact a penny for payment. In a similar vein there are those who think you should not hand the pointed end of anything sharp to a person or you will cut his

267

luck. Finally, many think that should you stir your food with a knife, you will surely stir up strife.

shavetail

Army slang for an inexperienced, newly commissioned second lieutenant.

shebang

A Western term referring to the entire collection, commonly used in the phrase, "the whole shebang."

sheepman versus skunk

A popular Western tale has to do with a contest in which the man staying five minutes in a particular tent would win $50. A cowman, a farmer and a sheepman all made the attempt. The first two were unable to stand the ordeal but as the sheepman was completing his time, a highly disgusted skunk was seen leaving the tent.

sheepmen

These figures of many legendary tales of the West were supposedly very much looked down upon by the cowboys who had preceded them on the range. Bitter arguments arose when fences were constructed by these newcomers to protect the sheep. They were never called shepherds because of the favorable religious connotation of Christ as a shepherd for they were much disliked. Their isolated life caused them to be subjected to many belittling remarks. For example, it might be stated, "Sheepmen ain't got no friends," to which the reply would be, "Don't want no friends." A cowboy was likely to say, "There ain't nothing dumber than a sheep except the man who herds them."

sheep shearing, Mexican style

In the Southwest the Mexican shearers believed it made their task easier if the sheep in groups of one hundred were squeezed into a small room where the heat from their bodies made them sweat copiously.

"sheep stealing"—winning over rival members

A common practice in New England, where there were

268

numerous Protestant sects, was for one minister to try to win over the members of another's congregation. Some "sons of thunder," avid evangelists, won over people to the new group by spellbinding and excitement of which there was a limited supply in most of the small towns of this area.

sheep superstitions

Our reference to the "black sheep of the family" as one who has brought dishonor to the family arose from the belief that a black sheep was bad luck and three black sheep meant a tragedy. On the other hand, the lamb has always appeared to be the symbol of innocence. The interpretation has been suggested that the "baa" of a lamb resembles most the sound of a man and that is why a lamb was used for a sacrifice instead of a person. Rams were considered lucky and also a symbol of fertility.

Sheridan's response

Legend has it that on an occasion when General Phil Sheridan appeared at church in Staunton, Virginia, the minister in the course of his sermon inquired of his congregation what they would do if the dead should rise and confront them. The General audibly remarked, "I'd conscript every damned one of them."

shift marriage

In parts of New England a widow upon remarrying might appear in her shift as a sign that her new husband was not assuming her obligations; therefore, the debts of her dead husband could be repudiated. In Connecticut it was required that such a marriage take place at a crossroads, and sometimes an additional requirement stated that the widow cross the King's Highway four times. Records of 1725 show a number of occasions when this ceremony was performed.

"Shirt sleeve to shirt sleeve"

This expression, attributed to Andrew Carnegie, has had widespread expression as meaning that though the father might leave great wealth to his son, by the time the grandson

269

was mature he had probably dissipated the wealth and was back to working in his shirt sleeves as his grandfather had done.

shirt tale boys

The general custom for young boys in the Ozark Mountains was to wear nothing but a shirt until they were twelve years old. Then as a concession to their growing maturity they started wearing blue jeans.

shoeflies

Detectives assigned to the job of checking up on the rest of the police force. *See* HEAVING.

shoemaker's awls as political symbols

The awl became a favorite weapon of the Know-Nothing Party, active before the Civil War, used to jab at voters of the opposition party. These activities were carried out especially in Baltimore, where enormous models of the awl were in display at their political meetings to intimidate those to whom they objected in the coming elections.

shooting star

If you see a shooting star you will have plenty of money if you say "money" until the star is out of sight. Another version claims that one must get his wish in before the star falls completely or the opportunity is lost.

"shooting up the town"

Cowboys coming into town used to make a practice of whooping it up and firing their guns. The origin of this action is thought to have started in imitation of a custom of the Plains Indians along the Missouri River. These Indians fired their guns upon approaching a group of people or a town in order to show that they had friendly intentions since they were arriving with their guns empty. Lack of familiarity with this custom sometimes brought disconcerting results when new officers at Army posts thought an Indian attack was imminent when only a loud welcome was intended.

270

shop signs

Many purposes were served by the products of the sign makers of the eighteenth and nineteenth centuries. These signs were important in a period when many were unable to read. They not only indicated the purpose of the shop by displaying a large glove, a garter, a chair, or a spinning wheel, but also helped in the determination of the location of neighboring houses—such as cater-corner from the "Sign of the Glove" or opposite the "Mortar and Pestle." Sometimes famous artists made their starts with sign painting. One of Benjamin West's signs still exists, a three-cornered hat and three-crown arrangement. Effigies were also sometimes used, such as that of Gambrinus, patron saint of brewers, Chinese mandarins and many Indians.

short sport

A term used for a Western trail boss who in counting over the number of "beeves" to be credited to an account would not accept an indiscriminate number.

shot-gun planting

The farms are so steep in parts of the Ozarks that the farmers had to work out some unusual way of planting. The old-timers insist they just used a shotgun to sow their seed.

sick book rider

Army slang for one who appears regularly at sick call formation with recurrent nonserious ailments.

Sierra, not the Sierras

Purists claim that it is wrong to refer to this magnificent range in the plural but insist that it is just one glorious range, the Sierra.

silkworm cocoons

In California wild giant silkworm moths spin cocoons five inches in length. The Indians of that region split these and insert a few pebbles in each. These are fastened, singly or in

271

groups, to the ends of sticks and are used as rattles or musical instruments for their special ceremonies.

silver bullet

In New England particularly it was understood that there was only one way to get rid of a witch and that was by piercing her with a bullet made of silver. There are numerous tales from this part of the country which "prove" the disposal of witches by this means.

singing bones

Many tales are based on the account of a cruel wife who kills her children and then feeds the meat to the father, but the singing of the bones gives the cruelty away.

singing to 'em

To the cowboy of the early West this was his way of indicating that he was on night duty watching the herd. The singing was in no sense to show his fondness for the cattle, nor to amuse himself, but to save himself a lot of trouble if the cows should get restless and leave their bed-ground and to save his boss money if the steers should mill around and lose weight. Of course, out of these circumstances some fine singing and songs developed, but many a cowboy had a miserable voice and a sorry assortment of songs. On the other hand, when he was really happy and carefree while he performed, he was said to be "singing with his tail up."

skidroad

Some of the early loggers were not too welcome to the more respectable elements of a town when they came in on a spree. At one time a district in Seattle where the "timber beasts" were restricted was designated as "skidroad." Here the loggers might be stripped of their funds and returned to their bunkhouses in a bad way. Original inhabitants claim it is a name used in other cities for the hangout of bums and homeless men. They claim the expression skidroad meant the road by which the logs reached transportation, a gargantuan railroad with huge ties over which oxen might haul loads of

272

logs. By transfer the term was later used for the area where some of the loggers "slipped" or were shoved along.

skim-alls

The Indians of Cape Cod tied sea clams to sticks and made hoes out of them. Others, used for skimming the fat from soups and similar jobs, they called skim-alls.

sleep superstitions

There have been those so superstitious about the direction in which a bed is to be placed for the best sleep that they carried compasses to make certain their heads were pointed north and feet south. Others put blocks under their beds to prevent the earth's currents from flowing into them while they slept. Another long-continued superstition held that if two persons slept together the stronger one lost some of his energies. Another common belief has to do with the harm some think comes from having plants in the bedroom because they are supposed (mistakenly) to absorb the oxygen.

sleepwalking superstitions

It is probably a carryover of the beliefs of primitive man, but many modern persons think that it is harmful to disturb a person walking in his sleep since his spirit or soul is not in his body and if awakened suddenly he might die. Another superstition states that the person in such a state cannot harm himself by falling or stumbling, though there is no positive evidence of this.

smith

A frog in the Okefenokee region which blows himself up and roars so lustily that he sounds like dozens of hammers striking against an empty barrel, making such a noise that the natives call him "smith."

smoking superstitions

There are those who claim it is unlucky to be offered a broken cigar, that you will run into trouble if your cigar burns unevenly down one side, or that some misfortune is impending if your cigarette keeps going out. If you catch a

273

smoke ring and put it in your pocket you will have money given to you soon. *See* TOBACCO.

smoking the peace pipe

All the Indians reverenced smoking as an important ceremonial, but among the Sioux if any one spoke during the smoking, the pipe was immediately dropped and no one dared use it again. They believed disaster would befall anyone who refused to smoke the pipe when it was passed to him.

snail water

A popular remedy used as practically a cure-all by colonial Puritan families. It was made by pounding snails and earthworms in a mortar and then boiling them in ale with various herbs.

snake head

In the early days of railroading a common accident to occur was the creation of a "snake head." This was a situation which developed because the track was made of wood to which a strap of iron was attached because metal was too scarce and too expensive to be used for the whole rail. It was not uncommon for this layer of metal to bend back and stop the train or even on rare occasions to poke up through the floor of the coach and harm the passengers.

"snakeroom"

The lumberjacks in the old days on the Michigan peninsula were known for their heavy drinking. They often drank up a season's pay in one great drunk when they came out of the woods. When they had reached a state where they were out cold, they were stacked up in a special room of the tavern called the "snake room," probably because of the condition they were in when they came to. It was against the law to put them out in the street for they would surely have frozen to death.

snakes

There are many popular and false superstitions connected with snakes, such as the belief that music can charm them

274

into quietude, or that a rattler always rattles before he strikes. There is no support either for the common belief that a snake hypnotizes his victim before striking.

Nearly all American Indian tribes have ceremonies involving snakes. In the Southwest immunization processes were undertaken to protect the young men who handled the snakes in these ceremonies and these individuals were usually isolated by those who thought they could spread the infection.

The Mojave Indians of southern California believe in a gigantic Sky-Rattlesnake who was killed but from whose blood a supernatural creature was created who had easy access to every tribe and favored war. Snake dances among the Indians often involved motions following a writhing course, with the coiling and uncoiling of a long line of dancers.

In some children's singing games the snake symbolizes the villain who then seizes one who becomes "It," as in "Black Snake, where are you Hiding?"

sneezing superstitions

The almost universal practice of saying "God bless you" when a person sneezes stems from an ancient belief that when a person sneezes his soul may have left his body and that such a salute might help to bring it back. In other respects a sneeze was looked upon as a good or bad omen according to the culture with which one was associated. Since some thought that sneezing indicated the presence of a foreign body or spirit, which might be transferred to others, sneezing was considered by them an evil omen. Taking snuff was a way of inducing a sneeze so that one could receive the good wishes of those around one, as well as expelling evil.

snollygoster

A term originating in the South in reference to a politician who wants an office regardless of party platform or principles.

snoose

A miracle product which makes strong men stronger but is dynamite to the weak was this food in the Paul Bunyan

275

tales. He decided to use it as a bait and a bribe for the whales he had rounded up in an especially excavated body of water in the Northwest. They were to make it possible for him to have his usual spring log run despite the fact that they had been faced with a terrible catastrophe in that instead of the usual rain only mud had fallen. Bunyan managed to fit pack saddles on each of the whales he had herded into his great corral. Each was then loaded with a great load of logs and one by one made their way down the Little Whale river which thereafter was known as the Big Muddy. A hundred-pound wad of snoose in the cheek of each whale made them docile and co-operative. The great blue ox, Babe, acted as "whale" dog and kept the whole herd in order.

"snowbirds"

Army deserters who joined the forces when snow fell and left in spring, having enjoyed free food and shelter during the winter. Since penalties were not strictly enforced, the deserters could get away with their performance. Custer claimed his regiment would have been a brigade if all the men he was supposed to have had, had remained in service.

snuffer

A device used in early times to trim the wick of a candle so that it would not flicker and gut the candle. Similar to it was a device that would extinguish the candle altogether.

sober-light

A Cape Cod expression for twilight.

sockdologer

A Western term implying something powerful. A teller of tall tales would use it to indicate a blow that would knock a man flat or in referring to a strong drink.

Sockless Jerry Simpson

A colorful Kansan politician active in the Populist Movement, Jerry Simpson was supposed to have said that he could not afford to campaign in silk stockings like the wealthy opponents he was fighting. This statement went over well with

276

his poor farmer followers and he was soon encouraging the newspapers to play up his sockless simplicity. He built up great popularity and in addressing huge crowds often made melodramatic entrances, such as coming in through a window and crawling over ladders to reach the front of a gathering. He became, it was said, "the greatest dry-land political sailor the Mid-West ever produced; no one could excel him in making political capital out of droughts and hard times."

soda fountain flavors

In the 1870's the early drug stores offered not only a half-dozen flavors, lemon, strawberry, raspberry included, but also one called "don't care" which was a mixture of odds and ends of all of these.

"soddies"

Sod houses in Kansas were made of grass bricks, usually ten by twenty inches square, containing well-matted buffalo grass. Some such houses lasted for thirty or forty years. Each "brick" was allowed to ripen before use, which usually cut its weight in half, to about forty-two pounds. The walls built up were by alternating bricks, first crosswise and then lengthwise.

sold his saddle

Since a cowpuncher's saddle is tailored to the individual's particular anatomy it will be the last item he will part with if hard put to it for cash. Therefore, when one says he has sold his saddle, it means he is really broke and can't get a loan. The meaning is sometimes carried still further to indicate disgrace or betrayal of a trust or even to suggest craziness.

son-of-a-gun stew

A stew popular with cowboys, usually called among themselves "son-of-a-bitch stew." If a calf were killed, the choice pieces such as the tongue, heart, liver, sweetbreads, and brains, were given to the cook to chop up fine and simmer in an iron pot with anything else that the cook had handy at the time. The longer it is cooked the better.

277

sooner

A term designating a citizen of Oklahoma. Originally it was a term of criticism of those who had crossed the line before the legal hour when new territory was being opened for occupancy. Later it lost its connotation of cheating and tended to imply enterprise and alertness. Ultimately it came to be used as a term of praise, in the same sense as prestige was claimed by the descendants of those who came over on the Mayflower.

Sorrow Songs (Trauerliede)

In Pennsylvania German lore these songs of suicide, hangings, and other choice events, rambling on through endless stanzas, form a fascinating collection. Set to some familiar tune, they were sung with morbid relish, detailing each weird circumstance, making the blood run cold with well-known horrors piled up in realistic recital.

sounding on the Mississippi

The boatmen on the steamboats operating on the Mississippi before the Civil War had an original set of terms to indicate the various depths they had to report to the captain. The first step was "passing the word," that is, telling the helmsman the depth after the "heaving of the lead." The "calls for the lead" were different for each level. That for the twelve-foot level was the now famous "mark twain," later used by the ex-boatman, Samuel Clemens, as his nom de plume.

spider

A host of superstitions center about the spider or his web. Some got their start from his activities, such as seeking out quiet isolated places like the cellar, suggesting that to see a spider means a peaceful time, or the casting of threads suggesting money-making and therefore encouraging the belief that you will have good fortune. To walk into a spider web means to some that one will meet a friend. The use of the web to staunch the flow of blood was common. The spider was a common ingredient in folk medicine: swallow a spider

278

with syrup to reduce a fever, tie one on the arm to cure ague, hang one over the infant's cradle to keep infection away, keep one in a walnut shell in the pocket to prevent the plague.

The Pawnee Indians had a Spider Goddess whom they regarded as the giver of fertility. They made use of a webbed hoop resembling a spider web to catch buffalo. Others trace the lacrosse stick to spider-web origin. In African folklore the spider is known as Anansi and is the trickster hero of a great quantity of folktales, many of which reached the United States, especially in South Carolina Sea Island tales. Anansi became Miss Nancy, the subject of many stories in the Uncle Remus category.

split nostrils for Indian horses

From an interesting document kept by Peter Pond of Connecticut before the Revolution and discovered years later when it was rescued from the flames, we learn of a curious custom followed by the Indians to increase the speed of their horses. They "split the nose up to the gristle of its head" enabling the horse to draw its breath more easily and become longer-winded.

Spring Fiesta

A celebration following the Mardi Gras in New Orleans, usually during March and April, mainly designed to focus attention on the camellias and azaleas then at the height of their glory. Tours are conducted through the lovely homes, where hostesses in appropriate hoop skirt or bustle serve tea and answer questions.

Special activities are concentrated around the "Vieux Carré," the French Quarter, a beautiful and well-preserved area showing the best of the old French culture. Included in the program is usually a project about "Courtyards and Crinoline," "Patios by Candlelight," "A Night in Old New Orleans."

spruce beer

A once popular custom in the Adirondack Mountains was

279

to collect the young branches of the spruce and boil them with sugar to make "spruce beer."

spruce gum

Adirondack spruce had its many uses but one of the more popular consisted of collecting it for its resin, an early predecessor to today's chewing gum.

stagecoach drivers

The drivers taking coaches over the National Road in our early history must have been very skillful considering the hard conditions under which they operated. They sometimes carried a load as heavy as twelve thousand pounds for a full day, making as much as fifteen miles an hour. It was claimed that one driver put whiskey in his horses' water so as to get greater speed out of them. The drivers were often flamboyant in personality and widely known by name. They were often as proud and independent as ships' captains and while they might accept treats by the passengers, would be indignant at tips.

stagged overalls

The standard outfit of the loggers in the early days included overalls that were cut short so that high boots could be worn for warmth and protection. The overalls were cut with an ax, and it would have been considered a sign of weakness if they were cut evenly, so they were always hacked with great unevenness.

stay husks

These were strips of maple slabs, hand-carved with hearts and flowers and used by the New England housewife to stiffen corsets.

Stetson hat created

Suffering from tuberculosis, the occupational disease of hatters, John B. Stetson, a Philadelphian, was visiting in Colorado in order to recover his health. Chancing to criticize the cumbersome, unsavory tents they were using he demonstrated how a fine material could be produced without tanning, or weaving.

280

He made a piece of felt out of rabbit's fur and then just for curiosity made it into a hat, which he wore around the mining camps. By chance a magnificent horseman saw the hat and admired it so much that he bought it for five dollars.

Returning home to his routine hat-making, Stetson continued to brood over the fine appearance the horseman had made in his hat. He also recognized that the increasing number of cattlemen were a potential source of good customers. He took a gamble and produced a hat he called "The Boss of the Plains," a fine broad-brimmed, natural-colored felt, of which he sent many samples to dealers in the Southwest and West. The hat was becoming and distinctive and soon was in great demand. The Texas Rangers adopted it and it soon became a characteristic part of a cowboy's attire. When John B., as he was popularly called, died at the age of 76 in 1906, he was making hundreds of thousands of hats a year.

The cowboy's weakness for the expensive hats produced by Mr. Stetson was not a matter of vanity, for in this one article he could find a continuous and indispensable value. If it were not of good quality, his life itself might be at stake. A brim which flopped down, blinding him, might cause him to be badly hurt. Among its numerous uses a few might be noted: container for oats for his horse, creating a draft for a fire, slapping an ornery cow into control. One never discussed the newness of a Stetson. The real test was its age. Some have been known to be in good service for twenty or thirty years.

stoopers

Those who hunt around among the debris at race tracks for "outs," that is, winning stubs which have not been cashed in, either thrown down by mistake or in unreasoned rage, or just lost. There are a lot of amateur stoopers who spend afternoons wandering around grandstands and the betting ring, picking up discarded tote tickets in the hope they will find a "live" one, one that they may collect some winnings on. There are professional stoopers too, sometimes referred to as "ground squirrels," who claim they do not do badly at all, averaging perhaps $100 a week according to some estimates. Some tickets have to be fitted together from a dozen pieces, requiring great skill and patience. These professionals are proud of the fact that none of these patched-up tickets are refused by the racing commissions.

straddlebug

A term applied in the South to a politician who takes both sides, or no side on critical issues.

straddling the liquor issue

In many a Southern state it has been the practice to "vote dry and drink wet." However, one Alabama politician found it wiser to antagonize no one. So he took the position that when he saw how homes were ruined and lives lost through liquor he was against it; but on a cold winter night when one could not get warm any other way except by imbibing a toddy, he was for it.

strawberries to be eaten

It was a Seneca Indian custom to say this about a person about to die. Strawberries were supposed to grow beside the heavenly road. According to their legend, mortal man would not have had them if the sky woman in falling through the hole in the celestial island had not grasped at the edges and brought down a vine with her.

straw used for warmth

Until the 1880's a matting of straw was laid under carpets to help keep the floors warmer.

Street-leading-to-the-woods

When Wilmington was taken over by the Dutch after 1651 many of the resident Swedes and Finns beat a trail escaping to the woods. At one time these "elopements" reached wholesale proportions. So numerous were these fugitives that a road was created which became a part of the federally supported National Road (or route U.S. 40) after it linked up with Baltimore.

"stretching the blanket"

A popular expression in the Ozarks for what in other parts

282

of the country would be called lying. However, it is to be noted that a sign often displayed in that part of the country states, "All the lies you hear about the Ozarks are true."

A story on melon growing shows how the blanket may be stretched. The growers of melons have difficulty with the speed with which the vines grow and the size of the melons. Some of them, therefore, have ordered little red wagons from Montgomery Ward upon which they place the melons so that they may be easily pulled along as the vines travel rapidly over the ground. Unfortunately the profits of the farmers are reduced because of the increasing expense of tires and axle grease for the wagons.

stumping

The West as a center for the spread of democracy as the frontiers gradually attracted more people, made a unique contribution to the stump or campaign speech. Speeches made for the uneducated were often intended to conceal the politician's motives as much as to reveal his position. Spicy anecdotes distracted attention from any shortcomings of the party or the platform. A general invitation to have a drink would often wind up the stump effectively.

stuttering beliefs

Many are so convinced that there is a connection between left-handedness and stuttering that they would refuse to admit it was a superstition. In the same category are the beliefs that tickling a baby on its feet will produce a stutterer, or that a stutterer is mentally retarded.

"Suet Gert"

In the 1890's a Chicago sausage maker was convicted of the murder of his wife who had disappeared into his factory. For years no one in that community would eat his brand of sausage meat from fear of its possible contents. The children introduced a gruesome song which they took a weird delight in singing: "He ground her up
Into sausage meat
And Suet Gert was her name."

surgical gloves, introduced

This was hardly a subject with which one would expect the topics of love and romance to be associated, yet the brilliant Dr. Halstead of Johns Hopkins did introduce a new departure in surgical practice because he had fallen in love with one of his nurses. It was customary then for doctors and nurses to make their hands sterile by prolonged scrubbing with germicidal soap and soaking them in a strong antiseptic solution. The doctor's wife-to-be had most delicate hands and the effect of the antiseptic was most painful. Therefore, after serious consideration, specifications were given for the provision of thin rubber gloves. So successful was the experiment that surgeons began to follow the practice. Thus thanks to a romance of the operating room, a new universal practice was developed.

Susquehanna navy

This was a derisive term used for small, but heavy boats operated on the Susquehanna to recover coal that had been washed down into the river. Centrifugal pumps drew the coal-laden muck out of the river like a vacuum cleaner. This accumulation was then dried out on screens and sold for industrial purposes.

swamp buggy

Navy slang for an amphibious tank.

swifts

These birds really live up to their names as they dart constantly about, so it is understandable why the superstitious think that if they see one it will make them lucky. The swifts of California follow the swallows of San Juan Capistrano with great regularity, appearing on October 23 and remaining until March 19, when the swallows return and take over the swifts' newly emptied nest after a battle royal. Then the swallows leave and the cycle repeats itself.

swimming steers

Many Texan cattlemen wanted to aid the Confederacy and did so by driving herds of cows to Mississippi or even to Alabama. One group of young men swam one thousand steers across the Mississippi at its widest and deepest point. To make this task a little easier one enterprising Texan, Colonel Cal Snyder, trained two steers to plunge quickly into a stream or river and lead the rest of the herd across. His activities had to stop when Grant captured Vicksburg and cut the Confederacy apart at the Mississippi.

T

Tabor's Opera House

In 1881 a theater was opened in Denver that was as lavish as money could make it. Tabor drove up on opening night and admired all the magnificent effects—except for one portrait he noticed on the lobby wall. "Who's that?" he demanded. Upon being told that it was Shakespeare he replied that he had never heard of him and wanted to know what he had ever done to help Denver. He then ordered that his own portrait be placed in that space instead.

tailor's goose

This was a heavy iron used by the "tailoress" of early colonial times to press clothes for the family. It weighed thirteen pounds or more and was long and slender in shape for the easier pressing of seams rather than the pressing of the whole article. It was made by the local blacksmith, with the handles wrought with many elaborate turns. This job was supplemented by pressing boards made of a certain type of wood that held moisture and thus automatically dampened the cloth being pressed.

tailor's spade

This was another little instrument used by the tailor. It was actually a miniature spade with a straight sharp end just the right length for cutting a man's buttonhole, which would then be bound with linen thread spun at home.

taking a man for a ride

An expression originating in Chicago, which was a more spread-out city than New York, therefore providing more of an

286

incentive to use a car or taxi for getting a man out of the way
—forever.

tallow dips

When the slaughter of meat animals was sufficient to provide our colonial ancestors with enough surplus grease to make
it worth while, housewives in both North and South would
make their dips when the weather was cool enough to cause
the tallow to harden. It took quite a bit of patience and skill
to make these necessary additions to better living, for many
households depended on the light from the flickering fireplace
for their only illumination. The great brass kettles would be
heated and then swung off the fire and with any sort of improvised wick the dips would be built up layer by layer as the coating hardened. Later, molds became available and hand dipping became unnecessary. Once the dip was ready for use,
there were still difficulties involved for it had to be placed in
a position in the room where its dripping would do no harm.

tall tale

An almost essential ingredient of folklore is the tall tale. One
definition calls it an exuberant combination of fact with out-
rageous fiction. Another writer points out that the teller does
not expect to be believed but does expect to heighten the effect
by adding many true and realistic details. Reminiscences include where possible reference to eyewitness corroboration or
avoid danger of contradiction by allusion to someone long since
dead. Next to local boastings and amusing incidents, the most
fertile sources of the tall tale are industry and remarkable in-
ventions, and the occupations, including all the innumerable
ways of making a living.

tame trout tale

In the Ozarks they have a popular tale that is offered to
gullible visitors. It is about a tame trout. He follows his owner
about and really becomes quite a pet. However, in crossing a
bridge one day the trout slips off into the brook and is drowned.

tapeworm

There was, and perhaps still exists, all over the United States

287

the belief that when a child has an enormous appetite and does not gain weight he has a tapeworm in his intestines which requires all the extra food and may even in time starve the host to death. Eating ground glass was held to be a cure. Other worm superstitions claim that if you step on a worm, you will have bad luck all day; if worms crawl out on the lawn in the daytime, you will have rain soon, if a measuring worm crawls over you, you get some new clothes. In order to cure ringworm you should pass your mother's wedding ring over it several times a day for nine days. There are many who believe that if an earthworm is cut in half each half will function as a separate worm.

Tar Heel

A term used for residents of North Carolina, probably derived from the fact that since pre-Revolutionary times the Carolinas have been producers of naval stores and centers for the distillation of turpentine.

tarpaulin tarradiddles

A Cape Cod expression for tall stories of which the following is a good example. Some ships sailing from Cape Cod harbors were so tall that when the sailors went up to furl the top royals they took their wives with them. Later they sent their grandsons down to report that the order had been carried out.

Taufschein (decorated baptismal certificate)

In Lehigh County among the Pennsylvania Dutch it was sometimes the practice to place a *taufschein* in the coffin of a dead person or even under the tombstone. The practice was probably based on the idea of having a passport to heaven to prove that one was a Christian, or had at least been properly baptized.

Teagues

A term for Irishmen, often used for the workers on the canals in the 1840's, who gained a reputation for being great drinkers and dying very young.

teamboats

A curious experiment was carried out in the early 1800's on the Ashley River at Charleston where a boat was driven by horse or mule power. The horses were taken on board the boat and were hitched to a beam about which they were driven in a circle. Through gears the power was transmitted to paddle wheels. It was a very economical source of transportation power and was quite popular for a while.

"Tea Stacks"

Henry Stacks was involved in an episode like the Boston Tea Party just before the start of the Revolutionary War. With a group from New Jersey and Delaware he burned some tea chests as a protest against the British authorities. He filled his pockets full of tea while taking part in the performance and thus earned for himself a name that stuck by him for the rest of his life, though applied in only mild derision. Actually when he was put on trial by the British for his participation in the destruction of the tea, his neighbors when called upon to testify could offer no evidence of his involvement.

"tell the bees"

In parts of New Hampshire it was a generally accepted practice that if a farmer died, the bees had to be told—that is, a shred of black had to be placed on the hive or they would swarm and leave the farm.

ten-in-one

A term used by traveling carnivals for a side show which had several acts under one top (tent).

ten-penny nail

This name was given to nails because they actually did serve as currency. Iron was very scarce and so the custom developed to use nails as a substitute for money. The weight of the nails determined their value.

tenterhooks

After the preparation of wool by the fuller (q.v.), the material still had to be dyed and stretched its full length, with weights attached to prevent shrinkage as much as possible. Bent iron tenterhooks or nails held the cloth in place while it was stretched out to dry in the sun in front of the fulling mills. Today we say a person is on tenterhooks when he is in "suspense."

Theodore Roosevelt

Paul Smith was the Adirondack guide who had the task of bringing Theodore Roosevelt out of the woods when President McKinley died. When asked how Roosevelt took the news of his succession to the Presidency, the guide said he did not tell him. When the newsmen inquired why not, he laconically announced, "He didn't ask me." Pressed to give additional information, he declared he was more concerned with the red-hot steam that was coming from the horses he was driving at such remarkable speed.

The Old Boy

"Speak of the Devil and he appears" is a popular folk expression, so if you refer by indirection he will not know you are speaking of him. In a similar vein, where it would be looked upon as unseemly to "take the Lord's name in vain," "gee," "gosh" or even "Good Lord" are acceptable.

they-got-me formula

When Westerners got together for a session of "tall lying" tales this type of ending might be one employed. The art was to build up to some seemingly impossible situation, then, at the highest point of suspense, pause. The listener finds it impossible not to demand a solution of the complication. The response states simply that there is no escape: "They got me" or "That's your lookout." For example, a story is built up to the point where a man is found to be lighting his pipe while hauling gunpowder. Pause. . . .

thousand mile shirt

The shirt of a railroad boomer was often given this title because as an itinerant worker he traveled light and supposedly wore the same shirt for a thousand miles.

290

thrown over the fence

Among the Pennsylvania Dutch after a young Amish man has been married, he still has to endure the final initiation into the ranks of the married men. This usually happens at the next wedding he attends. He may well hope that the rough and tumble horseplay will not result in serious damage, for broken legs have been suffered by those "thrown" over the fence. As further proof of having reached the married state he is now allowed to let his beard grow and he can earnestly hope that it will speedily reach the luxuriant abundance the Amish men are so proud of.

ticker tape reception

It is thought that the first time this popular Broadway reception was ever used was in 1910 upon the return of the popular Theodore Roosevelt from his African hunting trip.

tie one to that

After finishing his tale, a Western storyteller may conclude his turn with this expression, throwing a challenge to the next narrator to outdo him in adventuresomeness or exaggeration, if possible.

"tilter"

Before the Civil War, a young girl might be thought too young to wear a full hoop skirt, but would be permitted to wear half a hoop, a tilter, until she grew older.

timberhead talk

The stanchions of the barges which plied the Mississippi River were where the men squatted, relaxing between jobs, so that the talk arising in this area became "timberhead talk."

time telling in Cape Cod

In the middle of the seventeenth century there were few clocks on the Cape. Time was reckoned as suncoming, sun-an-hour, sun-two-hours, then midday, sun-four-hours-up, sun-three-hours-up, sunset, sober light (twilight), first-hour-night, second-hour-night.

291

Timothy Dexter

A hard-working tanner on Cape Cod, he was looked down upon by the thriving gentry of his town. Knowing his great desire to get rich, some local businessmen decided to unload upon him a quantity of warming pans they could not dispose of. He fell for the scheme and bought all the pans, which he shipped to the West Indies. There he made a great profit for with their long handles they were found to be ideally suited to the job of sugar refining. Rich at last, Dexter continued to provide material for later legends associated with his home and activities.

tip

Carnival term for "crowd." "Collect a tip"—gather a crowd together. "Turn the tip"—persuade the crowd. "A stick"—one who acts as a confederate of a concessionaire by leading the crowd to participate in the activity or by winning in the games of chance.

toad superstitions

The toad enjoys some of the consideration that the frog does in being reputed to bring good luck, but also has many beliefs associated with it connected with bad luck. A toad in the cellar brings bad luck, as does the killing of one, so a toad must be gotten rid of with care.

Many besides the Indians thought the toad poisonous and likely to cause a leg or arm to swell if touched.

tobacco

This plant, a native of the New World, was cultivated by most of the Indian tribes and used by all of them in ceremonial activities. Almost all have some legend telling of the way the sacred plant was originally obtained. Besides smoking the dried leaves, the plant was used also for medicinal purposes. It was claimed that chewing it would protect the individual from the plague. Little bags of ground-up tobacco were worn around the neck to prevent infections.

tobacco auction in Louisville

The bids for the tobacco were made by the hundred weight

292

and increased by twenty-five cents per bid. Eleven one meant $11.25 and eleven two meant $11.50. Eleven three would be $11.75. Any brief gesture, a nod, a wink, or the motion of a finger, indicated acceptance of a bid. Sticking out the tongue meant a seventy-five cent increase. If the bidder looked away it was an indication that the bidding was over. *See* COOPER.

tobacco canoes

On the tidewater rivers flowing down to Atlantic seaports, an economical way to transport tobacco was evolved by lashing two canoes together side by side and rolling eight or nine hogsheads of tobacco across their gunwales.

tomato superstition

For a long period of time people have thought that certain foods acted as sex stimulants or aphrodisiacs. Among these tomatoes were long considered an important one. They were originally known as "love apples."

Tom Quick, Indian Killer

Tom Quick was the subject of a legend popular among the Pennsylvania Dutch. He was the son of a Holland Dutchman who had settled along the Delaware in what is now Pike County. The family was at first quite friendly with the Indians but found relations strained during the French and Indian War. While crossing a lake the elder Quick was killed by a group of Indians. Witness to this action, the son swore to slay a hundred Indians in revenge. He proved as good as his word and stalked Indians, man, woman, and child, with wholehearted devotion. He is even credited with killing the very Indian who had slain his father, when the latter drunkenly revealed his deed, displaying buttons taken from the clothing of the elder Quick. When Tom was questioned about his cruelty to the children, he always produced the same reply, "Nits make lice." According to the legend, he managed to kill his hundredth Indian on his deathbed.

Tom Sawyer

An acquaintance made by Samuel Clemens when he visited

293

the San Francisco Bay area actually was named Tom Sawyer. He claimed his name was used by the author in his honor and kept a sign to this effect in the window of his establishment until it was destroyed in the great fire of 1906.

Tommy Knockers

Little gnomes who live in the heart of a bed of coal. Dressed in gray, they went around the mines knocking hammers on all the props to see if they were safe. If bad they would whistle to warn of a possible cave-in.

ton timbers

In the early lumbering period in Aroostook County, Maine, the trees grew to such heights that the term "ton timbers" was applied to the great square-cut beams, sometimes five and six feet in diameter, that were floated down the river to Canada, where the British bought them by the ton. In the 1840's their price was four dollars a ton but later went up to forty dollars. A single tree might bring as high as $1,000.

tooth superstitions

Some of these beliefs still commonly held are as follows: a clean tooth never decays; "baby" teeth need not be cared for; chewing tobacco will cure a toothache; wisdom teeth emerging before the age of twenty means a short life; drinking milk prevents decay; to have teeth well separated means you will have a fine voice.

tortience

The early dwellers on Cape Cod felt that there was a special relationship between a father and his baby daughter, which they called tortience.

Tote roads

When lumbering was still going on in Maine, the lumbering camps were supplied by oxcart from Bangor, nearly three hundred miles away. A dozen yoke of oxen might be needed on these carrying or "tote" roads. Stories are still told of a woman driver of such a supply train, "Henry Allen," who surpassed all the other drivers in "his" skillfulness. She not only cleared the roads of windfalls, but held off circling wild animals better than the best of the men. Not only were her essential supplies of molasses, pork and beans in great demand, but her entertainment was equally welcome. She carried her violin and introduced many a popular song, such as "The Wounded Hussar," "Flying Cloud," and "James Bird."

Towertown

The name used for a region in Chicago because of the fact that a famous tower was the only structure left in the area after the great Chicago fire of 1870. This region, on the north bank of the Chicago river, became in later years the center of an attempted renaissance of the arts slightly resembling Greenwich Village in New York. Towertown with its bohemian atmosphere was proud of the toughness of its city and contented with the provincialism of their residents. Still later Towertown became the locale of some of the most brutal of the gang killings in the Chicago Beer Wars.

tow heads

Term used for sand bars on the upper Mississippi which seemed to clog the stream in midchannel.

train delays

Exaggerated tales have always been commonplace about long train delays, but perhaps one of the longest delays ever encountered was after the Galveston flood, when a train of the Gulf and Interstate running from Beaumont to Galveston finally arrived three years late.

Tree of Hope

The wishing tree of Harlem was such a popular fetish that it had to be rededicated in 1941 and though it has been reduced to a mere stump it is understood that if you pat, kiss, or hug the tree your wish will come true.

trestle table

Planed boards were laid across sawhorses in the early Boston homes because they were so small it was not possible to have the table standing all day long and still be able to move around.

truck and dicker

When many New Hampshire towns were inaccessible to convenient shopping centers, they had a scheme for bartering farm produce, knitted goods and bags of rags for the manufactured goods they needed. They called it "country pay."

tuberculosis cures

In some of the backward areas of the Southwest the inhabitants still practice the eating of live snails and small frogs as an accepted cure of this disease. In other parts they may wear a rattlesnake belt for the same purpose, or eat the heart of a rattler fried. In dairy regions it was a common belief that butter made from the milk of cows pastured in churchyards or graveyards would serve as a cure also.

"tumble bug cat"

When manual labor on the levees came to an end on the Lower Mississippi, the Negro workmen used this term to describe a caterpillar tractor used to draw a Fresno scraping machine that was part of the modern-style levee repair job.

turnpike

Many of the improved roads in the colonial period were privately built and their owners were entitled to charge a toll for their use. A barrier was placed across the road which remained closed until the fee had been collected. The turning of this pole or "pike" led to the creation of the term turnpike for the highway itself. In some states there were interesting exemptions in regard to the payment of toll. In New England no payment was required on the way to church, to vote or for jury duty. In New York the blacksmith, the physician and the operator of the gristmill were not required to pay.

The Albany Post Road was often popularly called the Farmers' Turnpike. On Long Island there are two reminders of the old days; the Hempstead Turnpike and the Jericho Turnpike. The Lancaster Turnpike was one of the earliest to have a macadamized surface. It had been built in 1792. Recently the same term has been used for the Jersey and the Pennsylvania Turnpikes.

296

Turtle

In Indian mythology Turtle is commonly regarded as holding the earth in place. Just as Muskrat (q.v.) brought up the mud that led to the creation of the world, the Turtle holds it steady on his back. The Pueblo Indians think that Turtle makes the thunder and when they make rattles of turtleshells they think they retain some of this power.

There are many superstitions associated with turtles, many having to do with the turtle's having a very long life. Turtle oil has been popular in country areas for its supposed pain-reducing qualities and also for providing longevity. Turtleshells are often worn as good-luck charms.

Tush-ka-lusa's curse

A popular legend tells of an Indian chieftain in what is now Alabama who, upon learning of the accidental death of his son at the hands of one of De Soto's men, called down upon all white invaders the vengeance of the Great Spirit. There are those who see its fulfillment in one respect—the Black Warrior River named for this giant redskin, Tush-ka-lusa, has claimed at least one victim every year since that time.

"Tweetsie"

In the Grandfather Mountain section of the South this famous train was operated by the Eastern Tennessee and Western North Carolina Railroad. The line, first operated in 1882, was built by Yankee capital during the general renaissance following the Civil War. The narrow-gauge line provided the only transportation in that region until a heavy flood struck in 1940. The line was about to be abandoned when gas rationing and other wartime shortages made it worth while to continue it in operation, especially in the light of publicity showing the devotion of the surrounding population to its "little train." The ten-wheel engine, augmented by some narrow-gauge coaches, made its trips twenty-four miles each way between Elizabeth and Elk Park, North Carolina. Literally forward and backward, because, having no turntable, the train really did back up to its terminus.

297

two bits equal one quarter

In the early colonial days hard money was very scarce, so that in parts of the South where Spanish dollars were available, they might literally be chopped into "bits." Two such bits would be equal to a quarter of a dollar.

"Two-cent Church"

Kansas had churches established almost as soon as it had inhabitants. The religious life of the people permeates the communities. In Pfeifer (pronounced "pie-fur") one may visit the so-called two-cent church. When plans for the church were under consideration the parish priest of a group of Russian-German immigrants urged that each of his parishioners set aside two cents from the sale of each bushel of wheat for the financing of the church. Through good years and bad, with fluctuating prices, the practice continued until enough money was accumulated and the church was at last constructed.

two-dollar bills

So great is the antipathy of a large number of persons toward the two-dollar bill that cashiers have been known to ask a customer if he had any objection to receiving one in his change. Gamblers are supposed to be particularly prejudiced against them. Some persons try to counteract the bad effects by tearing a corner off the bill. The explanation for such reactions has been based upon many speculations. "Deuce," associated with the lowest card in the pack, is mentioned. The fear of those in limited circumstances that "twins" might be the bad luck threatened, is believed in the South. Though there are millions of such bills in circulation, many more could be used for their convenience and economy if this almost unconscious aversion were not so prevalent.

two-gun shooting

Old-timers in the West wore two guns and often drew both at once for display purposes. Despite the tales about the famous pistol duels of the 1880's and '90's, they probably did not shoot simultaneously. They were more likely to be concerned about

298

having some shots in reserve. Some men could shoot equally well with either hand, but others could reverse guns, often with lightning speed. The threat of firing two guns at once was in most cases just a fake.

type louse

Printer's pest. The tiny little creatures, so the story goes, hid away in the compartments where the type was kept, especially in the "fl" and "fi" boxes where they would be disturbed least. They would occasionally venture forth and eat what old type they could find. Of course they were blamed for errors in typesetting, for when they were gorged with lead they might fall on a key while copy was being set.

U

umbrella superstitions

The still commonly retained superstition that opening an umbrella in the house will bring bad luck probably has some foundation in the damage that might have been done to the household if the powerful springs of early days caused the umbrella to break something or hit somebody.

Uncle Sam

Uncle Sam Wilson, a Troy meat packer, supplied beef to the United States Army during the War of 1812. Supposedly the soldiers thought the stamp "U.S. Beef" meant "Uncle Sam's beef." Soon a caricature of Uncle Sam Wilson was used in cartoons to represent the United States and has been so employed ever since. Major Downing, a political figure popular in the time of Andrew Jackson, is also thought to have served as possible prototype for the personification of Uncle Sam. His folksy views and shrewd political observations began appearing in the Portland, Maine, *Daily Courier* in 1830.

Unsinkable Mrs. Brown

The tales about Margaret Brown, the wife of Leadville Johnny, varied and tremendous as they are, hardly kept up with some of the facts of her colorful life. Her husband made a fortune as a miner. Denver society, however, would not admit her to its select group so she traveled around the world, making her own society. Perhaps the most publicized incident of her unpredictable career had to do with her presence on the Titanic when it struck an iceberg. She happened to be fully dressed in an immense array of Arctic clothing with a gun in her enormous muff. Placed in a lifeboat with the others, she bossed the five men with her and then began the distribution of her clothing to the twenty shivering women. She covered three forlorn children with her priceless chinchilla wrap, and threatened to shoot anyone who did not help with the rowing. When picked up at sea and asked how she had managed, she announced, "I am unsinkable!"

Another dramatic story was started when she broke her engagement to the Duke of Charlot and disavowed any interest in a titled Britisher by stating publicly that the French were unbathed gallants and the British brandy-soaked.

"unwritten law"

The protection of Southern womanhood has long been an accepted practice, but in many parts of the South the husband's "right" of vengeance has been tolerated only if the action is taken immediately after the provocation.

V

vamoose

A common expression in the Southwest, meaning "Beat it" or "Get out of here." It is a popular corruption of the Spanish *"vamos"*—let us go.

Vanderbilt Legends

With the power that Cornelius Vanderbilt, the Commodore, exerted through his control of the New York Central, it is not surprising that many legends grew up about his activities. Perhaps the most famous is that having to do with his being questioned about the public's convenience, when he is supposed to have replied, "The public be damned."

Another incident tells of an occasion when he had promised a friend a thousand shares of his railroad stock. Learning that a bribe of some legislators was being considered to get through a law beneficial to the road and increase the value of the stock, he asked for the shares back, enjoyed an $80,000 profit and then reassigned them to the friend.

Another example of his meanness concerns the last episode of his life. He was suffering from an illness that caused his doctor to recommend champagne every day. Vanderbilt's comment was supposed to have been, "But wouldn't soda water do just as well? It's so much cheaper."

Commodore Vanderbilt had always been so much concerned with making money that he was a little disappointed that his son seemed not to have inherited his ability. But one day he was agreeably surprised. His son, William K., who was managing the family estate, made a deal with his father to buy fertilizer at $4 a load, when the generally accepted price

302

was only $2. His father did not have long to gloat over the advantage he had taken of his son, for it turned out the young man was expecting a scowload in return rather than the usual wagonload.

Venice treacle

A medicine popular among the Puritans. They would boil the pounded bodies of snakes with white wine and a mixture of twenty herbs. A little opium was then added. The liquid was drained off and put into a jar. It was usually administered to children for any illness, especially measles and whooping cough.

Virginia Military Institute Anniversary

On each May fifteenth there is a roll call taken of those students who served in the Civil War, in the last defense of Richmond, when the cadets, who were hardly adolescent, went into battle with tragic loss of life. As the roll is called an upperclassman steps forward and replies, "Dead on the field of honor."

voodoo

The Acadians scattered by the British were relocated in various places, some in Maine but many in the islands of the Caribbean. After much distress they finally reached the more congenial French environment of Louisiana. These refugees were saturated with beliefs in jungle magic, the efficacy of charms and the idea that one could dispose of those one hated by means of certain rituals. Many of these people drifted into the marshlands of Louisiana, where the land was cheap and available. Here, in inaccessible areas, they transplanted many of their voodoo customs in an isolation that assured their long survival. They employed charms and fetishes, but returned also to the teachings of the Catholic Church. Their folklore is full of tales involving practices of both. They observe all the correct details of their religion and at the same time light candles to propitiate spirits that may still be lurking around. In the city of New Orleans these activities culminate in the Mardi Gras celebrations.

W

wallpaper beliefs

Very little wallpaper was used before 1710 because there was a widespread belief that it was poisonous. Also it was very expensive to print and did not become really popular until after the Civil War.

wannagan

In lumbering talk this was the camp commissary where all sorts of necessities were sold.

war dances

The original purpose of war dances was to build up a frenzy to key up the tribe for its participation in a warlike activity, or to celebrate a victory already accomplished. They tended in time to become show-off pieces that gradually became associated with fertility ceremonies or rain dances. The steps might often include mimic encounters, involving boasting of great deeds previously performed.

warders

These devices are countercharms to release one from the harm imposed by another who has attempted to "conjure" one.

"warning out"

Puritan distrust of strangers was so great that new arrivals in Boston would be called upon by the sheriff and told that if they did not conduct themselves properly they would be expelled. This was in marked contrast to the lavish entertainment almost forced upon strangers in Virginia. As late as 1714

Boston was still preventing citizens from entertaining strangers without sending a full description of the persons involved and a statement of their reason for arrival to the authorities.

war stopper

Lord Sterling, William Alexander, a man of great wealth through his iron-making in northern New Jersey, was respected by both sides during the Revolutionary War. He was able to exert enough influence to enforce a temporary armistice, to allow time for his daughter's wedding, at which she was given away by the Governor and had as guests both King's men and Continentals.

warts

There is quite a body of material on the subject of the removal of warts by means of different kinds of charms. These usually involve the burying of something, such as a red string at a crossroads at midnight, or a stolen dishrag. There are also many still convinced that touching a toad will produce a wart, and that spitting on the wart every morning will cause it to disappear. Curiously enough, this practice actually seems to work and reinforces the superstition.

Some variations on this superstition exist. One states that if you wipe the wart with a dishrag and put it aside, when it rots the wart will be gone. Another states that you should tie knots in a string, one for each wart you want to disappear.

Washington Cathedral

This place of worship is the subject of a legend about a workman long associated with the construction, who wanted his wife to be buried in the new cathedral even though it was not yet finished. Though supposedly denied the request, it is claimed that he had her cremated and then sprinkled her ashes in some newly mixed cement.

Washington swore

When Washington was retreating from Princeton he ordered Charles Lee to delay the enemy, but Lee was so impressed

305

by reports of British strength that he retreated instead. He was falling back in some disorder when he encountered Washington. That was the day Washington swore, according to one of his generals, who states, "It was at Monmouth Court House on a day which would make any man swear. He swore on that day until the leaves shook on the trees, charmingly, delightfully. Never have I enjoyed such swearing before or since. Sir, on that memorable day he swore like an angel from heaven."

watered milk

Certain Irish settlers in the Housatonic Valley were suspected of diluting their milk sent to market. Though no one accused them directly, the comment was made that certain people were regularly "making the spring their best cow."

water hyacinth

Imported from Venezuela and exhibited at the New Orleans Cotton Exposition, this colorful plant was supposedly greatly admired by a lady who decided to introduce it into her home waters, the St. John River, about 1884. The brightly flowering bulbs entwined their roots into lovely floating mats which in time began to fill up the river and its tributaries. Soon the mass of foliage became far more than could be managed in the waters it was gradually choking off. It was harvested for a time as cattle feed but was soon discovered to have little food value. Ultimately these mats so blocked the progress of boats that the United States government had to spend over half a million to clear the river though the hyacinth goes right on flourishing.

watermelon cake

A popular Southern dish in which a rose extract was used to color the center and black currants or raisins sprinkled through it to imitate watermelon seeds. The outside was covered with a pale green icing made from pistachio nuts, often in two tones of green to imitate a Georgia melon.

306

water-soaked Yule log

In parts of Maryland in the eighteenth century it was the accepted custom that the slaves on the plantation did not work while the Yule log at Christmas time continued to burn. It was also an accepted custom, at which the masters winked, to have the chosen log buried for months beforehand in a swamp so that it would become thoroughly water-soaked and therefore take a very long time in burning.

wave around

If a rustler was at his fire busy changing a brand on a stolen calf and a stranger approached, he waved his hat in a semicircle from left to right, which meant that the intruder was not welcome. If this signal was not sufficient, a gunshot might be the next step.

weaker sex

The superstition that women belong to the "weaker sex" seems to be a pretty well exploded myth by the present time. Women's longevity and their resistance to disease have helped to defeat that idea. A related superstition also seems to have been thoroughly wiped out today—that is, belief in the incompatibility of beauty and brains. It is only fair to note that "strong back, weak mind" is equally outmoded.

weather prediction

An old weather prophet, asked for an estimate of Arkansas weather, declared he had given up predicting. When God ran the country he could do it, but now that the government was taking over he gave up. *See* GROUND HOG DAY, BEAVER, MUSKRAT, FROG, ONION, "WOOLLY BEARS," CODFISH SUPERSTITIONS.

wedding anniversaries

There has developed a practice of celebrating such anniversaries by a particular material according to the number of years. The gifts given are expected to be of substance associated with the year:

307

1 year—paper	9 years—pottery
2 years—cotton	10 years—tin
3 years—leather	15 years—crystal
4 years—silk	20 years—china
5 years—wood	25 years—silver
6 years—iron	50 years—gold
7 years—copper or wool	75 years—diamond
8 years—electrical appliances	

wedding cake superstitions

A very popular superstition decrees that if a girl puts a piece of wedding cake under her pillow she will dream of the man she will marry. Another common custom requires that the bride be the first to cut the cake if she is to be happily married. The bridegroom is supposed to help by placing his hand over the bride's thus symbolizing the cooperation their marriage is going to entail. The customary wedding breakfast also implies this idea of cooperation.

wedding customs

A tremendous collection of these customs could be collected for different areas of the United States and for people who carry on the traditions of the country of their origin.

In Virginia the wedding guests roll up the bride's stockings and throw them at her while she and her new husband lie on the bed. It is believed that the one who hits her on the head will be the next one married.

The country over it is believed that the girl who catches the bride's bouquet when it is thrown to the wedding guests when the bride leaves for her honeymoon, will be the next bride. Less commonly known is a superstition that if this young woman unties one of the "lover's knots" with which the bouquet is decorated she will get the wish she makes at that time.

Weft

When the whaling industry was centered at Sag Harbor a man's coat might be waved from a pole to indicate that a whale had been sighted. Later a flag or weft might be used for the same purpose in order for the whole town to prepare for participation.

Welsh Indians

An early legend developed about the first white men to settle in Tennessee. The tale stated that a blond, blue-eyed people wearing beards had settled in the interior before Columbus made his discovery. A Welshman, they claimed, was about to be given a sentence after having been captured by a strange tribe of Indians. He was supposed to be able to hear the debate and was astonished to note they were speaking in Welsh, whereupon he addressed them in the same tongue, condemning them for considering burning him at the stake. The tale concludes that he was released and adopted by the tribe as a brother. The account also becomes concerned about certain mounds and elaborate earthworks erected at various points along the river. Since the Indians disclaimed any responsibility, these were assigned to the legendary Welshmen.

A Cherokee chieftain, questioned about these stories by John Sevier, the first Governor of Tennessee, said he understood these early people were Welsh but after an exchange of prisoners they left the country and went on to the Missouri Valley.

The ancient records of the Welsh afford some evidence to reinforce this legend. The Welsh bards tell of ten ships that sailed for what was presumably America in the twelfth century. For all the unlikeliness of the situation, an American painter years later did find among the Mandan Sioux in the upper Missouri area some fair Indians with blue and gray eyes.

Western air superior

There are probably untold numbers of Westerners who would boast of the superiority of their part of the country, but there is one popular tale that proves the point. A Texan visiting up North became ill and was about to die when a friend rushed to his aid with a bicycle tire filled with Western air. The dying man immediately revived.

309

wet one's whistle
Middle-Western expression meaning to take a drink.

"whaleback"
As a transition was being made to the steel and propeller-driven cargo ships on Lake Superior, a Captain McDougal designed a curious ship for the American Steel and Barge Company. It looked like a huge metal cigar floating in the water, but served as an introduction to the modern type of steel cargo ship in use today. Successful as was this design, few of these "whalebacks" have survived the scrap heap because their loading devices were not adaptable to present-day self-loading.

whaling ships as reformatories
Wilmington, Delaware, town fathers sent young drunkards for a three-year cruise in her whaling fleet as a means of curing them, often with the connivance of well-meaning parents. How the Temperance Society came to think of a whaler as a moral sanitarium is not quite clear.

whing-ding
A social affair of a boisterous nature usually accompanied by much drinking, indulged in by the settlers of the early West.

whipping the cat
Before it was possible to buy "ready-to-wear" clothes in the stores, it was the custom in New England to have all clothing made in the home. However, occasionally young people became so proficient at the making of men's clothing that they might be asked out to farm areas to spend a fortnight making the family's yearly supply. This visit would be known as "whipping the cat."

whippoorwill
Since the whippoorwills are seldom seen and their weird call which gives them their name is often heard at nightfall or just before dawn, it is not surprising that a belief in them as birds of ill-omen has arisen. If a person makes a wish upon hearing the first call of the bird in the spring, and keeps the

310

wish a secret, it is bound to come true. It is suggested to avoid the tragedy that might come if a bird is heard near the home, that one should point a finger at it, as if attempting to kill it symbolically. This protection is supposed to help even if the bird is not seen. If two such birds are seen flying side by side, an unusual occurrence, it means a disappointment is due.

whip snake

In Southern and Southwestern United States there are those who believe that the whip snake or coach snake attacks human beings with its long tail and can lash its victims to death.

Whip the devil around the stump

In New England they used this expression to indicate that someone was able to enjoy the fruits of evil without having to suffer the penalty—to dodge punishment dishonestly but successfully.

whiskey as a cure for snake bite

Though this practice has long been looked upon with favor and some who have used it have survived, it has actually been found to be harmful because it speeds up circulation and causes the venom to spread more rapidly through the body. However, folklore still takes precedence over science in many circumstances.

whiskey for loggers

The men who worked in the lumber camps before the turn of the century had for the most part a great passion for liquor. Year after year they would spend all they earned in one grand spree when they came out of the woods in the spring. Many tales are told of the lumbermen's great thirst. An example involves a camp which by poor management ran out of supplies before the winter was over. A committee was sent on the long trip to town to replenish the food supplies. They finally returned to the starving woodsmen with several cases of liquor and a couple of loaves of bread. The classic response was: "What are we going to do with all that bread!"

Deprived of their favorite drink during Prohibition, they

311

resorted to fantastic substitutes: liniment, varnish, Jamaica ginger, cough medicine and similar products. One old codger sent in a message to the druggist that he wanted some *good* alcohol but the message was mixed up and he was sent wood alcohol. They found his body in the woods.

Whiskey Jack

Wisconsin has in Whiskey Jack a legendary figure patterned after Paul Bunyan. He was a raftsman seven feet tall who would pick up sections of a long logging raft and carry them wherever they were needed.

whistle-britches

An expression used in North Carolina for a small boy proud of his first pair of britches.

"whistle's moans"

According to song and fact, Casey Jones could just about play a tune on the sixty-one calliope whistle that was his distinctive trade-mark on his locomotive:

"The switchman knew by the whistle's moans
That at the throttle was Casey Jones."

whistling superstitions

Whistling is disapproved of in many occupations because of the bad effects it is supposed to have upon those involved, such as mining, in a newsroom or in the theater. A popular proverb shows the taboo as applying to women who were thought to have talked with the devil: "A whistling girl and a crowing hen always come to no good end." Yet another version of the same idea states, "Girls that whistle and hens that crow make their way wherever they go."

White deer of Onota

A popular legend of the Housatonic Valley is about a spotless white deer which came often, in the summer and autumn months, to drink at Onota. No Indian ever fired at this lovely creature for they believed that as long as she came back to them, "so long famine shall not blight the Indian harvest, nor pestilence come nigh his lodge, nor foeman lay waste his country." At the time of the French and Indian War an offi-

312

cer, Montalbert, was sent to the tribe to insure their support of the French. He heard of the beautiful deer and desiring to make a splendid gift to the King in order to advance his fortune, tried to get the Indians to help him capture their sacred deer. He was turned down with horror and warned of his danger if he continued to hunt her. However, he found an Indian so dependent upon drink that he was helped achieve his desired undertaking. He killed and skinned the deer and started on his way to Montreal. His helper, having sobered up, confessed what he had done and was speedily disposed of by his tribesmen. Montalbert and his baggage were never heard of again; and the tribe was never as prosperous again, though they mourned deeply and offered many supplications to the Great Spirit.

"White's town on the Lehigh"

This term was used to describe an unusual community on the Lehigh River at the turn of the century. The banks of the river were so steep that the Lehigh Navigation Company could not find quarters for the men working on a series of channels to carry the coal barges. Ignoring the narrow strip of land along the shore, they fastened three old scows together and produced "Whitestown." One scow was used for the workers, another for the managerial staff and another as kitchen and bakehouse.

whitewashing

Jersey brides in the seventeenth century had a never-failing article included in the marriage contract which assured her of "the free and unmolested exercise of the right to do the whitewashing."

Whitney Legends

Harry Payne Whitney had established a famous stable with race horses costing the then huge amount of $60,000. At one great dinner the Whitney groom brought into the great dining hall their host's equine favorite of the moment. "A shame," Whitney is supposed to have said to his wife later, "to let such a horse mingle with such company."

313

Mrs. Whitney went in for sculpturing. She donated many of her pieces for dedication in widely scattered public places. One, "To the Morrow," consisted of two nude figures twelve feet high poised at the end of a thirty-foot rainbow arch. At the dedication held in Times Square, Fiorello La Guardia announced that the group symbolized the great and powerful things aviation could bring to the world. However, Mrs. Whitney later confessed that the statue was intended to typify the spirit of youth looking into the future.

whittle

A cross between a shawl and a blanket. An article of dress worn in place of a heavy coat in New York City at the beginning of the nineteenth century by both men and women.

whoopee

The earliest cowboys may have uttered a sound resembling this in an attempt to call their animals. Eventually it came to mean that time men, not animals, got together and had themselves a good, usually uproarious time.

widow's vendue

When a "goodman" died on Cape Cod and left no resources for the support of his widow, the relicts were "farmed" out. The annual process of selling bereaved wives became known as the "Widow's Vendue or Vandue." About 1770 the town raised about three pounds for each widow offered. The bidder hoped to get his purchase price back through the labor of the widow, so that the old and feeble were often placed with difficulty, sometimes bringing only ninepence. A young and comely widow on the other hand might bring as high as ten pounds. Expenses for illness usually brought on a great "bickerfest." Should the community be required to pay the doctor if her guardians had overworked and underfed the widow? Often sums were agreed upon in advance if medical attention in excess of a certain amount was found to be needed or the widow would have to wait until her year was up and hope for better treatment from her next "buyer."

314

However, a few shrewd widows were able to exert a little mild blackmail and get their needs supplied "illegally."

widow's walk

Many of the homes around Cape Cod and along the Massachusetts seacoast were built by sea captains who recognized that their wives would be especially eager to know of their safe return home from the long sea voyages of the early days. So they had constructed on their rooftops, usually in front of the gables, a narrow space where a person could stand and perhaps take a step or two while peering out to sea. This was at first called the "captain's walk," but because so many of the sailor husbands failed to come home it gained the sadder name of "widow's walk."

Winchester quarantine

Ordinary cattle driven across country in the 1880's often carried a tick that gave pedigreed cows a fever. To prevent this "rough cattle" from spreading the contamination, some established ranches would not let these herds through their ranges. If persuasion was not sufficient to prevent the intrusion, Winchester guns were used upon those disobeying the settled ranchers.

Windham witch scare

In the midst of a political campaign in Windham, it was thought that the two candidates had won support from a group of witches. Great consternation was aroused over the situation, but upon investigation it was discovered that an army of frogs had moved into the only available water source outside the town. The small shrill-voiced frogs were those claimed to be campaigning for Dyer, and the deep-throated ones for Elderkin.

windies

These are the tall stories that were told by the cowboys, boastful accounts of activities that everyone understood had no relation to the truth. They were frequently retold until some developed into legends that almost acquired historical authenticity. See STRETCHING THE BLANKET.

315

windigo

This is the designation used by the Chippewa Indians for a member of their tribe who had been known to eat human flesh. No matter what stress led to the circumstances, he was outlawed for the action and cast out of the community. Tales of the tribes tell that a famished individual won the strength to avoid such action from the good spirits looking after him.

The legend spread in Maine that the windigo was a terrible creature upon whom it would be doom to look. The belief was so genuine that lumbermen secured a monopoly of certain jobs by scaring competitors out of the neighborhood through the simple device of tramping past their camp in fur-covered snowshoes and squeezing a drop of blood into each footprint, then spreading a rumor that a windigo was about. Among the Ojibwa a windigo is an ogre but not a cannibal, and serves as a means of frightening children.

wintergreen

The oil of wintergreen was looked upon as an important remedy in folk medicine, useful in reducing fever and in curing lumbago or a toothache. A tea was also brewed from the berries and given to check rheumatism or kidney trouble.

wipes

A Western cowboy's expression for his neckerchief, the square of a hundred uses, as a towel, dishcloth, sun breaker, hat holder, blind for cattle or bucking horse, bandages, and ultimately a shroud.

wishbone superstitions

It is still a very common practice to save the wishbone of a chicken or turkey and allow it to dry out. When it has become brittle, two persons each take a side and cause it to break apart. The one retaining the longer piece will have his wish come true. Pins or ornaments in the shape of a wishbone are considered to bring good luck and still have popular appeal.

316

wish book

When the western cowboy desired to bolster up his dreams, he drew his inspiration from one of the most widely read books of the West—the mail-order catalogue—which was read and reread with the greatest of care, not only for the ordering of the few things the cowboy could afford on his small income, but just to learn what was available in the outside world.

witch door

In some of the small towns of New Hampshire they constructed their houses with "witch doors," that is, they arranged the panels in the form of a cross to keep witches away from the household.

witch hazel

The Indians in New England brewed a tea from the bark of this shrub as a remedy that would stop bleeding of the stomach or kidneys. They steeped a solution of the leaves to strengthen the eyes. Its astringent water, it was claimed, would make a fine tonic to clear the skin. Sprigs of witch hazel could be used also for divining rods.

Wizard's Clip (Virginia)

Just after the Revolution Adam Livingston was visited by a sick man, whom the family took in and nursed, but who was obviously not going to live. Knowing he was dying, he revealed that he was a Catholic and asked for a priest. There was still considerable discrimination against Catholics in Virginia and Livingston would not have anything to do with "popery," so the man died without making a confession. Then strange things began to happen. Livingston's candles would not burn. He heard horses galloping in the night, but when he investigated they were all safe in the barn. His cattle sickened and his barn burned down. The family's best clothes had holes in them shaped like crescents. And in his dreams he saw the stranger. At last Livingston attained a more tolerant attitude. He sent for the priest he had once refused to call and made him the present of a field which the church

317

holds to this day. Here a service is held once a year and a mass is said for the dead man. Though the disturbances ended with the donation of the land, the area was known as Wizard's Clip for many years thereafter.

wohaw

When the Indians of the Plains saw oxen for the first time, they heard bullwhackers shouting "whoa, haw and gee" as needed to guide the cattle. The Indians gave the name "wohaw" to all the cattle they subsequently encountered.

wolf woman

Texas folklore includes an account of the circumstances surrounding a woman lost in the wilds who died after giving birth to a daughter. This child was supposed to have been raised by the wolves that found her. Years later, the details continue, the girl was recovered temporarily but eagerly escaped as soon as she could. Still later, she was glimpsed suckling two whelps. The final embellishment of the legend hints at the existence of "human-faced lobos (wolves)" among some of the rarely observed animals of the area.

wood-burner's influence on neighbors

When locomotives were still burning wood as fuel in the St. Clair region, it was the custom to phrase questions in terms of this activity. For example to inquire if a person wanted to eat, one asked, "Will you take in wood?" To inquire if a person was ready to go, one asked, "Is your steam up?"

woolen cloth making

In New Hampshire before 1880, melted pig's fat was worked into newly clipped wool by the women of the family in many of the isolated farm households. It was then carded with wire-toothed combs and spun on a big wool wheel, providing occupation during long winter days in the Hampshire hills. A flax wheel might also be used in this period.

"woolly bears"

This popular name has been given to the caterpillars of

318

moths of a great many species, though most are black at both ends with a reddish-brown mid-band which may vary in width from year to year. They are about an inch and a quarter in length, being hairy or woolly-looking in appearance. The width of the center strip has been used as the basis for prediction as to whether the winter will be cold or not. Though it has long been a basis of folklore, this system of prediction is now being seriously investigated as to its accuracy. The claims are made that the predictions are only expected to be correct for an average estimate of the weather, that an exceptionally cold snap may occur in a winter of average mildness and vice versa.

In the Ozark Mountains a variation in the folktale has developed. There the caterpillars are not considered for their weather-predicting characteristics but for a more practical use. There, it is claimed, they grow so large folk stretch them on walls or tan them for lap robes. They find them handier than buffalo.

wore 'em low

A Westerner who wore 'em low was one who had his guns easily available and it was generally understood that he meant business, and in most cases indicated a professional gunman willing to be hired for protection purposes.

work songs

These songs may be of great variety, love songs, complaints, lament, ballads, and so on, but they all have in common a desire to relieve the tedium of a monotonous job. The rhythmic nature of the songs was developed to accompany the task that was being carried on. It might be slow-paced or mournful, or gay and lively. Sometimes they are paced to the step of the individual doing the job or to the stride of the animal being used. There may be an action involved connected with the task, such as "heave ho" as ropes are pulled on, or spikes driven on a railroad construction job. Negro prison labor work songs involve poignant references, of misery, lonesomeness and hardships endured. Vendors' songs may also be included

319

in this category with the many colorful street songs that are gradually disappearing—unless the singing commercial can be said to be building up a new body of material.

worthless as a four card flush

An expression used in the West, borrowed from the game of poker, to indicate a condition that was really hopeless and useless.

"wreck ashore"

Along the coast of Key West it was commonplace for ships to run aground. In this situation it was customary for the one noting it to dash to the rescue, the first arrival becoming the "wrecking master" and obtaining a special fee. At the cry of "Wreck ashore!" a church could be emptied faster than by a call of "Fire." Even the minister might proceed to participate in activities.

writermarouster

A term used by some of the poorer-educated whites in the South to indicate a court order of eviction.

wrong side of the tracks

The common implication of this term is that a person is born or brought up in the less desirable part of the community and has to overcome this social handicap.

Wyoming Massacre

Near the present Wilkes-Barre is the Wyoming Valley, where in 1778 a bitter attack was launched by the Tories with their Indian allies against a group of Yankees trying to protect their lands. One of the strangest tales to emerge from this event had to do with two brothers fighting on opposite sides. One, a Tory, encountered his brother coming unarmed from the main battle where a frightful carnage was going on. Though this Yankee brother begged for mercy, he was ruthlessly shot and scalped by his own brother, whose standing even among the Tories was much diminished by this unnecessary cruelty.

320

Sixteen Yankee prisoners taken at the same time by the Tory's Indian allies were personally disposed of by an imposing-looking Indian squaw, a queen who had been friendly to the whites until her son was killed by the Yankees. Further lurid details were passed on by word of mouth for years afterward.

Y

yacky-yack

A century ago a yack was a Western term for a stupid person, but the modern application of the word is to what might be called stupid conversation. Some men find women's endless repetition of trivial topics a good illustration of "yack." A famous cartoonist sums up a typical performance by the conclusion—"and so far into the night."

"Yankee"

Among the earliest references to this term are those connected with "Yankee Doodle." It was employed as a variant to the expression "Brother Jonathan" in reference to a New Englander. The implication was that the "Yankee" was more rogue than fool; but also included was the idea of a cracker-box philosopher. The stage Yankee later developed was held to be an artificial creation. The commonest early picture of a Yankee was as a peddler hawking his own handiwork and notions, shrewd but with some degree of humor.

Yankee trickery

P. T. Barnum, known not to have been above trickery himself, was once caught by a Yankee trick. He was offered a rare "cherry-colored" cat which he purchased sight unseen. He found that he was the owner of a black alley-cat—black cherries being common in the East.

yarrow divination

If a girl wrapped flannel around a spray, placed it under her pillow all night and put it in her shoe in the morning, as she went out in the morning she could expect to encounter the man she was to marry.

yawning superstitions

There are those who believe that to yawn when you are not sleepy means that you will endure a disappointment. To others it means that the person near to them is disliked. There were some also who feared that while the mouth was thus open the devil might enter the body, so they quickly but surreptitiously made the sign of the cross in front of their mouths as a protection.

Yellow Dog Creek

This spot in Idaho got its name from an oft-repeated tale about a half-dozen Chinese who fled from Virginia City when they discovered a notorious gang of robbers liked to use them for target practice. On their way to the Columbia River they came upon a couple of prospectors, whom they murdered and whose supplies they took. Two of them put on the shoes of the dead men and they resumed their way. Unfortunately they encountered the prospectors' friends, who noting the shoes forced them to go back over their route until the murdered men were found. Then the Chinese were shot down, in the words of their executioners, "for the yellow dogs they were." Today the stream is still called "Yellow Dog."

Yellow Kid

One of the earliest comics created, it was drawn by Richard Outcault for the New York *World* in 1896 and became immediately popular—so much so that since the figure was colored a bright yellow to make it stand out on the page, and since it represented a rather low and vulgar level of humor, it is presumed that the term "yellow" journalism was thus born. The setting for the series represented a city's slum backyards and their inhabitants, who overflowed into nearby settings. Though distinctly not "genteel" in the eyes of the upper level of society, the antics of the "Yellow Kid" appealed to the earthy tastes of the average man.

Z

Zeller Legend

The Pennsylvania Dutch are proud of a tale about a family whose dwelling survived for almost two centuries. The founder of the family, Countess Clotilde de Valois, married a Jaques de Sellaire, but as Huguenots they felt the need to seek sanctuary in the New World. Their children were known as John and Henrich Zeller. The latter name was visible until recently upon the lintel of a barn dated 1745, its wood-mitered doors still held together with the wooden pegs of those days when metal was so scarce, and bearing a latch that had never been replaced. Here an intrepid descendant of the brothers, while removing milk from a well in the cellar, saw an Indian face reflected in the water. The tale varies as to how he disposed of him or how many accompanied him, but most accounts mention an ax and limit the deed to one Indian removed.

Zoetrope

A crude attempt at producing a moving picture popular in the 1880's, using a whirling series of cards and called the "Wheel of Life" in its advertising copy.